HIS BRAZEN BRIDE

"What are you doing?" he whispered.

"I think it should be fairly obvious." Claire's hands rose to rest against his chest; her gaze climbed to meet his. "I am attempting to steal a kiss from my husband."

"Here? Now?"

She pulled in a tight breath. Her courage threatened to fail her for an instant; then she pushed herself closer to his tempting male strength.

"Is this not the ideal opportunity?" she whispered seductively.

Sliding her hands up, Claire wound her arms about Jasper's neck and pressed her lips against his. Her kiss was not soft or gentle, but forceful and passionate. He responded in kind, and when the hot waft of his breath struck her moist lips, Claire felt her body tighten.

Slowly, she teased his senses awake, using her lips, teeth, and tongue, delighting when she wrought a husky moan of desire from deep in his throat. Though she had initiated the contact, Jasper now seemed to be in control. He held her firmly in place, kissing her fiercely.

Claire arched her back and pushed herself closer. She wanted to feel every last inch of him, to absorb the strength and hardness of his body into her own. She flicked his cravat loose, and then reached for the buttons of his waistcoat and began to unfasten them. The moment it was done, she started on his shirt, trembling with excitement when she was finally finished and had successfully freed it from his waistband. Inhaling deeply, Claire slipped her hands inside Jasper's open clothing. His skin felt hot, burning her trailing fingertips as they eagerly explored the contours of his chest. . . .

Books by Adrienne Basso

HIS WICKED EMBRACE

HIS NOBLE PROMISE

TO WED A VISCOUNT

TO PROTECT AN HEIRESS

TO TEMPT A ROGUE

THE WEDDING DECEPTION

Published by Zebra Books

The Wedding Deception

Adrienne Basso

ZEBRA BOOKS
Kensington Publishing Corp.

ZEBRA BOOKS are published by

Kensington Publishing Corp.
850 Third Avenue
New York, NY 10022

ISBN 0-7394-5440-4

Printed in the United States of America

To my editor, John Scognamiglio,
who always has the best story ideas
and thankfully is willing to share them!

Chapter One

London, England
Early Spring, 1817

It was a cool, misty, overcast day, yet the weather proved to be no deterrent to the bustling mix of human and carriage traffic gathered on the streets. The faint odor of mud and horses, the sounds of elegant coaches and merchant cart wheels rumbling, and the endless parade of pedestrians in all shapes, sizes, and manner of dress was truly a sight to behold.

The scene was unfamiliar to the young woman surveying it, and ordinarily she would have been pressing forward in her seat, anxious to have a better view of this strange, mysterious new world. But not today.

With a deep sigh of resignation, Claire Truscott Barrington, Lady Fairhurst, turned her head away from the carriage window and closed her eyes, shutting out the crowded London streets. If only it were as easy to shut out the guilt that crowded her mind, to ease the disappointment she felt within herself for the cowardly act she was about to commit.

A promise made is a promise kept. The haunting refrain whirled inside her head with such recurring frequency, it was a wonder that she did not begin to speak the phrase out loud. It started the moment she had been forced to agree to this journey, and it continued relentlessly throughout the two long days of travel. She wondered briefly if it would ease after she had completed her dastardly deed, yet she doubted her well-honed conscience would give it a rest.

The catalyst of all this momentous turmoil was at this moment seated across the carriage from her, snoring with vigor. With her black bonnet slightly askew, double chin quivering gently, and a stray wisp of gray hair cascading diagonally across her wrinkled cheek, the elderly woman looked harmless and fragile, but Claire knew better.

Great-Aunt Agnes had always possessed an overburdened sense of familial duty and an equally ferocious will that gave her the impetus to carry out those dictates. Unfortunately for Claire, age had not lessened the diminutive woman's temperament or softened her interfering personality.

It was purely by chance, and bad luck, that Great-Aunt Agnes had decided to make an unexpected stop in Wiltshire to visit her nephew's family before continuing on to her home in London. She insisted she was anxious to congratulate her great-niece on her recent marriage, though Claire suspected that was merely an excuse. Great-Aunt Agnes's real motive was to assess the qualities and characteristics of the new bridegroom and decide if they met her high, exacting standards.

And when there was no husband in residence to meet—well, that was when the fat hit the fire and Great-Aunt Agnes moved into action.

"It was a muddy nightmare the last time that I came home to London," Great-Aunt Agnes said, tapping her cane rhythmically on the carriage floor. "Though I know my coachman took care, it felt as though the carriage rattled and jarred over every rock and pothole in its path. It was almost a relief to get stuck in a quagmire, for it gave my old bones a rest from the discomfort. I am pleased to see the condition of the roads are much improved this trip. I believe we shall arrive at Lord Fairhurst's residence before full darkness has fallen."

Startled, Claire glanced up. She had been so lost in thought and worry, she had not realized her aunt was awake.

"I hope your driver does not encounter any difficulty locating the address," Claire lied, secretly wishing they could spend the better part of the night driving up and down the various London avenues without ever arriving at their destination. Or better still, get stuck in a rut of oozing mud, shatter a wheel, and abandon their journey. Forever.

"Lord Fairhurst's family resides on one of the most fashionable streets in Town," Great-Aunt Agnes said with a grudging sniff of approval. "My coachman is well acquainted with that section of London, so it will present no problem finding the appropriate home."

"How reassuring." Claire smiled weakly and pulled the edges of her cloak together, though she knew the numbness in her hands and the chill in her body were not due to the weather.

"I look forward to making Lord Fairhurst's acquaintance," Great-Aunt Agnes said with a self-satisfied grin. "At long last."

Inwardly, Claire grimaced, and then her self-preservatory instincts flared. It was going to take quick thinking, quick talking, and even quicker physical movement to gain entry to her husband's home. With

Great-Aunt Agnes by her side, it would be nearly impossible.

"There is no need for you to further delay your arrival home on my account," Claire said nervously. "The coach will deposit me practically on Lord Fairhurst's doorstep. I shall be perfectly fine on my own."

"Nonsense," Great-Aunt Agnes bristled. "No lady of breeding goes anywhere unaccompanied, even if she is a married woman."

"But I am arriving at my husband's home."

Great-Aunt Agnes's eyes narrowed. "All the more reason to be properly escorted. We might not hold an exalted title, but our family can boast generations of genteel breeding, as well as years of honorable service to the crown. Now that you are in London, 'tis important that you showcase *all* your assets, especially when you are dealing with Lord Fairhurst's family."

Claire's nostrils quivered with dread. No, this would never do. "Naturally you may accompany me this evening, Aunt Agnes," Claire began slowly. "However, I assumed you would prefer to wait until tomorrow to meet my husband, after you have had a proper opportunity to rest and refresh yourself from our long journey."

Claire's gaze flickered critically over her great-aunt's slightly rumpled traveling costume before deliberately twitching her nose as if she had encountered a strong, unpleasant odor. Great-Aunt Agnes immediately blushed, as Claire knew she would. Claire felt a stab of remorse at exploiting her great-aunt's inflated vanity, which was her greatest weakness, especially when there was no real truth to the implied criticism.

Yet, it had the desired effect. Great-Aunt Agnes's eyes widened as she caught Claire's meaning. "Well, I imagine we can make an exception, just this one time," the older woman replied, absently running her gloved hand over the miniscule wrinkles on her skirt. "Perhaps it might be best for me to meet everyone tomorrow. We shall arrange to spend the afternoon together. Just the three of us: you, me, and Fairhurst."

Knowing there was no possible way to respond to such a bizarre notion, Claire merely nodded vaguely.

Your word is your bond. Claire shivered again. She had always taken great pride in adhering to that simple principle. Throughout her twenty-three years she had encountered many individuals who treated such an ideal with cavalier disregard. She had consciously avoided them, believing they lacked character. Yet, now she was about to join their ranks.

Perhaps this was her punishment for being so uncharitable, for not understanding that sometimes circumstances pushed you to act in ways you would never consider. A dull pain settled on her chest as she pondered this, but then the carriage turned the corner and began to slow. Claire realized this was hardly the appropriate time for self-reflection.

They had arrived.

She sat upright, her spine not touching the back of the squabs, her hands clasped tightly in her lap as she waited for the vehicle to come to a complete stop. Her heart and mind were racing with distress. For one wild, impulsive instant she wanted to scream out the truth to her great-aunt, to explain why she could not possibly enter this house.

Ruthlessly, she squashed the cowardly impulse. Though in her heart Claire wanted to blame Great-Aunt Agnes for this interminable situation, she knew exactly where the responsibility lay—squarely on her own shoulders.

Claire's feet felt heavy as she climbed down the small carriage steps. Dusk had fallen, and beacons of bright candlelight shone from many of the windows in the large, stone mansion. They contrasted sharply with her bleak mood.

Fearing she might lose her nerve, she called out a hasty farewell to her great-aunt and rushed forward. The footman responsible for her luggage scrambled to extract her belongings from the coach. He was out of breath when he joined her at the imposing front door of the residence.

"Thank you for your assistance, Doddson. You may return to the carriage."

Claire reached out and pulled her satchel from the footman's grasp. She had brought only a few items with her, yet it was amazing how heavy three gowns, a pair of shoes, various undergarments, and nightclothes felt.

The servant gave her a puzzled look and moved as if he wanted to take the portmanteau back, but Claire stood firm.

"Thank you," she repeated. Then she nodded her head dismissively, indicating again that Doddson should return to the coach. If she were denied entry to the house, she wanted no witnesses who could carry the tale.

With another puzzled glance and a slight shake of his head, the well-trained footman removed himself. The moment she was alone, Claire raised her fist and pounded on the door. The sound echoed through the stillness of the evening, grating on her already frayed nerves.

Ever so slowly the door opened. Soft light spilled onto her person, illuminating, Claire believed, every one of her flaws: her considerable height, her modest and less than fashionable clothes, and her too full breasts and wide hips. Though she knew it was far wiser to have left her great-aunt in the coach, Claire momentarily wished she had her formidable relative standing beside her. There would be no question about gaining admittance with Great-Aunt Agnes leading the charge.

The stately looking butler who answered the door gazed down the length of his considerable nose and sniffed. "The family is not receiving callers at this hour," he announced in a haughty tone. "If you wish, you may leave your card."

Claire lifted her chin and gazed at him with stormy determination. "I am not here to visit the family. I only require a brief meeting with Lord Fairhurst," she declared firmly, and before the servant had a chance to decide if he was going to allow her inside, Claire pushed the door firmly with the toe of her boot and stepped forward.

"Miss!" The butler's gray eyebrows lifted in alarm.

Claire scrambled farther into the spacious foyer; then she turned and fixed him with a severe stare. "I know this seems most confusing and improper, but I can assure you that Lord Fairhurst will wish to see me. Immediately and discreetly. And most importantly, alone."

Though she forced herself to look confident and commanding, Claire's knees fairly shook as she waited for the butler to react. He considered her with a jaundiced eye for what felt like an eternity until finally jerking his head in an affirmative nod.

"Very well, Miss. I shall go and check if his Lordship is at home. Your name, please?"

Claire felt herself visibly flinch. She could not possibly tell the servant she was Lady Fairhurst. He would think her ripe for Bedlam and no doubt throw her immediately out of the house.

"My business with Lord Fairhurst is of a personal and

delicate nature," Claire insisted, trying to invest her voice with authority. " 'Tis best for all concerned if you do not announce me."

There was brief silence as the butler considered this latest request. Claire thought it a good sign that he had not ejected her outright, but her eyes traveled the length of the elegant, winding staircase just in case. If necessary, she had every intention of bolting up those stairs and searching for Lord Fairhurst on her own. She had come too far to be denied this meeting.

After another long minute of thought, the butler made his decision. "This way, Miss," he said grudgingly.

Claire allowed the breath to slowly escape from her lungs and resisted the ridiculous impulse to hug the servant. He would probably have a fit of apoplexy. She placed her portmanteau discreetly behind a marble pillar and followed closely on the butler's heels.

Under different circumstances, she would have appreciated the opulent and tasteful splendor of her surroundings. Even the hallway had high ceilings, with ivory-colored walls and gold trimmings. Though many candles had been lit, they could not entirely illuminate all the dark corners in this vast space.

The house clearly was furnished with an artist's eye toward quality. Everything from the paint and wallpaper on the walls, to the marble on the floor, to the paintings in the gilded frames was tasteful and expensive.

But all this beauty went unnoticed. As they walked through the mansion, Claire was focused on gathering her scattered thoughts and fledgling courage. She vaguely noticed the liveried footmen bowing respectfully as she glided past them. Finally, in the center of the second floor hallway, the butler abruptly stopped in front of a set of lovely, inlaid mahogany doors.

Claire felt a sinking in her stomach.

"The green salon, Miss." The butler turned one of the brass doorknobs.

Claire's hand shot out. She grasped the servant's arm, effectively preventing him from opening the door. "Is his Lordship alone?"

The butler stiffened and glanced down at Claire's hand. She reddened slightly, feeling the censure in that glare for her exceedingly inappropriate behavior. But she did not release her grip. "Is he alone?" she repeated.

"Yes."

"Good." Claire slowly relaxed her fingers and slid them discreetly off the butler's forearm. " 'Tis not necessary to announce me."

"I can hardly do that, Miss, since I am unaware of your identity."

Ordinarily, Claire would have blushed at the servant's sarcasm, but she was too distracted by her upcoming meeting to be bothered by the butler's low opinion of her.

With a nod of her chin, Claire signaled for the butler to open the door. The moment he did, she took a deep breath and sailed through the doorway on watery legs. The door clicked shut behind her with a resounding thud.

Upon her entrance, the man seated in an overstuffed chair set by the fireplace glanced up from the book he was reading. When she took another step forward, he rose to his feet, as every proper gentleman should, and bowed slightly, exhibiting the graceful manners that Claire had always appreciated.

Her eyes darted about the room, and she was relieved to note the butler had been correct—Lord Fairhurst was indeed alone in the room.

"Good evening, Jay." Her voice was not as steady as she hoped, but at least it did not quiver dreadfully.

Lord Fairhurst did not greet her as he usually did, with an open smile and an affectionate hug, his laughing eyes telling her he was glad to see her. Instead, he raised a cynical eyebrow and pierced her with an unfriendly, questioning stare.

Claire attempted a smile. When that failed, she cleared her throat. "Please, forgive my rude intrusion. I know this must be a great shock for you and a horrible inconvenience, but matters simply moved beyond my control.

"I promised, nay I swore to you, that I would never visit you in London unless you expressly commanded my presence, and now sadly I have broken that promise. I regret that most of all; but please, Jay, you must understand this unannounced visit could not be avoided."

Anxiously, Claire awaited his response. But Lord Fairhurst did not speak. Instead, he curled his fingers lightly around the handle of the gold-rimmed quizzing glass that hung from a ribbon against his chest, raised the glass to his right eye, and peered at her through it.

Surprised, Claire managed not to squirm under such glaring scrutiny. She had never seen Jay use such an item and could not decide if it was an affectation or a medical necessity.

Claire licked her dry lips. There was a chair nearby, but she continued to stand, since she had not been invited to take a seat. She tried not to concern herself too much about it because Lord Fairhurst clearly was distracted by her sudden appearance. He spoke not a word, but continued to stare at her through his glass in dumbfounded shock.

Fearing she had made a complete muddle of her explanation, Claire tried again. "This whole mess started last Sunday when Great-Aunt Agnes arrived most unexpectedly in Wiltshire. She was on her way to London but thought it would be appropriate to first visit the family. Naturally, we all realized her true intent was to meet my new husband.

"Even Mother thought it a brazen act, but no one dares to question my great-aunt, and never more so when her mind is set. Then, after she made this special journey for this specific purpose, I was unable to produce you. I explained you were in Town, and before I could voice an opinion about the idea, Aunt Agnes insisted on bringing me to London so we could be reunited."

"Reunited?" Lord Fairhurst abruptly dropped his quizzing glass. "With me?" He blinked slowly, then narrowed his gaze.

As usual, Claire watched his eyes, hoping they would give her a better indication of his true feelings; but they reflected annoyance, which unsettled her even more. She had expected he would be displeased, but she had not anticipated such a cool, distant response.

She took a slight breath and focused her wandering thoughts. "I tried every excuse I could think of to avoid the trip, but Aunt Agnes closed her ears and mind to all of them. My continued and vehement protests began to cause suspicions among my family. They had always thought it was most peculiar that you were called away so soon after our wedding and were just beginning to accept the unusual circumstances of our marriage. I could not jeopardize that progress by telling them about the true state of our relationship.

"Especially since Aunt Agnes kept insisting that a woman's place was by her husband's side in times of family upheaval. Even if she would have bothered to listen, I had no legitimate argument to refute her. The most I was able to do was stall our departure till the end of the week."

"So this is a time of family upheaval?" he asked, sounding quite astonished. "Dare I ask whose family? Yours or mine?"

"Well, both, I suppose." Claire let out a nervous laugh. "Though the notion that you have been called home to assist with a crisis that needed immediate attention is naturally a fabrication. We agreed having you summoned to London to deal with a family emergency was a reasonable explanation for you taking your leave so soon after our wedding."

He was quiet for a long moment. "How long ago were we married?"

"Three months."

"Where do we live?

"I live in a village in Wiltshire on a small estate I inherited from my grandmother. Since your unsettled nature leads you to nearly constant travel, you reside in various locations, including London." Claire took an anxious step forward. "Jay, I do not understand why you are asking—"

He held up his hand to halt her conversation, and she noticed the muscle in his jaw twitch. "You must indulge me, Madame. By your own admission you have arrived uninvited and unannounced. And I did listen politely and without interruption to your rambling about Wiltshire, the village, the small estate, Great-Aunt Agnes, and such. Surely, you owe me the same courtesy?"

"Yes, of course." Claire took a deep breath to calm herself. "Forgive me."

Her apology was automatic, a reaction to his demand that she exhibit proper manners. She was not sorry that she had given it, for it seemed to mollify him. Yet, truth be told, Claire thought Lord Fairhurst's probing questions were ridiculous.

She had often heard that husbands forgot things like birthdays and anniversaries, but Jay was acting as though he knew nothing about their relationship. It was most peculiar.

"What is my name, my full name?" he asked.

"Jasper Barrington, Lord Fairhurst."

He gave her a piercing, direct stare. "Why do you call me Jay?"

Claire lowered her chin and blushed. " 'Tis my pet name for you."

"We are married, yet we do not live together?"

"No. We agreed from the beginning that would not be necessary."

"Ah, so ours is a modern marriage? Not a love match?"

Helpless, Claire shrugged her shoulders, having no answers to give to such strange questions. Of course their marriage was not a love match. In fact, the only kiss they had ever shared had been the chaste pressing of lips at the conclusion of their wedding ceremony. How could Jay have not remembered?

A heavy silence soon surrounded them. It was an extremely uncomfortable moment.

She risked a glance at Lord Fairhurst. He had the oddest expression on his face. It was as if he were hearing these things for the first time, which made little sense, even though Claire would never refute the claim that theirs was a rather unusual marital arrangement.

"Do you wish to ask me anything else?" Claire asked quietly when the stretch of silence had nearly driven her mad.

"What?" Lord Fairhurst, who had begun pacing back

and forth across the room, turned his head sharply. "No, I believe I have heard more than enough."

Claire gazed at him, not knowing what else to say. Her limbs, nay her entire body, felt exhausted. She approached the nearest chair, but before she could collapse into it, Lord Fairhurst spoke.

"I must commend you, Madame. That was a most inspired, melodramatic performance. Claiming to be my wife was a bit over the top, but I suspect whomever hired you insisted upon it."

"Hired me?"

"Alas, you gave yourself away when you stated my full name. Only my close friends and family refer to me as Lord Fairhurst. The rest of society knows me as Viscount Fairhurst."

Claire awkwardly cleared her throat. "I do not understand—"

"Yes, yes, I've heard all that before," he replied impatiently. "The sweet, innocent, confused country bride. You do that part rather well. However, the joke is done and now you must depart. I promise I shall give a full accounting of this event to whomever contracted you to enact this little farce and assure them it was a stellar performance. Perhaps they will reward you with a bonus."

Claire felt the blood rush to her head. It warmed her cheeks and made her temples throb. She took a step back and grasped the edge of the chair to steady herself. The doubt niggling in the back of her mind that had been insisting all the while something was terribly wrong had now rapidly developed into a full-blown panic.

She gazed at Lord Fairhurst from his head to his foot, observing him with a critical eye. His hair was shorter and more conservatively styled; his face was slightly fuller. Yet, the barely noticeable bump on the bridge of his nose was visible, as was the small indentation in the center of his chin.

His clothes were expertly tailored and fitted, as usual, though a bit more formal and somber in color. It was to be expected that in this elegant environment he wielded a much stronger quality of power and authority, but there were no other obvious physical changes to his customary handsome appearance.

Puzzled, she took a few steps forward, and as she drew closer, a strange and totally unexpected thing occurred. Claire felt a rush of pure physical awareness shoot downward through her breasts and abdomen. Her heart began to flutter, and for an instant, she was robbed of breath.

She had always appreciated Jay's handsome looks. Blond hair, heavily lashed green eyes, a classic square jaw, and straight, bold nose. He was big and solid and masculine, and even though he could not seem to help his flirtatious and suggestive manner, she had never before reacted to his potent masculine charm in such a primitive, female way.

The Jay she knew made her feel safe, protected. It was the main reason she had agreed to marry him. Yet, somehow being with him in these rich surroundings made her heartbeat quicken and made her feel the most unusual and unexpected craving.

How was that possible?

"If you are quite through ogling me so shamelessly, Madame, I suggest you take your leave. My patience, a limited virtue in the best of circumstances, has quite vanished." He stalked purposefully to the door and yanked it open. "I have guests arriving in a few hours for a most important dinner party and announcement. I need to start dressing."

The sound of that deep, rich, *familiar* male baritone voice effectively cut through her wool-gathering. Claire slowly turned her head and felt a surge of dread push through her entire body. She knew she had come to the right address, to the right house. There could be no question as to the identity of this man. She knew he was in truth Lord Fairhurst.

And, yet, for some absurd and inexplicable reason, Claire also knew that although he looked and moved and sounded exactly like the gentleman who had stood beside her in the village church and pledged his vows of matrimony, this noble, arrogant, impeccably groomed man was most definitely and quite amazingly not her husband.

Chapter Two

For a moment, Lord Fairhurst feared the young woman would faint. She certainly was pale enough. Even her lips were colorless. She was taking in deep lungfuls of air, seeming to concentrate carefully on each breath. Her hands were clinging to the edge of his mother's favorite gilt chair as if it were her only lifeline. Jasper reasoned, if he tried, it would take all of his considerable strength to pry those fingers loose.

He supposed he should ask her to sit down, but he did not want in any way to encourage her to remain in the house. Her untimely interruption had already disrupted his schedule, and Jasper hated any disruption in his carefully planned day. Especially when later this evening a most important, life-altering event would occur.

"I shall have my butler fetch you a hackney coach," Jasper declared, deciding the best way to get rid of her was to provide a convenient mode of transportation. "In recognition of your worthy performance, I shall even pay the fare."

Feeling pleased with his more than generous offer, Jasper leaned his head out the open salon room door. But before he could summon his servant, a flutter of movement caught his eye. He turned his head and watched the woman slowly sink into the seat of the chair she had been holding so tightly. Her lashes fluttered, and her eyes remained fixed on the floor in front of her. Even at that angle, he could see her face was still alarmingly white, her expression incredulous.

He hesitated, trying not to be pulled in by her acting. Yet, her distress seemed disturbingly genuine. Jasper sighed loudly, and against his better judgment, shut the door and approached her.

She lifted her chin slowly, until their eyes met. "I have nowhere to go," she said quietly. "The only acquaintance I have in London is Great-Aunt Agnes. I dismissed her carriage when we arrived. I am certain by this time she has already returned home."

"It should not be a problem for the coach to deliver you to your aunt's residence."

The woman let out a short yelp of irony. "But I do not know her address."

Egad! Would this joke never end? It had gone far beyond its limited bit of humor ten minutes ago and was now beginning to reek, like three-day-old fish. For a moment, Jasper wondered who had decided to put this ridiculous prank in motion, but he soon concluded it was not worth the effort trying to establish blame. It was more important to end it. Immediately.

"Then I will instruct the coach to bring you to an inn." Jasper lifted his brow and could not resist adding, "Or would you prefer to be brought directly to Drury Lane?"

"I am not an actress!"

She gazed at him with stormy indignity. Lord Fairhurst was taken aback by this sudden burst of spirit and wondered if this show of temper was a direct result of the red-brown strands of hair he could see escaping from her unflattering bonnet. In his experience, the old cliché about women with red hair having a formidable disposition was alarmingly true.

Despite her somewhat plain appearance, that lovely hair sparked a thread of interest, and he took a moment to assess her female attributes. She was far too tall for his tastes, her face was too pointed and angular, and she had the most appalling taste in clothes. The color, quality of the cloth, and style were all wanting, though perhaps her outfit was a costume, part of her instructions to look like an affronted country maiden.

Her coloring, however, was pleasing: auburn hair; fair, creamy complexion; and startling blue eyes. Her lips were full and soft and seemed ripe for kissing. She carried herself gracefully, but with no overt awareness of her femininity.

Yet, her heavy traveling cloak could not disguise the fact that she had a well-curved figure and possessed a glorious bosom. He was surprised she was not flaunting it, for it was, in his opinion, her best feature. Under different circumstances, he probably would not have afforded her a second glance, unless she were wearing a low-cut gown.

A prickle of annoyance moved up Jasper's spine. He should not be ogling this woman's breasts. It somehow seemed disrespectful and boorish, not only to this poor creature, but to sweet Rebecca, the lovely young woman who would soon become his fiancée.

This type of behavior was more reminiscent of the old Jasper, the wild youth who cut an infamous path through the drawing rooms of society and the gaming hells of London. He had been a headstrong, unruly young man, flouting convention and public opinion at every turn. The more outrageous and scandalous the stunt, the more willing he had been to execute it.

It had been a passionate, dangerous, and wasted youth that surprised no one of the *ton*. This sort of hell-raising behavior was almost expected of a Barrington. He often imagined that society would have been disappointed if he had not been such an irresponsible young buck and had not provided the gossipmongers and disapproving matrons with hours upon hours of juicy tidbits of scandal to share and savor among themselves.

For years he did not know how it felt to enter a drawing room or ballroom without hearing the cluck of disapproving tongues, the swell of shocked gasps. The buzz of conversation usually hushed considerably as heads turned to watch him, hoping they would be able to witness firsthand the latest spectacle he would make of himself.

Jasper was the offspring of a couple labeled odd and eccentric by a closed and unforgiving society. His ancient family lineage, noble title, and substantial wealth had protected him from complete ostracism, and that knowledge had made him even more cynical and dangerous.

His older sister Meredith, a beautiful and accomplished woman, had practically been shunned by society until she unexpectedly married the Marquess of Dardington. Supported by her father-in-law, the Duke of Warwick, Meredith had unwittingly conquered and tamed the most stodgy and straitlaced London matrons.

It was Meredith's marriage that had opened Jasper's eyes to the possibility of change. He currently held the lesser title of viscount, but was, in fact, his father's heir and one day would become the Earl of Stafford.

Taking this responsibility to heart, Jasper emphatically decided it would be his mission to restore integrity to his family name, to show all of his critics that he not only knew the rules that governed polite society, he was more than willing to follow them.

For the most part, he had been successful in his task, over the years slowly and steadily erasing the memories of the past and replacing them with correct, proper behavior and attitude. The culmination of his plan was about to be achieved—marriage to a most suitable young woman, the type of individual he had always mocked and scorned in the past.

He supposed that is what made this ridiculous prank so amusing to his friends. The woman now claiming to be his wife was not merely unsuitable, she was a disaster. In her guise of a genteel country lady, she was everything he wanted to avoid.

Jasper consulted the ornate mantel clock. Damn, he was now significantly off his schedule. At this very moment he should be soaking in the bathtub, letting the steaming water ease the tension in his shoulders and back. Instead, he was being stonewalled by a barely attractive actress with a magnificent bosom.

What he really needed was a drink, but for the past few years Jasper drank only wine, and sparingly. He glanced down and realized he was drumming his fingers on the table.

"It appears we have come to an impasse, Madame," Jasper declared. "We both know full well you are not my wife. Perhaps if you tell me truthfully how you came to be here, we can end this little surprise visit on an amicable note."

The young woman tipped her head. She was chewing on her lower lip, turning it a deep, sensual rose color. "I am not an actress," she stated firmly.

Jasper ruefully considered it a measure of her talent that he nearly believed her. "Fine, you are not a professional woman of the theater, but rather a woman looking to earn an honest bit of coin. I do not judge you, Madame, but I am fast losing my patience. If you do not withdraw voluntarily, I shall have to remove you by force."

"You would not dare."

She glared at him with flared nostrils. The reaction surprised him. He had expected her to wilt back in her chair and raise a lace-bordered handkerchief to her watery eyes.

"This is *my* home. I shall *dare* anything I choose."

"I have done nothing wrong," she insisted. "Nothing. I do not understand what is happening. You are Lord Fairhurst, and you look and sound like Jay, yet you most assuredly do not act like him. I do not understand."

Her anxiety and confusion made him feel a twinge of guilt, and that annoyed him further. Plus, he really had no idea how to proceed. Though he had threatened her with bodily removal, he could not imagine himself hoisting her up like a sack of grain and carrying her out of the house, nor could he imagine watching several of his footmen perform the unpleasant duty.

Exasperated with the entire bizarre situation, Jasper threw himself into the chair directly opposite the beguiling stranger. After a moment, he lowered his chin and rested his forehead in the palm of his hand.

He should just throw her out of the house and be done with it, but there was something about her attitude and manner that stopped him.

As he was trying to gather his thoughts, Jasper heard the gentle swish of a silk skirt. Someone else had entered the room. Another wife, perhaps? Or was it the master of the joke coming to gloat?

Hoping it was the latter, so this nightmare would end, Jasper lifted his head.

"Forgive my intrusion, Jasper," a surprised female voice declared. "Cook wanted to consult with you about a change in tonight's dinner menu. Since Mother was busy, I volunteered to discuss it with you but was unaware you had company."

Lord Fairhurst sighed loudly. Perfect. Now his older sister Meredith was here to witness this debacle. Not believing his bad luck, Jasper tipped back his head against the top of his cushioned chair and placed the back of his hand over his eyes. Maybe if he pretended this was all a bad dream, when he lifted his head the two women would be gone.

Meredith had always been the constant, steady force in the family, the voice of calm and reason until he had decided it was his turn to assume that role. As a young man, she had gotten him out of more scrapes than he could count. It was rather lowering to realize he had not yet gone completely beyond that point.

"This is not a good time, Merry," Jasper declared. "Kindly tell Cook I shall deal with the menu later."

It was, of course, too much to hope that his inquisitive older sister would discreetly withdraw. Wincing at the intrusion, Jasper locked his jaw, lifted his head, and wryly observed Meredith settle herself on the adjacent brocade settee.

His sister was a stunningly beautiful woman. Age and birthing three children had not diminished, but rather enhanced, her looks. She was wearing a simple, yet fashionable, gown of lavender silk that set off the color of her eyes and the sheen of her blond hair.

The stranger was staring at Meredith with barely concealed astonishment, no doubt mesmerized by her striking looks. She seemed very conscious of her own dowdy appearance, realizing how the country mouse paled in comparison to the older, sophisticated beauty.

Once seated, his sister gave him a speculative look, then shifted her attention from him, to the woman, and back to him. Finally, she cleared her throat loudly. "You are being appallingly rude, dear brother. Please, introduce me to your guest."

Jasper's mouth tightened. There was no possible way to comply with his sister's wishes, for he did not know the woman's name. Still, there was no way to avoid the inevitable.

Lord Fairhurst let out a loud sigh and announced quite dryly, "My sister, Meredith Morely, Marchioness of Dardington, begs to be introduced. Regretfully, I cannot comply, since this young woman has not offered her last name or her Christian name."

Meredith's brow knit into a tiny frown. "Is she the relative of an acquaintance?"

"No," Jasper drawled lazily. He paused, pensively tapping a finger against his chin. "Apparently, she is my wife."

There was a brief moment of utter silence.

"How delightful," the unflappable Meredith replied. "I must ask, is this a sudden occurrence, or have you been keeping this marriage a secret for a long time?"

Jasper peeked over at the stranger, wondering if she would finally admit the truth, but she maintained a straight face, exuding remarkable calm under intense scrutiny.

" 'Tis a prank, Merry," Lord Fairhurst replied. "One I find not in the least bit amusing. Summers is the most likely suspect, though Monteguy might have had a hand in it, too."

"What unusual company you keep, brother."

Jasper shrugged, trying to remain unruffled by his sister's perceptive eyes. Over the years, he had greatly modified his inner circle of friends, but many of his youthful companions were now also men of rank, privilege, and power. It was impossible to avoid them, and their ridiculous idea of humor.

"When Hastings became engaged, they got him drunk and had a leg shackle, complete with a ball and chain, fastened to his ankle. It cost him a pretty penny and took nearly half the day to have it removed." Jasper's lips curled into a wry grin. "For some peculiar reason, it seems whenever the parson's mousetrap hovers around one of us, the rest of the bachelors get a bit nervous."

"So, acting like a bunch of imbeciles calms one's nerves?" Meredith inquired sarcastically.

"I did not say I approve or endorse these antics," Jasper replied defensively. "And since this prank was pulled on me, I can hardly be held responsible."

Meredith lifted her eyes to the heavens. "What happens now?"

"I wait for the orchestrator of this madness to reveal himself and pretend it was a hilarious and clever scheme, thus illustrating to one and all what a good sport I can be. In the meantime, my little wife departs so I can speak with Cook about the menu and attend to any other last-minute details for this evening's festivities."

Jasper turned his head and glowered at his "wife". She had remained silent and motionless for the past few minutes, but he did not doubt that she was listening attentively to each and every word. "Though getting this young woman to leave is a far more difficult task to accomplish than it sounds."

Being reminded of his lack of success in that area galled Lord Fairhurst into action. Jasper stood and narrowed the short distance between himself and the stranger. He reached down and took the young woman's hand in his, intending to assist her from her chair. But at his touch, she came alive. She shook off his grasp, then shot to her feet as if she had been fired from a pistol.

"I am not leaving until this mystery is solved, my lord," she said loudly. "My name is Claire Truscott Barrington, Lady Fairhurst. Or rather Viscountess Fairhurst. You, sir, are my husband. We were married three months ago at the village church. Reverend Clarkson presided over the ceremony, and he was so nervous he nearly misread the lines. We laughed about it together in the carriage on the way to the assembly that was held in our honor. You threw coins to the children who ran alongside the coach, and when they chanted and teased, you kissed me, ever so gently, on the cheek."

"Madame—"

She shook her head frantically and kept on speaking. Jasper remained silent, reasoning she would eventually run out of energy. He cocked his head to one side, folded his arms across his chest, and waited. Her breathing was short and shallow, and the words rushed, tumbled, and spewed from her lips like a waterfall.

"As bride and groom we led off the opening set of country dances. It was warm that day, despite the time of year. Nearly everyone in the village came to wish us well. We all ate and drank too much, and you made everyone laugh and then tear-up when you gave a toast to the health and happiness of your new bride."

She raised her arm and pointed an accusing finger directly at his chest.

"Your birthday is the tenth of June. Your favorite color is green. You like roasted guinea fowl, dislike peas prepared in any way, and insist upon having something sweet at the end of each meal, even breakfast. You have a large scar on your left wrist, shaped like a crescent moon. You told me it was a momento of a boyhood prank when you decided to try your luck posing as a highwayman.

"Amazingly, the driver of the coach took an eight-year-old boy seriously and halted the vehicle at your command, but when he realized you were merely a child, he struck the reins and took off. That sudden movement spooked your horse and you fell, hitting a sharp stone and cutting your wrist badly."

The last bit stopped Jasper cold. She continued speaking, but he had ceased listening. Something very strange was going on. There was too much truth and intimate detail for this woman to be reciting a script. His birthday was indeed on June 10th, and he did enjoy a good roasted guinea fowl, though it was not his very favorite meal.

He did not have an incurable sweet tooth, or possess a large, crescent scar on his left wrist as a result of a short-lived career as a highwayman. However, Lord Fairhurst was very well acquainted with someone who did—his identical twin brother, Jason.

Flabbergasted, Jasper turned and met his sister's eyes. They were round and wide, reflecting the same shock that was at this moment coursing through his body.

"My God," Meredith whispered. "This dear girl is married to Jason."

Releasing a steady stream of rambling dialogue had eased some of the tension throbbing in Claire's head. Speaking the words out loud had somehow made it real, had reenforced the memories of what she and Jay had shared, had assured her that their bond was solid and strong, even though she knew that something was very wrong.

It had been difficult to maintain a blank expression and remain calm when Lady Meredith had entered the room, especially since she and her brother had proceeded to discuss her as if she were not sitting right beside them.

Though not overtly derogatory, it had been a lowering and uncomfortable experience. Claire was pleased that she had been able to keep both her pride and temper in check, for each had been sorely tested.

Yet, the ordeal was far from over. They had listened to her tirade of memories because she gave them no choice. Yet, mercifully, something she had said must have struck a chord, for they were exchanging looks and remarks at a frantic pace.

Calling on all her willpower, Claire reined in her racing heart and schooled her features into an expression of interested detachment. It gave her a perverse sense of gratification to turn the tables on her reluctant host and his sister. For it was now the viscount and Lady Meredith who wore nearly matching confounded expressions.

"We have all had a great shock, but I believe that Jasper and I have managed to solve the mystery," Lady Meredith finally announced. She sank down gracefully on a chair and indicated that Claire should do the same. Lord Fairhurst remained standing, taking a position directly beside his sister.

Lady Meredith adjusted her skirts and gave Claire a friendly, encouraging look. "Now then, Claire. May I call you Claire?"

Claire nodded her head.

The marchioness smiled. "Good. And you must call me Meredith. We are, after a fashion, sisters."

Claire drew in a sharp breath and turned to Lord Fairhurst. He affected a grimace. She tilted her chin a little higher even as she felt the warmth flood her face. Though she had been insisting for the past twenty minutes that this man was her husband, more and more Claire was doubting that was true. It was an equally maddening, frightening, and utterly confusing situation.

"What do you wish to tell me, Lady Meredith?" Claire asked.

The older woman nodded eagerly. "It appears that you have made an honest and understandable mistake, for you are clearly not aware of all the facts. You claim that Jasper is your husband, yet he claims he has never before set eyes on you and believes you are part of an ill-advised prank."

Claire twisted the fingers resting in her lap tightly together. "There is no prank."

Lady Meredith clucked her tongue. "The prank, I fear, was played on you, Claire."

"What?"

"Lord Fairhurst and I have deduced that you are indeed married to a Barrington, a man who is a member of our family," Lady Meredith continued. "However, your husband, scoundrel that he is, neglected to mention that he has a twin brother."

Twins? They were twins? Claire felt her jaw go slack. She turned her head, but when her eyes met Lord Fairhurst's, she hastily lowered her chin. She had never in her life felt more embarrassed.

Twins! It was such a simple, logical explanation, yet it did not produce a simple, calm resolution to her situation. Instead, it presented another bizarre truth that made Claire's mind whirl with even greater confusion.

"I had no idea Jay had a twin brother. He rarely spoke of his family, and when he did, it was only in very general terms." Claire tried to let out a nervous laugh, but instead made an odd, mirthless sound. She could feel Lord Fairhurst's eyes focused upon her.

"Ah, so now you finally realize I am not your Jay," he said in a smug tone. "And by-the-by, your husband's name is Jason."

Feeling at a total loss, Claire slowly sank against the cushioned back of her chair. Her cheeks grew warm with heat, and for a moment, she felt completely disoriented. Jay, or rather Jason, had a twin brother! It was almost too much to absorb. This newest revelation put an odd and most unexpected crimp in her situation.

"Stop gloating, Jasper," Meredith admonished. "You are frightening Claire, and the last thing she needs is more distress."

"Sorry." Though he readily apologized, Lord Fairhurst's expression barely altered.

" 'Tis remarkable how much they look alike, is it not?" Lady Meredith grinned. "As boys they seldom had difficulty fooling their nannies and foisting the blame on each other for their misdeeds and raucous behavior, though they both got into trouble so often, I think they usually forgot which one was responsible."

"The nannies were easy," Lord Fairhurst interjected. "We were even able to fool Mother and Father on occasion. But never you, Merry."

"I caught on fast to your tricks." Lady Meredith let out a charming laugh. "It was more a matter of survival than skill. You were so wild and unpredictable, first as boys and even worse when you were young men. As I have told you more than once, the numerous gray hairs on my head are a testament to what I was forced to endure."

Claire was astonished to notice that Lord Fairhurst's eyes had warmed considerably. He leaned eagerly toward his sister, his posture more relaxed, his demeanor less threatening. There seemed to be real affection and regard between the siblings. Yet not, Claire suspected, between the brothers.

"I can see this has all been a great shock for you, Claire," Lady Meredith remarked in a sympathetic tone.

"Yes, it has, Lady Meredith," Claire answered. "As I mentioned, Jay spoke briefly of his family, and then only in very general terms. I do recall a reference he made to his brother, but the way he spoke of him led me to believe this brother was a much older man. A serious, dour, almost morose individual, nearly the exact opposite of Jay. A stickler for rules and propriety who was intolerably stuffy and quite a bo—"

Claire halted abruptly when she realized what she was saying and who she was insulting. Lady Meredith was regarding her with open amusement, a sweet grin on her lovely face. Lord Fairhurst looked ready to chew on nails.

"I imagine my brother portrayed me as a bit of a stuffed shirt," Lord Fairhurst said. Though his voice was calm, his nostrils flared in an expression that might have been anger. "What else would one expect from a grown man who has never experienced a crisis of conscience? Jason has always taken great delight in deliberately keeping the word *responsibility* absent from his vocabulary and his actions.

"He has repeatedly brought disgrace and dishonor to our family name, basking in his rude and vulgar behavior, despite our pleas to have a care for his reputation.

We have recently reached the alarmingly low point where revealing his name to others is now explanation enough for most of his rakehell antics. 'Tis a miracle, indeed, that any respectable family in society even bothers to acknowledge any of us."

"Jasper, enough," Lady Meredith chided.

Lord Fairhurst huffed for a moment longer, but held his tongue. Claire concluded this was hardly the first time this bone of contention between the siblings had been discussed.

"I need to see Jay as soon as possible," Claire declared, hoping the brothers would at least be able to conduct themselves civilly when they were in each other's company. She had worried that her sudden arrival would create an uncomfortable situation for her husband, but she never imagined how unpleasant things could become.

Lady Meredith turned a frowning face toward her. "Jason is not here."

"When is he expected home?"

"When the mood strikes him, I suppose." Lord Fairhurst replied. His tone held a mingling of mockery and scorn.

"Actually, I do not believe Jason is in Town," Meredith said. "Was he expected at the party this evening, Jasper?"

"No." Lord Fairhurst's expression darkened further. "Naturally, it would be too much for us to hope that our brother would be available to take charge of this messy situation. He always thinks 'tis best to leave that arduous chore to others."

"Jasper!" Lady Meredith exclaimed.

"I mean no insult, but this young woman is Jason's responsibility, not mine, thank the good Lord. However, something must be done with her." He removed a watch from his breast coat pocket and consulted the time. "I am horribly off schedule and have numerous items that need my immediate attention. Can you please handle this, Meredith?"

Claire's breath hitched in her lungs. How ridiculous to feel so rejected. She did not know this man; there was no reason to care about his opinion of her. Yet somehow it stung to be so soundly dismissed.

Still, she felt rather certain he would be singing a different tune once he knew the entire truth. Claire fleetingly pondered how to bring up the one extraordinary fact that would in essence change everything. The viscount's current state of annoyance would seem tame when he learned that astonishingly she really was his responsibility.

Hoping to soften the blow, Claire cowardly began by apologizing.

"Though as you clearly now know this was an honest mistake, I feel I must apologize for the difficulties I caused both of you this evening."

Lord Fairhurst's faint laugh held little humor. "Think nothing of it."

He bowed curtly, then pivoted on his heel and stalked toward the door. Claire followed behind him, scurrying to match his long strides.

"We seem to have put this rather odd puzzle of my marriage into place, my lord; however, there is one item I fear I must point out."

Lord Fairhurst stopped and turned his head, glancing at her over his shoulder.

"Yes?" His voice was vague and impatient, as if he had already dismissed her from his thoughts.

Claire looked back and forth, at Lord Fairhurst and his sister, wishing there was some way she could avoid telling them the entire truth. She knew the reaction to her news was going to be extreme, but there was no way to keep it from being revealed.

"Though I believe we have established it was Jason, and not you, who spoke the wedding vows, the name that is entered on my marriage license is Jasper Barrington, Lord Fairhurst."

She heard the marchioness gasp, but Claire's eyes remained riveted on Lord Fairhurst. Two spots of color appeared on his face, marring his handsome cheeks.

"What are you saying?"

"The same thing I have been repeating all afternoon," she replied miserably. "You are my husband. I confess I do not for the life of me understand it, but in the eyes of the world, I am Claire Truscott Barrington, Lady Fairhurst. Your lawful wife."

Chapter Three

Claire's head turned sharply at the sound of a knock at the door. Though she had been waiting for such a summons, it nevertheless jolted her nerves. Anxiously, her eyes gazed at the clock. Had it truly only been three hours since she first set foot in this house?

Lord Fairhurst had been tight-lipped with astonishment after she had revealed the final tidbit of truth about her marriage. Thankfully, Lady Meredith had been able to calm her brother's ire. The siblings had spoken together in low whispers while Claire helplessly watched, at a loss to explain how or why this had happened.

Then a servant had been called and instructed to escort Claire to a guest room. *It was better than being thrown out in the street,* she supposed. *But just barely.*

If only she knew Great-Aunt Agnes's address, she could leave this house and never again think about this family.

Are you losing your wits, as well as your nerve? Her fate was forever bound here, for she was in truth married to a Barrington man. But which one?

The knock sounded again. "They are asking for you downstairs, Miss. Will you come now, or shall I tell them to wait?"

"Just a moment," Claire called out. She took a deep

breath, feeling the butterflies she had struggled to contain break free and flutter wildly in her stomach.

Forcing her feet to move forward, Claire crossed the elegant room, pleased that she at least had been able to clean off the dust of travel and change into a fresh gown that a servant had somehow managed to quickly iron. It was the most fashionable garment she had packed, a fine muslin dress with a modest neckline, embroidered bodice, and high waist. It was also Jay's favorite dress, and Claire hoped wearing it would give her a dose of much needed courage.

Yet, when she reached the bedchamber door, she hesitated. Fearing she was losing her nerve, Claire closed her eyes and pressed her forehead against the thick, wooden door panel. Breathing deeply, she struggled to slow the racing of her heart, to ignore the doubt and fear that clung to her. Yet it trickled in icy drops down her spine, threatening to steal away the final bits of her dignity.

"Miss?"

Claire swallowed. She had done nothing wrong, yet she felt like a criminal for causing such an uproar in this household. At an early age, she had learned to think before she acted and to weigh carefully every scheme and wild impulse that entered her vivid imagination, fearing she would land herself in great trouble.

Thus, she had lived her life cautiously and carefully, regretting very little. She imagined most people would feel she was an equal victim in this bizarre situation, but Claire knew that if she had never set foot in this house, none of this would be happening.

Yet agonizing over it was a fruitless waste of time and energy. With deliberate force, Claire squared her shoulders and pushed away from the door, willing the pounding of her heart to slow. Unpleasant moments were best faced head-on. The sooner she arrived at this meeting, the sooner this mess could be untangled and she could move forward.

The moment she stepped into the hallway, a footman appeared from the shadows. He was the same young man who had escorted her to her room earlier. He gave her a curious glance, and Claire felt her face blush with color.

Though she had little experience with a household of this size, Claire imagined that servants were pretty much the same everywhere, and that any employee worth their salt would have heard about her arrival—and her outrageous claims.

She could only imagine what they all thought of this bizarre situation. And of her. But the servants were the very least of her worries right now, for when she entered the green salon a second time, Claire was unpleasantly surprised to discover the room held six occupants.

"Claire, you look charming," Lady Meredith said, immediately coming forward and slipping her arm supportively through Claire's. "I hope you were able to rest. Come, let me introduce you to everyone."

Claire greatly appreciated Lady Meredith's assistance, although her nerves were too shredded to form more than fleeting impressions of the individuals she met.

Lord Fairhurst's parents, the Earl and Countess of Stafford, were a striking couple. Well preserved for their age, they were fit and healthy, attractive and refined. Claire could see a distinct resemblance between the older couple and their son in looks, if not temperament. They greeted her kindly, with encouraging smiles and a warm handshake. She was grateful for their tolerance.

Lady Meredith's husband, the Marquess of Dardington, was tall, broad shouldered, and remarkably handsome. His haughty demeanor and distant greeting proclaimed his aristocratic heritage and clearly conveyed his suspicions about her character. Claire hoped he would refrain from voicing his opinions too vehemently.

As they swept around the room, the ladies paused in front of Lord Fairhurst. Naturally, no introduction was necessary. Claire curtsied, then lifted her head just enough so her eyes met his. Her heart gave a hard, solitary thump.

He had changed into evening attire. The black coat and formal satin breeches looked elegant and expensive, though she suspected he could be wearing humble workman's clothes and still look like a lord. His white cravat had been tied in an intricate knot, and his silk vest was a subdued pattern of silver threads on a slightly darker background.

The sight of him so masculine and powerful sent a wild reaction rushing through her. He was in appearance, she realized, the nearly perfect male specimen. Sparks flared and sizzled throughout her body, causing the most unusual and unexpected emotions.

Though he barely glanced at her, Claire experienced the oddest sensation that her destiny was standing before her. No matter what happened tonight, from this moment forward, she would never be the same again.

The sound of Lady Meredith's voice making the final introduction startled Claire, bringing her back to her surroundings.

"And this is Mr. Walter Beckham, our family solicitor."

Claire smiled faintly as the portly gentleman executed an awkward bow, then removed a snowy white handkerchief from his breast coat pocket and wiped the sweat from his brow. Claire could not help but notice that he looked nearly as apprehensive as she felt.

A moment later everyone was seated with the door closed firmly behind them.

"Shall we begin?" the solicitor asked.

All eyes turned automatically toward Claire. She frowned. "I am uncertain where to start," she said honestly.

Mr. Beckham gallantly came to her rescue. "Lord Fairhurst and Lady Meredith have already told us about the discrepancy concerning the name on your marriage license," he said. "Is it therefore accurate to state that you intended to marry Mr. Jason Barrington and not Lord Fairhurst?"

"Yes, of course." Claire lifted her chin and was discomforted to see the intense scrutiny everyone was affording her. She eyed them back warily, consciously clinging to her dignity.

"Perchance, do you have your marriage license with you?" the solicitor inquired. "I will need to examine the paper closely to determine its legal authenticity."

Claire felt her skin redden. "I left my home in Wiltshire with the intention of visiting my husband. I hardly felt it necessary to carry such an important document on my person."

"But you can produce it?" Mr. Beckham prompted.

"Naturally. The marriage is also recorded in the village church registry." Claire twisted her fingers. "But I can tell you with utmost certainty that the name of the groom is Jasper Barrington, Lord Fairhurst."

Silence fell as they all seemed to digest that most unwelcome bit of news.

Mr. Beckham once again removed his handkerchief and wiped his brow. "If that is indeed correct, this could be considered a marriage by proxy. Which would mean the young lady is married to Lord Fairhurst."

"Truly?" Lord Dardington asked.

The solicitor's fleshy double chin quivered as he nervously jerked his head up and down.

"Bloody hell," Lord Fairhurst groaned. "I'm going to strangle Jason. After I first pound him senseless."

"Jasper, such language. I know you are distressed, but there is no need to be vulgar," the countess admonished her son. "I am certain this was an inadvertent mistake that will easily be put to rights."

After exchanging a concerned glance with her husband, the countess then focused an appraising gaze on Claire, causing the tall black hair plumes nestled within the older woman's upswept coiffure to wave noticeably. "Do tell us how you met Jason, my dear, and how he came to be your husband. I am sure it is a wildly romantic tale."

Claire plastered on an innocent smile, wondering how vague she should be with her answers. Yet, even if she had any skill in weaving a tale, this was not a group that could be easily fooled. Best then to stick with the truth and provide as few details as possible.

"We had an unusually cold winter this season, with an unpredictable amount of snow," Claire began. "At the start of the new year, Jay was traveling through our village when the roads became impassable. Due to the deteriorating weather conditions, he was forced to stay a few days at the local inn."

Lord Dardington looked at her with raised brows. "You met him there? At a common inn? Were you also stranded?"

"Heavens, no." Claire swallowed convulsively. She did not appreciate the marquess's boldness or his implication of impropriety, yet his suspicions were not a total surprise. He had made his feelings rather evident when he met her.

"My family owns a modest manor house in the area, so naturally I was at home," Claire explained. "However, when Jay fell ill with a nasty cold and fever, I was summoned."

"To care for him?" the countess asked in a scandalized whisper.

"Gracious." Claire dragged in a tight breath. Is this what they really thought of her? The very idea of an unmarried woman caring so intimately for a male stranger made her feel light-headed. "I took no active part in Jay's recovery. Our local physician, Mr. Fletcher, tended to his needs. My mother is renowned for her gardening skills and the abundance of her annual harvest. Thus, we are blessed with an ample supply of medicinal herbs, which are freely shared with anyone in need.

"At Mr. Fletcher's request, I brought several packets of herbs to the inn. When Jay had recovered his health, he came to our home to offer his thanks to us all. It was then that we met."

"And no doubt instantly fell in love," the marquess remarked with a dismissive snort.

Claire stifled an angry retort. Her relationship with her husband was unconventional and unusual, but it was also private. The marquess had no right to cast aspersions upon it, even given these odd circumstances. Her anger continued to simmer until, from the corner of her eye, Claire noticed the cold glare Lady Meredith cast at her husband.

Knowing she had an unlikely ally made Claire's flagging spirits revive.

"I would like to ask a question," the countess said.

She bestowed an encouraging smile on Claire. "Our son's name is Jason. Why do you call him Jay?"

Claire returned the smile. "When he registered at the inn, he signed his name J. Barrington. When he was ill with fever, he was unable to tell anyone his full name, so we began to refer to him as Jay.

"After he recovered, I asked him what the initial stood for, but he refused to tell me. We shared many laughs as I tried guessing. In retaliation, I teasingly began to call him Jay, and eventually it stuck." Claire inclined her head. "I was therefore in no way suspicious on our wedding day when I saw my husband's name listed as Jasper."

There was a hum of conversation as everyone digested and discussed this latest revelation. Claire was grateful for this brief respite of scrutiny. It was exhausting to be the center of so much negative attention.

But her relief was short-lived. There were two individuals present who had not ceased watching, gauging, and judging her. Claire felt their gaze upon her even as they conversed together in low, serious tones. Head high, she glanced in their direction.

Seeing those identical expressions of stoic male reserve on the marquess and Lord Fairhurst made Claire more cautious. She had always prided herself on possessing a keen mind and quick wit, yet she knew she was out-matched when faced with the combined force of these two men.

Stiffening her spine, she braced herself for the next barrage of questions.

"You told me earlier this afternoon that you were married three months ago, yet you only became acquainted with my brother at the start of the year," Lord Fairhurst stated in an even, uninflected tone. "That is an exceedingly short acquaintance for two strangers to set their minds upon marriage."

"Yes, it was a very brief courtship." Claire's heart thudded uncomfortably, but she did not succumb to the temptation to lower her gaze. She knew the moment Lord Fairhurst suspected a vulnerability he would pounce, and she was determined to loyally keep Jay's confidences.

"Whirlwind romances are often the best kind," Lady Meredith interjected.

"Yes, they are," the countess agreed. "Though I am rather vexed that Jason did not inform us of his intentions to take a bride, nor did he bring her to Town so we could be properly introduced. At the very least, he could have written to us. After all, he knew how much we have all longed for him to settle down." The older woman glanced pointedly at Claire's lower abdomen. "And have a family."

Claire turned cold inside. There was not even the remotest possibility that she was carrying a child. It was the one regret she had had when agreeing to marry Jay—accepting the fact that she would never become a mother.

Drawing herself up, Claire waited for someone to make a sly comment about the oldest reason known to mankind for a hasty marriage. The hot denial hovered on the edge of her tongue, but fortunately it was unnecessary to express it, for no one had the audacity to directly address such a delicate subject in mixed company.

"I believe that Claire has told us all that she can about her marriage," Lady Meredith said, turning to glare at her husband and brother. "She can hardly be expected to answer questions about things she was unaware of when she took her vows, specifically why Jasper's name is on the marriage license. It seems rather obvious that only Jason can explain precisely what occurred."

"Exactly," the countess agreed. "We need to get in touch with him at once." She turned to Claire. "Where can he be reached?"

"I do not know where he is staying." Though she tried to avoid it, Claire could feel herself shrinking into the cushion of her chair. "Obviously, I thought he was in London, or else I never would have ventured into Town."

"What was his last known address?" Lord Fairhurst inquired.

"The only address I have is this one."

"Well, we all know that he is not here," Lord Fairhurst remarked dryly. "Where did he go when he left you?"

"I believe he was heading towards Scotland, but I cannot say so with any degree of certainty. His only remark to me on the morning of his departure was that he had not made a definite decision. He did, however, leave me with the distinct impression that he would be returning to London when the Season began."

Lord Fairhurst threw her a long-suffering look. "The Season is starting now and runs for months. It could be weeks before he arrives in Town."

Claire shrugged her shoulders helplessly. Lady Meredith had been right—Claire could hardly provide answers to questions that were an equal puzzlement to her, even if the proper and stoic Lord Fairhurst commanded it.

After a moment of brooding silence, Lord Fairhurst blew out a noisy breath. "I suppose that someone has to say it, so it might as well be me." He gazed sharply down at Claire, his expression almost grim. "You have a most peculiar marriage, Madame."

Claire felt the exasperation flare in her eyes. Even if

they were Jay's family, they had no right to judge her. "This arrangement suits us very well," she declared.

"How delightful that you are happy." Lord Fairhurst's voice was cold, hard, and flat. "However, this arrangement does not suit me at all. Why in the world did Jason use my name on that license? What could he possibly be thinking?"

The question was rhetorical and addressed to no one in particular. Now that she had learned the truth, Claire had a faint idea of what might have prompted Jay's action, but she was not going to share her theory with his family.

Besides, understanding the reasoning would not in any way change the situation. As her father often said, what's done is done.

"True, this is a devilish coil, but I believe the more important question is which brother is the groom," the marquess said philosophically. "What is your opinion of this matter, Mr. Beckham?"

The solicitor, who had remained silent and observant for the past ten minutes, bolted to attention. "Marriage by proxy is rarely used anymore, yet it is still a legal and binding agreement between two parties. In this instance, there is sufficient evidence that would support the claim of Mr. Jason standing up in his brother's stead and taking a bride on behalf of Lord Fairhurst."

"How is that possible?" Lord Fairhurst asked in a disbelieving tone. "When the wedding took place without my knowledge or consent?"

"Logically, one would assume that should be enough to end this discussion, but the law can be complicated." The solicitor smiled nervously, as if trying to ease the impact of his answers. "It should be possible to prove that the marriage is a farce, since you did not give your brother the authority to act on your behalf. However, he is your legal heir, and that muddies the waters a bit.

"I must study this carefully, but it might be best to have the union annulled, to make certain all legal ties between you and the young lady are completely severed. Though I must point out the process requires agreements from the Regent, as well as Parliament. It will take time. A considerable amount of time."

As she listened intently to every word Mr. Beckham uttered, Claire kept her eyes on Lord Fairhurst, studying his face, hoping to decipher his reactions. But his handsome features resembled chiseled granite.

"What if my brother were to claim her as his wife?" Lord Fairhurst asked. "Would that absolve me of all responsibility?"

"It might be helpful if Mr. Jason testified that it was his intention to marry this young woman," Mr. Beckham replied. "Then again, that might not be enough. If your name has been duly and properly recorded on the papers, it could be argued that you are the husband. That is why it might be best to petition the government to act in all haste and grant an annulment. With the support of several influential noblemen, dissolution of the marriage could pass through the House of Lords in a more reasonable time frame."

Lord Fairhurst's eyes narrowed. "Please, cease talking in legal circles, Beckham, and answer one question with a straight answer. Am I married to the girl or not?"

The solicitor licked his full lips. "I regret to say, my lord, 'tis not quite as simple as a yeah or nay answer."

"Then, pray, relate the complicated version. Very briefly." Lord Fairhurst's words reverberated through the room. "For in less than two hours' time I am expected to announce my betrothal to another woman. Clearly I cannot do that if I am already married."

Claire felt her jaw drop. She had heard the viscount and his sister discussing his upcoming announcement, and she also knew Lord Fairhurst was expecting guests for an important dinner party, but she had no idea he was intending to announce his engagement tonight. How horrifying! No wonder his anger and annoyance had reached epic proportions.

Mr. Beckham's eyes grew round with distress as he shifted uneasily in his seat. "I feel I must warn you that declaring your intentions publicly to wed would be ill-advised, my lord. At this time," he added hastily.

Lord Fairhurst shook his head sharply, angrily, as if trying to clear his mind. He left his seat and began to pace the room with restless energy. Eventually, he stopped at one of the windows and leaned heavily on the ledge. His fingers gripped the wood so tightly that his knuckles turned white.

After a few moments, he whirled around and looked straight at Claire. She recoiled at the expression on his face, feeling his accusing stare shudder through her body.

"Are you saying, Mr. Beckham, that I am married to this woman? And it will take nothing short of an annulment to dissolve this fiasco of a union?"

For a moment, no one spoke. Or dared to breathe.

Finally, Mr. Beckham gulped, letting out an odd, strangling sound from the back of his throat. "That is, indeed, a very real possibility, my lord."

It was the waiting, Jasper decided, that made each minute seem inordinately long, that grated so finely on his already worn nerves. The waiting, coupled with knowing he was about to do something hurtful to an innocent bystander, ruffled Lord Fairhurst's renown calm and added fuel to his growing ire.

Alone, pacing restlessly in the drawing room, he could hear the sound of arriving carriages, the hum of conversation and laughter, and the continual opening and closing of the front door. The dinner guests had begun to assemble, and he was not there with the rest of his family to greet them. This was *not* how he had envisioned this important evening unfolding.

Earlier, Jasper had sent his most trusted and reliable servant with an urgent message to Miss Rebecca Manning, requesting her presence in the drawing room for a private meeting before the party. No doubt the poor girl thought he was trying to orchestrate a stolen romantic moment between them, perhaps even the presentation of a precious piece of jewelry to commemorate their upcoming engagement.

Now he wondered if that engagement would ever occur. Sighing with frustration, Jasper glanced at the crystal whiskey decanter on the side table, wishing he could find solace in a glass of spirits. Yet he knew liquor would hardly be a comfort to him.

Breaking this news was one of the most wretched tasks he would ever be forced to undertake. He could not possibly insult his intended bride more than being in his cups when he gave her the disturbing news that their wedding must be postponed.

All thanks to the antics of his brainless brother. This latest stunt was merely a miserable reminder of the scandalous reputation his family had long held. And apparently deserved.

Jasper sighed with exasperation, yet it was more than

this difficult situation that had put him in such a state. Secretly, he worried that, despite his Herculean efforts, it might not be possible to alter the course of one's destiny, to escape one's heritage. No matter how tightly he held himself in check, how cautious and controlled he was in his manner and action, he was still a Barrington—an infamous Barrington.

From the doorway, the butler announced the arrival of Mr. Charles Manning and his daughters, Miss Anne and Miss Rebecca. Glancing up, Jasper saw his chosen bride standing in the doorway.

She was flanked on one side by her father and the other side by her sister. For an instant, he felt a spark of annoyance that she had not come to him alone, as he had instructed, but then felt grateful that she had valued her spotless reputation and good name sufficiently to challenge his request and brought along not one but two chaperones.

This caution and adherence to proper etiquette only reinforced Jasper's conviction that Rebecca was precisely the right woman to be his bride. Appearance, propriety, and adherence to society's strict rules would always rule Rebecca's life.

She looked enchanting in a gown of green silk that caught the candlelight and made her rich, dark hair shimmer. Her heavily lashed eyes were glowing with confidence and excitement; her refined face flushed with anticipation.

Rebecca's beauty was even more extraordinary when compared with the sister standing beside her, a woman who was slender to the point of thinness, with unremarkable brown hair; a long, oval face; and large, sad eyes.

"Good evening, my lord," Rebecca said softly. Her

lips curved into a beguiling smile. " 'Tis lovely to see you again."

Jasper winced. Her trusting innocence made his task even more difficult. She had no idea what was afoot. Indeed, how could any sane person imagine the bind he found himself embroiled in, or suspect that all was very much not what it seemed.

Burying these emotions, Jasper moved forward and welcomed Rebecca graciously, taking her gloved hands in his own and answering her graceful curtsy with a low bow. "Thank you for coming so quickly," he said. "I hope you were not terribly inconvenienced by my summons."

"More surprised than inconvenienced," Rebecca replied, broadening her smile and showing all her perfect teeth. "Women are a simple and curious breed. Your message was equally urgent and cryptic, an almost irresistible combination for any female."

He answered her smile out of politeness, then led her to his mother's favorite damask chaise. The moment she was seated, Rebecca gazed at him fully, a light of sharp curiosity in her sweet blue eyes. But she was a lady of proper breeding and did not indulge her whims; instead, she waited respectfully for him to speak. Jasper's guilt increased tenfold.

Standing on his feet, facing her squarely, Jasper spoke, " 'Tis my unfortunate duty to tell you that due to circumstances I cannot control, we are unable to announce our betrothal this evening as we had originally intended. However, I am hopeful the unexpected problem that is hindering our plans will be resolved shortly so we can move forward as we had agreed."

For a moment, it seemed that Rebecca did not understand him. "What are you saying? Why must we wait to announce our betrothal?" She blinked rapidly, her soulful eyes filling with tears. "Have you changed your mind?"

Anne moved forward and hovered protectively closer to her sister. "I am certain you have misunderstood, Rebecca," she said soothingly, before darting a glance of horror in his direction. "Lord Fairhurst would never do anything so crass and ill-mannered as breaking his word and jilting a woman he had promised to marry."

Jasper gritted his teeth at the backhanded compliment and braced himself for further scorn. "You are correct, Miss Manning. I have every intention of making Rebecca my wife; however, my brother Jason recently married, and there seems to be some confusion over the legalities of the union."

"But what does that have to do with your marriage to my daughter?" Charles Manning inquired. Short, bald, and filled with an overblown sense of importance, the elder Manning guarded his daughters tenaciously.

Jasper had never particularly cared for the man, but had given that dislike no more than a passing thought, because he reasoned he would see very little of him once he and Rebecca wed. But now he would have to deal with Charles Manning and not from a position of strength. Revealing the truth would place Jasper in the worst possible light and leave him in a position that was barely defensible.

"There is a slight possibility that the woman who spoke her vows with my brother is *my* wife."

"What!"

Knowing there was no choice, Jasper reluctantly repeated the words.

"You slick bastard!" Charles Manning shouted with open contempt.

The older man had been sitting silently watching

Jasper with cold, hostile eyes, but this revelation apparently catapulted him to action. With surprising agility for a man of his years and bulk, he leapt from his chair and lunged toward Lord Fairhurst. Jasper neatly dodged his lunge.

"How dare you toy with my daughter's affections?" Manning shouted. "You made promises, my lord, promises to my Rebecca that I intend to make certain you abide by. There will be no disgrace brought upon our name, no blackening of our reputation."

"Father, please!" Rebecca cried out.

Her sister Anne got to her feet and rushed forward, trying to hold their father back. Jasper could see the older man's shoulders rise and fall with frustration as he struggled to control his rancor.

In contrast, Rebecca had never looked more fragile and delicate. Her face turned pale as parchment, and her eyes were a mixture of confusion and fear—fear of the unimaginable, fear of being jilted and humiliated. Her lips quivered, and she pressed a hand to her forehead, completing the picture of maidenly helplessness.

It was in that moment that Jasper realized that he had never kissed her, had never once shared that significant intimacy. This was out of a sense of propriety, of course, and deep and proper respect for the woman that was going to be his wife.

She was a lovely woman. Many in society called her beautiful. He had chosen her to be his mate because she possessed the necessary qualities of character, and although he admired her beauty, he felt surprisingly cool and untouched by desire whenever he was near her.

And never more so than at that moment. She was such a delicate bloom, all gracious charm, mannerly behavior, and feminine dignity. She would make the perfect countess when the time came. Her usually chilly demeanor and self-contained emotions were to be admired; that was part of what made her so suitable to be his wife.

He wanted his wife to be predictable, prim, and even a bit dull. He preferred that she did nothing whatsoever to stir his sexual desire. He strongly felt that would add far more meaning to their lifetime relationship and would allow him to keep his own naturally passionate nature under control.

Yet, suddenly, he questioned if he could exist in such a life. *Would grace, dignity, and proper decorum be enough?*

Shaking off the odd direction of his thoughts, Jasper stiffened his shoulders and returned his full attention to the drama at hand.

"We must allow Lord Fairhurst to explain," Anne said. "Father, please be seated. For Rebecca's sake."

With a huff and a grimace, the older man complied.

"Please, my lord, tell us the rest," Anne requested.

Carefully, Jasper gave a brief account of what had transpired that afternoon, concluding with his instructions to Mr. Beckham to proceed with undue haste in discovering which brother was legally married to Claire.

"You might truly be wed to this woman?" Rebecca asked. Her voice was flat, emotionless.

Jasper inhaled audibly. "If that proves to be the case, I shall petition for an annulment immediately."

"All this never would have happened if your brother had any sense of responsibility lurking within his useless hide." Mr. Manning's stern accusation reverberated through the room.

"You forget yourself, sir." The faint lines around Jasper's mouth deepened with displeasure, and he had difficulty maintaining a steady tone. "I will allow that you have had a great shock and are understandably upset, but I warn you to have care with whom you insult in my home."

The older man blustered and postured a moment longer, yet wisely held his tongue.

Jasper dismissed him from his thoughts. Rebecca's distress remained his foremost concern. He observed her every expression, wondering what emotions were lurking behind those lovely blue eyes. She was undeniably hurt, yet whatever she was feeling was effectively hidden from view.

"Come along, daughters," Mr. Manning said stiffly. "We need to get home."

"But there will be questions if we do not make an appearance at the dinner party," Rebecca whispered.

"Let Lord Fairhurst answer them," her father responded bitterly. "I want you far away when the wagging tongues discover there will be no engagement announced tonight."

With her father and sister crowded protectively around Rebecca, there was no chance for Jasper to engage in a private word of comfort or to offer an apology.

Still, he could not help but admire Rebecca's composure as she strode out the door, a bit unsteady, but with her chin and nose in the air and her back rigid with dignity.

Unfortunately, from this vantage point, Lord Fairhurst missed the malicious gleam of anger and revenge in Rebecca's eyes. The woman he thought so self-contained and meek was seething with rage, nearly speechless with humiliation. And determined that this slight would not be easily forgiven or forgotten.

Chapter Four

"What do you mean Lady Fairhurst is gone?" Squire Dorchester roared at the quaking servant standing before him. "Gone where?"

"To London, sir." James, the squire's servant, replied timidly.

The young man waited nervously for the next explosion of rage, cursing his foul luck at being the one who drew the short straw and was thus saddled with the misfortune of being the bearer of such odious tidings.

The drawing of straws or the flipping of a coin, when one could be found, were the only methods the squire's beleaguered household staff could devise to fairly distribute these oftentimes dangerous tasks. Though there were few of the merchant and gentry class in the village who would credit such a tale, the quick tempered squire was not adverse to striking his servants. And never more so than when he was given news that angered him.

"How the hell did she get to London?" Dorchester's handsome face contorted in sudden alarm. "Did Fairhurst return and take her away?"

"No, sir. There has been no sign of Lord Fairhurst for months. Lady Fairhurst traveled to Town with Mrs. Humphrey, her great-aunt."

The squire let out a disgusted snort. “Interfering old bitch. I thought she was dead.”

“No, that was her sister, Mrs. Hathaway, who passed on last winter,” James supplied helpfully, regretting the words the moment they left his mouth. The squire never wanted to hear anything from a servant except a direct answer to a question.

James’s eyes darted desperately about the room. He calculated the distance to the door, dismayed to realize it was a good fifteen paces away. Hunching his shoulders, the servant began to discreetly slink toward it, preparing to break into a run on a moment’s notice.

If he did not have to support an elderly mother, who broke down in tears every time he suggested they leave the village where she had lived her entire life, James would have long ago escaped the squire’s employ. It was a dreadful house to work in—long hours of hard, demanding work; pittance for wages; and a constant environment of fear.

The squire was a man who lived by his own rules. He was rude, tyrannical, spoiled, and a lecherous womanizer. Over the years, he had been involved in countless indiscretions with women of all classes, but he was too clever to ever let even a hint of scandal or misconduct touch his name.

An unrepentant villain who possessed the devil’s own luck, he somehow managed to keep this seamier side of his nature a secret from the good folk of the community. Few knew about the black heart that beat beneath the handsome exterior, and his servants often commented the squire would probably kill to keep it that way.

“When did Lady Fairhurst depart?” the squire asked, his tone quelling. “This morning, at first light?”

James’s heart thumped so loud it felt like it was about

to burst from his chest. Saints preserve him, the answer to this question was going to earn him a bruised cheek, a bloody lip, or a broken nose. Or perhaps all three.

When the rumor had reached the servants that Lady Fairhurst, the former Miss Claire Truscott, had left the village, they were at first pleased to hear she had so neatly escaped from the squire. In the servants' quarters, there was laughter and snide remarks and more than one tankard of ale raised in salute to this kind and well-liked lady.

It was only when they all realized this news would have to be given to the squire that the jesting and celebration ceased. For three full days they had kept silent, but there would be no avoiding the unpleasant truth now.

"Is there something wrong with your hearing, man?" the squire said in a deceptively quiet voice. "I asked you about Lady Fairhurst's departure. When, exactly, did she leave?"

"I don't know," James squeaked, trying to make himself smaller as he inched ever closer to the door. His hands were quaking.

"Idiot! Find out!" The words were shouted with such rancor and disdain that James braced himself for a savage blow.

But the servant had miraculously managed to put just enough distance between himself and his bellowing employer that the swinging fist fell short of its mark. Knowing he would never again get such a blessed reprieve, James bolted for the door.

Richard Dorchester, or Squire Dorchester as he was called by the locals, watched the wiry young man sprint away with detached interest. He worried for a moment that he might be getting soft, remembering how in a rage he had once grabbed a servant who was attempting to crawl away, held him by the neck, and beat him until the fellow had winced and cried and begged for mercy.

But today he had not felt the need for such harsh treatment. Better instead to wait for the servant to uncover the information he wanted before teaching him a much needed lesson. It would serve as a good example to the rest of the staff.

Damn Claire to hell for all the bother she was causing! The woman was starting to possess his very soul and invade his every waking thought. For the briefest of moments Dorchester cursed his body's unrelenting demand that he completely possess and dominate the elusive Lady Fairhurst, wishing only to be free of the madness that burned through his heart.

Resentful of this physical betrayal, he tried to tell himself she would be a disappointment, as so many others had been, but deep down the squire never really believed it.

Thus, his obsession was fueled.

Ever since Richard reached maturity, women had been throwing themselves at him. As a callow lad he had been eager to learn and experience all that was offered. The lessons soon led to sensual fulfillment, then quickly to sexual excess.

He had never been a disciplined young man, and this lack of control drove his carnal cravings to the edge. Within a year of reaching his eighteenth birthday, he had bedded every married woman in the county who was so inclined to such activities. It became a game to indulge in casual dalliances and torrid affairs, taking everything and giving nothing. Yet he remained careful to never cross the lines of propriety while in public, ever mindful of his reputation and position.

Spinning sideways, Dorchester studied his profile in the large mirror hanging above the fireplace. The gray eyes that gazed back were cold and unfeeling; the mouth was a thin, hard line.

Shaking his head, the squire realigned his features, donning the persona he wore whenever he was in public busy focusing his efforts on a prospective female conquest. The transformation was nothing short of miraculous.

His handsome face softened into an expression of easy charm. Even though his jaw was shadowed by a day's growth of facial hair, he appeared friendly and approachable, a man of quiet, fashionable elegance.

Imagining he was staring at Claire, Dorchester's lips curved into a seductive, heart-stopping smile—part wolfish, part enticing. His eyes became alive with interest and charm, while they still held that hint of wickedness that never failed to let a woman know he thought she was incredibly desirable.

Richard lifted his head and straightened his stance, admiring the cut of his jacket, the intricate knot of his fine linen cravat, and the smooth line of his breeches. Everything was perfect, just as he demanded.

To achieve this latest style of fashion and keep his wardrobe developed to the highest degree, the squire had all his clothes made in London. The garments cost him dearly, but he could afford them. The running of his estate was overseen by a dedicated, frugal manager who knew he would be dismissed, without a reference, if the funds to indulge the squire's passions were ever unavailable.

Though he abhorred work and physical labor of any kind, the squire possessed imposing physical size and strength. Beneath the fine clothes, his body was strongly muscled, with a wide back and shoulders, strong calves, and strong thighs.

Richard had a physical beauty and a magnetism that drew both men and women to him like flies to honey. This intense attraction at first surprised him, for he knew he did nothing to warrant such adoration, yet this oftentimes fawning popularity gave him a heady sense of power and self-importance.

Once given a taste of such regard, it became impossible to give it up. The safest course would be to abandon his excesses and lead a more moral existence, but Richard never considered taking that path. Instead, he did exactly as he pleased, yet guarded his reputation so fiercely that not even the highest sticklers suspected anything was other than it appeared. In fact, nearly all would be shocked to discover he lied as easily as he breathed.

Shaking his head at the gullibility of his foolish peers, the squire poured himself a full glass of whiskey. He took a long swallow, feeling the comforting burn trail down his throat and join the fire already churning in his gut.

Just thinking of her always brought forth this reaction. Her. Claire. The one person who had successfully avoided his carefully spun web, who had the gall, the sheer effrontery to reject his overtures.

That self-possessed lady had never been taken in by his charm or flattery. If he believed in such nonsense, he would blame it on cruel and capricious fate, but there was nothing random about Claire's dislike of him.

He drank a second glass of whiskey and allowed the bitter memories of her to rush through him. Like his own, Claire's family had lived in the area for generations. They boasted a fine pedigree of respectable and occasionally noble ancestry, and Claire's mother enjoyed a position of leadership in the quaint society of the community. Her father was a gentleman of moderate means who provided a comfortable life for his wife and three daughters.

Previously, Richard had only brief encounters with them, finding them to be staid and annoyingly moral. Then he met Claire at a village celebration when she was a young girl of sixteen and he a more mature man of twenty-three. There were other, prettier girls in attendance that day, but the moment Richard had clasped Claire's delicate hand in his own, he felt a jolt of emotion unlike any he had ever experienced.

He knew in that moment that he wanted her—and for more than just a brief affair. She was initially flattered by his regard, yet took pains not to encourage his attention. That whet his appetite further and quickly brought his all-consuming need to posses her to a rash and dangerous level. He was a man who did not believe male fidelity in marriage was required, yet for a brief time, Claire had actually incited thoughts of monogamy in him.

Assuming she would be honored by his courtship, he confidently went to call on her at her family home. But Claire was not honored. She refused to see him, sending her mother to make excuses. Frustrated by her lack of interest, Richard set out to find out everything he could about Claire and was dismayed to find she had a beau—dismayed, but not deterred.

Fortunately, the young man who had captured her heart had foolish notions about duty and obligations and felt it was an honor to serve his country. Richard's military connections proved most useful in this instance—he was able to get the lad shipped to an area of the Peninsula that was embroiled in the heaviest fighting. It took less than a year for the fellow to obligingly get himself killed.

With his rival safely out of the way, there was no need for haste. In fact, Richard decided it would be better to wait until Claire got older and feared becoming a spinster before approaching her, thus making it easier to secure his desire.

But nothing from that point on had gone according to plan.

Footsteps reverberated in the hall, and the squire snapped himself away from his musing.

"Well, what have you found out?" Richard testily snarled the moment the servant was in the room. He crossed his arms over his broad chest, waiting impatiently.

"Sir?"

"About Lady Fairhurst," he clarified.

The servant paled. "Nothing else just yet, Squire."

Dorchester raised an eyebrow. "Then why are you here pestering me?"

"You have a visitor." The servant cleared his throat. "Mrs. Clayton has come to call."

Lydia? What the hell was she doing here? He had not sent for her. In fact, their brief, torrid affair had ended months ago.

"Did you tell Mrs. Clayton that I was not at home?" the squire asked, repeating the standard response that he instructed the staff to give to any and all unattended and uninvited female guests who came to call.

"Yes, sir, I explained that you were unable to see her. Three times. But she was very insistent, claiming she would wait as long as necessary."

Richard bristled with irritation. What the hell was

happening to his household? Clearly, he had become far too lenient with them. First, they had been lacking the necessary information about Claire, and now they were letting Lydia bully them. After this meeting, he was going to have to go below stairs to the servants' hall and knock a few heads together. Literally.

"Since you appear to be incapable of getting rid of Mrs. Clayton, wait fifteen minutes, and then bring her to me," Richard instructed, glaring hard so the servant would feel the extent of his annoyance.

The young man lowered his head and backed nervously out of the room, assuring the squire that he had made his point. This pleased Richard, until he realized he would now have to deal with Lydia.

On the day Claire married Lord Fairhurst, Richard, needing a distraction, began his seduction of Lydia. She was different from the majority of his conquests in that she was younger and was reported to be in love with her husband. She had also possessed a great many sexual inhibitions when he began the affair, and he had thoroughly enjoyed shattering each and every one. It gave him a perverse sense of power to change a naive, demure female into a woman who craved decadence.

But as with so many of his relationships, after the affair started, Richard soon became apathetic and abruptly ended it. Lydia had been shocked, reading far more into their dalliance than he was inclined to give. She had made one pathetic attempt to rekindle the spark of sensuality between them and was soundly and cruelly rejected for her efforts.

As the weeks passed with no further contact, Richard assumed he had made his feelings clear. Hoping that had not changed, yet suspecting it might have, he now waited to greet his former mistress.

When she entered the room, he deliberately made no attempt to stifle his groan of displeasure. "I should greet you with a friendly embrace and tell you that I am glad to see you, Mrs. Clayton," he drawled in a sarcastic tone. "But I made myself a promise that I would try not to lie so early in the day."

Her chin lifted proudly. She was a dark, young beauty, with striking features and a lush figure. She looked very fetching in a muslin dress with a loose, floating skirt and a low-cut bodice that showcased her ample bosom.

"I would not have come if it could have been avoided," Lydia replied stiffly.

She took a seat without being invited and, for a lengthy interlude, sat in silence and simply peered at him. Richard, adapt at reading female emotions, quickly recognized the underlying agony of doubt and fear that coursed through her. It peaked his interest.

"Why are you here?" he finally asked.

She took a shuddering breath. "I think, no, I am certain that I am increasing. I have been afraid to consult a doctor or a midwife, but all the signs are present." She took another deep breath. "I believe the child will be born sometime in the coming autumn."

Though his gut lurched, the smile appeared effortlessly on Richard's face. "Aren't you the clever girl? Congratulations. I'm sure your husband must be proud and pleased to be anticipating the arrival of his first child."

The look she gave him was pure venom. "I have not said a word about this to him. How can I? The babe is not his. 'Tis yours!"

"Don't be a fool. Our little affair ended months ago. You cannot possibly know who fathered this brat." The squire lifted his chin to a sharp angle and glared at her.

"When a married woman gives birth, her husband is the child's legal father, regardless of how many men and how many times she has spread her legs."

Lydia hissed in a breath at the insult. "I see that you have not changed one bit. Tedious, offensive, and a prized prick."

Richard laughed. "You should know, my little pet."

Seeing her simmering anger caused the squire's own ire to slightly dim. Even at her worst, Lydia was no match for him. He saw her brow furrow and noticed that her mouth had narrowed in a grim line. He chuckled again. Why did women have to be so bloody theatrical about everything?

"Mr. Clayton strikes me as the type of man who expects his wife to happily breed dozens of offspring," Richard said patronizingly. "If you play your cards right, he'll probably shower you with gifts when you share your good news."

Her back visibly flinched. "There was an accident when Mr. Clayton was a boy. The result is that he can function as a man, but cannot father any children. He told me of his condition before we married."

"Yet you married him anyway. How noble of you, Lydia."

Her eyes flashed at him. "If I tell Mr. Clayton that I am expecting a baby, then he will know I've been unfaithful. He will be furious and in all likelihood leave me. My family will be shamed by the scandal and shun me. I cannot survive on my own, especially if I am responsible for the care of an infant."

Richard let out an exaggerated sigh. "I still don't see how any of this can possibly concern me."

"The child is yours, Richard!"

"Even if that is true, it makes no difference. I shall

never acknowledge it." He shrugged. "If it troubles you so much to confess your sins to Clayton, then get rid of the brat."

"What?"

The squire sighed with annoyance. "You heard me. Get rid of it. There are potions, herbs, medicines that can be ingested to rid oneself of an unwanted babe. If you are too squeamish for such measures, go away just before your condition begins to show. Make up some tale about visiting a sick relative or some other such nonsense and have your child in seclusion and anonymity. After it is born, give it away or put it in a foundling home and return to your husband unencumbered."

"How could you even suggest . . . such a monstrous . . . a wicked . . . ?" She had to swallow twice before she could finish. "I would never be able to live with myself if I even considered something so horrid."

Richard shrugged his shoulders again. "Keep it, get rid of it; tell your husband, don't tell your husband. Whatever you do is of no consequence to me, Lydia. As I said, this is not my concern."

Her arms closed about her lower abdomen in a tight, protective gesture. She held that pose for a long moment, then turned her head toward him. She was white faced.

"What if I make it your concern, Richard? What if I involved you in a ghastly public scene, revealing to everyone our affair and the consequences of that immoral union?"

"Lower your voice."

Her eyes turned dark and full of menace. "You would not like that, would you, *Squire Dorchester?* To suffer such hideous embarrassment; to lose your stature in our humble little village; to be revealed to all for what you truly are, a common adulterer. A man who lacks all sense of morality, all sense of conscience and honor."

"Bloody hell, you bore me, Lydia."

"You think I am bluffing, don't you? You think that I will keep quiet because my reputation will suffer also, perhaps more than yours." She raised her hands dramatically. "Though I have long tried to deny it, I know the damnation of my soul began the moment I let you touch me. I am beyond redemption, yet I foolishly thought if I came to you today, you would help our innocent child. I should have known better."

"Yes, you should have," Richard agreed smugly.

"Finally an honest answer from you," Lydia said with a bitter laugh. "The first I've ever been given."

Richard turned, giving his back to her. This discussion was starting to bore him. Her threats of blackmail were disconcerting, yet he suspected they were a bluff, a bitter attempt to extort money. Besides, as he had repeatedly said, it truly was none of his concern. Deciding it was time for Lydia to leave, he turned and moved toward her. Yet, when he came closer, he did not particularly like the sudden gleam that entered her eyes.

"Preparing to throw me out, Squire?" Her voice held an edge of hysteria. "I would advise against it. My life is crumbling around me, and I can assure you if it spirals into a scandal, I shall take great delight in pulling you down with me."

Rage knotted his gut at her audacity to threaten *him*. Richard reached out and grasped Lydia's forearm. He dug his fingers into the delicate flesh, applying pressure until he felt the bone beneath.

"You will keep your mouth shut about our past acquaintance, or so help me, you will regret it for the rest of your miserable life."

Her eyes grew wide with alarm. "You are hurting my arm," she whimpered.

"I shall hurt far more than your arm if you do not do as I say." And to emphasize the point, his free hand swung out. Open palm, he struck her across the face so hard that she almost fell off the chair. "Do you understand?"

Lydia's chest heaved in a sob. She let out another whimper and looked as though a sick feeling was beginning to spread through her.

"Do you understand?" he shouted again.

Lydia squeezed her eyes shut and nodded her head.

Slowly, Richard released his grip. She trembled and shuddered, obviously trying to compose herself. He pulled himself away.

"Get out of my sight," he growled. The physical roughness had stirred him, but he would not lower himself to fornicate with her again.

"I think I might be ill," Lydia declared piteously, holding a hand to her mouth.

"Not in my drawing room," the squire insisted. He reached out to hustle her from her seat and she flinched.

"I do not need your help," Lydia cried out, batting clumsily at his hands.

The squire backed away slightly, preparing to move quickly if Lydia exhibited any signs of heaving. He noticed that she needed to use the arm of the chair to steady herself as she got to her feet. Good. Perhaps now she had learned her lesson.

As she shuffled, defeated, to the door, Richard could not resist one final warning. "I expect my sterling reputation to remain intact, Lydia. If it suffers in any way, I will know who is to blame."

A look of pain and fear on her face was her only response. Yet Richard still regarded her with a bit of unease. Though he knew he had completely intimidated and frightened her today, emotional women were always an unpredictable lot.

Though he tried to tell himself otherwise, Richard knew Lydia's condition *was* his concern, and he needed to proceed with caution. It would not be prudent for him to go chasing after Claire in London until he made certain that Lydia, the nagging thorn in his side, did as she was told and kept her mouth shut.

Chapter Five

Claire woke early after a surprisingly restful sleep. The room she had been assigned was spacious and comfortable, boasting a large four-poster bed, a luxurious carpet, and an attached dressing room. With the aid of a footman, she had returned here directly after the meeting with Lord Fairhurst's family and their solicitor, thankful to have such a comfortable sanctuary at her disposal.

Initially, it had been a relief to be alone. Claire had even managed to eat a few bites of the hearty dinner served to her on a tray in her chamber, though it sat uneasily in her stomach. Once her meal was over, the silence and solitude encouraged her thoughts to stray to the drama unfolding in the house. Though large and sprawling, Claire could hear the faint sounds of rumbling carriages and the buzz of numerous conversations as the guests started arriving for the party.

The sounds haunted her, making the events of the day all too real. Ever the glutton for punishment, Claire had opened her bedchamber door and crept to the end of the hall. Pressing herself against the wall, so as not to be seen, she listened openly, straining to hear snatches of conversation as the guests gathered in the downstairs foyer. But she was too far away to distinguish anything more than the occasional word or phrase.

Fearing discovery, Claire was forced to return to her room. Reading was impossible, and she had no needlework to keep her hands and mind occupied. A maid arrived to help her prepare for bed, and although she would have liked to know more about the members of the household, Claire did not engage the girl in conversation.

Thinking she would toss and turn until the early morning hours, Claire nevertheless climbed into bed and propped herself against the comfortable pillows. The sheets smelled faintly of lavender, and the cheerful fire kept the chill from the room.

Though she strained again to listen, Claire heard no further signs of the evening's festivities. Surprisingly, she somehow fell asleep before all the guests departed. And slept through till morning.

Stretching her arms above her head, Claire rolled onto her back. She pulled the heavy coverlet up to her chin, keeping her body warm and snug beneath the covers. Broodingly, she stared at the elaborate blue silk bed hangings, not sure what to think or, more importantly, what to do now that morning had arrived.

What new horrors would this day bring? Perhaps it would be best for all concerned if she remained in this bedchamber, hidden away from all but a few faithful servants. The scandalous family secret.

Claire was thoroughly ashamed of the part she had played, albeit unwillingly, in the ruining of last night's party. She knew she would take to the grave the memory of the expression of horror and anger on Lord Fairhurst's face when he discovered he might, indeed, be her husband.

And his poor betrothed! Claire could hardly imagine how his lordship's chosen bride reacted when she was given the dismaying news that her marriage must wait until all the legalities could be sorted out. Claire shut her eyes and muttered a short prayer, asking for forgiveness, and hoped the disappointment Lord Fairhurst's intended experienced would eventually fade and the joy and anticipation that every bride deserved would replace the distress.

But what of your bridal joy?

Claire shook her head, wondering why such an outlandish thought popped into her mind. All dreams of a loving marriage had died years ago on the battlefield with Henry. She had committed herself completely to him; she had loved him with all her heart, body, and soul. Even if there had been other suitors, Claire firmly believed she could not possibly marry a man who was not Henry.

And then Jay arrived.

He arrived with a perpetual gleam of humor in his eye and a kind, understanding heart. Their friendship grew quickly. He, too, had known the pain of heartbreak, had suffered the ultimate disappointment. For each of them it had been a tremendous relief to discover someone with whom they could unburden their woes, confess their hurts, and confide their sadness without fear of censure. Or even worse, platitudes of advice and admonishments declaring all would be well and they would soon forget.

There had never been any romantic illusions connected to their marriage, and Claire found that to be a great relief. She had entered into the union with her eyes open to the reality of her situation, grateful Jay was aiding her in her time of need, and pleased that she would finally have an opportunity to live an independent life.

The modest bequest left to Claire by her maternal grandmother could only be claimed if she were a married woman. Though meant to be a kind and generous gesture, it was a bitter reminder year after year that the means to live her own life existed, yet they were frustratingly held just beyond her grasp.

If Henry had survived the war, her life would have been very different. But he had not, and Claire had come to accept her impending spinsterhood, determined not to spend the remainder of her days brooding over what could not be controlled.

And then one fine, cold, January afternoon, Jay announced to the odious Squire Dorchester that he was going to marry her. And Claire, equally speechless and intrigued by the prospect, had not denied it.

Ever the gentleman, Jay had insisted she was doing him the greatest of favors by becoming his wife, and he often joked that he was the one making the best of the bargain. Claire knew that was a gallant falsehood, yet had blindly agreed that she was indeed offering her husband something he claimed to desperately need—freedom from the persistent and relentless expectation of his family and peers to take a wife.

But why had he used his brother's name, and title, when they married? She was never a person who aspired to marrying a title and embracing all the trappings that came along with it. The notion that Jay might think it mattered to her was distressing, yet deep down Claire suspected it was not she that Jay felt the need to impress.

A gentle knock sounded at her door. Claire sat up in her bed. "Come in."

The same maid, Mary, who had attended her last

night entered the room, carrying a small tray. She set it carefully down on a bed side table. Claire's nose twitched with interest as she smelled the hot coffee and spied the neat squares of buttered toast. Back home, no one was ever served breakfast in bed unless they were ill.

"I brought you a bit of food to get your morning started," the maid said. She was a middle-aged woman with a stocky build and a no-nonsense air. Claire had liked her almost immediately. "A full breakfast is set out in the dining room each morning for the family. Though if you prefer to have a more substantial meal sent up, I can fetch a footman and make the arrangements."

"This is fine for now, Mary," Claire replied, though a knot of anticipation began to form in her stomach at the mention of the family.

While Claire forced herself to take a few sips of the hot coffee, Mary bustled about the room, opening the heavy window curtains, checking the fire in the grate, making a slight adjustment to the flower arrangement on the corner table.

"Have you decided what you will wear this morning?" The maid's voice emerged from the wardrobe, where she was busy inspecting the neatly hung and freshly pressed garments.

After seeing the quality of fashion worn by Lady Meredith and the countess, Claire suspected the servant was shocked by her meager belongings. She winced, feeling more and more out of her element. "I trust you to select the most appropriate garment."

Apparently, it was the correct thing to say, for the maid nodded her head approvingly.

Feeling restless, Claire left the bed. She sat on the low stool in front of the dressing table and gazed into the mirror. Heavens, her hair was in a complete tangle, with large sections of unconfined waves tumbling down her shoulders and curls sticking out at odd angles. Though she had slept for many hours, here was proof she had spent a good portion of the night tossing and turning, for her hair had been neatly braided last night.

With a sigh, Claire tugged out the ribbons and tried to fix it.

"I'll attend to your hair," Mary insisted.

Meekly, Claire handed the maid her brush. With characteristic efficiency, Mary soon had it styled and pinned into place.

As Claire left her bedchamber and walked to the dining room, she tried to tamp down the rising flood of uneasy feelings. Mary had mentioned that it was usually the countess and, on occasion, her daughter Lady Meredith partaking of breakfast at this relatively early hour. Claire fervently hoped that was the case today, uncertain if she was ready to face any male members of the household on a nearly empty stomach.

Claire paused a moment before the closed dining room doors. Lifting her hands to her face, she ruthlessly pinched her cheeks, attempting to add a bit of color. The last thing she wanted was to enter the room looking pale and martyred. She then smoothed the fabric of her skirts and patted her hair to make certain everything was properly in place. She might not be the most fashionable woman at the table, but there was no excuse not to be well-groomed.

Upon her entrance, Lady Meredith flashed her a bright smile. "Good morning, Claire. I am so pleased you were able to join us. Not everyone can manage rising so early in the day."

For a brief moment, it seemed as though Lady Meredith was going to hug her, but then withheld the impulse.

Claire pasted what she hoped was an appropriate smile on her face and moved forward. Somehow she was going to conquer the almost crippling sense of awe that swept through her whenever she was in the company of the members of this family.

Still, it was all rather confusing. After all, how did one behave with in-laws who might not be in-laws?

The delectable odors wafting from the covered dishes on the sideboard provided the perfect distraction. Deciding the trick was to behave as if she belonged, Claire obligingly followed the footman and instructed him to fill her plate with a variety of the morning offerings.

"Would you like some coffee? Or perhaps some hot chocolate?" the servant inquired.

"Chocolate, please." Claire seldom enjoyed the luxury of chocolate, and never in the morning. It was reserved as a special treat, carefully rationed among Claire and her sisters to ensure that everyone received an equal share.

It was therefore a challenge for Claire to keep a casual attitude when a cup of the rich beverage was poured for her and the sizable china pot it came in was left in easy reach. Even the beverages offered in the household once again emphasized the vast difference between her style of living and Lord Fairhurst's.

"You have been out riding, Lady Meredith?" Claire asked politely as she began to eat her breakfast.

"Just once around Hyde Park," Lady Meredith said. "My husband does not enjoy waking this early in the morning, so it is a wonderful way for me to get some fresh air and exercise on my own."

"And stop in and visit with me for breakfast before returning home to your brood," the countess said.

Lady Meredith smiled. "Yes, I will admit it helps to have a clear head when greeting my children."

"But I thought you were residing here, with the rest of your family," Claire said, surprised.

"When in Town we stay with my father-in-law, the Duke of Warwick," Lady Meredith explained. "Though he spoils my girls so disgracefully I might have to reconsider the arrangement."

"How many children do you have?"

"Three. All girls." A mischievous gleam lit Lady Meredith's eyes. "Initially, my father-in-law complained mightily about not having an heir beyond my husband, but now he has decided if I do not bear a grandson, he will petition Parliament so my eldest daughter can inherit the title."

"How extraordinary." Claire blinked, thoroughly intrigued at the notion of a woman inheriting such an important position of wealth and prestige. "What does your husband say about his father's plans?"

"He tells me that he fully intends to keep producing females, so he can watch the duke knock heads with the monarchy, the nobility, Parliament, and whomever else gets in his way," Meredith replied. She reached for another slice of toast and smiled. "Though they have managed to form a strong bond, my husband and his father are far too much alike to avoid spirited conflict."

"It happens in the best of families," the countess interjected.

"Oh, yes," Claire hastily agreed.

The countess nodded, then her face took on a pensive expression. "Did Jason speak often of us?"

Claire bit the inside of her cheek to keep from saying anything impulsive. Both women were being kind and clearly trying to put her at ease, yet her loyalty remained with Jay. Even if it was eventually concluded that they were not indeed husband and wife, he deserved her silence.

Besides, Claire had a feeling his family would be shocked to know they were part of the reason Jay took her as his wife. He was weary of being pressured to marry. His heart had been broken, and his family refused to acknowledge his pain and respect his wishes to avoid any entanglements with proper ladies.

Fortunately, Lord Fairhurst arrived, interrupting the conversation. He too was dressed for riding in thigh-hugging breeches, a white linen shirt, a bottle-green coat, and black Hessian boots polished to a mirror shine. Claire could not tell if he had just taken a ride or was waiting to eat his meal before venturing out.

There was neither a drop of sweat nor a speck of dirt or dust anywhere on his person, which should have indicated he had not yet been riding. Yet Claire realized she would not be at all surprised to discover he had just finished a spirited cantor about Town. The man was simply too stubborn and too proper to ever be anything but impeccably groomed.

He was also devilishly handsome.

An unexpected quiver coursed through Claire's veins. This uncontrollable reaction whenever she was within a few feet of him was starting to grate on her nerves, especially when Lord Fairhurst's reaction to her presence seemed to verge on the edge of general annoyance.

"Good morning." Claire replied to Lord Fairhurst's greeting, hoping to sound casual and at ease.

"Don't let me interrupt your conversation, ladies," he said, taking a seat beside his sister.

A footman served him a plate of food, then rushed to the kitchen to retrieve a fresh, hot pot of coffee.

"Claire was telling us Jason's opinion of his family and his life in London," the countess explained.

Claire shifted in her chair. "Actually, Jay said very little about either." She shrugged apologetically at the countess, whose face was lined with disappointment.

Lord Fairhurst pursed his lips together. "My brother enjoys discussing many topics, but his favorite subject has always been himself."

"That's unfair," Claire said.

"And untrue?" Lord Fairhurst asked, a challenge lighting his eyes.

Claire paused, her fork halfway to her mouth. "Well, I will confess it was hardly difficult for me to get Jay to reveal certain things, especially what caused him to be in such doldrums."

"A woman," Lord Fairhurst replied smugly. "With Jason it is always a woman."

"Jasper!" the countess said, blinking in astonishment. " 'Tis most indiscreet to speak of other women in front of Claire."

Claire put down her fork, resting it against the edge of her china plate. She could not stand the looks of pity and distress the two women were casting her way, especially when they were so unwarranted. It was clear they all expected her to act like a jealous, affronted wife. The notion was so absurd it was nearly laughable, but, of course, Jay's family could not know the truth of the matter.

"It was hardly a secret that Jay wanted desperately to put the past behind him," Claire said. All eyes turned to her. Clearly more of an explanation was expected, yet Claire had no intention of elaborating. "Please, I have already said far more than I ought."

Lady Meredith frowned at her. "I would not ask you to betray a confidence. However, would you at least tell us if the woman causing Jason such distress was named Elizabeth?"

There apparently was no need for her to answer. The surprised expression Claire could not contain, coupled with her reddened cheeks, let them all know Lady Meredith was correct.

"Good God, is he still spouting off about that nonsense with Elizabeth?" Lord Fairhurst asked in an annoyed tone. "I thought he had finally outgrown it. How tedious and infantile. And unsurprisingly typical."

Claire jumped to her feet, scraping back her chair with her knees. "I will not have you make light of Jay's suffering. I know that you are upset with him, and with good reason, yet that does not give you the right to belittle his feelings."

"My heavens," the countess remarked, looking at her with astonished approval. "Such a spirited defense, and after Jason has treated you rather shabbily. Your character shines through in adversity, Claire, and your loyalty is to be admired."

"However misplaced it may be," Lord Fairhurst added dryly. He lifted a slice of buttered toast to his lips, bit off a sizable piece, and chewed quietly, a thoughtful expression on his face. "Still, you are *my* wife, at least for the time being, and therefore obliged to share your secrets with me."

Claire had to fight to keep her expression blank. The countess had just given her a compliment. It would certainly be bad form to now discredit her opinion and begin shouting at Lord Fairhurst like a fishmonger.

"This is hardly my secret to share, though I realize now that Jay's regard for Elizabeth is something you are all aware of," Claire replied, as she slowly sank down in her chair. She took a small breath and struggled to find the correct balance of words. "Therefore, I will confirm it was Elizabeth who caused him great distress. Yet I am certain you will agree that anything he has said to me about her was told in the strictest of confidence. I must honor his privacy and ask that you respect my decision not to betray his trust."

Her response seemed to raise some hackles. "I suppose he told you that his heart had been broken?" Lord Fairhurst drawled.

Claire avoided looking at him; instead, she concentrated on the dwindling chocolate in her cup. "Jay might have made a passing remark or two about a romantic disappointment."

"A remark?" Lord Fairhurst let out a bark of laughter. "Jason has been known to go on for hours and hours about the fair Elizabeth. It is all a bunch of rubbish and nothing more than a good excuse for drinking himself under the hatches."

"How can you be so heartless?" Claire blurted out. "She married another. Jay was devastated."

"Indeed." Lord Fairhurst lifted his linen napkin and dabbed at the corners of his mouth. "Perchance, did my brother happen to mention that this marriage took place five years ago?"

"Five years?" Claire choked back the warm chocolate she had been sipping. "I was under the impression that Jay's heartache had been a more recent occurrence."

"Well, it was not," Lord Fairhurst declared flatly.

Claire bowed her head. "The passing of time may lessen the openness of the wound, the intensity of the ache, but does not completely heal the pain. That remains forever."

"Spoken by the voice of experience," Lord Fairhurst said in a surprisingly kind tone.

She caught his gaze and colored, embarrassed to reveal so much of herself. "My own heartache is not the issue, though it did help me to understand and empathize with Jay's feelings about Elizabeth."

"What happened to your young man?" the countess asked sympathetically.

"He was killed on the Peninsula. We spoke of becoming engaged when he came home from the war, but he never returned."

"How dreadful for you." The countess sighed. "We are all sorry for your loss."

"It was a long time ago." A sad expression touched Claire's lips. "A lifetime ago."

"Was he someone you had known for a considerable amount of time?" Lord Fairhurst asked.

"Yes." Claire lifted her chin. She let the memories slide over her. "Henry was the son of our neighbor. We had occasional contact as children and discovered many shared interests as we grew older. It surprised no one that we eventually fell in love."

"Then it would have been a good match," Lord Fairhurst said. "The sum of my brother's relationship with Elizabeth consisted of a handful of dances at several different balls, a shared supper at a costume party, two carriage outings in Hyde Park, and an endless stream of unanswered letters. In truth, he barely knew her."

"Well, there was that nasty business the Season they met," the countess interjected. "Jason did save the poor girl from the clutches of a madman."

"True, my brother proved himself to be a man of character and honor and contributed greatly to saving Elizabeth's life," Lord Fairhurst conceded.

"Careful, my lord, you almost sound proud of him," Claire chimed in. She had heard the story of Elizabeth's rescue and was impressed with the part Jay had played. It was good to discover that his family also acknowledged his valor.

"I would like nothing more than to admire my brother, but he makes it exceedingly difficult at times." Lord Fairhurst idly stirred the contents of his coffee cup with a silver spoon. "And I would give far more credence to his romantic suffering if I believed it to be sincere. Jason has long been enamored with the *idea* of loving Elizabeth. She is a fine lady of good character who prefers to live a very quiet, ordinary, and dare I say, dull life. Away from society, away from fashion, away from the glaring eye and wagging tongues of the beau monde.

"Thankfully, she also possessed the good sense to realize that Jason would have be bored within a month of their marriage. So she wisely married a man who was far better suited to her personality and expectations of life. I have heard they are very happy."

Claire felt her jaw tighten. "Jay did not see it that way. He firmly believed they were meant to be together, yet she gave her heart to another."

"That may have been the case five years ago, but Jason decided it would be far easier to dwell on the disappointment than to move forward with his life," Lord Fairhurst said. " 'Tis very easy to fall in love with a beautiful, attractive young woman, but it is far more difficult to love her. To sustain the emotion, to allow it to mature and grow, to be unselfish when necessary, to bend at times and stand firm at others. Only when you have experienced such love, and then lost it, are you entitled to such misery."

Claire looked at Lord Fairhurst in fascination. She

never expected that under his proper, cool exterior he was such a romantic. She wondered if he loved the woman he intended to marry this way and felt a brief stab of envy at the notion.

"Love is a complicated matter of the heart and mind," Lady Meredith said. "Those of us who are lucky enough to find it have learned it must be nurtured, as well as cherished."

"Was yours a love match, Lady Meredith?"

"Not initially, but it most definitely is now," she replied with a smug grin.

The countess sighed. "All this talk of love is making me miss your father," she complained. "He is spending the day away from home with his scholarly brethren. I fear I will need a distraction or else I shall become quite maudlin."

"We could go shopping," Lady Meredith suggested. "I am sure Claire would enjoy seeing Bond Street."

"A perfect idea," the countess agreed enthusiastically.

Lord Fairhurst seemed to take this as his cue to leave and rose to his feet. "I have numerous business matters to attend to this morning, so I must leave or else I shall be running late all day. I wish you all a pleasant morning."

He touched his hand to the edge of his forehead, made a mocking half bow, and strode at a purposeful pace from the room.

Though she tried valiantly not to, Claire's eyes remained glued to his broad, retreating back until he was gone from her sight.

As much as she would have loved to see the London shops, Claire was not keen on the idea of venturing out with the countess and Lady Meredith, fearing the famed

Bond Street would prove to be just another place where she would feel out of place. But the stubborn set of the countess's jaw left little room for arguing, and without knowing precisely how it happened, Claire soon found herself stepping through the front door of one of the most famous and exclusive dressmakers in Town.

They were welcomed with open arms and overflowing, slightly overbearing, compliments. Next came a great deal of tongue clucking and exaggerated exclamations of horror as Claire was examined from head to toe. She was unsure if that was due to her rustic clothing, her plain appearance, or the vague explanation of how she was related to the countess and Lady Meredith.

However, Claire's nervous bewilderment soon turned to excitement as she was caught up in the newness of the experience. The clerks, as well as the proprietress, literally fawned over the countess. Anything and everything was done to please her, and no task was considered too challenging or too difficult.

After Claire's measurements were taken, the three women looked through numerous fashion plates. The proprietress, Madame Renude, made subtle suggestions, but she deferred her opinions about cut, style, and fabrics to the countess.

Claire was occasionally consulted, but often overruled. Thankfully, the countess favored high-waisted, loose-flowing gowns, a fashion that Claire felt comfortable wearing. Deciding she needed to assert herself, Claire took a considerable amount of time selecting the fabric and trimmings for the gown, marveling over the quality and color choices.

In the end, she was pleased to realize that an outing she initially feared would be bewildering and tedious was actually a great deal of fun. However, Claire soon learned that the countess had no intention of stopping at buying one gown. Or two.

The list of necessary items the countess insisted be purchased made Claire's head spin: morning dresses, afternoon dresses, dinner gowns, ball gowns, carriage dresses, walking dresses. It seemed that no matter what the occasion or circumstance, a well-bred woman of the beau monde was expected to own, and wear, the correct garment.

There were no prices on any of the dress patterns or fabrics, making Claire even more nervous about buying anything. After discreetly examining the quality of the fabric and the expert needlework of the dresses, Claire shrewdly realized that only a woman who need not concern herself with costs frequented this establishment.

Claire was not, nor had she ever been, that kind of woman. Though raised in comfortable circumstances, there had been two other sisters and her mother to be properly clothed. At an early age, Claire had learned to appreciate the beauty of quality items, as well as the need to exercise restraint when acquiring them.

Apparently, restraint was not a word the countess ever used. Gown after gown was ordered, and cost did not appear to be of any concern to either the countess or Lady Meredith. The moment Madame Renude left them to fetch another bolt of cloth, a nervous Claire broached the subject. It was dismissed with a vague smile.

"My son has very deep pockets," the countess said. She fingered a piece of a red silk cloth. "He has also acquired a ridiculous talent for making money, something I am almost horrified to admit he learned from his sister."

Claire turned an assessing eye toward Lady Meredith. The older woman shrugged. " 'Tis true, though naturally we never speak of it outside of the family."

For some peculiar reason the idea of being part of a family secret made Claire feel privileged. For all their arrogance and bossy mannerisms, the Barringtons were a very charismatic group, and Claire was honored to be entrusted with their confidence.

Though feeling tired, Claire managed to endure another hour of shopping in good humor. Yet it was a great relief when the countess at last returned her gold lorgnette to her reticule and announced they were finished.

The sun was shining when they emerged outside. Claire felt a stab of regret when she spied their carriage parked in front of the dressmaker's shop. There would be no opportunity to enjoy the fresh air and allow it to blow away some of the cobwebs in her tired brain.

Claire was also honest enough to admit she would have liked to indulge in a bit of vanity by strolling down Bond Street in the fashionable new outfit the countess had practically bullied Madame Renude into selling them. It had been commissioned by another patron, but the countess decided it would look much better on Claire, and after a few alterations, the outfit was fitted to her.

The countess suggested she wear it home, and Claire had been eager to comply. It was by far the prettiest, and most expensive, garment she had ever owned.

But Claire's thoughts about her new outfit were soon diverted when her eyes beheld the figure of Lord Fairhurst a short distance away. She recognized him immediately. He was on foot, walking toward them at a clipping pace.

He had not yet seen them. Claire concluded if she turned her companions around and headed directly for the carriage, their paths would never cross.

Her feet never took a step.

"Ladies," Lord Fairhurst said, touching the brim of his hat courteously. "Have you finished with your shopping?"

The countess laughed. "Shopping is not something that a lady ever finishes, Jasper. She merely pauses momentarily to regain her strength."

"Well, my strength is nearly gone," Lady Meredith said. "I am more than ready to quit for the day."

"You are still recovering from the birth of my newest granddaughter," the countess said sympathetically. "We need to get you off your feet as soon as possible."

"Marissa is almost five months old," Lady Meredith replied with a laugh. "I can assure you 'tis not my infant daughter who has left me feeling so tired."

"Nevertheless, it would be best for you to be relaxing inside the coach." The countess turned to Lord Fairhurst. "Claire has been abundantly patient, hiding her exhaustion to spare my feelings. Take her for a stroll. The fresh air will do her good."

Lord Fairhurst's handsome face took on a decidedly sour expression. "I think the less that I am seen about Town in Claire's company, the better."

" 'Tis only a few blocks, Jasper. I'll send my maid as a chaperone for propriety's sake," the countess replied. "Naturally, we must be circumspect regarding Claire's unique situation and use sound judgment, but there is no need to hide her away."

"I disagree."

"Jasper! I insist that you stop being so difficult." The countess clasped her hands to her bosom. "Your stubbornness is quite draining."

Lord Fairhurst raised his eyebrows and gave his mother a frosty look. "I am hardly being discreet if I parade her down Bond Street like a prized calf."

"Gracious! What a vulgar reference, comparing a lady to livestock. A calf? Apologize at once, Jasper."

"Mother, you are overstepping your bounds."

The countess stiffened. "If you are going to be so stubborn, then I shall apologize for you."

"Truly, there is no need," Claire interjected, her face burning with embarrassment.

No one paid her any attention. The three began a heated discussion, their voices kept to a low, well-cultured tone, yet the emotions behind the words were strong and forceful.

"I'm sorry, Jasper, but I find I agree with Mother," Lady Meredith said. "Acting as if we have something to hide will arouse everyone's suspicions and bring the gossipmongers out in full, vicious force."

"Precisely," the countess exclaimed. "We all know there is no way on earth to keep a secret in this Town. The best we can hope to do is control the information as it spreads."

"Then it would be wise to keep Claire's existence a secret," Lord Fairhurst said.

The countess let out an exaggerated sigh. "Don't be ridiculous, Jasper. We have just spent the better part of four hours in Madame Renude's establishment. By the end of the day, the beau monde will be well informed about the mysterious female relation that bought an entire new wardrobe and had the bills sent to you."

There was an awkward little silence. Claire cleared her throat loudly. They all gave her a quick glance, then resumed the conversation.

"Does Madame Renude know Claire's identity?" Lord Fairhurst asked.

The countess looked highly insulted. "I am not a fool, and neither is Madame Renude. She was wildly curious about Claire and hinted broadly about her suspicions, but she would never risk offending me by pressing for information. I can assure you that none of us gave anything away."

"And I can say with certainty that Madame Renude will never guess the truth of who I am. The story is far too remarkable to even be imagined."

Claire did not realize she had spoken aloud until all eyes turned in her direction. She fully expected to be on the receiving end of an icy stare, yet it never materialized. Claire assumed it must be a trick of the afternoon light, for it seemed as though Lord Fairhurst was looking at her with something other than contempt.

"We really cannot stand here and argue the point any longer," the countess said. "Your sister needs to get off her feet."

"My carriage is several blocks away," Lord Fairhurst offered.

"Ours is closer." The countess gazed at her son. "Is it really too much to ask you to reward Claire with a few minutes of fresh air? The stroll to your coach should take but a moment."

Lord Fairhurst barely had time to voice his further objections. The countess turned to her daughter. She forcefully linked her arm in Lady Meredith's and forged her way toward the waiting coach. In the blink of an eye, the countess and Lady Meredith disappeared inside the vehicle.

Claire was highly conscious of Lord Fairhurst, large, solid, strong, and silently standing beside her. She knew he must be furious. She could see his fingers flexing into fists at his sides and could hear his foot tapping a sharp tattoo on the pavement.

Coolly, he turned and offered her his arm. Knowing

the alternative was to be left on Bond Street with only a maid to guide her, Claire gently rested the tips of her fingers on his sleeve and, against her better judgment, allowed herself to be led away.

Chapter Six

Meredith peered out the carriage window as it started down the street and saw her brother and Claire, arm in arm, strolling cautiously in the opposite direction, both looking decidedly uncomfortable. A wave of wariness spread through Meredith at the sight of their glum expressions, and she wondered if it had been the right thing allowing the couple to be alone, with only a maid for a chaperone.

"Well, that settles it," the countess said as she clapped her hands together with delight. "I suspected it to be true and now I have seen the unrefutable proof. All that is needed is a strategy to gain us more time."

The countess smiled and nodded approvingly, shifting away from the carriage window where she, too, had apparently been observing the couple. Stretching her torso, the still grinning countess lifted her arm high above her head, then pounded her knuckles insistently on the interior roof of the coach.

"What are you doing, Mother?"

"Getting John Coachman's attention. He must turn the carriage toward Mr. Beckham's office."

"We are going to see the family solicitor?"

"Yes." The countess seemed fair to bursting with excitement. "I feel a great need to know what else Mr.

Beckham has discovered about the validity of Claire and Jasper's marriage."

"Can it not wait until later in the week? We spoke with Mr. Beckham less than twenty-four hours ago. I doubt much has changed in that short time span."

"Oh, but it has, Meredith. And all for the better."

The look that came into the countess's eyes made Meredith suddenly wary. "What do you mean?"

"Claire married Jason, yet as we all know, there is something very odd about their marriage. And I am not referring to the fact that Jason signed the license with his brother's name and title."

The countess leaned forward, her eyes bright. "For years, my dear son has been using his infatuation with Elizabeth as a shield to avoid an emotional attachment to a female. I always believed that once he found the right woman, that barrier would shatter completely." The countess paused. "Claire is not that woman."

"Jason apparently thinks otherwise," Meredith insisted. "He married her."

"Did he?" The countess cocked her eyebrow. "Or did he wed her by proxy to Jasper, knowing he had found the perfect mate for his brother?"

"Jasper and Claire?" Meredith's brow puckered in doubt. "Jason is not that far thinking or devious to set up such an elaborate plan, nor would he have the first clue as to what sort of woman would interest his twin. Jason was probably drunk during the wedding service and signed the wrong name accidentally. And even if he did sign Jasper's name, the marriage cannot be legal."

The countess bristled with indignation. "Jason is impetuous and daring and far from perfect, but he is not a drunken lout. He loves his brother dearly, despite the estrangement of their relationship these past few years."

"I suppose you are referring to the disagreements and shouting matches they have engaged in since Jasper turned into such a prig?"

The countess huffed. "Jasper's change of habits has had some positive influences."

"I agree it is wonderful that he no longer excessively drinks and gambles, but it seems as with everything my brothers do, Jasper has gone to extremes with propriety. He is stuffy and stodgy and so tightly in control, I worry if there is any passion or joy left in his heart."

"Maybe that is to be Claire's role," the countess said. "To bring the joy and passion back to Jasper's life."

"A rather tall order for an unsuspecting woman who believes herself married to Jasper's brother," Meredith replied, but she could tell her words had little effect in convincing her mother this theory was absurd.

"Obviously, Jason has not yet told Claire all the details of his plan," the countess said. She spoke slowly and carefully, as if she were forming her opinion at the same time she was voicing it. "Claire's visit to London was unexpected. She said repeatedly that she had promised Jason she would never come to Town unannounced. That could explain how things got off to such a rocky start."

It was all so ridiculous, Meredith hardly knew how to respond. "You honestly think that Jason had some grand scheme concerning Claire and his twin, and Claire came to Town and spoiled the surprise?"

"Yes, 'tis possible it happened just that way."

Feeling stunned, Meredith pressed a gloved hand to her forehead. The workings of her mother's mind were truly amazing. "The legalities of Claire's marriage are confusing enough without adding all these ridiculous, baseless suppositions. Enough, Mother. Your absurd theories are starting to make my head spin."

The countess patted her daughter's shoulder. "I, too, felt similar confusion until I saw Jasper and Claire at breakfast, and again just now outside Madame Renude's shop. Then, suddenly, it became crystal clear.

"There are sparks between those two. Interest, excitement, even passion are all there, simmering just below the surface. I saw it quite clearly last night, though at the time I was uncertain what to make of it. After seeing it again today, I realize with the right encouragement and a touch of luck, the sparks between these two will most certainly flare."

Meredith slowly spread the fingers that were pressed against her face and peered through them at her mother. "Need I remind you that Jasper has already chosen a bride?"

"Ah, yes, the impeccable Miss Rebecca Manning." The countess repeatedly tapped the tip of her index finger against her chin. "What do you think of Jasper's choice?"

Meredith hesitated, feeling uncomfortable criticizing someone she barely knew. She took a slow breath, and then lowered her hand to her lap. "Miss Manning seems like a respectable young lady. She has had a quiet, sheltered upbringing and behaves in a proper, though somewhat staid, manner."

"Exactly! Such a tedious young woman." The countess shuddered. "I do not care for her much, either. There is something not quite right about the girl, though I cannot precisely explain it. More importantly, she is absolutely the wrong woman for Jasper."

"That is hardly kind, Mother. We barely know Miss Manning."

"I highly doubt she will improve upon further acquaintance." The countess lifted her chin. "Stop glaring at me with such a scolding look. If we cannot speak candidly to each other, then who will we share the truth with, Meredith?"

The marchioness continued to glare at her mother, silently appraising her. They had not been especially close when Meredith was growing up. Although it was never in doubt that the countess loved her three children, she preferred to spend her time traveling the world with her husband, who had an affinity for antiquities and a passion for visiting exotic lands and places.

The result was that Meredith had practically raised herself, and then had been forced to keep her wayward twin brothers in check. Her parents had returned to England when Meredith's daughter, their first grandchild, was born. The absent parents who had exhibited only a passing interest in their children soon became doting grandparents and expressed little interest in leaving home.

Initially pleased to have an opportunity to forge a strong bond with the parents she had always loved, Meredith was lately starting to wonder if the time had come to suggest they take a trip abroad—a nice, long trip.

"Whatever the truth, I think we must agree that this unholy mess is best left to sort itself out," Meredith declared.

The countess stared at Meredith for a moment, then averted her gaze, pretending interest in a very small stain on the skirt of her cloak. The telling gesture made Meredith very uneasy. "You are suddenly very quiet, Mother. I fear you are plotting something."

"Plotting? Gracious, that has a rather sinister tone." The countess gave her a puzzled, slightly hurt glance. "I am merely looking out for the interests of my sons, which is my solemn duty. Who can possibly fault a mother for doing what is expected?"

Meredith grimaced. She leaned back against the upholstered squabs, suspicious of the expression on her mother's face. Anyone who tried so hard to look innocent was most assuredly up to no good.

All too soon Meredith learned the direction of her mother's thoughts. Their carriage came to a stop in front of a stone building in the fashionable business district. Though they had no appointment, it took but a few minutes for the countess and her daughter to be shown into Mr. Beckham's office.

As they entered, Meredith almost felt sorry for the poor fellow. He was nervous and flustered. He blushed and stammered and bowed so low, she feared he might lose his balance, tip over, and land on his bottom.

Clearly, the lawyer was unaccustomed to having two aristocratic women in his office, especially because he had just met with them last night. Meredith calculated that this was probably the most time he had spent with them since becoming the family solicitor ten years ago.

"Ladies, I am honored to welcome you to my humble office." The solicitor pulled two chairs closer to his desk, huffing and puffing and nearly exhausting himself with the effort of moving the heavy furniture. Then with an unexpected flourish, he withdrew a large linen handkerchief from his breast coat pocket, wiped the fine layer of dust from the top of the cushions, and indicated that the women should be seated. "It was hardly necessary for you to make the journey here. If summoned, I would have hastened to your residence."

"We were shopping and thought it would be more efficient if we came to you," the countess explained.

"Ah, shopping. A favorite female pastime." The solicitor cleared his throat. "How may I be of service this afternoon?"

"We have come to hear the latest news on my son's situation."

If Mr. Beckham felt any surprise at the countess's request, he hid it well. "Indeed, there is good news to report. I have been researching all the legalities and reading the case law on proxy marriages. I was hoping to call upon Lord Fairhurst in a day or two, once I have reviewed all the specific documents regarding his difficulties."

The pleasant expression on the countess's face turned to something greatly resembling a scowl. "And what have you discovered?"

"If this were a legal proxy marriage, Mr. Jason Barrington's name must also appear on the marriage certificate as Lord Fairhurst's representative." The solicitor placed his palms flat on the desk he was seated behind and leaned forward. "From what Miss Truscott has told us, she signed a standard marriage certificate, containing her name and the groom's name. Once I verify that, Lord Fairhurst will be in the clear and, thankfully, any thoughts of annulment proceedings can be dropped."

"I presume you are moving swiftly to verify this situation?" the countess asked, her hand straying to the broach at the neck of her gown.

"With all haste. I have put my best clerks on the case and am supervising their work personally."

The solicitor beamed with pride, but his expression soon turned to distress as the countess removed a lace-edged handkerchief from her reticule and pressed it to her lips.

" 'Tis as I feared," she whispered, dabbing at the edges of her eyes with the linen.

"You are displeased, my lady?"

"Oh, not with you, sir. Clearly, you are a fine attorney, skilled and ethical. My nerves are overset by the entire incident, and I was hoping that you could somehow—"

The countess broke off in mid-sentence. She swallowed convulsively, trying to fight back the emotions. Mr. Beckham sprang up from behind his desk and hurried to her side. Once there, however, he seemed even more confused, terrified to offer any physical comfort and unsure what else was proper in these highly unusual circumstances.

"You must tell me what has upset you so completely, my lady."

The countess turned toward the lawyer, her face a mask of long-suffering martyrdom. "I need your help, Mr. Beckham. You are the only one that I can turn to, the only one who I can ask. Will you help me? Please?"

"I shall do whatever you ask," he answered gallantly, his chest puffing with pride.

"I thank you, kind sir. You are a true gentleman."

Meredith lifted her gloved hand to her mouth to hide her smile. Poor Mr. Beckham. He stood no chance against her mother, who was a master manipulator. He clearly had no idea he had just agreed to aid her mother without knowing what she required.

The solicitor returned to his seat behind his desk. The countess took a few more moments to compose herself. Meredith moved to the edge of her chair, anxious to hear and watch the next scene in this continuing drama. Why, it was almost as much fun as attending the theater.

"After much thought and consideration, I have decided that it would not be such a tragedy if my son were to stay married to Claire," the countess announced.

Mr. Beckham frowned. "Unfortunately, because he did not use his legal name when he took his vows and signed the license, Mr. Barrington is not married to Miss Truscott, just as Lord Fairhurst is not married to her. However, there is nothing that would impede Mr. Barrington from marrying Miss Truscott in the future, provided he used the correct name on the license."

The solicitor smiled at the countess, but his apparent attempt to lighten the situation with a dash of humor fell flat.

"I do not want Claire to be married to Jason," she replied forcefully. " 'Tis Jasper, Lord Fairhurst, who should be Claire's husband."

Mr. Beckham's smile froze on his face. "But Lord Fairhurst has made his position in this matter most clear. He has instructed me to extricate him from this situation as soon as possible, and I shall do so within a day or two. He stated several times, and quite emphatically, that he does not wish to be married to Miss Truscott. And he is not!"

"How can he know what he wants," the countess declared airily. "He barely knows the girl."

"My lady, I cannot withhold information from my client." The solicitor crumpled the edge of a paper that was resting on his desk. Both his manner and tone suggested he was severely rattled. "I have already given Lord Fairhurst my word that I will handle the matter. To *his* satisfaction."

Meredith watched in amazement as a confusing flicker of emotions played across her mother's face. She was surprised, displeased, and finally determined. The transformation occurred in a flash, but because she was watching so closely, Meredith caught it. She imagined Mr. Beckham was too distraught to be aware of anything except his own sense of panic.

"You misunderstand, Mr. Beckham. I would never ask you to compromise your ethics." The countess tilted her head to one side. "However, it is a mother's prerogative to want the best for her children. What I need is time. Your efforts to resolve this marital dilemma must continue. At a remarkably slow pace. An amazingly slow pace. A snail's pace, if you will. I want Lord Fairhurst to think long and hard about his future and his future wife."

Mr. Beckham stared mutely at the countess. He was clearly uncomfortable with her request, but he had already given his word. There would be no recanting unless he was prepared to diffuse a nearly hysterical female fit.

"I suppose I could give everything a second and even third check before proceeding," he said, though he seemed stricken by the very notion.

"Excellent." A sly smile crept across the countess's lips. "Or perhaps you could take a holiday? A few weeks away from the office will no doubt do you a world of good."

Mr. Beckham's face turned red. "I never leave Town at this time of year."

"No?" The countess cast a regretful look at the solicitor. "Well, if you think it is best for you to stay in London, I shall trust your judgment. I have full confidence in your abilities to handle this in the way we have agreed."

The solicitor stood. It was hardly a subtle hint, and under ordinary circumstances, this lapse of manners would have offended the countess, but she barely looked surprised as she too got to her feet. Meredith decided her mother must be feeling generous in her victory.

"You have my gratitude, Mr. Beckham, as well as my deepest respect." The countess patted his sleeve in a maternal way. "Thank you, my good man, for bringing a touch of comfort to a bruised mother's heart."

With her exit line dramatically delivered, the countess sailed majestically from the office. Meredith followed on her mother's heels, catching a final glimpse of the hapless Mr. Beckham. He looked utterly bamboozled.

Meredith managed to hold her tongue until they were alone in the carriage.

"After witnessing that little performance, I have decided that my oldest daughter Stephanie comes by her flair for dramatics quite naturally," Meredith said. "Apparently, she inherited the inclination from you, Mother. I dare say you missed your true calling in life. Had you decided to pursue it, you would have been a great success on the stage."

"Rubbish." The countess let out a superior smirk. "I would never do anything so vulgar as to trod the boards. What I did this afternoon in Mr. Beckham's office was for my son. Clearly, Jasper is in desperate need of romantic assistance, though he will never admit it. Therefore, it is up to me to decide what is best for him. As a mother yourself, Meredith, I would expect that you of all people would understand."

"Understand is not the same as condone," Meredith stated flatly.

The countess's face grew tight with concern. "Are you going to say anything to Jasper?"

"No. I will keep the events of this meeting to myself." After a slight pause, Meredith added, "For now."

Though she agreed in principle with her mother's opinion, she felt a bit uneasy with her tactics. Still, she reasoned it would do no harm to keep silent. Jasper was a grown man with a strong will and an even stronger sense of determination. He would not be forced into a relationship that was repugnant to him, no matter how hard their mother pushed.

Content with her decision, Meredith relaxed and watched the traffic on the busy street, feeling blessed that her mother cared enough about her children to take their happiness so seriously and doubly blessed that her parents had been out of the country when Meredith's own marriage had taken place.

Lord Fairhurst could not remember a time when he was more uncomfortable. It felt awkward and unnatural to stroll down the street with Claire on his arm. She was taller than most women of his acquaintance, which should have made it easier to carry on a conversation without straining his neck, but Jasper had nothing of significance or interest to say.

Her posture was stiff to the point of rigidity, as she unsuccessfully attempted to keep her skirts from brushing against his boots. The touch of her hand against his arm was so light it was barely perceptible. Her fingers scarcely skimmed the fabric of his greatcoat. Given how desperately she tried to distance herself, Jasper was amazed she was even able to keep in step with him.

The sun had managed to break free of the early morning clouds, and beams of sunshine played over the street. Though he had grown weary of the wet, gray days that had dominated this week and last, Jasper almost wished it were raining. Then the suggestion of a stroll could have been easily dismissed, and he would not be in this position.

Desperate to alleviate the awkward silence, Jasper began to point out the various landmarks they passed. Claire made appropriate murmurs of acknowledgment, but he had no idea if she found this bit of sightseeing completely fascinating or a total bore. She scarcely looked in his direction, and when she did, it was with a guarded expression on her face.

"I notice that you have changed your outfit. Is that one of your new ensembles?" Jasper finally asked, feeling the need to introduce a neutral topic of conversation.

"Yes." He saw her lips twitch before she glanced down at herself. "Madame Renude protested my wearing it home from the shop, claiming the garment was not properly fitted, but your mother and sister insisted. They both assured me it looked fine."

Jasper grudgingly admitted that the walking dress did, indeed, flatter Claire. It was a bold patterned fabric, but the deep colors gave a richness and elegance to the dress, and the colors complemented Claire's skin tone. It fit astonishingly well for an outfit not custom made. She was shapely in the right places, and the garment emphasized that fact most charmingly.

"Your mother and sister are turning me into a woman of fashion." Claire smiled, as though it was the most outlandish thing she had ever heard. "Well, at least they are trying."

"Do not allow them to change you too much. The adage that women must suffer for beauty was no doubt concocted by a female with no looks to speak of."

"That would explain a lot of the more peculiar fashions," Claire replied with a slight smile. "Some of the dress plates we examined offered garments that seemed uncomfortable, as well as outlandish. I cannot imagine anyone wearing them without looking ridiculous."

Jasper smiled inwardly, remembering some of the outfits he had seen. "The most undistinguished, insipid society event is made far more palatable by these so-called height of fashion costumes," he explained. "And 'tis not only the women who provide such amusement. I've seen dandies dressed in the most appalling combinations of bright colors and in clothes that are so tight, they appear to have been sewed into their breeches and jackets. Not to mention shirt points so high and stiff, the fellow cannot even turn his neck."

"Normally I would accuse you of pulling my leg, but after my morning in the dress shop, I know you are being truthful. I am willing to go to some lengths for fashion, but will exercise restraint and avoid the more extreme changes that were suggested by your mother, such as cutting my hair." She caught his eye. "And while I appreciate and value your mother's and sister's advice, I am more than capable of making my own decisions. Thankfully, I am not feebleminded."

"Will and wits might not be sufficient when dealing with my mother." Jasper paused for a heartbeat, then leaned closer. "She can be a bully at times."

Claire's eyes, locked on his, widened. "A family trait?"

"One of our better, and stronger, ones," he shot back.

"That does not surprise me in the least."

They both laughed, until Jasper, remembering he was in a public street, pulled back. He drew in a sharp breath and glanced around, relieved to note they were not being observed by any of their fellow pedestrians. Then, unable to stop himself, Jasper's gaze returned to her face.

Claire's cheeks flushed with color, and he noticed her eyes were sparkling with humor. She looked very pretty and remarkably young.

Quite unexpectedly, he felt a frisson of physical awareness. It affected his equilibrium in a most peculiar way, mostly because he did not understand it. His body seemed to spring to life, to pulse with anticipation. A normal male reaction to an attractive woman, yet somehow this feeling was different. It was unique and possessed a depth that was as unfamiliar as it was unsettling.

With ordinary female attraction, Jasper would simply wait and will the feelings to fade from his body and mind. Eventually, they would. He viewed this as a triumph, knowing that after years of indulging his every passion, he had finally succeeded in training himself to exercise this tight, strict control.

Yet, curiously with Claire, the feelings and images were stronger and far more compelling. He was still able to control them, but in a jolt of insight, Jasper realized the true danger of this predicament. The discovery made his heart slow to an erratic thump. It was highly possible that the attraction would not fade, but instead grow.

But why? What was it about this woman that set him on edge?

He knew far prettier women, far more sophisticated women, and even more fascinating women. Yet it seemed that somehow Claire possessed the power to cause him to lose his much valued control.

As if trying to run from the feelings, Jasper stepped along more briskly. Claire was forced to tighten her hold on his arm to keep pace. They crossed the thoroughfare and strode down the street.

"My carriage is on the next street," Lord Fairhurst announced. "I can instruct the driver to take you back any number of different routes. There is far more of interest for you to see in London than the shops on Bond Street. Are there any particular sights you wished to view?"

"I want to see everything."

Her voice was a breathless whisper. Jasper knew that was due to the near sprint they had just completed to the carriage, but the husky intimacy made him think of other, more delightful ways to cause such a reaction.

He thought of kisses, soft as butterfly wings, but powerful enough to send a strong stirring of heat and wanting throughout their bodies. The eagerness, the enthusiasm that fueled a lingering fascination, a quickening desire that stoked the sensual fires that he *knew* would spring between them.

Jasper was suddenly conscious of a definite ache. He took a deep breath and stepped back, wondering if physical distance would help ease the tightness. It did not.

"I will instruct my driver to take you by Westminster Abbey," Jasper decided. "You can appreciate the architecture and get a sense of the great history of the place even viewing it from the carriage window."

Her eyes widened. "Aren't you coming?"

Lord Fairhurst shook his head forcefully, not liking the pleasure he received from the sound of disappointment in her voice.

He placed his hand on her elbow and was about to assist her into the carriage when the sound of a familiar female voice calling his name shot a prickle of awareness up his spine. Fearing to verify the identity of the speaker, Jasper nevertheless turned his head and found himself gazing into the eyes of the last person he expected or wanted to see. Of all the rotten luck!

"Miss Manning. Miss Rebecca." He snatched his hand off Claire and made a bow to the newcomers, cowardly wishing it were possible for the ground beneath him to open up and swallow him whole. Unfortunately, that was not an option.

Neither Rebecca nor Anne curtsied in response to his greeting. Instead, the women stared at him in speechless shock. He saw Rebecca's eyes flick to Claire, then widen when she somehow correctly guessed Claire's identity. A faint blush tinged Rebecca's skin. She opened her mouth briefly but closed it again, without speaking.

Jasper wondered how he could possibly avoid a scene that would scandalize the *ton* and be the talk at every society event of the evening, yet he found it difficult to think with Rebecca and her sister staring at him like a pair of tragic characters from a Greek chorus.

"Rebecca—" Jasper said, but she had turned sharply away. She stumbled down the street with ungainly haste, hurrying toward her father's coach. Her sister Anne scrambled to keep pace.

Jasper swallowed a curse and started after her, but was drawn back when he felt a tug on his coat sleeve.

"I assume you are acquainted with the ladies?"

Jasper stopped, then turned, struggling to mask his anger. "I was, though I wonder now if they will acknowledge me at any event, or instead give me the cut direct. 'Tis no more than I deserve, given the disgraceful way I treated them."

"But you were perfectly polite. It seemed that their manners were the ones lacking." Claire stared up at him for a long moment, clearly not connecting with his meaning. Jasper was forced to explain.

"Miss Anne Manning is the elder of the two sisters. She was dressed in the gray pelisse. The other young lady was Miss Rebecca. She is the woman I planned to marry." He shifted his head so he was gazing directly into her eyes. "That is, before you became my wife."

The moment the carriage door closed behind her, Rebecca's temper erupted.

"How dare he?" She threw her reticule forcefully on the carriage floor, then stomped on it in anger. "Out in public with that creature after promising me that she would be quickly gone from his life. And did you see the way they were acting with each other? Cozy and intimate, speaking in discreet, exclusive tones. I had to call his name twice before he even turned to acknowledge me. It nearly caused me to lose my breakfast."

"Truly, Rebecca, it was not that bad," Anne said. She bent over and rescued the squashed reticule, lifting it off the floor and placing it in her lap. "Lord Fairhurst seemed equally distressed at the unexpected meeting."

"Of course he did, you fool!" Rebecca hauled in a tight breath. "He hates to have attention drawn to him, especially if it involves anything that smacks of impropriety. Now I wish there were more people present to witness the encounter."

"That's illogical," Anne contended. "Lord Fairhurst would never—"

"Shut up!" Rebecca gave an exasperated hiss and turned with an upraised hand, posed to strike. "If you utter another word in his defense, I swear I shall slap you silly."

The threat effectively stopped any further comments from Anne. Her lips quivered with uncertainty, and for a moment, Rebecca felt the urge to slap her sister anyway, knowing she would receive a sense of pleasure from the act.

Rebecca's stomach coiled with nausea. She had not expected to have such a violent, jealous reaction. In truth, she cared little for Lord Fairhurst, agreeing to the match mostly to please her father and, more importantly, to remove herself from his influence.

Fairhurst had many qualities she desired in a husband. He was wealthy, possessed a title and was heir to an even higher position, was handsome and relatively young, but most important, Rebecca knew Lord Fairhurst never intended to love her, and she knew with certainty she would never love him.

Yet, that apparently did not preclude her from feeling possessive about him. Seeing him with that woman had unleashed all sorts of raging emotions. Fortunately, she had held them in check while on the street. Though tantrums were her speciality, Rebecca never indulged in them unless she was far away from prying eyes.

Though the carriage felt airless, Rebecca pulled down the window shade. A fleeting madness gripped her, and she released the emotion, spewing out her distress. "Is this to be my life? Forced to endure anguish and humiliation day after day while Fairhurst parades about Town with this woman?"

"He was merely assisting her into a carriage," Anne said timidly. She reached across the carriage interior and squeezed her sister's hand. "Perhaps it was a chance encounter."

"My God, you are an idiot," Rebecca said, shaking off Anne's feeble attempt at comfort. "It was his carriage.

Did you not see the emblem emblazoned on the door? 'Tis no wonder you have never married, or even had a single offer. You have a feeble mind, sister, that matches perfectly with your mousy looks."

Anne flinched at her sister's words and bit her lower lip. Rebecca ignored her sister's bowed head and trembling hands. Her mind was occupied with far more pressing problems—namely, her own survival. She had been naive and foolish last night to take Fairhurst at his word. There apparently was far more to this situation than he had previously told her. And when taking into account today's incident, it seemed doubtful that Fairhurst was going to do everything possible to honor their betrothal.

After all, it had never been officially announced. The negotiations had been completed and the financial arrangements had been decided, but no papers were signed. Handled correctly, Rebecca knew she could escape the worst of the scandal and place it all squarely at Lord Fairhurst's feet. Exactly where it belonged.

Slowly, Rebecca lifted the shade and peered through the carriage window. The storm of her emotions had finally begun to settle, but the need for revenge still lingered. She held tight to the power of it, knowing it would drive and sustain her in the coming weeks.

A sudden chill moved over her and Rebecca smiled. Everything was going to work out for the best. The stabbing dread she had initially felt at the idea of losing Fairhurst was gone, replaced by a strong, intense need to be cruel.

And that, she understood completely.

Chapter Seven

"Are we home?"

Jasper nodded to Claire, marveling at how natural the words had fallen from her lips. Home. But this was his home, a family property that had belonged to generations of Earls of Stafford. It was not her home, nor would it ever be. As eldest son and heir, he would someday inherit the property, together with the title. His twin brother Jason would always be welcomed, for it was a substantial mansion boasting numerous rooms, as well as fifteen bedchambers, but Jason would never have the right to call this dwelling his home.

It also would never be home to Claire Truscott, unless somehow she remained Lady Fairhurst, and one day became the Countess of Stafford.

The very idea jolted Jasper. Especially because it did not instantly feel so totally repugnant.

The carriage door swung open. A liveried footman pulled down the steps and offered his arm to Claire. She descended gracefully from the coach, and Jasper followed quickly on her heels.

He had not originally intended to ride back to the mansion with her. Restless and wanting to be alone with his thoughts, he had planned on placing Claire and the maid inside the coach, and then walking over to his club.

But Rebecca's unexpected appearance had altered everything. After the incident on the street, spending time at the club held little appeal for Jasper, especially because the possibility that a fellow club member had witnessed the chance meeting was a very real fear. Women might be accused of relishing gossip and scandal, but Jasper knew that men enjoyed the activity equally.

So Lord Fairhurst had reluctantly climbed into the coach and endured a carriage ride fraught with silent tension. Now that he had finally arrived home, he wanted nothing more than to retreat to the comfort of his study and decide how to fix this latest mess. If it even was fixable.

Yet even that small pleasure was to be denied, for the moment he and Claire began climbing the interior staircase, the butler handed her an urgent message that had been delivered earlier.

She unfolded the note and read the apparently brief message. Her face paled, then tensed.

"Bad news?" Lord Fairhurst asked.

Claire glanced up. "Of a sort."

"Is it from my brother?"

"No. The note is from my Great-Aunt Agnes. I told her she could call on me today." Claire's eyes filled with apprehension. "As you might remember, she has been most anxious to meet my new husband. In fact, she was expecting to be received by both of us this afternoon."

Jasper did remember her many references to Great-Aunt Agnes yesterday afternoon, but because he had believed at the time that a practical joke was being played upon him, he had paid little attention to the particulars.

"If you care to receive any visitors, you may use the gold salon. Cook will be pleased to serve any refreshments you require. Just ask thc butler to make the arrangements."

"Will you be joining us?"

Jasper barely hesitated. "No. But do send Aunt Agnes my regrets."

His tone was sharper than he intended. Yet, surprisingly, it did not seem to upset Claire. She was standing on the main staircase, one step above him, causing their heights to be nearly even. She was gazing at him and waiting, her eyes never leaving his face, as though she expected him to change his mind at any moment.

The gesture put Jasper's back up. Just because she was in need of his help did not obligate him to come to her rescue. It was his twin brother, Jason, who had always been far better suited to the role of knight errant. Jasper usually kept a tighter leash of control on his impulsive actions.

The silence stretched taut, apparently along with Claire's nerves. "Aunt Agnes will be very disappointed if you do not make an effort to meet her," Claire finally said. She paled even more. "And highly suspicious."

"That is hardly my problem."

Claire licked her lips, her gaze flicking from Jasper's eyes to her note, then back again. She, apparently, was not about to allow herself to be dismissed out of hand. "It could very well become your problem if Aunt Agnes catches wind of our rather unusual situation."

Jasper raised his eyebrow, uncertain if she had just uttered a veiled threat. "Then I suggest you tell Aunt Agnes the truth. The sooner, the better."

Claire appeared to smother a nervous grunt. "The

moment Aunt Agnes knows the truth, the entire world will be privy to our secret."

"Ask her to be discreet. For the sake of the family."

"Father says asking Aunt Agnes to keep a secret is tantamount to taking out an ad in the newspaper," Claire said, as she tucked the note into the pocket of her new gown. "I believe she truly is incapable."

"Then I shall leave it to you to decide how best to cope with this delicate situation, since she is a member of your family," Jasper said.

Claire's shoulders rose in a gentle shrug. "Even if I were so inclined to share this confidence with my aunt, what would I tell her? I married Lord Fairhurst. Does that mean that you are my husband? Or is Jay?"

Jasper raised his fingers to the bridge of his nose and pressed hard. "I am paying one of the finest legal minds in the country a ridiculous sum of money to answer that very question. I promise the moment I know, I shall rush to share the results with Great-Aunt Agnes."

Muttering a curse, Lord Fairhurst executed a bow, made an about-face, and retreated to the sanctuary of his study. He dutifully buried his nose in a variety of business correspondence for the next hour, but eventually admitted he was comprehending little and accomplishing even less.

The house was quiet. Apparently, his mother was still away from home and would most probably remain so until this evening. At least that would afford Claire the opportunity to greet her elderly relative in private, though if the old woman was the bona fide terror Claire indicated, that might not be the ideal situation.

He tried to dismiss it all from his mind. Yet try as he would, Jasper could not remove the picture of Claire standing on the staircase in her pretty new outfit, looking forlorn and utterly lost as he so ungallantly abandoned her.

She had not begged, or cried, or insisted that he help. She had used none of the usual feminine tricks; in truth, it seemed that she used no deception at all. She stated her case as forcefully as she could, and when he refused her request, she accepted it with quiet dignity. Yet Jasper had clearly seen that at his refusal, some of the light went out of her eyes.

Suspecting he would probably regret it, Lord Fairhurst nevertheless took a deep breath and left the privacy of his study, concluding that it was damn inconvenient to have a conscience. Claire was alone when he entered the gold salon, seated on his mother's favorite settee, her hands in her lap and her eyes on her hands.

"Your guest has not yet arrived?" he asked.

With an air of distraction, Claire glanced briefly in his direction. "Aunt Agnes is always five minutes late. Never more, never less. She will therefore be here in precisely two minutes, so if you wish to avoid running into her, I suggest you leave immediately."

Jasper gazed at Claire for several long moments. "My brother and I are very different men. We might be nearly identical physically, but we are hardly interchangeable."

"No one knows that more than I, my lord," she replied with a rueful grimace.

"Then how do you suggest I fool your aunt into believing that I am Jason?"

"You are willing to help me?" Claire asked.

Jasper tried to shut out the look of relief and surprise on her face. He was not doing this solely to aid her, but rather he was doing it to keep the circle of scandal from growing ever wider. Or so he told himself.

"I give you fair warning, Madame. I shall not lie to anyone for you."

She lifted her chin and looked directly at him. "I would never ask such a thing," Claire responded with indignity.

"Then what do you propose?"

"Given the circumstances, our only course is to tell the truth. However, we must do so with great care and selectively."

"Lie by omission?"

A look of guilt flashed across her face. "Aunt Agnes knows that I have married Lord Fairhurst. And are you not Lord Fairhurst?"

"I am not the man you married," Jasper said.

"That is not what I asked."

Her voice was firm, but her eyes were troubled. It gave Jasper's rigid sense of morality a boost discovering that she too was uncomfortable with this approach. But he knew it was the only sensible course and clearly the lesser of two evils.

"I shall introduce you as Lord Fairhurst," Claire continued. "Aunt Agnes will assume the rest. We shall avoid any direct questions that would force either of us to lie about our relationship. Is that acceptable?"

Jasper nodded his head. "Since my brother is in part responsible for this mess, I shall consent to a brief meeting with your aunt under these terms."

"Thank you." She raised her hand as if to shake on the agreement, but lowered it before following through. "When Aunt Agnes is present, one seldom needs to speak very often. Though I should warn you that she will question you unmercifully on subjects of a delicate nature, such as the state of your finances and your views on political issues."

He stared down at her. "I can handle myself."

"I fear you might discover that you have met your match, my lord," Claire answered. "Though advanced in years, Aunt Agnes has a keen eye and a sharp mind. We must avoid arousing her suspicions at all costs." Her brow furrowed. "To that end, do you think you could try to be a little less stiff?"

"I beg your pardon?"

Claire responded in a softer tone. "I am a romantic, and everyone in my family knows and teases me about it. The story of my whirlwind courtship with Jay is a subject much discussed among the small society in our village. With each retelling it has grown until it has reached epic proportions. And believe me, Aunt Agnes has heard every detail, no matter how exaggerated. If you behave in your usual stiff manner, she will never believe that I willingly married you."

She gave him a doubtful, sidelong glance that sent a shiver of indignity up Jasper's spine. How dare she accuse him of being stodgy? He was tempered and controlled, always the perfect gentleman. Did she seriously expect him to act the smitten husband? In front of an audience?

"Precisely what level of intimacy do you require, Madame? Should we be locked in a passionate embrace when your aunt arrives, or do you suggest something more radical? Unbuttoned and disheveled clothing, along with heavy breathing and flushed skin, perhaps?"

His words painted a seductive, steamy scene, yet his tone would have made icicles shiver.

Claire's head lowered. "I meant no insult. If you could merely refrain from glowering at me, that should do the trick."

Her obvious remorse struck a cord of guilt. Jasper

opened his mouth to apologize for his crude remark; then he noticed the slight movement of her shoulders. Good Lord, he'd made her cry! Feeling even greater guilt, he leaned forward in his seat. He was just about to extend his handkerchief to wipe away her tears when he caught the glimmering of her white teeth.

Bloody hell! She was not weeping, but rather trying to choke back her mirth. 'Twas only the sound of a discreet cough that saved her from a scathing tongue-lashing. Lord Fairhurst looked over her shoulder and saw his butler standing to one side of the open door.

"Mrs. Agnes Humphrey," the servant announced in a serious tone.

Great-Aunt Agnes swept into the room, her eyes darting curiously about the elegantly appointed surroundings. She was short and round and dressed entirely in black. Though clearly a woman of advanced years, she had an obvious, robust energy. Her features were strong and prominent; even as a young girl she would have at most been labeled handsome. If he had encountered her on the street, Jasper realized he never would have believed she was related to Claire.

He rose automatically to his feet and straightened his shoulders; then he wondered if he should assume a more casual air.

"Aunt Agnes, how wonderful to see you." Claire crossed the room and kissed her great-aunt on the cheek, and then turned to Jasper. "May I have the pleasure of presenting Lord Fairhurst?"

Great-Aunt Agnes acknowledged his bow of greeting with a short huff; then she lifted her chin and looked down her nose at him as if he were a nasty character. "I have been waiting a long time to meet you, young man."

"I, too, have heard a great deal about you, Ma'am," Jasper replied, keeping his tone sober and polite.

At Claire's urging, Great-Aunt Agnes took a seat. Jasper, who remained standing, raised one arm to rest on the mantelpiece above his head and assessed the situation.

With her black skirts billowing about her and her gaze fixed firmly on his face, Jasper quickly concluded that Claire had not exaggerated. Great-Aunt Agnes was a formidable opponent. She seemed to possess in abundance the gall shared by many elderly individuals who believed their advanced years gave them the right to say anything they wanted. A few flattering words and good manners were not going to be enough to make a favorable impression.

Yet Jasper was not so easily discouraged. With almost grim resignation, he set himself to be totally charming. He asked about her journey, the weather, and a favorite subject of all elderly women he had ever met, her health.

Great-Aunt Agnes would have none of it. She grilled him like a freshly caught salmon and did not even have the decency to look shamefaced about it. Instead, she glared at him as if she had bestowed some great gift upon his person by asking him so many pointed questions.

"I certainly hope that you will prove yourself to be a gentleman worthy of my great-niece's hand," Great-Aunt Agnes bristled. "I must say, I am not impressed with how you have conducted yourself thus far, though I am willing to give you an opportunity to redeem yourself."

Jasper's lip twitched. Her words expressed the exact sentiments he would have conveyed to his brother, if given the chance. He eyed his foe with a new respect; then realizing that he and Great-Aunt Agnes shared such a similar thought pattern aroused Lord Fairhurst's sense of the ridiculous. He could not resist answering, "Claire is indeed a rare treasure. I promise I shall endeavor to do better in the future."

Claire's brow rose at his pronouncement. She reached out and hastily pulled the bell rope; then she instructed the answering footman that they were ready for refreshments.

The tea tray was brought in, and they all conversed politely on inane topics in front of the servants. For once Lord Fairhurst regretted that his staff was so efficient, for he knew the moment they withdrew the inquisition would begin anew.

"I believe a husband and wife should live together, Lord Fairhurst," Great-Aunt Agnes insisted the moment the servants departed.

Jasper regarded her with a faint smile. "That is often the usual arrangement."

"And will that be your arrangement?"

"We shall see," Claire interjected. She lifted the tea tray and swung it toward her great-aunt. "Please try a scone. Cook makes them with dark currants for extra flavor. They are simply delicious."

Great-Aunt Agnes accepted the treat her great-niece pressed on her, but left it untouched on her plate. Her gaze once again roamed over Lord Fairhurst. "You must tell me why you had to travel all the way to Wiltshire to find a bride. Were none of the London misses to your liking, my lord?"

Jasper stiffened. Was it possible that she had heard some of the gossip about his upcoming betrothal to Rebecca? Great-Aunt Agnes did not travel in the same circle of society, but unsavory tales had a nasty way of finding their way to all sorts of ears.

He regarded the older woman's shrewd expression. No, if she had heard even a whiff of scandal, she would have confronted him with it the moment she arrived.

"I did not travel to Wiltshire to seek a bride, but came away with one nevertheless." He turned and gave Claire a smoldering look. "I suppose one could say it was out of my control."

"Ah, he is a romantic!" Great-Aunt Agnes declared. She clasped her hands together in delight and smiled broadly.

Claire laughed a little uncertainly. Lord Fairhurst turned his gaze to her. She looked steadily back at him, her lips tight, her eyebrows slightly raised, as if she had no understanding of what he was doing.

Jasper smiled, deciding this visit was starting to become amusing.

"Well, your attitude and affection for my niece renews my hope, young man." Her tone had softened almost imperceptibly. "Though I was never blessed with any of my own, I'd not be adverse to holding Claire's child in my arms at least once before I die."

Claire passed one hand over her face and turned bright red. "Aunt Agnes, do you like my new dress? I went shopping with His Lordship's mother and sister this afternoon, and they both insisted it was perfect for me."

"The pattern is rather bold for your coloring," Great-Aunt Agnes replied, barely glancing at her niece. "Though it is a flattering style."

"I like it," Jasper interjected.

"Do you?" Great-Aunt Agnes darted him a sly glance. "And what about children, Lord Fairhurst? Do you like them, too?"

"Aunt Agnes, please."

The older woman shrugged innocently. "I am merely saying that I want a few great-nieces and-nephews to comfort me in my old age."

"There are many things we all want, Aunt. Alas, life is not always so accommodating, and we do not always get what we wish." Claire patted her elderly relative's hand affectionately. "Or deserve."

After a moment's hesitation, Great-Aunt Agnes nodded her head in solemn agreement. Jasper was impressed. Claire had managed to put Great-Aunt Agnes in her place without sounding like a spiteful child retaliating for an insult. The tide of conversation was now successfully turned, and Claire was in charge. For the rest of the visit, Great-Aunt Agnes allowed herself to be led away from her preferred topic—him—and discussed the state of other relatives' lives. Since he knew none of the individuals they talked about, it was only necessary for him to look mildly interested and nod occasionally.

As Great-Aunt Agnes prattled on, Jasper let his mind drift. He really did owe the old biddy a debt of gratitude. She had unknowingly prevented him from committing the crime of bigamy, which would have created a scandal far worse than the one that was brewing.

If not for her interfering ways and bullying attitude, Claire would never have come to London, and Jasper would not have learned about his brother's marriage. Or rather his marriage, for more and more it seemed possible that Jasper could be the bridegroom.

Finally, the visit came to an end. After a hug for her great-niece and a nod in Jasper's direction, Great-Aunt Agnes left the same way she came, with her nose in the air and a regal swish of her skirts.

"Well, that was not too bad," he ventured.

"Compared to what?" Claire asked dryly. "The Spanish Inquisition?"

Jasper sniffed. "I suppose she can be a bit overbearing."

"Yes, a bit." A small smile appeared at the corners of Claire's mouth.

"I think she liked me," Jasper said.

That remark earned him an amused glance from Claire. "You were quite charming and exceptionally patient." She looked archly at him. "Thank you."

"Only quite charming?" he pressed.

"Remarkably charming," she replied. "And that is the extent of the compliments you will be receiving from me, my lord."

Jasper joined her in a small laugh. The mild annoyance he had early felt toward her was gone, replaced by a strange, almost desperate tenderness. Her face was close to his, and Jasper became very much aware of her warmth and femininity. He decided to throw her off balance.

"You know, I missed your wedding. As it stands, I might very well have been the groom." He reached out and took one of her hands in his. "I think it only fair that I kiss the bride."

Such a declaration would normally draw a blistering set down, yet no words of protest were uttered. Encouraged, Jasper lowered his head and touched his lips to hers—soft, warm, and featherlight. He knew often the lightest touch could give the greatest pleasure.

A tingling sensation began at the point of contact and quickly spread throughout his body. He tasted her lips and inhaled her essence. She had a spicy, sensual scent he could not ignore. She sighed against his mouth and he pulled back a fraction. Then, because they were tempting him beyond measure, he brazenly licked her closed lips.

At the same time, his hands reached out and touched her face, the fingertips running over her delicate eyebrows and soft cheeks. Pulling back, he rubbed his nose lightly across hers; then he pressed his lips more firmly, deliberately enticing her, coaxing her to open her mouth so that his tongue could slip inside and mate with hers.

He felt her tremble against his body and he molded her curves closer to his hardness. Raw sensation burst to life within him. Her mouth was a delight of sweetness—wild, wet, and hungry. Her tongue dueled with his, eager to participate. Jasper slid his hand along the base of her neck and cradled her head, holding her in place to receive more of his attention.

The heat intensified. He tried not to let it take control, but the feel and taste of her fed his desires. Pleasure burned throughout his body; blood was pounding through his veins in a hot, demanding rhythm.

In this brief, unguarded moment, Jasper caught a glimpse of the passion she offered, the passion she was capable of igniting and experiencing. And in that instant he was awoken to the truth. He wanted this kiss to become something more.

Yet deep inside, some small shred of sanity remained. He knew he was doing something unthinkable. With great reluctance, Jasper lifted his head. She blinked dazedly up at him and swayed. He caught her shoulders to steady her. She drew in a sharp breath and glanced around. Almost by instinct, she placed her hands against his chest, though she did not push him away.

Claire half smiled. "I think that was most unwise."

Jasper knew she was right. It was perhaps one of the

more inappropriate actions of his life, kissing his brother's woman. Yet for once his conscience was not concerned about propriety. Rather, his male vanity was pricked at her reaction.

"Was is truly so unpleasant?"

She shivered. "No. It was actually rather spectacular."

Then, with a mysterious smile, she turned and walked away. Jasper gazed at her departing back with narrowed eyes and tried to untangle his motives. Why had he kissed her? Was it merely payback for her early remark about him being stodgy? Or was it some sort of twisted revenge against his brother for placing him in this untenable position?

Or, most disturbing of all, was he losing a bit of his famous control and indulging in the passion Claire so effortlessly inspired?

Claire could not say, with any degree of certainty, why she allowed him to kiss her. She was normally a very steady person, yet it seemed that whenever she was in Lord Fairhurst's company, she felt the urge to do something utterly mad.

It would have been wonderful to say that it was he who initiated everything, that it was he who was wholly responsible for the kiss, but Claire was honest enough to admit she shared equally in the blame, for he had given her ample opportunity to say no. And the thoughts running through her mind had been screaming yes!

She had not reacted physically to any man since Henry. On the surface, it seemed that Lord Fairhurst would be the last person with whom she would develop a passion. He was rigid and strict, stuffy, and usually disapproving of her. Yet she always seemed to react to his nearness with a heightened awareness of her female soul and a slight shortness of breath.

Claire pondered this oddity as she walked up the stairs to her chamber. Once in her room, she went to the windows and pushed back the velvet drapes. The sun was beginning to set. Soon the garden would be bathed in the eerie light of dusk, the tight buds waiting for the warmth of the morning sun to bring forth their full, rich blossoms.

The garden held the promise of spring, the hint of beauty yet to come. It seemed a fitting metaphor to Claire's growing feelings for Lord Fairhurst.

The thought depressed her. The heavy push of emotions lodged in her breast were a testament to the attraction she had felt toward Jasper from the start. It made no real sense, but feelings of this sort never did.

She looked out at the view of the garden and drew in a deep breath. She had no right to these emotions. Lord Fairhurst belonged to another, as did she. Her relationship with Jay was not of a romantic nature, nor would it ever be, but that was the bargain she had struck.

That was the bargain she would keep.

At least now she had a memory. It had been a very long time, indeed, since a man had pressed his lips to hers. Jay might be considered the rake of the family, but the kisses she shared with Jasper informed Claire that Lord Fairhurst knew how to satisfy a woman.

The very idea left Claire feeling weak-kneed. Resolutely, she vanquished the thought, and images, from her mind. She spent the remainder of the evening in her room, deciding it would be better to stay in her chamber than to sit silently at dinner. Besides, she was schooling herself to become accustomed to the aloneness. It was not an altogether pleasant evening, nor was it horrible. It was what it was—the reality of her future.

Occasionally, when she could not control her thoughts, Claire would again remember the fiery embrace of the afternoon. But close on the heels of delight was the constant warning. *I must not kiss this man again. He is not mine, nor will he ever be. To follow that path will only lead me to heartbreak.*

Unfortunately, what the mind knows cannot be dictated to the heart. As she feared, Claire stayed awake half the night, and when she at last drifted off to sleep, her dreams were filled with the memory of seductive kisses and hard, lean, male strength.

Chapter Eight

During the coming days, Jasper tried to busy himself with business matters. He spent a considerable amount of time with his secretary and man of affairs, but the men were so competent, and Lord Fairhurst so organized, that they quickly ran out of items to discuss.

He reviewed accounts from his country estate in York, Haverford Grange, which produced a sizable portion of his income, and then read several reports on various business ventures that were actively searching for investors. Most were far too risky for his tastes, and under normal circumstances would never have been considered, but Jasper welcomed the distraction and read every page.

Though he told himself it was merely a precaution, Lord Fairhurst also deliberately avoided Claire. The house was large, so chance meetings were rare, but to ensure his seclusion, he began taking his meals at odd times of the day and night in the privacy of his study or his chambers.

For the first time in his life, he felt uncomfortable and uneasy in his own home.

It would have been a relief to throw himself into the distraction of social events, but that too was to be avoided. Lord Fairhurst was unprepared to answer any questions from friends and subtle inquiries from acquaintances about the state of his relationship with Rebecca.

He sent Miss Manning flowers daily, together with a note of remembrance, yet she never acknowledged the receipt of either. He thought her silence most telling and was beginning to wonder if he would be given a chance to make things right between them. Or, on the days when he felt more tired than a man his age should, if he really wanted to set things back on course.

And that revelation distressed him most of all.

The one person that he was anxious to see, his solicitor, Walter Beckham, was puzzlingly unavailable. Never being one who tolerated inefficiency, Jasper summoned the lawyer to his home for a meeting, composing the missive so that it would be impossible for it to be ignored or refused.

When Mr. Beckham was announced, Jasper remained seated behind the leather-topped desk that dominated the far end of his private study. Through hooded eyes, he watched as the solicitor advanced across the room, his uneven gait betraying an elevated level of nervous agitation.

Jasper feared that meant the news would not be good. Unfortunately, he was correct. Yet it was not only the disappointing progress that Mr. Beckham had achieved that distressed Lord Fairhurst, it was the manner in which he delivered the information.

"Your complacency in this matter has me worried, Mr. Beckham. Have I inadequately expressed my desire to see this problem swiftly resolved?"

"Not at all, my lord. You have been most clear about your wishes." The solicitor darted him a nervous grin; then concentrated on shuffling the numerous papers in his lap. "This is a highly unusual, complicated case. It will take time to maneuver around the many legal obstacles."

"I am not expecting miracles," Jasper replied, though his tone suggested that was precisely what he expected. "Nor do I profess to understand all the complications of the law. Still, I am a logical man, and it seems that it should be fairly simple to prove that I cannot be married without my consent, even if the person involved in the incident is my twin brother and heir."

The solicitor bowed his head closer to the papers in his hand. "As you said, my lord, the law is complicated."

"But I must know my legal position as soon as possible."

"Yes."

"I am a man caught in limbo, Mr. Beckham. I cannot move forward until this matter is settled."

"I understand."

Lord Fairhurst lowered his voice. "Then do something about it."

Mr. Beckham cleared his throat. "Yes, my lord."

With a slight frown, Jasper watched him leave. The meeting had not gone at all the way he had hoped. Plus, there was something about Mr. Beckham's nervous attitude that was troubling. The usually talkative lawyer had been miserly in his answers and had had difficulty meeting Jasper's eyes when speaking.

Lord Fairhurst had never questioned the solicitor's skill or honesty, yet he was left with the distinct impression that the man was hiding something.

"Am I interrupting?"

Jasper glanced up and spied his brother-in-law, the Marquess of Dardington, standing in the doorway. "No, come in. I need a distraction to keep this day from becoming totally soured."

"I noticed Beckham leaving," the marquess remarked. He seated himself on one of the more comfortable chairs near the fireplace. "I take it the news was not encouraging?"

Lord Fairhurst scowled. "Hardly." Jasper strode to the sideboard, greatly feeling the need for the mellowing aspect of alcohol. Deciding it was more than necessary to break his restrictive rules on spirit consumption, he poured two glasses of port, then silently handed one to the marquess.

There was no comment from his brother-in-law about the early hour or the generous serving, and Jasper was reminded why he liked the man so damn much.

"The Bow Street Runners I hired on your behalf have confirmed that the marriage between Jasper Barrington, Lord Fairhurst, and Claire Truscott is duly recorded in the village registry. They also noted that the Truscott family is well respected and liked within the community," the marquess reported.

"What about my brother?"

"He left Wiltshire directly after his wedding, presumably to come to London to assist with a family crisis. Since we know that is not what happened, the runners are investigating other possibilities, but it will take time and more than a dash of luck for them to find him. The trail has gone cold." The marquess shot him a look over the rim of his glass. "Do you think Jason has come to harm?"

" 'Tis too early to say. My brother has disappeared for long periods of time on several occasions." Lord Fairhurst took a sip of his drink, then let out a bark of laughter. "Of course, he has never before left me with a wife."

The marquess quirked a brow. "So she is yours?" he asked. "Is that what the solicitor told you?"

Jasper gazed down at the dwindling contents of his glass. "Not directly, but his nervous agitation made it abundantly clear that it will not be easy to disengage myself from her. I fear it will most likely have to be an annulment. Or, God help me, a divorce."

"Rotten luck." The marquess shook his head sympathetically. "Though I cannot see it coming to that, given these circumstances. Actually, I cannot believe a legal marriage truly exists between the two of you. Would you like me to ask my father's solicitor to look into the matter? He has a reputation for a sharp legal mind and is very discreet."

" 'Tis a very tempting offer, but I would rather not involve anyone else at this stage. However, if Beckham fails to produce satisfactory results by next week, I shall ask you to arrange a meeting with the duke's attorney." Lord Fairhurst gulped down the last of his drink and deposited the empty glass on the edge of his desk. "And now I must make a visit to the Manning household. I have to tell Rebecca that things remain in a legal coil and our plans to become engaged must wait."

"Bloody hell!"

"Exactly." Lord Fairhurst pushed himself from the chair and stalked to the sideboard. The temptation to refill his glass was strong, but he resisted it. Being a good host, he did offer a refill to his guest, who also declined.

Rising to his feet, the marquess extended his hand. "I wish you luck."

Jasper stepped forward and shook his brother-in-law's

hand. "Thank you. I have a sinking feeling that I am going to need it."

Lord Fairhurst was kept waiting for fifteen minutes before being admitted to the Mannings' formal drawing room. As he paced the hallway, he wondered if the slight had been ordered by Rebecca's father, but when he entered the drawing room, he discovered that only the two women of the household were present. Mr. Manning was not in attendance.

Rebecca sat stone-faced in an armchair by the fire. Her sister Anne was on the nearby chaise. After a somber greeting, Jasper was rather reluctantly offered a seat. He sat on a chair that offered him a clear view of his intended bride. Refreshments were not offered nor was any concession made to see to his additional comfort.

Jasper grimaced inwardly. This chilly reception was a far cry from what he usually received. Much had changed since slipping from his role as potential suitor. Now he was rightfully viewed with suspicion and distrust.

"I met with my solicitor earlier today," Lord Fairhurst began.

Rebecca's chin rose abruptly, and her eyes flared with hopeful excitement. "Is it over? Are you at last free of that horrid woman?"

Jasper tried to ignore the feeling of dread that slid through him. "I am afraid the news is not very encouraging."

"Oh." Rebecca sagged against her chair.

Her face was the picture of disappointment. If she

was trying to make him feel guilty, she was doing a first-rate job.

"Though it has not yet been confirmed, the marriage my brother undertook using my name appears to have legal substance. It must be dissolved before we can proceed with our own nuptials."

"Will you have to seek an annulment?" Anne asked.

"That is the preferred course, but if it is not granted, then I must petition for a divorce." Though he spoke to both women, his eyes never left Rebecca's face.

"Divorce?" She spat out the word like a bitter pill. "I cannot marry a divorced man. The scandal would be unbearable. I shall be cast out of society. Forever. No person of social standing would ever receive me."

"I do not believe it will come to a divorce, though I must in good conscience warn you of the worst difficulty we might face. Our circumstances are so unique that many are bound to show us sympathy and consideration. It might be rough going initially, but I am certain we can weather the storm. Together." He looked into her eyes. "The *ton* has a short memory, and I have powerful and influential relatives and friends. I am confident that we will gradually be accepted again in the finest homes of the beau monde."

"And what are we to do in the meantime? Rusticate in the country?" Rebecca made a dismissive sound. "That is not acceptable."

Lord Fairhurst weighed his words very carefully. "We are not officially betrothed. I still have high hopes that we will make a match, but I cannot say with any certainty when that may occur."

For a moment Rebecca did nothing but stare at him, and he almost wished she would open her mouth and shout. At least that would release some of the tension that was suffocating them all.

"I am sorry this has been so difficult for you, Rebecca," he added quietly.

"Difficult?" The flash of her eyes startled Jasper. He expected her to be upset, but the depth of her rage was an unwelcome surprise. "I have been humiliated, my lord. Waiting in near seclusion like a docile servant, while you parade about Town with that female on your arm."

"That was a most unfortunate incident," Lord Fairhurst replied, defensively. "And entirely innocent. If you would allow me to explain, I—"

"Unfortunate for whom?" Her frozen eyes narrowed. "You, my lord? Getting caught with your lady-love?"

"Rebecca!" Anne's appalled voice echoed through the room. "Lord Fairhurst is a gentleman. He would never do anything so vulgar."

"Did my eyes deceive me the other day on Bond Street?" Rebecca asked.

"What you saw and what was happening appear to be very different," Jasper said, trying to remain calm and patient. "In your distress, you have jumped to numerous exaggerated conclusions and turned an innocent, insignificant incident into a melodrama. There is a simple explanation that—"

"How dare you!" An angry flush crawled up her neck. Rebecca raised her hand and slapped it across his cheek. "Do not make light of my suffering. You have no idea of the anguish I have been forced to endure."

She lifted her arm higher, poised to strike again, but when she swung toward him, Jasper grasped her wrist and held it tightly, preventing contact.

"One I will allow, given your heightened emotional

state. But only one." He bent his head and spoke softly, so only she could hear. "I know this is distressing, but try to remember you are a lady."

She paled. "How dare you cast aspersions on my character?"

"I cast no aspersions, Miss Manning. Your actions and attitude are testimony to your lack of character."

He probably should not have stated it so bluntly, but Jasper's patience had reached its limit. He had expected her to be upset, but he was unprepared for such an emotional, vicious attack.

"Remove yourself at once, Lord Fairhurst." She rose, her face a rigid mask. "And do not bother to ever return, for you shall not be received."

"Oh, Rebecca." Anne's voice was a wail of remorse.

"Good-bye, Lord Fairhurst."

Rebecca's dismissive tone should have produced a bleakness inside him, but instead Jasper felt an odd sense of relief, as if he had just dodged a bullet.

Jasper gave a curt nod to the footman who held the door as he exited the Manning household. For the final time. Once on the street, he pulled his hat down and eased on his driving gloves.

Years ago, he had always driven his own team about Town, but when he had decided he needed a more conservative, respectable image, Jasper had abandoned the task. Deciding the activity might calm him and help him consider his next move, Lord Fairhurst relegated his surprised driver to the back of the coach and took up the reins.

When he arrived home, Jasper did not immediately go inside, but instead circled around the house and entered the rear gardens through the back gate. Even in hibernation the rose garden was a thing of beauty.

The neat rows of bushes, surrounded by well-tended, formal shrubbery, were healthy and lush, covered with tight buds that seemed ready to burst into bloom at any moment.

He strolled down a gravel path, then turned the corner of the hedge and saw Claire. She was sitting on a garden bench in a secluded alcove of greenery; a leather bound book rested beside her. She had removed her bonnet, and the full rays of afternoon sunlight were directly upon her head.

Claire clearly enjoyed the sensation, for her head was tilted toward the sky and her eyes were closed. To offset the warmth of the sun, she was slowly fluttering a fan near her face to create a small breeze.

She looked content and relaxed, with nothing in her face betraying the strain of the last few weeks. Jasper hesitated a moment. It was not proper for them to be alone, especially in a secluded area, yet it seemed cowardly to turn tail and run.

He was still a few yards away when he spoke. "Good afternoon. I see that you are enjoying the sunshine."

Claire's head whirled in his direction. Her eyes popped open in surprise. She quickly tugged on her bonnet and straightened her skirts, knocking the book to the grass in her haste.

"Lord Fairhurst, you startled me."

"Sorry. May I join you?" he asked, as he lifted the book from the ground and held it out to her. He sensed her indecision, her surprise at his request. After all, he had done everything he could to avoid her the past week.

"Of course." She moved to the edge of the stone bench to make room. "This is your garden."

He had not intended to sit so close beside her, but it

would seem rude if he ignored the place she had created for him.

" 'Tis very peaceful back here," Jasper mused.

"Yes, it is rather amazing how a touch of quiet, natural surroundings can provide a wonderful escape." She turned toward him. "And it looks as if you are very much in need of one, my lord."

He could not suppress an ironic smile. "So, it is that obvious?"

She nodded. "Bad day?"

"Challenging. I have just come from calling upon Miss Manning. Earlier in the afternoon, I met with my solicitor."

"The expression on your face and the tone of your voice tells the rest of the story." She let out a quiet sigh. "The news is not good, is it?"

"We might need a divorce," he said glumly.

"Oh, goodness, I am so sorry. How perfectly dreadful for you."

"And you."

For a moment, she looked perplexed. Then, amazingly, she smiled. "Oh my, I believe I shall become quite notorious in Wiltshire. I will be the first divorcée to ever set foot inside the village square."

"This is very serious. Divorced women are often shunned by polite society."

"Then I am fortunate not to live in polite society. A small community does have its share of gossip-hungry folks, but I already know that those who are rigid and intolerant will be loudly disapproving and those who are loyal friends and family will support me." A stricken look crossed her face. "I fear you will have a much harder time than I. Can we try for an annulment instead? 'Tis hardly ideal, but carries far less scandal."

"We have no grounds. If you were underage or it could be proven that you were forced against your will to take your vows, then the marriage could be easily annulled."

"What about non-consummation of the union?"

Her cheeks had heated to a bright red. She was clearly mortified at the notion, but had raised the topic in hopes of aiding him. Jasper was touched by this selfless act.

"I appreciate that you would be willing to subject yourself to such acute embarrassment for my sake, but non-consummation is not a guarantee of annulment. It would have to be proven that the husband was incapable of performing the marital act." Jasper cleared his throat. "I believe my pride has suffered enough without subjecting myself to official court documents stating such a lie."

"No one would believe it anyway," she muttered.

The compliment brought a smile to his lips. "Thank you."

The color in her face deepened when she realized he had heard her remark. He marveled again at how sweet she was, how genuinely kind and considerate she was, and how, despite his determination not to, he liked her. Very much.

She had the power to stimulate his mind and his senses, but more importantly, she made him laugh. Sometimes at himself.

"I am sure your solicitor will be able to find an easier, less shocking way to dissolve this union," Claire said. "Even if it is your name on the marriage license, I can testify that Jay was the person who signed it, making it a forgery. There must be a legal contingency to dissolve a union under those circumstances. If not, women all over the country would be marrying themselves to powerful, wealthy men by forging names on marriage certificates. I imagine the Regent alone would have hundreds of wives."

"Hundreds?" Jasper smiled as he pondered that absurd notion. "I have met the Regent on numerous occasions, and I can assure you that any female with an ounce of common sense runs in the opposite direction when she encounters our prince."

"Oh, dear." Claire's eyes widened, and they shared a quiet laugh. "Still, we must leave it to the lawyers to sort out, though I'll own it feels like time has been suspended."

Her statement gave him pause. It was past time he remembered that he was not the only one affected by this situation. "Are you longing to return home?"

"Not really." She dipped her chin for a moment, seemingly embarrassed by her answer. "Before arriving here, I had never ventured more than a few miles away from the village where I was born. Though I have seen only a glimpse of the city, I am enjoying my time in London."

"You have done some sightseeing?"

"Oh, yes. Both your mother and sister have been excellent guides. I have been to the Tower of London and Westminster Abbey and have also viewed the paintings on display at the Royal Academy. They were marvelous and proved to be a wonderful distraction from my worries." Claire's brows knit together in a small frown. "But I should return home, so that you may assume your normal routine and restore some order to your life."

It was probably better if she did leave, but Jasper discovered the notion unsettled him. Though he had been avoiding her, there had always been an odd comfort in knowing she was near, available almost instantly.

What would await her upon her return to Wiltshire? How would she explain the bizarre change in her circumstances to her family and friends? Though she joked about the notoriety of being a divorced woman, he knew it would not be an easy road.

Jasper's mind raced forward to an impulsive idea that his highly developed common sense immediately rejected. Yet the idea lingered, persistent and possible, nagging at his brain.

His connection with Rebecca Manning was severed. His need and desire for a wife remained. Though she would likely claim otherwise, his family owed Claire some protection. His brain twisted and turned as he tried to decide what they could do for her.

There was only one answer. And it was now within his power to act upon it. If he dared. Common sense, be damned!

"Are you in love with my brother?"

It was the most direct question anyone had ever asked her. And, in some ways, one of the easiest to answer, for the truth was abundantly clear. Yet, Claire hesitated. The moment dragged on, and as Lord Fairhurst continued to stare at her and wait, she knew she would have to say something.

"I have a great affection for Jay," she hedged.

"Affection?"

"Yes. And a deep regard."

"You once told me that you were a romantic," Lord Fairhurst said, his eyes never leaving her face. "I would think a woman with such a nature would require far more than regard and affection from her husband."

The intensity of that stare made Claire hot and a little nervous. "What we require is not always possible to receive," she whispered. "I needed a husband and Jay needed a wife, and thus we agreed to marry."

"Yet somehow my idiotic brother made a mess of it." Lord Fairhurst reached out and adjusted the brim of Claire's bonnet, exposing her face more clearly to his gaze. "Do you still need a husband?"

Claire gulped. What did he mean? His face was calm, almost remote, but his gaze was intense. Claire shivered. He could not possibly be offering himself in the role of husband? Could he?

Her heart pounded at the very thought. Marriage to Jay had been a practical, business arrangement. Marriage to Lord Fairhurst would be completely different, for reasons she did not fully understand. What was it about him that made her knees weak? That made her burn to reach out and touch him? That made her long to brush her fingers tenderly along his square jaw and press her lips against his?

"I married to secure a modest inheritance from my grandmother," Claire said, in a voice far softer than she liked. "And to avoid the persistent advances of a neighboring squire, though in truth it was Jay who felt strongly that the man was a danger who could not be ignored."

Lord Fairhurst grimaced. "My brother has a talent for rescuing fair maidens."

"Apparently."

"But now it is my turn to be the hero." A sudden, inexplicable gleam shone in his eyes. "Would you consider becoming *my* wife?"

Claire was glad that she was seated, for if she was standing, surely her knees would have given out. "What about Miss Manning?"

The viscount frowned. "She has decided it would be best not to continue an association with me."

"I am so sorry."

"There is no need." Remarkably, Lord Fairhurst sounded almost cheerful. "I warned her that I might be facing a divorce and she found the notion very distressing. Can't say that I blame her. I do not find the idea very palatable, either."

"I see." Claire was surprised at how strongly the disappointment rushed through her. Lord Fairhurst was nothing if not a practical man. Now that he was no longer beholden to Miss Manning, the easiest way to avoid a scandal and a messy, public divorce would be to stay married to her.

"If you marry me, you can legitimately keep the title of Lady Fairhurst. In fact, one day you will become the Countess of Stafford. In addition to my rank, you will be entitled to a considerable portion of my wealth."

Claire smoothed her skirt over her knees. "And what of Jay? How can I so callously abandon him?"

"You are not abandoning him. If Mr. Beckham is correct, you never were married to my brother."

It was not what Claire wanted to hear. It made the reality of her situation too bleak and distressing. Yet she knew it was the truth. "Jay and I shared a unique relationship, agreeing from the first to live separate lives, apart from each other. Is that also what you desire?"

He stared at her, expressionless. "No, I do not wish to have a marriage of convenience. As firstborn and heir, I have far greater responsibilities than my brother. In addition to the more mundane household duties, I need a wife who is comfortable in society and is willing to attend important social engagements, as well as host similar events."

"I am hardly qualified," Claire protested. "I have neither the training nor the necessary connections to move in aristocratic circles."

"Nonsense. You are a lady of good character, breeding, and intelligence. My mother and sister can guide you through the more intricate and delicate rules of the *ton.* I have no doubt you will be a great success."

His confidence in her ability was flattering. But there were other aspects of this proposal that needed to be clarified. Claire drew a breath to speak and discovered she could not inhale enough air. "Will you want children?"

"That is something we will need to consider." He broke his granite expression and smiled quite charmingly. "Jason is my heir, so the Barrington line is secure, though I will confess I have never thought needing an heir was a good reason to produce offspring.

"One only has to look to my sister Meredith to see the fault in that reasoning. She has birthed three children, all girls. Not an heir in the lot. The decision to have children must be mutually agreed upon. I am not opposed to it, but I would like to leave that discussion for the future, when we have come to know each other better."

Claire curled her fingers into the hard stone of the garden bench. It was not a bad bargain. He was offering her far more than she ever dreamed possible. She had discovered that she liked living in London, at least for part of the year, and she was eager to explore the world of glittering society.

She was not as confident in her ability to take the beau monde by storm as Lord Fairhurst was, but Claire was shrewd enough to realize that with the proper guidance, and his connections, she could at the very least be a modest success.

And what about her ever-growing feelings for him? Was it folly to let herself believe that someday he could come to care for her? That they could have a real marriage, based on companionship, respect, and affection? That there might even be children to love and nurture?

Claire licked her dry lips. "I shall need some time to decide. I must consider everything you have said most carefully, my lord."

"Of course. 'Tis a big step." He smiled encouragingly, seemingly relieved that she had not rejected him outright.

"There is something, however, that I must tell you."

"Yes?"

A lump caught in Claire's throat. For an instant, her voice froze, but with effort, she pushed the words out. "I am not a virgin."

"I see." His left eyebrow lifted. "Apparently, my brother remained with you at least one night after the wedding."

"Oh, no. 'Twas not Jay. He and I never, that is, we did not even—" Claire ceased speaking abruptly when she realized she was babbling. She felt the heat rise in her cheeks and feared she must be nearly crimson with embarrassment.

"If not my brother . . ." Lord Fairhurst's voice trailed off as he left the rest of the sentence unspoken. Silence loomed, then Lord Fairhurst suddenly straightened. "Was it that young man? The one who was killed on the Peninsula?"

"Yes."

The single word seemed to echo through the garden. It took a great effort, but Claire kept her head high. She had never breathed a word to anyone about the extent of her relationship with Henry, always believing she would take this secret to her grave. Though she knew it was necessary, it felt ridiculously intimate to confess it to Lord Fairhurst.

His prolonged silence made her lift her shoulders defensively. She wished he would say something. "Perhaps you would like to withdraw your offer, my lord?"

"No." He turned toward her. "Though I would expect that once taken, you will honor the vow of fidelity."

Claire bristled. "Of course. As will you."

"Me?"

"I know it is fashionable for men of noble birth to keep mistresses and dabble in affairs with other married ladies. But I cannot respect a man who conducts himself in that manner. And I cannot marry a man I do not respect."

"I assure you, there will be no cause to worry about my fidelity," Lord Fairhurst insisted.

Because you will keep me sexually satisfied and utterly sated.

Claire blinked and shook her head, knowing such shocking words had not been uttered from his lips. They were in her thoughts.

And his smoldering gaze.

A fleeting madness gripped her, and Claire had to fight hard against the urge to lift herself toward him and press her lips to his. Thankfully, there was no opportunity to act upon her wild impulse.

"I await your answer to my offer," he declared.

Lord Fairhurst executed a cordial bow, then walked off toward the house, the sunlight gleaming on his blond hair and his long-legged stride confident and strong. Though he did not turn and look back, Claire sensed he was very aware that she watched his every step.

Chapter Nine

That night, Claire dreamt of children. Handsome, sturdy-limbed little boys with a proper attitude and formal manner and sweet, darling little girls who giggled and smiled whenever you drew near. They played together beneath a tall oak tree, running around and around the thick trunk; their laughter floating on the mist of a spring morning.

Her children. Fathered by Lord Fairhurst. Jasper.

Claire woke abruptly, her heart pounding in her chest. Her dreams had revealed the secret desires that her mind could not accept. It was more than an infatuation, more than a passion, more than a passing regard. She wanted Lord Fairhurst to be her husband.

Claire nearly fell out of the bed at the realization, for it was an extraordinary truth to be faced. She, a woman who usually approached life with both feet planted firmly on the ground, had somehow let her imagination take flight. Claire's mind raced over the great risk she was seriously considering, the major change in her life that would forever alter her destiny. Did she possess the courage to embrace it?

The road ahead would not be easy. She worried how Jay would react when he learned of the sudden change in their relationship—from wife to sister-in-law. But deep down she knew that Jay was the least of her worries.

Already, her feelings for Jasper were taking control of her actions. He could be somber and stiff at times and seemed determined to keep his emotions at arm's length. Yet, she had glimpsed far more beneath that formal facade: A keen sense of responsibility tempered by a good and true heart.

Claire firmly believed Jasper possessed the ability to love, and if she were very lucky and very clever, he might come to love her. It was a heady thought, indeed.

It was also madness. Utter madness. And yet, although every practical instinct within her screamed to abandon the notion, Claire decided that marrying Jasper was what she truly wanted. And though it was an idea fraught with bizarre difficulties, she could not bear the idea of missing this chance to become his wife.

Claire spent the first part of the morning in restless anticipation. Now that she had made her decision, she wanted to inform Jasper that she would accept his offer so they could move forward. She also rather desperately wanted to squelch the nagging trace of fear that echoed in her mind—the fear that during the night Lord Fairhurst had thought better of the idea and changed his mind about marrying her.

She took extra care with her attire. Before leaving her chamber, Claire stole a moment to glance at herself in the wall mirror. She was wearing one of her new gowns, a muslin day dress of light pink. It brought out the color in her cheeks and made her eyes sparkle, and for an instant, Claire saw the reflection of a stranger.

She shook her head at her whimsical attitude, knowing a few fashionable gowns and a flattering, updated hairstyle did not truly change a person. Yet she knew that she was a far different woman than the one who had entered this house more than a fortnight ago.

The servants directed her to the library, and after being assured that Lord Fairhurst was alone, Claire entered the room without being announced.

Lord Fairhurst stood with his back to the door. He was swaying to and fro in an odd rocking motion and appeared to be contemplating the brightly burning fire in the hearth. When he made no move to turn and greet her, Claire assumed he had not heard her enter the room.

She loudly cleared her throat.

"Thank God you have finally returned," he cried out as he turned.

Claire gasped in utter surprise. In the crook of his arm, Lord Fairhurst awkwardly held an infant.

"I thought you were Merry," he said glumly. "She came for a visit, but the nursemaid suddenly became ill and my sister had to help the poor woman to an upstairs bedchamber. She left me with the baby."

"So I see."

"She's only been gone a few moments, but it feels like hours." He let out a huff of breath, then moved closer. "This is Meredith's youngest daughter Marissa. Would you care to hold her?"

"Me?" Claire practically stumbled backward. "I know nothing of infants."

"But you are a woman," he said, following her.

"So? My gender gives me no innate abilities." Claire crossed her arms protectively beneath her breasts. "Besides, the child seems perfectly content. I fear if you move her, she might become distressed."

"You could be right." Lord Fairhurst tilted his head and glanced down at the bundle in his arms. "Damn

Dardington. The marquess spends far too much time catering to his children. This little minx is used to having a man cart her around, acquiescing to her every whim. It bodes ill for her future."

"I think you should be pleased that she is so easily amused. And quiet." Claire wrinkled her nose. "Babies can make a terrible racket when they are upset."

"Oh, she did that when she arrived. I'm surprised you did not hear her."

"My chamber is on the opposite side of the house."

"Ear-splitting shrieks of that volume carry rather far," Lord Fairhurst reported in a wry tone. "I expected a troop of Bow Street Runners to come charging through the door at any moment to investigate the racket."

The infant made a short, grunting noise, as if she knew they were talking about her. Claire smiled and drew closer.

"She is very pretty. 'Tis hard to believe such a tiny, delicate creature can cause such a ruckus." Reaching out, Claire touched the small dimple on the baby's elbow. The chubby, pale, perfect skin was as smooth as silk.

She ran her fingertip back and forth over the softness until the baby broke into a wide, toothless grin. A longing for what was missing from Claire's life suddenly washed over her, causing her to shiver.

"I think she likes you," Lord Fairhurst commented.

"Don't sound so amazed," Claire said in a shaky voice. "A lot of people become fond of me upon first acquaintance."

"Ah, is that a veiled criticism of me? Because it took so long for me to recognize your finer qualities?"

His remark made her blush. His approval should not matter quite so much, but it did. For a moment, she studied him, letting her gaze dwell on the picture he made standing in the center of the elegantly paneled library with the babe nestled in his arms. It should have looked ridiculous, yet somehow it seemed to fit.

She swallowed hard. Claire had made her decision. There was no need for idle chatter; in fact, she believed Lord Fairhurst would prefer that she be direct. "If your offer still stands, then I shall accept it. I would like to marry you."

"What?" Lord Fairhurst stumbled, losing his footing and nearly dropping the baby.

"Goodness!" Claire leapt forward, thrusting her arms out instinctively. But the infant was secure, and Lord Fairhurst remained on his feet.

At that moment, the door burst open and the countess sailed into the room. "I have just been informed that my granddaughter is here. My heavens, what are you doing with the baby, Jasper?"

"I believe that is rather obvious, Mother." Lord Fairhurst straightened his shoulders and gave a haughty sniff. "I am caring for her."

"You are holding her like a sack of grain."

"She is voicing no complaints." He shifted the baby's weight closer to his chest. She snuggled against the softness of his jacket and let out a happy gurgle.

"I am sorry to have left you for so long, but the poor nursemaid was in dire circumstances, and I could not leave until help was summoned," Lady Meredith declared as she too rushed into the room. She was uncharacteristically disheveled and slightly out of breath, and Claire concluded that she must have run the entire way. Apparently, Lord Fairhurst also took note of his sister's appearance.

"There is no need to call out the Life Guards, Merry.

I am perfectly capable of caring for one small infant," he said in an indignant tone.

"And I thank you for doing such an excellent job," Lady Meredith replied graciously, reaching out as if she were itching to snatch her daughter back.

With a great show of reluctance, Lord Fairhurst relinquished the child. She went willingly into her mother's arms, but then arched her back and twisted her head, straining for a look at her uncle.

Lord Fairhurst smiled. "Why, the little flirt. Dardington is going to have his hands full when she turns sixteen and is presented to the Queen."

Lady Meredith groaned. "We must not speak of such things in front of my husband or else his hair will fall out and the scowl between his brows will forever mar his handsome face."

"With three daughters I suspect he is in for some very interesting years ahead," Lord Fairhurst said. " 'Tis good to see a former reprobate so thoroughly domesticated." Jasper smoothed the fabric on the front of his jacket, adding, "And, amazingly, I am about to join his ranks."

Saucer-eyed, both Lady Meredith and the countess turned sharply toward the viscount.

"You are going to be married?" Lady Meredith asked. "To whom?"

Lord Fairhurst moved closer to Claire and placed his arm around her waist. The simple, possessive gesture was clearly his unspoken answer. Silence settled over the room.

Claire shivered. She could feel the warmth of his fingers as they rested on her hip. Deep within her, primitive emotions began to stir, but she was distracted by nerves as she waited for the countess and Lady Meredith's reactions.

"Goodness, this is rather sudden," Lady Meredith declared.

Ignoring her daughter's less than enthusiastic remark, the countess clasped her hands to her bosom and grinned broadly. "I am delighted by the news. Simply delighted. Congratulations."

"Thank you, Mother."

Arms outstretched, the countess hurried across the room and embraced her son. She next extended both hands to Claire's and squeezed them tightly as she kissed her on each cheek. Claire was relieved to note that when the countess pulled back, her eyes were shining with happiness. The knot of nerves in Claire's stomach eased slightly.

"Are you doing this because you believe that you are in truth already married and cannot easily obtain an annulment?" Lady Meredith asked. "Or because you fear you will need a divorce?"

The concern in her voice stung. Claire had believed Lady Meredith had grown fond of her, yet she seemed tense and distressed.

"Meredith!" the countess scolded. "What an ungracious remark!"

"I am merely trying to ascertain all the facts and the reason for this very sudden decision," Lady Meredith replied.

Claire noted that the countess tried to hold her daughter back, but Lady Meredith shrugged off her mother's restraint and came to stand directly in front of Lord Fairhurst.

"Have you fallen in love with each other?" Lady Meredith asked, as she stared into her brother's face.

Lord Fairhurst raised his eyebrows. "While I certainly appreciate your concern, dear Merry, I must insist that my feelings for Claire and hers for me are our private business."

My Lord! Claire felt herself turn hot, then cold. It was a perfectly acceptable answer, if somewhat formal.

"What about Claire's marriage to Jason?" Lady Meredith asked.

"According to the message I received this morning from Mr. Beckham, there never was a legal union between Claire and our brother," Lord Fairhurst said. "Therefore, I am free to take her as my bride. We shall be married by special license as soon as possible. I will instruct Mr. Beckham to purchase the document from the Archbishop of Canterbury today."

Lady Meredith appeared to hesitate before saying anything else. She shifted the baby in her arms from one side to the other, then cleared her throat.

"If this is truly what *you* want, Jasper, I also offer my felicitations and wish you happiness in your marriage."

Rather solemnly, Lady Meredith kissed her brother's cheek. Though hampered by the infant in her arms, she also managed to give Claire a hug.

Relieved to have cleared this hurdle, Claire sighed deeply, then turned toward the man at her side. She looked into his eyes and saw contentment. Or so she believed.

Claire lifted her eyes heavenward and uttered a short, silent prayer, hoping she was not fooling herself into seeing only what she wanted to see. She prayed that, for everyone's sake, she was not blinded by her attraction and longing for him into making a colossal mistake.

Rebecca Manning dressed carefully for the Williamsons' ball. It was by far the biggest event of the

Season and her first public appearance at a society event since the night of Lord Fairhurst's dinner party. It was therefore even more important that everything be perfect.

Her new gown, a sparkling creation of white silk shot through with threads of gold that shimmered when she moved, had been selected with the intent of looking especially good on the dance floor. For she intended to dance nearly every set tonight, partnered each time with a different elegant, eligible gentleman.

She had stolen her sister's maid in the early afternoon to help her prepare for the ball. The girl had a way with hair, and Rebecca wanted her tresses placed in a sophisticated, elegant style. After much discussion, she allowed the dark strands to be dressed in a high topknot, with several curls left to cascade along the side of her face and rest elegantly along her neck.

Her lovely appearance boosted her confidence and gave her the courage to face what lay ahead. Tonight, Rebecca was determined to be seen by one and all—carefree, happy, and looking her very best.

If she had the unfortunate happenstance to meet Fairhurst, she would bend her knee ever so slightly in a shallow curtsy, then tilt her chin in arrogant indifference, acting as though he were an insignificant nuisance. No matter how closely they were observed, no one of the *ton* would ever be able to say they had witnessed her humiliation and discomfort.

Rebecca knew there had been various rumors about Fairhurst and herself swirling about, though none of the cowards circulating these tidbits had had the audacity to confront her directly. Oh, no, that was not the way it was done among the beau monde. There were whispers and innuendos, exaggerations of facts, and titillation at the possible suffering of some poor individual.

Those little snubs and small slights were done with such skill that the victim could never say with any great certainty what had occurred. But the feelings of unease and humiliation were quite emphatic.

Above all else, Rebecca was determined that she would not fall prey to such circumstances. She would do everything within her power to ensure that she did not lose her social standing in the *ton,* or even worse, become an object of scorn and pity.

The Williamson mansion was one of the oldest in Town, a great sprawling building built on a large parcel of land near the edge of the city. It was an impressive dwelling, with numerous large, airy rooms; long, winding staircases; and a ballroom with a ceiling gilded in gold leaf.

After greeting their host and hostess, Rebecca and Anne descended the massive marble staircase and entered the ballroom. Their father abandoned them the moment they passed through the golden archway, muttering something about visiting the card room.

"Father." Anne made a weak plea, but Charles Manning was already gone.

"Stop looking so pitiful," Rebecca whispered in an exasperated tone. "If they sense your fear, we shall be eaten alive. Now, take a deep breath and smile. You must look as though you do not have a care in the world."

" 'Tis hard to smile and nod and pretend we do not notice the women gossiping behind their fans," Anne moaned.

"You hardly have cause to complain, since it is me and not you they are staring at," Rebecca hissed. Her stomach churned with nerves, but she kept smiling until her cheeks ached.

They circled the outer edge of the ballroom. It was too early for all but the most ardent couples to take to the floor. The sizable orchestra was playing enthusiastically, and those who were indulging in the dance whirled and dipped under the twinkling lights of the chandelier. These lucky few seemed to be having a marvelous time.

Rebecca hoped it would not be too long before she was asked, for she much preferred dancing to chatting and making small talk.

"Should we make our way to the other side and greet the dowagers?" Anne asked.

Rebecca turned toward the gaggle of older women, clustered in a prime viewing spot. They were seated in a semicircle facing the center of the room, so as not to miss a thing. Rebecca wished she had the nerve to send them all a quelling glare, but it was foolish to antagonize them.

"Egad, no. I want to stay as far away from that nest of vipers as possible," Rebecca declared, as she plucked a fluted crystal glass of champagne from the silver tray of a liveried servant.

Anne nervously unfurled her fan and began cooling her face with it. "Oh, dear, it seems as if every eye in the room is focused upon us."

Rebecca tried to summon her patience, but failed. Anne's nervous hovering made her feel even more unsettled. She downed the contents of her glass, then turned to her sister. " 'Tis no wonder that everyone is staring. You look a fright. That gust of wind as we left the coach made a shambles of your hair. You need to make a trip to the ladies' retiring room and fix it at once."

Anne blushed scarlet and snapped her fan shut. “Goodness! You should have told me sooner.” Her hand crept nervously to the top of her head.

“You cannot fix that mess here!” Rebecca hissed.

“Oh my. Will you come with me?”

“No. I dare not risk being cornered in the retiring room by some gossip-minded female.”

“But I cannot leave you here alone,” Anne protested.

Though she seethed inside, Rebecca’s face gave away none of her annoyance. Pasting on a whimsical smile, she turned toward her sister. “ ’Tis far preferable to be left alone in the ballroom than to be standing here with you when you look as though you have just been pulled through a hedge!”

Anne’s chin trembled. Fearing her sister might begin blubbering at any moment, Rebecca reached down and gave her a sharp pinch on the arm. Anne squealed, then with a meek cry of distress, disappeared.

Rebecca tried to summon up a scrap of sympathy at the sight of Anne’s misery-ravaged face, yet none was forthcoming. Her sister really was something of a nitwit. She and Anne had never been very close. Their sisterly bond was nothing more than a sense of duty. They were very different individuals, sharing none of the same friends, and none of the same likes and dislikes.

At first it was awkward to be alone in the ballroom, but then Rebecca realized she had stood there for a full five minutes and no one seemed to be noticing her.

“Miss Manning!”

Rebecca lifted her chin and pasted a smile on her face, then decided she need not bother. It was Gertrude Hawkins pushing her way through the crowds. Poor Gertrude was a perpetual wallflower, and at twenty-five, firmly on the road to spinsterhood.

"Good evening," Gertrude said, as she reached Rebecca's side. She paused a moment to catch her breath, then looked around. "Are you here alone?"

The question was galling enough, but Gertrude's look of pity and concern plunged Rebecca into a foul mood.

"I am waiting for my sister to return," she replied, dismissively staring into the distance, hoping Gertrude would take the hint and leave.

"Has Lord Fairhurst arrived?"

Rebecca's head turned sharply, wondering at the insult of that remark. But Gertrude's guileless expression made her realize it was an honest question. Gertrude was a female who existed on the fringes of society and that extended to her knowledge of the latest gossip. She apparently was unaware of the change in Rebecca's relationship with the viscount.

"I have no idea if Fairhurst has arrived, nor do I have the slightest interest if he plans to attend."

"Oh, dear." Gertrude moved her fidgeting hands through the air as if they could somehow help her figure out how to respond.

"Pray, do not let me keep you from the other guests," Rebecca said briskly. "I am sure there are many gentlemen anxious to fill your dance card."

Gertrude glanced down at the blank card that dangled from her wrist and sighed, but the sigh soon turned to a tittering giggle. Too late, Rebecca realized that Gertrude had a perfect view of Rebecca's identically empty dance card.

" 'Tis best to circulate among the outer edges of the ballroom when the set begins," Gertrude said solemnly. "That way you can avoid looking like a wallflower."

Of all the nerve! For a moment, Rebecca feared she might suffer a fit of apoplexy. She was completely outraged by Gertrude's presumption, especially because it tapped into her deepest, most secret fear.

"Coming from you I am certain it is tried and tested advice," Rebecca replied, baring her teeth in a feline grin. The action served the purpose of completely intimidating Gertrude. She made a feeble excuse and scurried off.

The moment Gertrude left, Rebecca sagged against the wall, feeling suddenly quite ill. If she had difficulty tangling with the likes of Gertrude Hawkins, what chance would she stand when she faced a real tyrant, like Lady Hartmore or Mrs. Standish?

Rebecca shivered, and then wondered if she had made a mistake coming to the ball. Perhaps it would have been better to ease into the social whirl slowly with a few outings to Hyde Park, and then some afternoon visits to friends and relations. Jumping headlong into the social fray may be too much of a strain on her already tattered nerves.

Deciding she needed a few moments alone to compose herself, Rebecca slipped quietly from the room, hurrying down the hall until she reached a set of French doors that led to the outside terrace. There was no one in sight. It was a cool evening, but lanterns had been lit and strung across the patio for those guests who desired a bit of fresh air, or privacy.

Rebecca closed her eyes and shuddered, admitting she badly needed both.

"Are you cold?"

Rebecca's eyes flew open. She had believed she was alone, yet standing before her was an unknown gentleman. Even in the limited light she could see he was handsome and well-turned out. His broad shoulders were clothed in evening black; his gray silk waistcoat shimmered softly in the glow of the lantern light; and his cravat was tied in a simple style, with an elegant diamond pin accenting the white cloth.

He possessed all the necessary elements of a civilized, cultured gentleman, yet there was something about his eyes that intrigued her. They were sharp and watchful, yet lurking in their depths was faint amusement.

"Are you cold?" He repeated the question and took a step closer. When she did not answer, he rotated his shoulders. It took a moment before Rebecca realized he was removing his jacket to offer it to her.

"No, please." She raised her hand in a staying manner. "I am fine. The cool air is a welcome change from the stuffiness of the ballroom."

He ceased his movements and smoothed the garment back into perfect alignment. "I suppose the night air is refreshing. I am certain a lady as lovely as yourself has been dancing since she arrived at the ball."

Rebecca's eyes narrowed suspiciously, wondering if he mocked her, but his manner and continence seemed sincere.

"Actually, I have not yet taken to the dance floor."

His brows lifted in amazement. "I should think your suitors would be coming to near blows to fill up your card."

Normally, Rebecca would have answered such a remark with a flirtatious toss of her head, but the mention of a dance card was a rather sore subject tonight. "My dance card is none of your concern, sir. And this conversation is most improper, since we have not been introduced."

She turned her head dismissively in the direction of the garden, but she could see very little. The night lurking beyond the terrace was black. A breeze stirred the air, causing a distant rustling of the hedges on the edge of the garden.

"Something tells me that you are not the type of woman who always follows the rules of propriety."

His remark pricked her already sensitive nerves. "Whatever makes you say such a thing?"

" 'Twas daring for such a beautiful woman to come out here, alone." He smiled, charmingly. "Daring and provocative."

Watching his eyes drift suggestively over her, Rebecca felt her breath catch. He was no longer an elegant, handsome gentleman, but rather a large, predatory figure. She fought to suppress a shiver, but this reaction was not due to the cold. Heat rose in her cheeks, and she hoped the light was dim enough to hide it.

Though his expression remained innocent, his eyes were most assuredly not. They flared with scorching heat that had a profound, disturbing effect on her body. Rebecca tried to ignore it, and him, but then his gaze wandered to her bosom. She felt her temper rise at his insolence, but fear of discovery kept her voice low. She inclined her head haughtily. "If you will excuse me—"

"No." Steely fingers closed over her wrist. "Not until you tell me your name."

"I will not." She drew in a deep breath and held it, almost daring him to challenge her.

The pressure of his fingers increased ever so slightly. It was a subtle reminder of how vulnerable and defenseless she was against his masculine strength.

She glanced around. There were no other guests in sight.

The stranger continued to hold her in place and stare at her oddly, intensely enough to make her squirm. Yet for some peculiar reason, Rebecca did not believe she could look away.

His smile came easily. "Relax. I won't bite."

She let out a nervous snap of laughter. "I am not foolish enough to believe you."

"Smart lady." His tone remained playful. "Yet if you were truly frightened, you would scream."

"I still can."

He shook his head. "If you meant to call for assistance, you would have done so five minutes ago."

Involuntarily, she glanced down at their hands. His fingers were long and elegant, yet their strength was obvious, especially when contrasted with her delicate wrist. "You sound far too experienced in such matters for my liking, sir. Do women often scream when in your company?"

"Only in the throes of ecstasy."

What! Rebecca's face felt hot. The boldness of his remark stunned her. She pulled her upper body away, but he leaned close enough so that his breath caressed her cheek.

"This conversation is entirely inappropriate," she bristled.

"Perhaps. But you like it. And you like me. I can tell."

"Like you? That's laughable. I know nothing about you. I do not even know your name."

"Then allow me to introduce myself, fair maiden." Still holding tightly to her wrist, the stranger executed a faultless bow, then drew himself up to his full height and stared down at her. "I am Richard Dorchester, recently arrived from Wiltshire. My friends call me Squire Dorchester and something tells me that you will soon be among their numbers."

Chapter Ten

The nuptial service was an exceedingly private affair, held at Lord Fairhurst's home, with only the immediate family in attendance. Claire spoke her vows in a quiet, unwavering voice, yet she felt as if she were in a dream. Lord Fairhurst was courteous, but distant, except for a moment at the end of the ceremony when their eyes met, and each acknowledged that something momentous and irreversible had just taken place.

A festive breakfast was served, and everyone tried just a little too hard to be merry. Claire appreciated the efforts of her new family, who had been nothing but patient and kind to her. She worried briefly how she would explain the bizarre change of husbands to her own parents, but reasoned that all they ever wanted was her happiness, and if she could convince them she was content with her choice, they would accept her new circumstances.

On their wedding night, and each night after, the newlyweds slept in separate rooms and separate beds. Lord Fairhurst was taking very much to heart his decision to wait until they were better acquainted before becoming intimate. The arrangement distressed Claire more than she cared to admit, but for the time being, there seemed little she could do to change it.

Valiantly, Claire tried to temper the rush of impatience she felt when she was with Jasper. Her body often trembled at his nearness; the sensations of desire occasionally eclipsed her ability to think rationally. She was more than ready to leap with all her heart, body, and soul into this marriage, but Lord Fairhurst was taking a more cautious approach.

The first week of their marriage passed swiftly. Once the wedding announcement had appeared in the paper, many members of the *ton* came to call. There were curious stares and pointed questions, but Lord Fairhurst distracted, stared down, or charmed away the inquirers. Claire soon came to have a greater respect for her husband's position and his ability to navigate the murky waters of society.

Tonight was Claire's formal presentation to the beau monde. It was decided that a ball hosted by the Duke of Warwick, Meredith's father-in-law, would afford the new viscountess the most social clout, and the older gentleman graciously offered his hospitality. Lady Meredith supervised all the important details, from the invitations to the music to the food, and Claire was grateful for her sister-in-law's support.

As they stood in the receiving line greeting the guests, Claire's nerves slowly began to diminish, though she hardly enjoyed feeling so conspicuous. *Why must everyone be so incredibly surprised that the viscount has at last taken a bride?* Together with the endless exclamations of shock were the many not-so-subtle looks cast her way and the calculated expressions of astonishment that seemed to be saying, *why would Fairhurst marry you, an ordinary-looking nobody from the country?*

At last they were permitted to leave the receiving line so the dancing could begin. The full orchestra of formally dressed musicians seated on the dais at one end of the room ceased tuning their instruments and waited for the signal to start playing. Claire concentrated on masking her fears as the duke, a handsome, imposing older gentleman, led her to the middle of the smoothly polished dance floor.

She barely had time to appreciate the candlelight shivering over the gilded ceilings and walls and the perfume of hundreds of flowers filling the air. Her face ached with the smile she held, and although she appreciated the duke's steadying arm, she secretly wished she could affect his manner of haughtily well-bred nonchalance.

The music swelled up from the orchestra and, for a moment, Claire panicked. She was not ready. She glanced up to find the duke regarding her with a steely eye.

"Now is not the time to let your courage fail, young woman," he declared, placing one hand on her waist. "If they sense your fear, the jackals will attack."

"I know that only too well, Your Grace." Claire shrugged helplessly. "Though I suppose this might be a good time to mention that I do not know how to waltz."

The duke's jaw grew taut. His other hand, poised in the act of signaling for the dance to begin, returned to his side. "Are you joking?"

"Yes." The hammering of her heart against her ribs slowed, and the first genuine smile of the night filled Claire's face. "But I feel better knowing that your composure can be ruffled upon occasion, too."

The duke stared at her for a long moment; then his eyes softened, and his face broke into a large grin. "Aye, if you have the courage to tease me, you can take on any one of these malicious tabbies."

Without further ado, the duke commanded the orchestra to play. He was a tall man, fit for his years, and a skilled dancer. Under his guidance, she managed to execute the steps with ease. Although she found it to be an agreeable experience, Claire was nevertheless relieved when the dance ended and she was passed off to her next partner, until she realized it was the Marquess of Dardington.

Lady Meredith's husband had attended her wedding ceremony and the breakfast that had followed, but his congratulatory wishes had been less than enthusiastic and noticeably tempered with restraint. Claire could hardly fault him for his honesty, yet she wished he would at least give himself time to get to know her before deciding he disliked her so much.

Fortunately, this was a country dance, with intricate steps and twirls and little chance for private conversation. At its conclusion, her father-in-law claimed her for a cotillion, and after that, a distant male relative of the duke's partnered her in a spirited reel.

" 'Tis time for me to claim a dance with my bride, Berkley," Lord Fairhurst told her partner.

"Yes, indeed," Lord Berkley said with a bow. "She is a lovely girl, Fairhurst. I hope you realize what a lucky fellow you are to have her."

Although Claire appreciated Lord Berkley's remarks, she did not have the faintest idea what she had done to earn such praise.

"Berkley's always had an eye for a pretty lady," Lord Fairhurst whispered in her ear, as if reading the question crowding her mind.

"He must be sixty. Or more," Claire replied.

"That doesn't mean he can't still appreciate a beautiful woman, or enjoy having a few minutes of her exclusive attention."

Claire felt the color rise in her cheeks. She was unsure if it was the result of making a conquest of a man of such advanced years, or if it was due to hearing her husband refer to her as *beautiful.*

Jasper had offered a modest compliment when he first saw her this evening, remarking that she looked appropriately aristocratic, which was not precisely the effect she was hoping to create.

Though she was too proud to tell him, Claire had selected her outfit for this evening with her husband in mind, choosing a cream-colored silk gown trimmed in green and gold with a wide, low neckline and a fitted bodice. Satin slippers adorned her feet, a cream-colored fan dangled from her wrist, and her hair was dressed in soft curls that tumbled about her ears and nape.

Claire was not a vain woman, but she knew tonight she was looking her best. It would have been marvelous, of course, if just one glance at her would have shattered Lord Fairhurst's control, but, alas, that was not to be. Still, his acknowledgment of her appearance gave Claire hope that he would not survive the night without succumbing to a kiss. Or two.

But the kisses would have to wait until they were alone. Claire's thoughts were soon diverted from kisses as her husband led her onto the dance floor. The other couples moved aside, forming a space around them. Every eye in the room was focused on them, but it was more than the fixed scrutiny that made her nervous.

Threads of panic rose inside Claire, and her senses went on full alert. Something tense and charged seemed to be permeating the air around them. Turning her chin,

Claire caught sight of Miss Rebecca Manning, who was staring intently at them.

Since Miss Manning had not gone through the receiving line, Claire was therefore unaware that her husband's former flame was in attendance. Feeling she needed to do something, Claire nodded her head slightly in greeting.

She saw an odd confusion pass over Miss Manning's face before she turned to the gentleman at her side. A pillar blocked Claire's view of Miss Manning's companion, yet for some strange reason Claire thought he seemed familiar.

It made her uneasy, though she could not explain why. She risked a glance at her husband to see how Lord Fairhurst was reacting to the curious looks that were sent their way. He was clearly ignoring them, his handsome face set in purposeful lines and his expression so confident, arrogant, and lordly it served to warn off any who approached.

"I assumed we would generate some curiosity, but must they all stare?" Claire whispered.

"You knew there would be gossip and speculation," he said.

"Yes, but not to this extreme." Claire blew out a small breath and tried to ignore the flare of annoyance she felt. "Gracious, will the music never start?"

"In a moment." Lord Fairhurst's eyes never left her own. She admired his composure, which was far superior to her own. "I believe they are looking so closely to see if I will revert to my scandalous ways."

"At this precise instant? What could you possibly do in the middle of a ballroom that would be scandalous?"

He chuckled suddenly. "I could snatch a bottle of champagne, tip it to my lips, and down the entire contents in one long gulp, or pinch a dowager in an inappropriate manner on a most inappropriate part of her person."

Claire eyed him askance. "Why do I get the feeling those antics are not conjured from your imagination, my lord?"

He laughed again, and in that instant Claire realized that the music had started and they had begun to waltz. They danced alone for several minutes before the other couples joined in, smiling into each others' eyes, looking like a pair of newlyweds in love. It was an exhilarating moment.

"So, you do not find my wild, misspent youth offensive?" he asked, expertly weaving them in and out of the other dancing couples.

"High-spirited antics demonstrate a lack of judgment, which is a common affliction among male youth," Claire declared, as she tipped her head back to gaze more fully into his face. "I doubt anyone suffered any serious injury from your pranks."

"You are too forgiving."

"Not really. But now you have peaked my interest." Claire kept her tone light and flirty, her expression teasing and mischievous. "Tell me something positively shocking about yourself."

Lord Fairhurst smiled. "You are only asking because you do not believe I will have anything to tell you."

"Quite the contrary, sir."

"Very well." He lowered his head and whispered into her ear. "I once fought a duel."

"A duel?" Claire stumbled slightly, nearly missing a step. "Truly?"

"You are supposed to be horrified, not intrigued," he responded.

"I am?" She tilted her head to one side and considered the matter carefully. "Well, I am not horrified. Did you fight over someone you loved?"

"My sister."

"Ah, so you were defending Lady Meredith's honor?"

"Yes, against Dardington's insults."

Claire's jaw dropped. "You challenged the marquess?" she asked in amazement. "Swords or pistols?"

Jasper shook his head and laughed. "You are a bloodthirsty wench. If I knew that, I would never have revealed my sordid past to you."

"You were delighted to reveal this scandal about yourself," she responded with sudden insight. "It allows me to know something of the man you truly are."

He stiffened at her remark. "I am no longer a wild, irresponsible youth who risks everything on some wild impulse."

His voice was chilly, his tone clipped. Claire was surprised to realize she had struck a nerve, but she had no intention of letting the matter drop. By the time the waltz ended, Jasper appeared to have forgotten their conversation, but Claire remembered every word.

"Come, I am free for the next set. I wish to hear the rest of the story of your duel." Claire practically dragged her husband to the open French doors, but once they reached them, they were forced to pause. "Drat, 'tis raining."

"Rather steadily," Lord Fairhurst added as he stuck his head out-of-doors. When he pulled back, droplets of rain clung to his hair.

Claire sighed heavily and brushed away the moisture that had fallen on the viscount's broad shoulders. A sharp knot of disappointment shot through her. "Perhaps we can find a quiet corner or anteroom where we can steal a few minutes of privacy?"

It was a bold request, even for a wife. Claire half expected to hear a lecture on propriety and decorum, but Lord Fairhurst surprised her.

"The duke has a most impressive conservatory. And I know where he keeps the key."

"A conservatory?" Claire smiled hopefully. "Filled with plants and flowers? Do you think the duke would mind if you showed it to me?"

He squeezed her hand, then tucked it beneath his elbow. "Come."

Though excitement gripped her every pore, Claire allowed herself to be meekly led away, not noticing how keenly they were being observed by one individual in particular.

The conservatory was located on the first floor of the mansion, in the same wing as the ballroom. It was a large, dome-shaped structure with glass walls and a glass ceiling. True to his word, Lord Fairhurst was able to locate the key, which hung near the entrance door.

He lit a candle to illuminate the room, which was thick with plants and flowers and exotic foliage. He led the way down the central aisle, and Claire followed willingly, after first closing the door behind her.

When they reached the deepest curve of the window, they halted. Outside, the night was pitch black. Claire could hear a steady pelting of raindrops as they struck the glass walls. The smell of flowers and vegetation and dampness wafted around her, creating an almost otherworldly atmosphere.

After a minute of fumbling, Jasper lit two lamps, casting just enough light to locate a sitting area containing a sofa and several chairs. He indicated that she should be seated, but Claire declined.

Instead, she circled the area, reaching out with her fingertips to touch some of the more exotic-looking foliage. Her slippers moved softly on the tiles; her silk skirts rustled gently. She knew he was watching her.

Claire's chest felt tight. She turned toward him. Jasper leaned against the wall and grinned; his image reflected in the glass. It was a most eerie reminder that he was a twin, that there were two men who possessed nearly identical handsome masculine attributes.

Yet Claire had no difficulty distinguishing which man stood before her. Broad shouldered, yet thin at the waist and hips, he made an imposing picture. Beneath his evening coat his arms were muscled and defined, but, amazingly, this manly physique was tempered by an air of elegance and refinement.

Claire felt her heart falter. In an instant, she forgot about the ball and society and her nerves and all the other odd bits that had worried her since agreeing to be Jasper's wife. She thought about kissing his lips, his chin, his neck, his throat. She thought about caressing and fondling his broad shoulders and chest, stroking the strong muscles of his thighs, and touching the hard maleness between them.

She imagined having him inside her body.

The sensations crowded in to distract her from everything except her true feelings for her husband. She wanted him. She desired him on the most primitive, basic, and intense level. The realization jarred something inside her and pushed her practical, levelheaded nature toward a deep, erotic need.

She had heard that desire could masquerade as love, but in this instant, Claire felt very sure of her feelings.

She both loved and desired her husband. Perhaps if they assumed a more normal physical relationship some of the tension between them would be released.

It was unthinkable for a lady to be so forward, even if the man in question was her husband. Yet, in that moment, Claire learned something about herself. She discovered that she could be ruthless when she wanted something. And she wanted her husband. Here and now.

Boldly, she approached him, not stopping until she was crowding him against the glass wall. Heat, beckoning and enticing, immediately bloomed between them.

"What are you doing?" he whispered.

"I think it should be fairly obvious." Claire's hands rose to rest against his chest; her gaze climbed to meet his. Immediately she was held in thrall by his extraordinary green eyes. "I am attempting to steal a kiss from my husband."

"Here?" A strained expression settled over his face. "Now?"

She pulled in a tight breath. Her courage threatened to fail her for an instant; then she pushed herself closer to his tempting male strength. Oh, my goodness. He had an erection.

"Is this not the ideal opportunity?" she whispered seductively.

Sliding her hands up, Claire wound her arms about Jasper's neck and pressed her lips against his. Her kiss was not soft or gentle, but forceful and passionate. He responded in kind, and when the hot waft of his breath struck her moist lips, Claire felt her body tighten.

Slowly, she teased his senses awake, using her lips, teeth, and tongue, delighting when she wrought a husky moan of desire from deep in his throat. Unfulfilled passion was thick between them; the smoldering embers were poised to burst into flame.

Their mouths melded, and their tongues dueled as each vied for dominance. Though she had initiated the contact, Jasper now seemed to be in control. He held her firmly in place, kissing her fiercely, his one hand resting at the nape of her neck, the other cupping her buttocks, pulling her harder against his erection.

The tips of Claire's swollen breasts were crushed against the muscled planes of his chest, creating a piercing sensation even through the layers of fabric. It left her feeling restless and edgy and drove her craving to an even higher pitch.

Frustrated, Claire arched her back and pushed herself closer. She wanted to feel every last inch of him, to absorb the strength and hardness of his body into her own. She flicked his cravat loose, and then reached for the buttons of his waistcoat and began to unfasten them. The moment it was done, she started on his shirt, trembling with excitement when she was finally finished and had successfully freed it from his waistband.

Inhaling deeply, Claire slipped her hands inside Jasper's open clothing. His skin felt hot, burning her trailing fingertips as they eagerly explored the contours of his chest. She was fascinated by the hair that covered his body, the satiny dark nipples nestled beneath the springy curls, and the solid strength of his sculpted muscles.

The sensation of running her fingers over his skin was so erotic that it wasn't until Claire felt the cool breeze on her own nipples that she realized Jasper had pushed down the fabric covering her breasts, leaving her upper torso wantonly bare.

"My God, you are beautiful," he said in a hoarse whisper.

She drew back just enough to catch his eyes. The stark emotion in his face brought her close to tears. "So are you."

They reached for each other at the same moment. The mating of their mouths was carnal and impatient. Jasper's hand slid beneath the curve of Claire's breast, and his head dipped down to her chest. She squealed and jumped when his wet lips closed over her nipple, his tongue tracing and tickling the sensitive flesh.

He showed no mercy, suckling one breast and then the other. He placed tender kisses on the tips of her wet, hard nipples, and then blew a warm breath across her entire chest. Claire cried out as she felt a wave of heat spiraling downward and felt her body start to convulse.

"We must stop now, or else it will be too late," he said, breathing the words against her cheek.

For Claire, it was already too late. A rising heat of longing had washed through her the moment their lips first met. "Why must we deny our passion?" she asked, running her fingers over the front of his black satin breeches. His shaft continued to swell and lengthen.

A muscle worked in his jaw. "Bloody hell, you make me crazy."

The torment in his voice haunted her. "Jasper." Tenuously, she lifted her hand to his face and stroked the contours of his firm jaw. Her hand was visibly shaking. "I am your wife."

His eyes had darkened and turned fierce, but she glimpsed the desire shining from their depths—the desire for her.

She feathered light kisses along the underside of his

jaw, nuzzling and nipping at his throat, and waited breathlessly for him to make his decision.

"This is most improper," he growled, his voice ragged.

"Yes."

He groaned, his shoulders trembling. "And impossibly delicious."

"Oh, yes," she breathed.

He bore down on her, and Claire felt her knees buckle. He wrapped an arm around her back and held her steady as his kisses sent a frantic urgency careening through her body.

Claire's fingers literally attacked the buttons on his breeches. Jasper's harsh intake of breath told her of his increasing excitement as she released the final button. In seconds, the full throbbing length of him was in her hands.

Emboldened, she explored this masculine prize, running her finger over the velvety tip, her palm down the thick shaft, and finally cupping the twin sacs of his testicles in her hands. She rolled them gently, causing his penis to jerk.

Labored breaths echoed through the glass-enclosed air. Claire felt Jasper quiver and shudder as she continued caressing his strength, fascinated by its turgid length and engorged size.

Jasper's hands skimmed the curves of her hips, and then Claire felt him lift her skirts, spreading her knees wider as he stepped nearer. He quickly stripped her of her undergarments. Her breath came in great gasping moans. She could hear whimpering sounds of frantic anticipation and realized they came from her own throat.

"Should we move to the sofa?" she gasped.

"I don't want to waste the time."

"Standing up?" She heard the stunned amazement in her voice as he reversed their positions and pushed her back against the glass wall.

He answered with a low growl. "I shall stand, my lady, and you shall be pushed to the heavens."

Claire shivered as his hand caressed its way up her inner thigh until his nimble fingers found her core. She writhed shamelessly against him, opening her legs wider, so his teasing fingers could find their way through the folds of her femininity to stroke her.

A gasp of pleasure burst from her lips as he entered her body with first one finger, then two. She gripped his hair and moaned. He touched her in ways she never imagined, until she was nearly drowning in heat and longing. She felt like she was fighting for every breath, while each fiery stroke left her clinging to sanity.

He thrust deeper and faster, and she knew what was coming next. She closed her eyes, then gritted her teeth and tried to pull back. "No. I want you with me this first time."

He sucked in a loud breath. His hands stilled. Claire let out a whimper as he followed her command and removed his fingers from the apex of her thighs, dragging them tantalizingly through the wet thatch of curls. Cradling her bottom in both hands, Jasper lifted her high in the air.

"Wrap your legs around my hips."

Claire's passion-soaked brain gave pause. It was wicked, unthinkable. But she did as he commanded, placing all of her trust in this man she loved. A searing blaze of desire made her stomach muscles clench as their bared flesh pressed together for the first time.

Claire's eyes remained on Jasper's as their bodies came together. She felt her body stretching, but there was no pain as he pressed forward, hard, hot, and much larger than she realized.

"Are you all right?"

Claire bit her bottom lip and tried to answer. When words failed, she simply nodded her head and rocked her hips slightly. It was all the answer he needed.

He pressed deeper, holding her in place, though in truth she had no wish to escape. Her body arched and bowed, but he did not stop, pressing deeper and deeper, until she was so filled with him she could barely breathe.

He waited a moment for their bodies to adjust, and Claire gloried in the magnificence of this ultimate intimate experience. He was sheathed to the hilt inside her clinging warmth, and she loved the feeling. The ache that had been a dull throb was now filled with something vital and strong.

Jasper pulled himself back until they were nearly separated. Claire whimpered in distress as the ache of longing and demand for completion swamped her. Frantically, she tried to push herself back. Jasper gave a wicked laugh and entered her again, repeating the motion over and over.

He tormented her until her flesh was throbbing and sizzling with sensation, until she could not think, could barely breathe. Claire began to tremble, her head falling back against the glass wall behind her.

Her entire being seemed to tingle and throb. She mindlessly rocked her hips upward to pull him deeper, and he answered forcefully, thrusting hard into her body. Claire's breath caught, and he brought her over the edge; her flesh spasmed into exquisite, perfect ripples of pleasure.

The tightening of her inner muscles triggered his climax. He closed his eyes and groaned, giving one final powerful surge. Claire's lips curved in a satisfied smile as she felt his warmth flood her. She wrapped her arms tighter around him and held on, until the tension slowly drained from her body.

He waited a long time to disengage himself, and Claire relished this intimate entwining. Slumped over his broad shoulders, she felt boneless and sleepy, her limbs unable to move. With considerable effort, she adjusted her position so that her head lay against his chest. Sighing with contentment, she smiled and listened to his heart beating against her ear.

Finally, he lowered her carefully to the ground. She continued to cling to him, not wanting this blissful moment to ever end. Then Jasper's deep, measured voice broke through Claire's languid thoughts.

"I must ask the duke for a copy of the building plans to his conservatory. I've decided I need to start construction on one for our London residence immediately."

Chapter Eleven

Claire's infectious laugh echoed off the glass walls of the conservatory. A burst of happiness filled Jasper at the sound, but the joy soon faded and his brain started to function again.

What the hell had he just done? Made love to his wife, for the first time, at a ball given in their honor, in a location where they could be discovered at any moment! Holy Christ!

Jasper's head was swimming. How had he allowed himself to be seduced so thoroughly? How had he allowed his self-control to be so utterly and completely lost? Where was the famous control he was so proud of developing, the all-important sense of propriety and decorum he longed to achieve?

Gone. It disappeared in an instant, like a puff of smoke. Dread flooded through him, together with the realization that he was not really a changed man. His wild, impetuous, destructive nature was not gone or tamed. There had merely been nothing there to challenge it, until Claire, with her alluring smiles and fiery kisses, entered his life.

When he had brought Claire out to the conservatory, he had never expected anything like this to happen. He had deliberately kept his distance since their wedding, figuring they both needed time to make adjustments to their wedded state before moving on to an intimate relationship.

But what he really had been doing was avoiding temptation, and avoiding risk. He had made an emotional retreat from Claire in order to save them both. He shook his head, trying to make sense of it, but it was impossible to find logic or reason in passion.

His gaze rose and met hers. Claire's blue eyes were wide and brimming with unasked questions. Cowardly, he turned from her and began to button his shirt. He was not ready to discuss what had just happened. Truthfully, he doubted he would ever be ready to have that conversation.

Jasper stuffed his shirt back into his breeches, then fumbled with the ends of his limp cravat. Knowing it would be impossible, he did not attempt to recreate the intricate configuration his valet had tied earlier in the evening. Instead, he formed the fabric into a simple knot. Though a small detail, Jasper knew there would be some at the ball who would notice the change in his appearance, but he doubted even those jaded minds would hit upon the true reason for the difference.

Once he was finished putting himself in order, Lord Fairhurst wordlessly turned to assist Claire. She jumped slightly when he touched her bare shoulder, but then willingly accepted his help.

As he fastened the long, neat row of small buttons on the back of her bodice, Jasper saw the faint marks his fingers had left on the creamy white skin of her shoulders and back. Tangible evidence of his passion—and loss of control—it also was a stark reminder of her vulnerability.

He stood for a moment staring into space. He imagined she was bruised and sore in other places, too. Unbidden images sprang to mind, and Jasper felt another surge of longing shoot through him.

Hell, the last thing he needed is more erotic pictures swirling in his head. Every nerve in his body was still humming; pleasure still coursed through his veins. Though a part of him was appalled at his lack of control, another equally strong part was more than prepared to mate again with his alluring wife.

Somehow he managed to stop himself from pinning Claire against the glass wall, covering her mouth with his own, and pressing his hard body intimately against her softness. Digging deep, Jasper pulled his sense of propriety to the forefront, hoping that would stifle his emotions, but he could not completely abandon the odd proprietary feeling and sense of possession he now felt toward Claire.

He had wondered how he would feel about her lack of virginity when he finally consummated their marriage. Initially, it had irritated him, knowing she had so deeply loved another man. But in the end, Jasper was surprised to realize it had made very little difference.

Who was first was not nearly as critical as who would be last. On that there would be no compromise or question, and the thought relieved Jasper of any lingering distress. Claire was now his and would always remain his. Until death parted them.

The conundrum lay in the fact that it was far more than sex. Jasper shook his head and laughed silently. All of the early years of reckless and wild copulation *had* indeed been useful, for they showcased the difference most blatantly.

Making love with Claire involved a darker need that existed inside him. By indulging this need, a link had been forged between them that was stronger than his common sense and his sense of propriety. It left him uneasy, knowing part of him had relished the intimacy, part of him had craved it, and part of him had been humbled by it.

"I have never done anything like that before," Jasper said suddenly. "Completely abandon myself to my carnal desires in such a public place, with the risk of discovery at any moment."

"This is a first for me also," Claire retorted. The edge in his voice seemed to make her wary, yet her eyes were sharp as they met his.

Guilt surged through Jasper. He did not mean to hurt her feelings or to imply that he believed she often engaged in such rash behavior.

"I found it to be rather extraordinary," he replied in a spurt of honesty.

She seemed startled at his admission. An odd sense of desolation swept over him. After what they had just shared, it seemed almost criminal that they should feel so unsure of each other. Recklessly, Jasper swooped down and kissed her neck. It was an acknowledgment of his sexual satisfaction and an apology for acting so distant. Claire seemed to understand, for the tightness in her shoulders relaxed.

He made a move to leave, but she touched his arm. "Can we stay just a little longer? 'Tis rather pleasant, being alone here in this hushed room."

He peered over her shoulder and gazed at the clock that stood in the corner. It was late. They really should leave. He opened his mouth to deny her request, then stopped.

Though it was the last thing he wanted, Jasper drew up a chair. Once Claire was seated, he fetched a second chair for himself. "We can only stay a few minutes, though, I'm fairly certain by this time everyone has noticed our absence."

Claire wrinkled her nose at him. "Does it really matter so much? What they think?"

He shrugged.

She smiled. "I would have thought that a man brave enough to fight a duel with the Marquess of Dardington would have the courage to face down the gossip of even the fiercest matron of the *ton.*"

Despite his lingering anxiety, Jasper felt his lips curve up in a slight smile. She really was fascinated by his duel. He suspected she would not be satisfied until she heard the entire story. Because it would provide an excellent way to avoid discussing the intimacy they had just shared, Jasper was more than happy to indulge her.

"We never fired a shot," Jasper announced.

"Ah, so it was swords." Her eyes were lit with sinful amusement. "How marvelously barbaric."

"No, it was pistols, and as I said, neither of us fired a shot."

Claire's face broke into a confused frown. "Why?"

"Merry broke it up before either of us was able to pull the trigger."

"Lady Meredith was present at the duel?" Though there was no one about, Claire lowered her voice to a whisper. "I thought only women with, um . . . well, you know . . . fast reputations attended such events."

"My sister was hardly an invited guest," Jasper bristled, remembering all too well the combination of shock and anger he had felt when Meredith had charged up the hill, shouting at the top of her voice for them to cease immediately. "However, she somehow managed to discover not only where and when the duel was being held, but with her usual impeccable timing arrived in time to stop it from occurring."

"How extraordinary." Claire's eyes grew round with astonishment.

"Dardington and I had already squared off and were poised to fire when Meredith approached."

"What a sight to behold! Lady Meredith must have been nearly frightened out of her wits. If you had fired, she could have easily been struck by a stray bullet. 'Tis amazing she was not injured." Claire's cheeks turned a little pink as she looked more closely at her spouse. "You are wearing a most devious smirk, my lord. What are you hiding?"

Jasper ducked his head. "Perhaps there is a bit more to the story," he admitted, letting his eyes drift over a particularly lush plant. "Meredith never was in any true danger and, alas, my courage in this instance was false. The duel was staged. Though I'll own it was not the easiest thing to do, I was able to stand and stare down Dardington's gun barrel because I knew he was going to fire his shot wide, and I, in turn, was going to deliberately miss hitting him."

Claire raised an eyebrow. "The duel was staged?"

"Exactly."

"Why would you pull such an elaborate ruse?"

Their eyes met briefly as Jasper recollected the incident. "My sister was being unreasonable about marrying him, so Dardington had to force her hand."

" 'Tis rather extreme, though in truth it does not surprise me. Dardington strikes me as a man who gets what he wants."

Jasper broke into a wicked grin. "He is not the only one I know who possesses such a talent."

Claire blushed crimson, and he knew she had caught

his reference to their recent sexual encounter and his acknowledgment of her part in the incident. As he rose to his feet, Jasper tried to keep his laughter muted, to spare her any further embarrassment. But she must have heard his mirth, for her face remained a bright hue.

They left the conservatory arm in arm, in a companionable mood. The ball was at its zenith when they returned. Intimate groups of guests clustered together along the edges of the room, watching, observing, and chattering. The large wooden dance floor was crowded with colorful silk and satin gowns of every shade, made all the more vibrant as they dipped and swirled under the brightly lit chandelier.

This opulent collage of color contrasted sharply with the black splashes of the gentleman's evening coats and lent an air of elegance to the entire assembly. As he escorted Claire across the ballroom, Jasper tried to ignore the disapproving glances and tittering smiles that were pointedly sent their way.

Yet, it soon became obvious that nearly everyone was in a fervor of speculation as to exactly what Lord Fairhurst and his bride had been doing. Jasper knew his only hope was to brazen it out. It took discipline, but armed with the knowledge that what really happened would never be known by anyone, he was able to enact the charade.

"Has someone claimed this dance with you?" Lord Fairhurst asked, knowing he needed to separate from Claire as soon as possible. He had already spent far too much time in his wife's company this evening. The wagging tongues would never cease if they remained together.

"I am uncertain," Claire answered. She fumbled with the card that dangled from her gloved wrist, then lifted it close to her face and squinted. "Gracious, many of these gentlemen have atrocious penmanship. I can barely decipher the names of some of these entries."

Mindful of the watching eyes, Jasper attempted to peer over her shoulder and casually read the dance card. The problem was, in addition to the dance card, he had an excellent view of Claire's luscious breasts partially exposed by the low-cut bodice of her gown.

"I recognize Lord Quimby's name beside the cotillion," Jasper choked out, tamping down his suddenly pounding pulse. "I will assist you in locating him."

He held out his arm, and Claire dutifully clasped it. "Which set are they dancing now?" she whispered, as they began to slowly circulate along the outer edge of the ballroom.

Jasper tightened his mouth into a grim line. "I have no idea." He stopped, then reconsidered their plan. "Perhaps it would be better if you found a quiet corner and waited for your partners to come to you."

"All right."

Grateful for her easy acquiescence, Jasper surveyed the ballroom, searching for an appropriate chaperone with whom to leave his wife. He noticed his mother laughing, and no doubt flirting, with the Earl of Richmond on the opposite side of the room and quickly decided to steer clear of her.

Fortunately, he soon spied his Aunt Louise clustered in a semicircle of cushioned chairs surrounded by an imposing group of matrons. She was his mother's eldest sister, a stickler for all that was proper and correct, and the perfect choice for a chaperone.

The daughter of an earl and wife of a viscount, Aunt Louise could be outwardly icy at times, yet Jasper had faith that Claire would be able to charm the older woman in short order. And once charmed, she, in turn, would leap to Claire's defense if anyone so much as breathed an insult in his bride's direction.

"Ah, Fairhurst, at last. 'Tis about time you brought your bride over for an introduction," Aunt Louise scolded, when Jasper escorted Claire across the ballroom to greet her.

Jasper bowed and presented his wife; then he waited for his aunt to pass her verdict. In her typical fashion, Aunt Louise made them wait. With great exaggeration, she raised her long-handled lorgnette to her eye and regarded Claire through it.

Jasper could not help but admire how his wife was able to stand so still and quiet when that damnable lorgnette was turned upon her. There had been numerous times throughout his youth when he had wished to pull the object out of his aunt's hand and crush it under the heel of his sturdiest boot.

"She's a bit long in tooth, Fairhurst," Aunt Louise proclaimed, after making a final sweeping assessment of Claire's person. "I would have expected you to select a young chit right from the schoolroom, so you could mold her into the kind of wife you need."

"Aunt Louise." Jasper folded his arms across his chest and bestowed his sternest glare upon her. "Claire is a most suitable—"

"And spirited choice," Claire interrupted. "Where would the fun and challenge be if Fairhurst married a naive milk and water miss? He would be bored before the month was out."

Aunt Louise's lorgnette lowered as her eyebrows soared, but that reaction did not seem to deter Claire.

"May I take the seat beside you, my lady?" she asked. "My husband longs to visit the card room but fears leaving me on my own. As I am sure you are aware, the *ton* can be so cruel and narrow-minded when it comes to accepting newcomers."

Without waiting for an answer, Claire placed herself squarely in the chair next to his aunt. For several long moments the older woman sat silently, languidly moving her fan. The battle lines had been drawn. Jasper practically held his breath as he waited for either a smile or an explosion of outrage. One never could be certain with Aunt Louise.

"Your bride is an original, Fairhurst," Aunt Louise declared. "Even if she is a bit cheeky."

"She learned it all from me, Aunt," Jasper said.

The older woman let out a bark of laughter. "That sort of brass 'tis not taught, but rather inherited. I predict you shall have thoroughly incorrigible children. Just as you deserve."

Realizing that was his cue to leave, Jasper bowed and retreated. After the crush of the ballroom, the idea of escaping to the card room, and male company, was rather appealing, even though he no longer gambled. Once among his fellow gentlemen, Jasper accepted a glass of whiskey he had no intention of drinking, declined a smoke, and set about trying to relax in one of the soft leather chairs.

The room was smoky; the conversation civilized and subdued, accented only by the occasional clink of coins as the players placed their bets. Normally, he would have enjoyed the atmosphere, but Jasper found himself feeling edgy.

Aunt Louise's mention of children had unwittingly turned his thoughts toward the begetting of his offspring, which brought to the forefront the memory of what had transpired but an hour ago in the conservatory and its implications for his future. The control he so prized was a myth, for he had utterly lost the fight against his impulsiveness and given into his desires.

This placed his entire view and expectation of marriage in a totally different perspective, because he had honestly never expected to be embroiled in such a torrid physical and emotional involvement with his wife. Given all that he knew of her, Jasper would never have believed that Claire possessed the confidence to seduce him so openly and brazenly.

And he also never believed that he would have enjoyed it so much.

The faint buzz of whispered conversation began the moment Lord Fairhurst and his bride returned to the ballroom. Yet, as the speculation ran rampant among the guests, there was one observer who did not need to guess what had kept the couple away from the ballroom for a scandalously long time.

There was one individual who was all too aware of what had occurred between the viscount and his bride. One individual who had grown distressed when they had initially left the party and did not return. One person who had searched among the many rooms of the mansion until they had located the conservatory, had discovered the door was unlocked and ajar, had heard muttered voices and strange sounds, and had been compelled to investigate.

This person had silently, stealthily followed the path in the moonlit glass room and there had seen, most clearly, the aftermath of what had no doubt been an utterly disgusting interlude between the couple—rutting together like two heathen animals, behaving like lower beings without class or breeding.

The stab of disappointment was strong; the pain so intense the individual had almost cried out their distress, and thus almost revealed their position. But self-control had prevailed, and they had slipped away the same way they had come—quietly and undetected.

With each step, the rage coursed through their body, so strong it left a bitter taste in the mouth. Heart racing, palms sweating, pain rolling over them like waves, they had sought privacy in a dark corner of an empty hallway. Slumping to the floor in distress, they tried to convince themselves that the pain would fade, that the wounds they had just received would heal. But that would take time, considerable time.

"You have imbibed more than your share of drink this evening, sir," a female voice scolded. "Best return the glass to the servant while it is half full."

"Shut up," Squire Dorchester retorted.

He shot Miss Rebecca Manning a warning scowl before downing the contents of the glass he held in his hand in three long swallows. And then, just to annoy her further, he summoned one of the duke's servants and accepted a tumbler full of whiskey from the stone-faced liveried footman.

"You are acting very unwisely," Rebecca declared. She lifted her chin, folded her arms, and then huffed in that superior air that set Richard's teeth to grinding.

"I said shut up! I despise women who nag. They are pathetic, utterly pitiful, boring little creatures who cannot hold the attention of a man without resorting to continual whining."

Predictably, Rebecca's face crumbled. God, she was so ridiculously easy to torment at times. Yet, surprisingly, that did not lessen Richard's enjoyment of seeing her suffer.

"I am only trying to protect your reputation," she said defensively, though her voice held a hint of uncertainty.

"When your assistance is required, I will tell you," he snapped, knowing she was actually more concerned about her own reputation than his.

"This is London, not some sleepy village in Wiltshire," she pressed. "The rules are different."

Her implication that he was not gentleman enough to conduct himself properly at this level of society stung all the more because it held an ounce of truth. Richard felt Rebecca staring at him and knew she was waiting to see if her barb hit its mark. He kept his face impassive to deny her the satisfaction and maintain the upper hand in their relationship.

He had danced with several other women this evening, including her mousy sister Anne, but had deliberately avoided guiding Rebecca onto the floor, knowing it would anger her. She sought now to gain her revenge with this slight, but he would not allow it.

In the few weeks of their acquaintance, Rebecca had fallen quickly under his spell. He had recognized in her a kindred spirit of selfish determination, and he knew how to manipulate it to his advantage.

"What do you know of tonight's guests of honor?" Richard asked.

"Only the usual gossip." For an instant, he thought he saw her stiffen with tension, but then Rebecca waved her long, narrow, gloved hands dismissively. "Fairhurst is a stickler for propriety, and his wife is a nobody from the country."

"They just married?"

"No, they just announced their marriage. 'Tis unclear when the ceremony took place," she replied in a slightly exasperated, uninterested tone.

Richard took a sip of his whiskey, then stared broodingly into the glass. He had learned little that could aid him since coming to London, and the frustration was starting to take its toll.

"I spied your father looking for you earlier," the squire said.

"Oh?" Her lips curved deviously. "Perhaps I shall go and find him and leave you to your whiskey. And solitary company."

"I think you should. He might take pity upon you and partner you in a dance."

Her eyes darkened, and Richard waited for the explosion. But apparently Rebecca was learning to play the game, because she let out a disdainful sniff, then stalked away.

For an instant, the squire thought to follow her, but then he stopped. It wasn't good to let her think she had any control over him. Initially, he had required her assistance to gain entry into the more exclusive parties of the Season, but now that he was established with a few key hostesses, the need was not as great.

Still, Richard was reluctant to abandon her altogether, knowing she could prove useful in the future. Besides, the squire had already decided he was going to seduce Rebecca. It seemed likely he would have to remain in London longer than he anticipated, and he could not possibly wait that long without having a woman in his bed.

He might even dangle marriage in front of the silly

chit to gain her initial cooperation. Though the idea of forcibly taking her virginity also held great appeal.

Bored now that Rebecca was no longer available to torment, Richard skulled along the edges of the ballroom, searching for a glimpse of Claire. The rush of emotions he had felt upon seeing her for the first time since arriving in London had nearly overtaken him.

Prickling sensations of heat had streaked over his skin at the sight of her so elegantly dressed, so cooly composed, so regally beautiful. It was a strain, but he was able to control his aggression until the tension gripping at him eased.

He was not yet ready to reveal his presence to Claire. This was the first society event she had attended, and Richard predicted there would be other, more advantageous opportunities to confront his prey. Preferably when she was alone.

A bell chimed the hour loud enough to be heard above the swell of conversation. The orchestra had taken a break, allowing the guests an opportunity to mingle and gossip before supper was served. Richard strutted among them, nodding to those he now knew, enjoying his newly established place among this formidable, elite group.

His wanderings eventually brought him to the gentlemen's card room. He entered on a whim, but he was quickly brought up short by the sight of Viscount Fairhurst seated comfortably in a leather chair near the fireplace.

The cold fury of intense hatred and the burning desire to inflict bodily harm washed over Richard. The prudent course of action dictated that the squire leave, but he had swallowed just enough whiskey to cloud his judgment, and so he ignored that instinct.

"Fairhurst."

The viscount glanced up. "Good evening."

His expression was vague, dismissive. To Richard's eye, insulting.

"Where is your wife?"

Ah, now that caught his attention. Fairhurst placed his drink on the table and slowly rose to his feet. The two men were similar in height, lean and well built, though Fairhurst's shoulders were broader.

"I take exception, sir, to a stranger inquiring after Lady Fairhurst."

Richard flushed at the curt tone. "How interesting that you do not recall my name, since we have met on more than one occasion," the squire replied, his fists clenched at his side. "And I have known your wife more years than you."

"My apologies." Fairhurst paused, sending a side glance toward the small crowd of interested gentlemen that were unabashedly listening to the exchange. "Apparently you are a rather forgettable fellow."

Without wasting a breath, Dorchester burst forward and grabbed Fairhurst by his lapels, shoving him up against the paneled wall. Jealousy consumed his entire being, obliterating the cool composure he had always relied upon to prevent him from creating a scandal and revealing his true nature. But the thought of this man treating him as if he were nothing and nobody and then taking what was rightfully *his* caused this blinding anger.

"Remove your hands," Lord Fairhurst said in a strong tone. "You are drunk, sir, and therefore entitled to the courtesy of a warning. However, if you do not release me by the time I cease speaking, I shall take great delight in putting a bullet through your thick skull tomorrow at dawn on Harrows field."

Though the need to commit a heinous and violent act against his enemy sang through the squire's blood, a glimmer of self-preservation still remained in his mind. Fairhurst was no London dandy. It was said that he was rather high in the instep these days, but his reputation with both pistol and sword was not to be ignored.

With great reluctance, Richard eased his grip on Lord Fairhurst, then stiffly took a step back. There were a few disappointed grunts from the audience of men, now denied the possibility of bloodshed. The squire nearly called out to assure them that given time he would do battle with the viscount, but even he would not be so foolish as to threaten Fairhurst in so public a manner.

His temper under control, the squire turned to leave, but Lord Fairhurst moved quickly, bringing them face-to-face to square off for another moment. "One word of caution before you go."

"What?"

"If you ever pull a stunt like that with me again, you shall not leave the room in the same condition that you entered it."

Richard's jaw flexed. "A threat?"

"No." A hint of a smile curled the corners of Fairhurst's lips. "A promise."

Chapter Twelve

"What can you tell me about Squire Dorchester?"

Claire paused in the act of lifting a forkful of buttered eggs to her mouth and stared at her husband. They were alone at the breakfast table, being the only two members of the household that rose before noon, even after returning home very late from the previous evening's ball.

"Squire Dorchester?" Claire slowly set down her fork, and the uneaten eggs slid unceremoniously back onto her plate. "There is a gentleman by that name who lives back home."

"So I've gathered." Lord Fairhurst signaled the footman for a refill of coffee, then complained the brew was not hot enough.

Claire let out a small sigh of relief, pleased to have Jasper distracted from the topic of Squire Dorchester. But he turned toward her the moment the footman left to fetch a fresh pot of coffee, and she realized with dismay that Lord Fairhurst was waiting until the servant was out of earshot before continuing.

"I had a most unpleasant encounter with Dorchester last night at the ball."

"I had no idea he was in Town." Claire shifted uneasily in her chair. "I have known him for many years. For some odd reason, the squire seems to have taken a liking to me. When I was younger, he even briefly attempted to court me. But my heart was already pledged to Henry, and I refused any attention Dorchester tried to pay me."

"Did that anger him?"

"I never got that impression." She paused and considered her words for a moment. "There was always a bevy of women who demonstrated a marked interest in him. He is the richest man in the county, as well as a handsome, well-turned out gentleman. My lack of regard should have been barely noticed. There were numerous other women who were flattered if he cast an eye in their direction."

"But not you?"

Claire shook her head. "I have always felt uneasy around him, though in truth I can offer no concrete explanation for the feeling. Many people, including my own parents, think the squire is someone to be admired. After Henry died, they harbored great hopes that I would make a match with Dorchester, but I knew that would never happen."

"Because of my brother?"

"In part. Though their acquaintance was brief, Jay was the only person who shared my aversion to Dorchester. I believe one of the reasons he asked me to be his wife was to protect me from the squire."

Lord Fairhurst leaned forward. Concern filled his eyes. "Protect you? Did something happen? Were you harmed or threatened?"

"Oh, no." Claire's heart turned over. His caring attitude warmed her, soothing her insecurities over his usual formality and distance. "Jay developed an intense dislike for the squire. He advised me to remain cautious and alert whenever Dorchester was around and to never allow myself to be alone with him."

Claire glanced at her husband. There was a frown forming in his eyes.

"I wish you had told me this earlier."

She smiled, trying to soften his ire. "I hardly saw the need. The squire is of no importance in my life."

"That is not how he sees it."

Startled, Claire widened her eyes. "How do you know that?"

After a discreet glance toward the footman who had entered the dining room carrying a fresh pot of coffee, Jasper returned his gaze to Claire's. "He made a point of telling me of your long acquaintance last night."

She opened her eyes even wider. "He did?"

"Yes. His attitude was both possessive and belligerent. He was quite annoyed when I did not recall his name, and he tried to instigate a fight."

Claire took a deep breath and silently lectured herself not to overreact. "He must have thought you were Jay."

"Obviously. Fortunately, the squire was too far in his cups to be observant of the differences between me and my brother." Lord Fairhurst fingered the newspaper that had been brought to him earlier. He always read it while enjoying a solitary breakfast, but in deference to Claire joining him this morning, it had remained neatly folded and untouched. "My ignorance put me at a disadvantage last night, and I was planning on avoiding that in the future; hence my questions."

"I am so sorry. I never thought to warn you." Claire dropped the rest of her uneaten toast onto her plate, next to her now cold eggs. "I had heard that the squire made occasional trips to Town, but I never dreamt our paths would cross. I am very surprised to learn that he was at the duke's ball last night. Quite frankly, I never knew he had connections in such exclusive circles."

Jasper's mouth twisted into a grimace. "His appearance last night is something of a mystery. I consulted with my sister, since she organized the affair, and confirmed that Dorchester was not among the invited guests. He must have come to the ball as someone's escort."

"That seems logical. He would be an excellent choice for the role, since he is such a handsome and well-turned out gentleman."

"So you have mentioned. More than once."

Jasper's expression was placid, but a fire glittered in his eyes. If she did not know better, Claire would think Lord Fairhurst was jealous. They sat in silence for a minute as the footman cleared their dirty dishes from the table.

When the servant retreated to a respectable distance, Claire spoke. "Since we have no notion of how long he plans to be in Town, I think we must assume there is a good chance we will encounter Dorchester again."

"I fear you are right." Jasper regarded her with steady, unsmiling eyes. "If he somehow discovered the truth about our marriage, would he use the information to cause us trouble?"

"Nothing would delight him more." The thought caused a cold shiver to run down Claire's spine. "The squire is highly regarded in our small community, yet I have often questioned his true character. I have no specific proof, but I believe he is a man capable of great malice."

"Then we must guard our privacy and hope the squire has other interests to occupy his mind." Lord Fairhurst wiped the corners of his mouth with his linen napkin before tossing it onto the table. "My brother has always had good instincts about people. 'Tis obvious he thought the squire was trouble, and after meeting him I must concur. I therefore second Jason's advice and request that you avoid Dorchester, and if you are forced into his company, make certain you are never alone with him."

Though it seemed like an excessive precaution, Claire nodded her head in agreement. She truly had no particular liking for the squire and was more than happy to agree to avoid his company.

"There is one other thing," Claire said as Lord Fairhurst stood, clearly intending to leave.

A muscle tightened in his jaw, but he sat down, this time in the chair closest to Claire. "Yes?"

"This is probably not worth mentioning; however, you said earlier that you wanted to know as much as possible about the squire."

"I do."

Claire fingered the handle of her delicate china coffee cup. "Jay told me he believed the squire was very impressed by the aristocracy and their titles. I did not give the matter much thought, but after discovering that it was you and not Jay who held the rank of viscount, I formed a theory about why Jay might have used your name and title when he married me."

"To impress Dorchester?"

"Or intimidate him." Claire pitched her voice very low, so only Lord Fairhurst could hear. "Since Jay and I had always planned to live apart, he might have believed the title of Lady Fairhurst would elevate my status in our small community enough to protect me from the advances of any unseemly gentleman, like the squire."

"Men like that tend to take whatever they want, regardless of a woman's situation." Lord Fairhurst's face remained concerned. "What are your plans for today?"

Claire blinked at the sudden change of topic. "I agreed to accompany your mother to Bond Street this afternoon." She dipped her chin and smiled. "Though I promise I will refrain from purchasing anything."

He stared at her with indignation. "I understand that you need an entirely new wardrobe befitting your new station. Though I applaud fiscal responsibility, I would not wish to deny you the pleasure of shopping."

"Your generosity is most appreciated, but I can assure you that my maid will be unable to stuff another article of clothing into my wardrobe. 'Tis fairly bursting with more garments than I can ever hope to wear."

His eyebrow went up suspiciously, and Claire realized that after living with his mother's extravagance for so many years, it was difficult for the viscount to understand a woman refusing the opportunity to indulge herself.

"You have my permission to buy anything that strikes your fancy; however, there is one thing I must insist upon when you leave this house," Lord Fairhurst said. "You will be careful."

It was a statement, not a question, and his tone made it clear that he expected to be obeyed. Meeting his eyes, Claire graciously inclined her head. "I expect you to also be on your guard. After all, Dorchester approached you, not me, last evening."

Lord Fairhurst's eyes seemed to darken at her words. Claire was unsure if that meant he was pleased or angry by her comments, but soon realized she did not care. With Dorchester in Town, it was important that the viscount remain vigilant. She would be remiss in her duties as his wife if she did not remind him of that fact.

"I can handle myself," he declared with a superior air.

"I know," she replied. "Though I would prefer that you were not put in the position of having to defend yourself, verbally or physically."

The very notion of Lord Fairhurst coming to harm turned her blood cold. He was close enough to touch, and Claire found she could not resist the opportunity. She raised a hand and gently, tentatively laid her fingers along his cheek. "I hope you have a pleasant day, my lord. I look forward to hearing about it when I see you tonight."

"Jasper," he replied. His eyes grew warm as he stared at her. "When we are in private, I want you to call me by my name. I like hearing it fall from your lips."

"Jasper," she repeated in a throaty, flirting voice, feeling his gaze sear her from head to toe. She glanced about for an instant, pleased to discover the servants had all left the dining room. Boldly, she drew a teasing finger down his lean cheek. "Is your name the only thing that comes to mind when you contemplate my lips? For shame, Jasper."

He did not show even a flicker of surprise, but the little smile that played along his lips let her know he knew exactly what she was doing. Without further comment, he leaned forward, pressing his lips to hers.

Though his kiss was now familiar, it still had the power to tempt her. The pressure increased and Claire felt herself beginning to melt against him. She curled her arms around his neck and moved as close as she could, frustrated that she was hampered by the section of dining table that stood between them.

He started teasing her with his tongue, making her body burn to be pressed against his. As he deepened the kiss, it gave her a glimmer of hope, not that he was falling in love with her; she was not confident enough to dream that could be happening. But here at least was hope that he wanted her.

Claire was conscience of a warmth rising from within her. Her senses began to swim as she gave herself over to the sheer delight of the experience. She liked Jasper's kisses. Very much. They were not too wet or sloppy, too forceful or hard. They were tantalizing and beguiling and made every bone in her body feel weak.

Finally, Jasper drew back. Claire was joyful to see that he was looking at her with distinct hunger. It made her heart sing.

"Until tonight," he whispered.

Claire sat alone at the table after Jasper left, pink faced and slightly breathless. It had been, without question, one of the most thrilling ends to breakfast she had ever experienced, and she wanted to bask in the glow for as long as possible.

Her mind had felt clouded when she first arrived in the dining room this morning. Last night she had been unable to sleep, made restless by her own expectation that Jasper would come to her room, even if just to sleep.

When he did not appear, she was forced to come to grips with her feelings and admit that she wanted him to come, needed him to come. She had believed that in the conservatory at the duke's ball they had formed a meaningful bond, but was suddenly unsure if that was the truth or merely her deepest wish.

It had been an act of love for her, and she had hoped at least an act of pleasure for Jasper. Yet, he hardly seemed as if anything had changed between them when she entered the dining room earlier. It was the first time they had been alone since leaving the conservatory last night, and Claire's heart had plummeted when her husband greeted her with his usual stiff formality and politeness.

But their conversation had taken an interesting twist that highlighted Jasper's concern for her and, more importantly, had ended with a passionate kiss—several kisses, actually.

Those kisses had left her feeling edgy—and hopeful. She wanted more. More kisses, certainly. Together with the pleasure they promised, she also wanted a future that was more than wistful dreams.

"We are not receiving callers this morning, Squire," Rebecca announced. "My father and sister are both away from home."

Richard lowered his eyes, hiding the gleam of excitement he could not yet control. "How unfortunate. Will they be gone long?"

"For several hours."

Richard's pulse leaped in anticipation. She thought she was playing the coquette, making herself unavailable to him, and thus heightening his interest. Yet, Richard reasoned that if Rebecca truly meant to deny him an audience, she would have sent a servant to impart the news. Instead, she had come herself to inform him that she was alone.

What amazing good fortune. After hearing some fascinating gossip earlier this morning, he had been racking his brain trying to devise a way to get her alone. But now any additional plotting was unnecessary. This perfect, unexpected opportunity had arisen, and the squire had no intention of wasting it.

"I require only a few moments of your time, Miss

Manning." He flashed his most enticing smile, and then lowered his voice to a caressing whisper. "Surely you can spare a minute or two for a dear friend?"

Her tongue darted out, and she licked her lower lip in nervous hesitation. Calmly, Richard waited. He knew she had been strictly brought up; the rules of decorum and propriety had been drummed into her head at an early age. But he had been working his wiles on her for several weeks, and the cracks in her discipline were starting to show.

A more prudent, cautious woman would turn and walk away, but Rebecca was sufficiently intrigued to hesitate. It would not take much more to push her into abandoning good sense.

Richard was glad he was wearing his newest garments, a costly outfit of formidable elegance. His morning coat was dark brown, his breeches ivory, and the waistcoat was pattered with ivory and brown stripes. His black Hessian boots were polished to a high gleam, and his white cravat was starched and simply tied.

He struck a pose in the Mannings' front foyer and allowed Rebecca to examine him thoroughly, confident he looked like the epitome of a London buck. After assessing his physical attributes, her eyes anxiously scanned his features, as though she were searching for some sign of his mood. Richard kept his expression pleasant and open.

"We can retire to the library," she finally decided. "For a few brief moments."

Richard bowed his head in acceptance. Swallowing his smirk of triumph, he followed her at a respectful distance, doubly pleased to note there were no footman standing guard in this area of the house.

The scent of leather bindings and stale smoke assaulted his nostrils the moment they entered the room.

Tall, narrow windows let in a surprising amount of light, and the golden glow contrasted sharply with the austere gray carpet. Books lined three of the walls, reaching nearly to the top of the twelve-foot ceiling. The neatly stacked volumes were aligned so precisely, it seemed obvious that they had never been removed from the shelves.

Richard walked past Rebecca and positioned himself in the center of the room, facing the south windows, with his back toward her. "Close the door behind you and lock it."

"Why?"

"I do not want any of your servants interrupting our discussion."

He modulated his voice just enough to align her suspicions and peak her curiosity. Fearful his eyes might reveal his true intent, he held his position facing away from her until he heard the door shoved closed and the lock click into place.

Only then did he turn and face her.

"Why are you here, Squire?" Rebecca asked, setting her shoulders mutinously. "What do you want?"

"Answers."

"About what?"

"Your past."

He felt a spurt of triumph as a stricken look crossed her face.

"My past? Whatever do you mean?"

Determined to call her bluff, he inched closer. "I discovered something most interesting while I was examining the horseflesh at Tattersall's earlier this morning."

"Concerning me?" Rebecca interrupted. "How vulgar for you to have been a party to such a discussion."

"Oh, I can assure you, only the finest of gentlemen participated in the conversation," he insisted.

She pulled in a startled breath. "Gentlemen? Are you saying there were several men discussing me?"

"At least five, and all showed considerable interest." He laughed at her obvious discomfort. "Naturally, I intended to put an immediate stop to the conversation the second your name was mentioned, but, alas, the discussion turned far too enlightening."

"I am certain I have no idea what you are talking about."

"Truly?" He smiled, not at all fooled by her grand show of indifference. "Well, you can imagine my surprise when I learned that you were expected to announce your betrothal to Lord Fairhurst sometime this Season, but then he suddenly produced a wife, and talk of your union was quickly relegated to the gossipmongers."

Rebecca's muscles tensed, but somehow she managed to favor him with an icy stare. "Are you jealous?"

"Hardly."

"No matter. My involvement with Lord Fairhurst is over and is certainly no concern of yours," Rebecca stated in a crisp, clipped voice.

"You are wrong. Anything regarding Lord Fairhurst interests me."

Color filled her cheeks. "What?"

He laughed, amused at her shocked expression. "I came to London in search of Fairhurst, and his bride. And on my second night in Town I stumbled across you, his former beloved, escaping the scrutiny of a ball by hiding out in the garden. Is it coincidence that brought us together? Or fate?"

"Purely bad luck, Squire."

"I think it was fate. Yet you tried to cheat me of it

when you claimed to know nothing of Fairhurst." He dropped his voice to a lower pitch in an attempt to hide his growing ire. "Explain yourself."

"I do not need to explain anything, sir. Especially to you."

"I beg to differ." He held his smile in place, but Richard's hold on his temper was slipping. Rebecca must have sensed his escalating mood, because suddenly she lunged for the door. But Richard had already anticipated her flight.

He bounded after her, managing to intercept her before she escaped. Grabbing her by the waist, he lifted her and carried her across the room, setting her atop the desk. He trapped her legs between his thighs.

Wildly, she flayed her arms, beating at his chest with her closed fists. "Release me at once!"

"Not until I am ready." He caught her hands and manacled them together behind her back with one of his own. Her awkward position caused her chest to thrust forward. Unable to resist, Richard reached out with his free hand and cupped her breast.

Rebecca screamed.

"You've been holding out on me," he snarled. "Dallying with noblemen, secret engagements, pretending to be the grand little lady. I bet you aren't even a virgin anymore."

"How dare you say such a thing!"

She began to struggle anew, and Richard laughed. His excitement grew. Lord, she was such a little spitfire. He was mad enough to exaggerate his claims and took delight in how his words tormented and humiliated her.

"Afraid?" His voice was edged with mockery. "You should be. 'Tis very foolish to lie to me. It makes me very angry. And now you will learn the penalty for duping me."

He curved her over his arm and kissed her, assaulting her mouth, demanding a response. When she refused to open her lips, he sunk his teeth into her lower lip until she cried out.

Richard's tongue thrust rhythmically into the depths of Rebecca's mouth and her struggles slowed, then ceased. She opened her mouth wider, and he greedily plundered her softness. With a strangled cry of passion, Rebecca took a handful of his jacket in her fists and held on, pressing herself closer.

Richard could feel her breasts, full and warm, crushing against his chest. Grasping her wrist, he slid her hand down between them to rub the bulge in his breeches.

Tearing his mouth from hers, he breathed hotly into her ear. "See how I can make you feel? How I can give pleasure and withhold pleasure on a whim?"

Rebecca shuddered, then slowly withdrew her hand. Sliding off the desk, she struggled to regulate her breathing. Then she drew further back, taking several long steps away from him. "And I can do the same to you, sir," she declared with a smirk of triumph.

Her arrogance challenged him. How dare she consider herself his equal? Or far worse, his superior?

Richard's cold, penetrating glare bore into Rebecca as he stalked toward her. "I am not yours, Madame; however, I have just proven to both of us that I can take you whenever the mood strikes me."

"I make my own choices," Rebecca stated in a raw voice, flinching as Richard drew near.

He enjoyed seeing her fear. The more her lips trembled, the harder and stiffer his cock grew. "I can have you whenever I wish," he declared, curling his mouth into a twisted sneer. "And I can discard you just as easily."

"I am a lady," Rebecca retorted. Her voice was strong, but she averted her gaze and began to slowly inch toward the door.

His arm snaked out and grasped her wrist. He felt Rebecca recoil instinctively, which caused him to tug harder. His grip tightened further, and she whimpered, releasing trembling sobs from the back of her throat as he pulled her into an unyielding embrace.

He ran one hand down the length of her torso, lingering on her full breasts. "You are no lady, Madame. You are my whore."

Richard felt her cringe in his arms. Gleefully, he continued. "I have every right to take you, to use you, to do whatever I wish with you because I know you will come back for more. Every time."

"I will not!"

The scent of her fear, mingled with sexual excitement, filled his nostrils. He was a man who had perfected the art of torment, and this was precisely the kind of situation that drove his depraved appetite into high gear.

Deciding he simply must have her, Richard swung Rebecca off her feet and deposited her on the floor. He pushed her so that she was lying facedown on the rug, with his knee centered squarely in the small of her back.

Talons of passion clutched at him. Roughly grasping her hips, Richard lifted Rebecca to her knees, arranging her limbs until she was bent over at the perfect angle. With a groan of mounting excitement, he moved closer, then tossed her skirts up over her head.

Her body was now brazenly presented for his attention. He attacked her flesh like a man starving for food, stroking, kneading, grasping. When the fabric of her petticoats heeded his progress, Richard tore at them, smiling with pleasure upon hearing the violent sound as they ripped apart.

With one hand, Richard opened the fall of his breeches and poised behind her. He noticed her fingers clenched in the thick strands of the carpet as she tried to stay balanced. When her breathing grew shallow, Richard knew she realized his intent.

The lush globes of her breasts had fallen out of her low-cut bodice. They swayed to and fro, too tempting to resist. Greedily, Richard reached forward and pinched one luscious peak. Rebecca yelped in surprise and tried to twist away. Richard smiled, then pinched the other nipple even harder.

She whimpered in distress and tried to crawl to the door, but he held her firmly in place. "Relax, my little bitch. I'll soon have you panting and screaming with bliss."

Reaching down with one hand, he spread the delicate lips that guarded her womanhood. Rebecca flinched, let out a strangled cry, and redoubled her efforts to escape.

"I usually prefer my women on their backs with their legs in the air," he grunted. "But you are special enough to take this way."

"Don't!"

Kneeling, the squire positioned himself to enter her squirming body. Rebecca continued to struggle and whimper and her actions drove him out of his mind with savage lust.

She hissed in pain as he started to push inside, then let out a sharp scream when he made his first full thrust. Her body, tight and dry, struggled to accommodate him.

It fired Richard's blood to know she could barely take his hard length.

"Stop," she sobbed brokenly. "You are hurting me."

Her agony, coupled with the slight burning sensation surrounding his cock, was sheer bliss. Richard lunged forward again as hard as he could, and Rebecca squirmed beneath his savage thrusts. Her frantic movements and whimpers of pain brought his excitement to a frenzied pitch.

"Had enough," he cried, gripping her buttocks and driving into her.

She groaned. He smiled.

Though tormenting Rebecca was bringing him deep pleasure, Richard knew he could not push her too far. In order to maintain his control over her, it would be necessary to bind her to him completely. And that could not be accomplished with pain.

Deciding it was necessary to begin the next phase of Rebecca's initiation, Richard slowed his thrusts, reluctantly leaned forward, and placed a tender kiss on her neck. Her body tensed further, almost in shock, but he repeated the gesture over and over until she was trembling each time he flicked his tongue on the sensitive skin.

He murmured sweet, tender words like a witless, love-hungry fool, nearly choking as he whispered each ridiculous, flowery phrase. Yet his continued efforts soon brought a subtle change in Rebecca. With almost dispassionate skill, he caressed and teased her body until she began to match his mating rhythm. Just as he had planned and calculated, her fear had turned to passion, her pain to pleasure, and her cries now echoed with desire and need.

Rebecca's muscles stretched and tensed. She began

panting and groaning, surging back against him, willingly impaling herself on his hardness. Her feminine passage was slick and hot, instead of rough and dry. Richard drove himself deeper and deeper until he could feel her body start shaking and realized with amazement that she was about to climax.

The tension inside him coiled as his own release beckoned, hardening his body as he thrust harder, faster, more powerfully. With a strangled cry he gave one last, deep surge against her lush, curved bottom and spilled his seed inside her.

Just as his shuddering ended, Richard felt her body convulsing around him. He held himself completely still, waiting impatiently for the pulsing to subside, for the strangled groan that sounded from deep in her throat to end.

Frustrated that he had to appease her desire, feeling alone and empty, Richard roughly pulled himself out. Rebecca let out a cry of distress; then with a pitiful moan, she collapsed completely on the carpet and rolled onto her side.

The ribbons that had fastened her hair were dangling over her face, the top half of her gown was pulled obscenely low, and the shreds of her petticoats clung to her legs.

Her eyes were heavy with shock and weariness, her cheeks were flushed, and her mouth was trembling. He waited for her reaction, uncertain if she would attack him, break down in hysteria, or crawl away.

Richard leaned back on his haunches and began to fasten the top buttons of his breeches. His breath was still coming in hard gasps. The air was thick with the fragrance of lust and violence.

Once he had put himself to rights, he looked again at

the woman sprawled on the carpet. Her legs had fallen apart, and he saw a dark smear of blood on the white skin of her upper thighs.

"Not bad for a virgin," he remarked with a chuckle. "Though I expect you will improve over time."

With a deep sigh, Rebecca rolled onto her back. Her red lips opened slightly, her white teeth glistened, and her eyes fluttered open. There was something about her eyes that was remarkably different. They seemed to burn into his flesh. Cautiously, Richard pulled away.

Then, remarkably, her legs parted in blatant invitation. She gave him a pleading look, stirring her hips in a provocative manner. "If I am to improve, then I need to practice. Will you try again, sir? I find that I am not yet satisfied with our morning's activity."

Chapter Thirteen

Lord Fairhurst entered White's, the most exclusive of London men's clubs, precisely at four o'clock in the afternoon in a fit of aggravation. He had spent a good part of his day trying to ferret out information about Richard Dorchester and had learned precious little of importance.

Hopefully his brother-in-law, the Marquess of Dardington, had had better luck with his inquiries. They were due to meet at the club this afternoon to share information. A quick scan of the room revealed that Dardington had not yet arrived. Jasper fervently hoped that was due to the fact that his brother-in-law was more successful in this quest, and not reflective of Jasper's own anxious, early arrival.

A waiter discreetly approached Jasper as he waited in the doorway. "May I serve you some refreshment, my lord?"

Fairhurst slung his greatcoat over the servant's outstretched arm, and then handed over his hat. "I am meeting the Marquess of Dardington. Bring us a bottle of your finest claret the moment he arrives."

"As you wish, my lord." The waiter bowed respectfully and disappeared.

Jasper cast an eye at the leather chairs clustered

around the dark mahogany tables, searching for a quiet alcove. The moment he spied a suitable location, he headed directly toward it, exchanging only the barest of greetings with the various gentlemen who called out to him, displaying an unusual lack of common courtesy.

Jasper seated himself in a comfortable chair near the fireplace, facing the entrance. The marquess did not possess the same diligent sense of punctuality as Lord Fairhurst, yet he could be counted upon to arrive within an acceptable time frame.

"I hope you haven't been waiting long," Dardington said as he approached the table. "I needed to stop at the jeweler and pick up the bauble I commissioned for your sister's birthday. It was difficult to make a final decision about the design, but the jeweler exceeded my expectations after I told him that I have always liked how my beautiful wife looks draped in sapphires."

The marquess absently patted his breast coat pocket, and Jasper could clearly discern the outline of a large box. He could only speculate on how magnificent and expensive this little "bauble" was, for the marquess was more than generous with his wife. It was acknowledged among society that Lady Meredith possessed one of the finest jewelry collections in all of England, rivaled by few except for royalty.

"You spoil my sister rotten," Jasper declared.

"She is more than worth it." The marquess grinned smugly. "These trinkets please her. Besides, Meredith has always been very adept at saying thank you."

Jasper managed a smile through his sudden stab of envy. His sister's marriage had begun on even rockier footing than his own, yet clearly they had made a great success of it. Perhaps he should ask Dardington for his jeweler's card.

A waiter interrupted the conversation by promptly delivering the wine that Jasper had requested earlier, then quietly asked if anything else would be needed. He was dismissed with a casual wave and the men were left in private.

"Despite an exhaustive morning of calls and conversations, I have had little success in uncovering anything noteworthy about Squire Dorchester." Jasper leaned back in his chair and tried not to look as anxious as he felt. "What have you heard?"

The marquess took a sip of his drink before speaking. "By all accounts, the man is a perfect gentleman. He comes to Town several times a year for fittings with his tailor and to partake of society, though this is the first year that many of my acquaintances have been introduced to him.

"According to those who claim to know him best, Dorchester possesses a keen knowledge of horseflesh, is known to be a gaming partner who has the grace to lose just a bit more coin than he wins, is obliging enough to dance with a less than attractive sister or ward if asked, and is inclined to pick up the tab after a round of drinks or a hearty supper."

Jasper drummed his fingertips on the top of the table. "Claire mentioned that he holds a similar reputation in their community, but both she and my brother feel there is something unsavory about the squire."

Dardington considered, then shook his head. " 'Tis hard to make an assessment of the man's character when I have not had the opportunity to look him in the eye. Yet my own reckless bachelorhood makes it difficult for me to fathom the existence of such a paragon. No gentleman is that perfect or proper unless he is the dullest sort of man." The marquess grinned. "Except for you, perhaps."

"No longer." Jasper frowned at his brother-in-law, amazed at how calm his voice sounded. For a considerable time now he had dealt with nearly all situations in a manner that would keep his reputation above reproach, regardless of his feelings.

But now reputation and propriety were taking a far distant second to his emotions in any matter pertaining to his wife.

"No one had the courage to state it bluntly to my face last night or even this morning, but I was definitely left with the impression that Dorchester's behavior in the card room was considered *my* fault," Jasper continued.

The marquess's eyes met his with a touch of sympathy. "I too had heard such rumors, but thought it best not to mention it to you."

A small spurt of anger rose in the back of Jasper's throat, but it quickly faded. " 'Tis of no importance. The days when I was so ridiculously stiff-necked about such things are coming to an end."

"I am very glad to hear it. Still, it seems unfair that you are garnering the lion's share of the blame for Dorchester's boorish behavior." Dardington shrugged his shoulder's philosophically. "I suppose some men lead charmed lives."

"Dorchester is the kind that makes his own charm."

A frown touched the marquess's brow. "If what you suspect is true about his real character, then he is a clever man, who could cause some real trouble. He believes that you, not your brother, married Claire months ago in Wiltshire, so the squire is bound to think it odd that your marriage is only now becoming known throughout society, and that you have waited so long to acknowledge her as your wife."

"If questioned about it, I can only hope that I am better

at manipulating the truth than Dorchester, even though I believe he has had far more practice at it." Jasper finished the small drink he had poured for himself. "The last thing I want is for Claire to be touched by any scandal."

"Back to protecting the family reputation?"

"She is my wife, Dardington. Her feelings are most important to me."

The marquess cleared his throat. Then he placed his hands on the table and leaned closer. " 'Tis a rather amazing feeling to find a woman you wish to see sitting across the breakfast table every morning, is it not?"

Jasper nearly dropped the empty glass he held. Dardington had clearly gotten it all wrong. "It is not uncommon to have a proper regard for one's spouse," Jasper said stiffly. "There are many in our class who would benefit greatly by adopting a similar attitude."

The marquess laughed. "I have known you for years, yet I would never have taken you for a man who allowed his heart to rule his head."

"I would hardly classify myself in that category," Jasper replied in a huff.

The marquess looked unconvinced. Jasper replayed the conversation in his head and realized he wasn't being truthful. This was harder than he thought, admitting how much Claire had come to mean to him.

"I did discover one potentially troublesome fact about Dorchester," the marquess said, brushing away the lock of hair that fell over his eyes. "His nearly constant female companion these past few weeks has been Miss Rebecca Manning."

Jasper let out a low whistle of surprise. "That could be trouble. Miss Manning is not feeling kindly disposed toward me these days. Not that I blame her. She has every right to feel hurt and angry. Though it could not be avoided, I treated her shabbily."

"A woman's scorn is not to be taken lightly," the marquess declared. "In addition, Miss Manning is one of the few people outside the family that knows the truth about your marriage."

Jasper set aside his empty glass. "She cannot say a word about it, for if she tells anyone, she too will be embroiled in the scandal."

"Not if she paints herself as the affronted maiden," the marquess countered. "Such a tact could elicit sympathy for her position, especially from other females."

Jasper shook his head. " 'Tis far too late for that approach. If she wanted it known, she would have leaked the truth about our relationship within days of learning about Claire."

The marquess stared at him skeptically through the veil of smoke drifting through the air. Though they were seated in relative seclusion, so many gentlemen availed themselves of the opportunity to enjoy a peaceful cheroot or pipe of tobacco that the rooms at White's were often clouded with smoke.

"Nevertheless, I recommend you stay on your guard," Dardington suggested. "Women sometimes pick the most damn inconvenient time to be dramatic. The activities of the Season are starting to reach a frantic pace. With musical evenings, soirees, several major balls every night, plus daytime teas, luncheons, picnics, and at-homes, there is no way to avoid seeing Dorchester or Miss Manning."

"I promise to be careful." Jasper rubbed his chin. "It might be advisable to employ a few discreet Bow Street men to keep a watchful eye on the squire. What do you think?"

"I strongly agree. My father has excellent connections in that area. I'll have him arrange things for you. Discreetly, of course."

"Thank you."

The two men tousled momentarily over the bill. After Jasper signed it, they left the club together, promising to meet again at the same time the next afternoon.

Lord Fairhurst's coach was waiting in its customary location on the busy street. He set about completing the remainder of his errands, and then returned home. As he handed the family butler his greatcoat and hat, Jasper realized the evening candles had already been lit.

Drat! It was far later than he thought. "Have my mother and Lady Fairhurst left for the theater?" Jasper asked.

The butler nodded. "Twenty minutes ago, my lord. The earl decided to stay at home for the evening. A new shipment of books on the architecture of the ancient Greeks arrived today. The earl has retreated to the gold drawing room with several of the volumes. Will you be joining him for dinner later this evening?"

"Probably," Jasper muttered unhappily.

A well-produced theatrical performance was one of the few society diversions that Jasper did not find tedious, and he regretted being absent from tonight's event. But he regretted even more the missed opportunity of introducing Claire to the delights of a professional London production.

When the outing had first been discussed, Claire had confided to him that her experience of the theater was limited to the rare appearance of a traveling troupe of actors in the village and the yearly Christmas pageant enacted by the youngsters of the community.

She'd been filled with excitement at the prospect of attending a Covent Garden event, and her enthusiasm had heightened Jasper's own anticipation of the evening, not only to enjoy the play, but to relish Claire's reactions.

He suspected she would not sit politely, affecting a faintly bored and disinterested countenance, like so many of the others in the audience. Instead, Claire would most likely listen raptly to every word and show an honest, open appreciation of the skill in which the actors delivered their lines.

Jasper entered the drawing room and found the earl seated in comfort near the fireplace, engrossed in a book.

"Brinks told me that my wife and Mother have already departed for the theater," Jasper remarked as he brushed some imaginary dust from his trousers. "I was hoping to accompany them tonight, but the traffic on Bond Street was nearly impassable, and I arrived home too late."

The earl looked up and blinked distractedly for a moment, his mind clearly still wandering the streets of ancient Greece. Jasper paused while his father's brain switched back to the present.

"I got the impression that your wife wanted to wait for you, but of course your mother wouldn't dream of being late," the earl replied, closing his book and setting it aside. "You know how crowded it becomes, and she is determined to avoid the crush by whatever means she can devise."

"Were they alone?"

"No. Lord Berkley was with them. He's a good sort and can always be counted upon to escort your mother to these things." The earl attempted to stifle a sigh. "I find his conversation deadly boring, but your mother thinks he is very droll and amusing. Apparently, he knows a considerable amount about ladies' fashions and exhibits a great wit when critiquing a female's ensemble."

The earl looked completely mystified by the very notion, and Jasper had to agree with his father on this point.

"Why didn't you go with them? I thought you liked the theater?"

"I do. But I know that if I want to enjoy a play, I cannot bring your mother with me. 'Tis maddening how she must always leave before the end of the performance. Thankfully, Berkley never seems to mind."

"Did Mother mention if they were attending any parties after the play?" Jasper asked. "Or going somewhere for supper?"

"She said nothing about that, though I suspect they will come directly home. Going to the theater usually gives your mother a headache."

Jasper's brow lowered in annoyance. "If she doesn't like the crowds, is not especially interested in the performance, and gets a headache, why does Mother bother at all?"

The earl stared at him in confusion. "Everyone attends the theater. 'Tis expected. However, tonight, your wife wanted very much to see the performance, so your mother made the arrangements."

"I wish they had waited for me," Jasper replied glumly.

"It was probably best for you to stay behind. Or if you absolutely must go out tonight, attend another event," the earl advised. "It might look suspicious if you are seen so often in your wife's company. It just isn't the thing."

The door opened and both men turned toward the doorway. Jasper looked at the butler, and then looked past the servant to the gentleman striding confidently into the room.

"What a delightful surprise to find you both at home, though I cannot fail to notice that you resemble a pair of elderly maiden aunts, all cozy inside for an evening of embroidery and gossip. Why aren't you out enjoying the many social delights of the Season?"

There was a moment of stunned silence as the two men simultaneously examined their uninvited guest. Finally, the earl sprung into action.

"Jason, my boy!" The earl moved forward and grasped his son's arm. "You scoundrel. Where have you been? We've got half of Bow Street scouring the countryside looking for you."

Jason grinned sheepishly. "I've been traveling, Father." Jason's smile faltered when he turned toward his sibling. "Fairhurst."

"Good evening." Jasper's heart lurched at the sight of his twin brother, but he displayed no emotion. For weeks he had been almost desperate to speak with Jason, but now that he was finally here, Jasper felt uneasy and uncertain.

They had been nearly inseparable when they were boys and even closer as they became young men, spending practically every waking hour together, testing their limits, and breaking all the rules of polite society. Yet, somehow, somewhere, they had taken diverging paths.

Jasper had consciously turned away from the irresponsible behavior, the nefarious habits, and indulgent lifestyle, whereas his twin embraced an excess of indecent pleasures and immersed himself in vice.

Though the diversions so eagerly sought by his twin seemed almost tawdry to Jasper, it did not diminish the feelings of brotherly love that had been strongly forged between them since birth. And he mentioned his sincere hope that someday, despite their differences, they could restore their friendship and mend the rift between them.

But first there had to be explanations—and accountability for actions that made little sense. Marrying a woman and using his twin's name and title was a good place to start.

With his hidden emotions running high, Jasper politely shook his brother's outstretched hand. Then he took a deep breath, drew back, raised his arm, clenched his fist, and punched his brother square in the nose.

The Covent Garden Theater was one of the most popular in London. Claire could hardly believe she was actually there. She was enchanted by the entire experience from the moment she stepped out of the carriage, climbed the long staircase, and passed through the heavy curtain screening the doorway to the family's private box.

Though subjected to numerous, wide-eyed stares from the other patrons, Claire settled herself in one of the seats at the front of the box, determined not to miss anything. Yet, as she took in all of her incredible surroundings, Claire felt a sharp pang of regret that Jasper was not by her side.

She had secretly been hoping that he would surprise her and somehow magically appear, but as the music started and the curtain lifted, Claire knew he was otherwise occupied for the evening. Though she repeatedly told herself it was the way things were done in his world, husbands and wives leading separate lives, his absence diminished a part of her joy.

Fortunately, the actions on the stage quickly drew her in—she was soon so enthralled by the drama on the stage, she barely recalled that she was in the theater. When the curtain came down at the end of the first act, Claire clapped enthusiastically and even let out an unladylike shout of *bravo* to show her appreciation.

As the candles in the large chandeliers were lit, Claire noticed many of the ladies in the other boxes gathering their shawls and reticules. Claire, having no need to use the ladies' retiring room and no wish to parade in the corridor, was hoping she would be allowed to remain in the box alone.

The arrival of an attendant carrying a chilled bottle of champagne and a tray with three glasses solved Claire's dilemma rather nicely. With a smile, Lord Berkley eased the cork from the bottle and poured three long flutes of the bubbling liquid. Glasses in hand, the three toasted the performance and the excellent company.

A few friends and acquaintances entered the box to talk to the countess and Lord Berkley. Claire, content sipping her champagne, did not mind being excluded from the conversation. When addressed, she smiled and nodded politely, easily deflecting the common question regarding the whereabouts of her husband.

For her own salvation, she pretended to be unaware of the many pairs of eyes avidly watching her, though Claire could not help but wonder what their real thoughts were behind their oftentimes false smiles.

At the start of the second act, Claire felt an odd sensation grip her, a persistent, eerie feeling of being observed. She peered curiously into the darkened theater, but soon realized it would be impossible to verify if she was in truth under scrutiny.

Deciding she was just being fanciful, Claire drained the last of the champagne in her glass and dismissed the chill that swept down her spine. So far it had been a lovely evening, and she was determined that nothing would unnerve her tonight and spoil her enjoyment of the play.

As the play progressed, Claire was eventually able to

tune out the babbling of those individuals who had miraculously lost interest in the performance and were now rudely gossiping among themselves.

Suddenly, Claire felt a sharp tap on her shoulder. She turned in alarm and beheld the countess motioning toward the exit.

"Is something wrong?" Claire whispered in a concerned voice. "Have you taken ill?"

"Oh, no, dear. How sweet of you to worry." The countess smiled. "It is time for us to leave."

"Now? You wish to leave before the end of the performance?"

"Naturally. 'Tis the only way to avoid the crowds and traffic. The lower lobby can become quite suffocating when it is jammed with so many people."

"But we will miss the best part, when Laertes and King Claudius and Queen Gertrude and Hamlet all die." Claire turned beseechingly toward Lord Berkley, hoping for an ally to support her argument.

"Ah, so you are familiar with the story. Delightful. It is therefore unnecessary for you to wonder about what happens next," the older gentleman said.

"Precisely." The countess agreed. "If you want to refresh your memory on the particulars, I am certain Jasper can assist you in finding a copy of *Hamlet* in the library at home. He owns a complete set of all the Bard of Avon's works and has read them several times."

Claire opened her mouth to protest, but the countess had already left, and Lord Berkley was politely holding the heavy curtain aside waiting for her to do the same. With great reluctance, Claire picked up her beaded reticule, cast a final, longing glance toward the stage, and followed her mother-in-law into the semicircular corridor running behind the boxes.

Lord Berkley soon joined them, gallantly offering each lady an arm. The empty corridor allowed them to easily walk three abreast down the long staircase, through the lobby, and out the front doors.

Outside on the pavement, Claire was forced to admit on this point her mother-in-law had been correct. When they arrived, there had been a long line of coaches traveling at a slow crawl to the front of the theater, but now the street was nearly deserted. All that could be seen was a small blur many blocks away.

"Ah, that must be our carriage approaching," the countess announced. "John Coachman knows that I always like to leave the theater no later than eleven o'clock. I must commend him on his punctuality."

Claire, thinking about the well-staged and, no doubt, superbly acted final scenes of the play she was missing, was paying limited attention to her surroundings until she heard the rattle of a fast-approaching coach. She looked up in startled surprise and beheld a heavy, old-fashioned, black carriage at the end of the road.

It swayed drunkenly, careening wildly from side to side. Claire blinked, hardly believing what she saw. She was not standing in the roadway, yet somehow managed to be directly in the path of the heavy, out of control vehicle.

The thud of flying hooves echoed in her ears as Claire stood frozen in place, watching with wide-eyed horror as the grim-faced coach driver tried to rein in the wild team of horses.

"Watch out!" a male voice screamed.

She heard the voice and registered the extreme danger, yet shock and fear held her immobile. Try as she might, she was incapable of moving. Her head buzzed, her lungs felt tight, and her breath came in great gulping gasps.

As the coach barrelled ever closer, the final thought that struck Claire's mind was that she would never see Jasper again. Never hold herself close to his chest and rest her head against his broad shoulder; never tenderly or passionately kiss his lips, or feel his arms wrapped around her body in warmth and comfort.

The horrific rattle of the wheels hitting cobblestones paralyzed her utterly. And then, amazingly, miraculously, Claire felt a pair of strong hands grip her shoulders and haul her backward a mere split-second before the coach flashed past.

Abruptly, the street was silent. It took a few moments for Claire to realize that disaster had been averted—that she was still in one piece, with all her limbs intact, frightened, but unharmed. She staggered sideways, but the arms that held her were like an iron bar keeping her upright.

In the distance, Claire could hear the countess's voice battling hysterics, and the deep, soothing tones of a male voice—Lord Berkley?—encouraging her to remain calm. The hysterics slowed and Claire was grateful the older woman was listening to the advice and winning control over her emotions.

Claire lifted her chin and stared at the stars in the night sky; then took a deep, full breath. There was dampness in the air, perhaps it would rain later, despite the twinkling stars. She pressed her hand to her mouth to smother the jerky, nervous laughter that suddenly bubbled to the surface.

How bizarre to be thinking about rain when she had nearly been trampled to death! If not for the courage of a stranger, she would never again have had the chance to feel the cool wetness of falling raindrops on her skin.

Claire turned, trying to thank her mysterious savior, but she lacked the strength to perform such an awkward motion. Deciding to allow herself a few more moments to recover, she remained sprawled in the stranger's arms.

And then she felt the hand planted in the small of her back glide downward over the curves of her bottom.

In light of the fact that her life had just been saved, Claire decided to ignore the gesture, but when the same hand very deliberately molded and squeezed her behind, she knew she could no longer pretend ignorance.

"I must thank you, sir, for your brave rescue." Claire tilted her head back and glanced up.

Her rescuer met her eyes and smiled wolfishly. "How very fortunate that I was here precisely when you needed me, Lady Fairhurst."

"Squire Dorchester? My God, is it really you?" Claire whispered in shocked disbelief. He tightened his hold, and Claire struggled to fight down the faintness and giddiness that threatened to overtake her.

"Are you pleased to see me?"

His eyes gleamed like polished steel. He grinned again and moved his hand suggestively over the lower part of her body.

Claire shuddered with revulsion. Her skin felt icy, her stomach hollow. She sucked in a deep breath, frantically gathering her wits. But the shock of her near-fatal accident and the identity of her rescuer proved too difficult to overcome. The darkness closed in on her mind; her eyelids fluttered shut; and for the first time in her life, Claire fainted.

Chapter Fourteen

Claire, shrouded in a fog of unreality, recalled little of the carriage ride home. The countess held her hand and babbled soothing nonsense, trying to offer comfort. Lord Berkley fidgeted nervously, asking her continually if she was all right, and then repeatedly calling out to the driver to hurry.

The familiar sight of the brightly lit mansion nearly had Claire in tears, so anxious was she to be inside the security of its strong stone walls, and safely enfolded in her husband's arms.

A footman stepped forward to assist her from the carriage. Claire nodded her thanks and concentrated fully on subduing her chattering teeth and keeping herself upright on her very unsteady legs. It seemed grossly ironic that the most difficult part of her ordeal should occur now, well after the danger had passed.

With the countess and Lord Berkley flanking her on either side, they entered the drawing room. Claire found herself moving quickly toward the tall, broad-shouldered man standing near the fireplace.

"Jasper," she whispered.

The man turned and, for an instant, Claire was so overwhelmed by surprise and disbelief she was speechless.

"Claire, good God, what has happened? You are as pale as a ghost."

It was not her husband that stood in front of her, yet the sound of that dear, familiar voice broke Claire's resolve to contain her emotions. She hiccuped a sob and started to move.

"Oh, Jay, is it really you?" Ignoring the others in the room, Claire launched herself into his arms. "I am so glad to see you."

"You are?" Jason smiled. His arms closed around her, and Claire snuggled closer to the safety of his strength. "What a relief to discover you are not furious with me," he continued, "I never expected such a warm reception. I thought you'd want to plant your fist on my face, just like my brother."

Claire pulled back and examined Jay's face carefully, noticing for the first time the swelling around his nose and the bruising under his eyes.

"Jasper did that to you?"

Jay's smile faded. "It was a cheap shot. He caught me unawares. First he embraced me in a welcoming hug; then when my guard was down, he punched me in the nose."

"Jasper is at home? Where is he? Has he already retired to his bedchamber?"

"I am right here, waiting to see how long it takes you to remember which brother is your rightful and legal husband."

Claire turned. Lord Fairhurst's jaw was set, his expression disapproving. He was glaring at her and glowering at Jay. Oddly, these emotions made him appear far more human, almost vulnerable.

"Would you be so kind, brother, as to remove my wife

from your embrace?" Jasper asked in a clipped, stiff tone. "Immediately."

Jason, ever the rebel, ignored the request. Claire darted a quick glance at her husband. His expression was still tight and granite-jawed. She opened her mouth to try and smooth over the tension, but her mother-in-law spoke first.

"I am afraid you will have to save your jealousy for another time, Jasper," the countess lectured as she touched her son on the arm, signaling him to pay attention. "Claire has had the most horrific experience. Less than an hour ago she was nearly killed, practically trampled to death in front of the theater by a runaway coach."

Hearing the words spoken aloud brought on a rush of frightening memories for Claire. She felt her knees weaken, but she was glad her mother-in-law had explained the situation.

"Are you certain you are unharmed?" Jay asked in a deeply concerned voice, as he tightened the reassuring arm he continued to hold around Claire's shoulders.

"I confess to being a bit shaken up, but otherwise I am fine," Claire said with a tighter voice than she wished.

She risked another quick glance at her glowering husband, prepared to encounter a mask of aggravation, but instead he appeared gravely concerned. Her throat ached at his genuine distress, and for one mad impulsive moment, she wanted to throw off Jay's arm and launch herself at Jasper.

But the stoic Lord Fairhurst also looked vastly unapproachable, and her shredded nerves could not take the pain of a possible rejection.

Lord Berkley took the men aside, presumably to relate a less emotional accounting of the tale. But within moments, Claire saw the older gentleman pull a handkerchief from his pocket and wipe the sweat from his brow. His complexion was ashen, and his hands were visibly shaking.

Claire tried to ignore their whisperings. The butler solicitously left a tray of filled brandy snifters. For a moment, Claire was tempted to drown her fears with the expensive liquor, but she felt a headache forming behind her eyes and knew the strong spirits would only worsen the pain.

Instead, Claire collapsed on the settee. After downing one of the goblets of brandy, the countess took the seat beside her. The women waited in silence for the men to return.

Claire stood the moment the gentlemen approached, moving from foot to foot to ease her discomfort. The countess rose with her, squeezing her hand in support.

The earl cleared his throat. "Well, it certainly sounds like it was a nasty accident, but fortunately it all worked out in the end. We would like to personally extend our thanks to the gallant gentleman whose quick reflexes and bravery saved you from being injured, though I suppose in all the confusion no one thought to ask the fellow's name."

Claire hesitated. The last thing she wanted was more drama, but the full truth had to be revealed. "I know the man who came to my aid."

The countess's neatly arched eyebrows shot up. "You do?"

The skin between Claire's shoulder blades began to twitch. Knowing there was no easy way to phrase her response, she simply blurted it out. "The gentleman who pulled me out of the path of the coach was Squire Dorchester."

"What?"

The exclamation had come from Jay, but Claire barely concerned herself with his reaction. She stole a sideways glance at Lord Fairhurst.

Jasper's gaze darkened. The news seemed to affect him physically. His hands clenched and unclenched, and he breathed shakily as his anger exploded.

"At breakfast, less than twelve hours ago, I told you to be careful and avoid the odious squire," he said furiously.

Claire felt the sting of his words shake her already rattled composure. She gazed at him in disbelief. She had expected his anger but had not anticipated that he would tell her it was her fault. Did he truly think she had courted the squire's attention?

Claire had always hated confrontations, especially those enacted before an audience. She gritted her teeth together, refusing to speak another word.

"Who is Squire Dorchester?" the earl asked.

All eyes turned to survey Claire. She stirred restlessly, yet gave no answer. The ever gallant Jay came to her rescue.

"The squire is a neighbor of Claire's, and I have long held suspicions about his true character."

It took little encouragement for Jay to elaborate on his opinion of the squire. As they were all trying to comprehend the magnitude of the incident and the implications of the squire's involvement, Claire slipped away from the group. The countess soon followed.

"You need some rest, my dear," the countess declared. She leaned forward and pressed a kiss on Claire's forehead. "Go up to bed. I'm sure that everything will seem far better in the morning."

Touched by her obvious concern, Claire managed a melancholy smile. Though she put up a brave front, there were lines of worry etched on the countess's face that made Claire even more jittery. Maybe time alone, snuggled in her bed, would help contain the fear that still held her in a tight grip.

With the men otherwise occupied, it seemed like a good time to escape. Unnoticed, Claire left the room and climbed the stairs slowly, wishing she felt as certain as her mother-in-law that all would be fine.

A half hour later, Lord Fairhurst left the drawing room. Exhausted, yet knowing he would get no sleep even if he tried, Jasper stepped onto the third floor of the mansion and moved toward his wife's bedchamber. Though he had seen with his own eyes that she was physically unharmed, he needed to speak with her for a moment to make certain.

Claire was partially undressed when he entered the room. His eyes quickly scanned the corners for her maid, but he soon realized Claire was alone.

"Goodness, Jasper, you startled me."

Claire's eyebrows drew together in a frown. She was in the process of removing her stocking. One of her legs was already bare. Leaving the wisp of silk on her other leg, she stood erect, allowing her chemise to cover the limb.

Jasper bowed. "I apologize for the intrusion, but I require a few moments of your time."

She let out a dejected sigh. "If you have come to lecture me on my inappropriate behavior toward Jay or my lack of sense regarding Squire Dorchester, I must insist that you wait until tomorrow. I fear my nerves truly cannot sustain anymore of your husbandly concern tonight."

Her voice was weary with bitterness. Jasper was not quite sure how to respond, especially since he did, indeed, wish to speak about both matters. A wave of guilt crashed over him.

Damn his emotions! If jealousy had not consumed him the instant he saw Claire in his brother's arms, he would have been able to properly comfort his wife. Instead, he acted like a prized fool, condemning her of things he knew she was not capable of doing and increasing her distress tenfold. Though he knew he had sounded like a spiteful child, he had been unable to contain his tongue or his actions.

Jasper turned to leave, then stopped. His conscience gnawed at him, urging him to say what truly needed to be stated, even if Claire was still too upset to forgive him.

"My behavior earlier this evening was inexcusable. I can offer no explanation for treating you so shabbily, but hope you will, in time, be able to accept my apology."

His words were uttered in a stiff, jerky manner. This was harder than he thought. Claire was watching him with confusion and a hint of suspicion. He turned away, raking his hand through his hair.

"Wait!"

Her voice was strangled with surprise. Instinctively, Jasper obeyed the command. He turned to look at his wife, moving closer to the glowing fire so he could see her face. She was staring at him in what might be considered fascination.

"Why did you punch your brother?"

Her question caught him off guard. But maybe that

was exactly what he needed. Maybe if he explained the depths of his fiery emotions, she would understand the necessity of keeping them firmly under control.

"I have been angry at Jason for so long, I can hardly cite a single reason for reacting so violently to his sudden appearance."

"Did your anger then extend to me when you saw me greet Jay with an affectionate hug?"

Jasper crossed his arms over his chest. "I did not see you greet him. I arrived to discover you locked in an intimate embrace."

"Intimate? With a room full of relatives?" She clucked her tongue. "That was hardly the situation. Though I suppose if one were very cynical and jaded, it might have looked improper."

"It did."

Claire flushed. "You were completely wrong in your assessment of the situation. From the moment I arrived home tonight, my thoughts were centered on finding you. I ran to Jay, thinking I was running to you." She came toward him, standing so close he could see the sparkle of firelight in the depths of her eyes. "I was looking for *you,* Jasper. I wanted *you.*"

Jasper felt the muscle in his jaw tighten. The one thing he disliked more than dealing with his naturally high-spirited emotions was discussing them. But Claire deserved to know the truth.

"I was racked with guilt because I was not there to protect you from danger. And I was not only angry, Claire, I was consumed with jealousy at the sight of you so comfortably enfolded in my brother's arms."

Claire sighed. "I have told you repeatedly that Jay is nothing more than a dear friend. That has not changed."

"Logically, I can accept that as the truth. Emotionally, it has proven to be a far more difficult adjustment."

For a long moment, she stared into his eyes. The cloud of weariness that appeared in her face earlier gradually lifted and was replaced by a look of sheer wonder. "It brings me great happiness to learn that you care so much about me, Jasper."

Her words were like a sharp knife cutting across his flesh. Like most women, Claire viewed this as something positive and wondrous. But it was not. This type of passionate emotion was dangerous and needed to be harnessed and controlled.

"You did not appear very happy in the drawing room," Jasper said, his mind filled with the memory of her anguished face.

"I was upset from my ordeal."

"And I made you feel worse. My jealous nature caused my disgraceful behavior. I hurt you, Claire, and that is truly the last thing you deserved." Jasper took a short breath, trying to rid himself of the sick feeling squeezing his heart. "I know that there are many people, including members of my own family, who think that I am cold and controlling. And they are correct. I deliberately distance myself from everyone. I strive each day to keep my passions and emotions under strict control, or else these feelings will overrun my common sense and sense of decency, and others will suffer because of my weakness."

There was a slight hesitation before she asked, "Was it an honest reaction?"

"My jealousy?" He frowned. "It was immature and undisciplined."

"Yes, but it was also an honest expression of your feelings," she replied breathlessly.

He shook his head. She did not understand. "That level of intense emotion will ultimately prove to be a destructive force."

"Oh, Jasper, is that truly what you think?"

To his ears, her voice sounded ragged and desolate, yet inexplicably she was smiling.

"Claire—"

She pressed her fingers to his lips. "Would you kiss me? Please?"

Jasper hesitated. Sex was not the answer. It would only confuse the issue. But she was regarding him with such open delight, it seemed cruel to deny her a simple kiss.

Jasper's mouth descended to hers. Her lips were soft and sweet, moving in a welcoming, knowing response. He knew if he pressed deeper, he would find the hunger, simmering and soft, within her. Tantalizing her with his lips and tongue, he allowed her one firm, long, satisfying kiss.

A kiss that set his aroused body aching.

Keeping an iron band around the passion he was feeling, Jasper broke the kiss; then he pressed his lips to the exposed curve of her neck. With a sigh, he drew Claire's head down to rest on his shoulder. She breathed contentedly and feathered several light kisses along the underside of his jaw.

Another sigh of pleasure escaped from his lips. Though he knew he shouldn't, he liked how she needed to kiss him, needed to stay close to him. Her gentle caress made his flesh feel as if it were alive with sensation and need, and the low, ragged sound in her throat made his senses quiver and heat.

He looked down. The top laces of Claire's chemise were loosened, and the curve of her breast moved as her unsteady breathing continued. Trying to distract himself from that beguiling sight, Jasper slowly smoothed her unbound hair, enjoying the velvety feel of it against his skin, the way it ran through his fingers like fine silken threads.

She snuggled closer. Jasper placed his hand on Claire's shoulder, slid it down her arm, and gently enfolded her left hand with his.

Claire stood perfectly still. He lifted their joined hands and studied how well they fit together.

"I am very glad that you are my husband, Jasper."

He tried to control the wave of emotion that swept through him. At times he had not been the best of husbands and they both knew it. But, obviously, Claire was willing to forgive and forget his past mistakes. It was an equally humbling and frightening thought.

"It is amazing to me that you continue to believe in me, in the strength of our future together," he remarked as he brought her hand to his mouth, brushing his parted lips over her soft knuckles.

She smiled. "You are a good man, Jasper. You have a level head, a deep sense of honor, and a true heart. All you lack is the confidence to trust those instincts."

Was she right? Could he really experience the depths of his emotions without losing control of himself?

"We Barrington males are an eccentric, wild lot," he said. "I fully expect to be the one that will finally succeed in breaking that unacceptable pattern."

"There is nothing wrong with being different."

"True, but there is something very wrong about being destructive."

Claire sighed deeply. "Jasper, your emotions are not destructive. You are confusing the indiscretions of your youth with the qualities of your personality. I have no doubt that you were once restless and aimless, as well as careless and cynical. But those traits are barely evident. You have matured into a fine man, who at his core is devoted to his family and his honor. I only wish that you would allow your heart its freedom, too."

His heart? Did she actually believe that he had one? The dinner he had shared with his father several hours ago rumbled uneasily in his stomach, while a nagging voice in his head shouted at him to turn around and flee. Yet, somehow, Jasper held his position.

He looked down at his wife. Her gaze was steady and inscrutable. "So, you are interested in my heart?" he asked.

"Very much." She lifted her shoulders in a tiny shrug. "I will confess that my reasons are rather selfish. You see, I have fallen in love with you and would like very much for you to one day reciprocate my feelings."

"In love?"

She nodded. The lump of emotion clogging his throat swelled. Jasper tried to swallow past it, but could barely get his throat muscles to cooperate.

He tried to think of mundane things to distance himself from the moment, but his heart and inner will would not allow it. He settled into his thoughts and let the possibilities slip into his mind.

He dreamed of companionship with Claire that included physical fulfillment and joy, that allowed him to let his pure and intense emotions to reign free, that allowed him to return her regard and affection and love with every bit of his soul.

It was something he had never believed possible for himself, so he had never wished for it, never contemplated it. Yet, as he examined all the facets of this incredible opportunity, Jasper realized it was what he truly wanted.

Maybe he had been too rigid in his thinking. Maybe it was possible to experience the emotions without allowing them to completely overcome him. Claire certainly trusted him enough to believe it was possible.

He tightened his jaw. "I do not believe I can change my attitudes and behavior overnight. You will have to be patient with me."

She stared at him a long moment, as if not quite understanding him. "Patient?"

"I promise it shall be worth the wait," he said quietly.

She went perfectly still. Even her breathing became inaudible. "I always knew that it would be," she finally answered, pulling her hand free and smoothing it across his chest. "I love you, Jasper."

His eyes locked with hers. She raised herself up on her toes and waited, an expectant look on her face.

Her declaration jolted him in a way he had not expected. Over the years there had been other women who had spoken those very same words, much to his discomfort. But hearing Claire state her feelings caused a different reaction.

I love you, too. The words welled in his chest, pushed up to his throat, and settled on his tongue. But he could not utter them. A part of him wanted to return the declaration, but it was too new, too fresh in his mind and heart.

So, instead, he decided to show her—to say with his body what was in his heart. Bending his head, Jasper touched his lips to hers. Eyes closed, he savored the taste of her sweetness, while his tongue tempted and seduced.

He ran his hand down her body, skimming the curves

and hollows of her luscious flesh, following the ridge of her hipbone, and turning finally to the inside of her thighs. "You are trembling," he whispered.

"Because of you."

She leaned her forehead against his chest. Her hair felt silky and soft beneath his chin. He inhaled deeply. The enveloping scent of her skin sent the hunger twisting sharply through him.

Reaching down, Jasper gathered the cloth at her thigh in his fist, then pulled Claire's chemise up and over her head. It stuck momentarily around the swell of her breasts, but the laces had been loosened enough that with a few persistent tugs, it broke free.

One of her silk stockings remained in place, clinging seductively to her shapely leg at mid-thigh. He took a moment to drink in the sight of her looking so wickedly sexy, naked except for the scrap of glimmering fabric on her leg.

She lifted her foot playfully so he could remove it. He willingly complied, then dropped slowly to his knees. His hands slid down her hips, around her body, and closed possessively over her bare bottom.

Taking a firm hold, he kneaded the tender flesh for a moment, then pulled her hips forward. Her musky scent ignited his senses. Her body was pulsing hotly; her delicate flesh pink and moist and waiting for his mouth.

Though the position he assumed made his erection ache with longing, Jasper ignored his own needs and concentrated solely on Claire's pleasure. His time would come soon enough. First, he wanted Claire to experience perfect bliss.

Boldly, he reached through the tangle of soft curls at

the apex of her thighs with the tip of his tongue, lovingly stroking the soft, sweet flesh they concealed.

"Jasper!" Claire gasped, trying to pull away from his kiss.

He would not allow her. He locked one arm firmly beneath the cheeks of her bottom and supported her, holding her steady and in place while his tongue stroked and probed and lapped at her softness.

He heard her breath catch sharply, then for one moment she stopped breathing entirely. Easing her thighs wider, Jasper continued his assault, exploring the swollen folds between her thighs with delicate reverence.

Each time he felt she was on the brink of release, he would ease back, kiss the edge of her stomach, lick the top of her thighs, flick his tongue in a trail of fire down the inside of her leg. Then, once she was calm, he would start again, setting his tongue against her sweet pearl, teasing and tantalizing her, building the tension and need until the passion once again claimed her.

Her hips twisted and tilted, her fingers dug into his hair and clung tightly to his skull, and still Jasper tasted and teased, nudging Claire to greater and greater heights of pleasure. He heard her panting his name; then she made a sound that was shattered delight.

Jasper sighed with satisfaction and continued to suckle and lave her delicate flesh until Claire cried out again, sobbing in the intensity of her second climax.

He savored her contractions, speaking sweet words of nonsense as they eased. As if her legs could no longer support her, Claire slowly sank to the floor, collapsing against him. Jasper pulled her close, cradling her within the circle of his arms.

It was a wild, erotic feeling to be holding a naked

woman while he remained fully clothed. Her skin, still in the last flush of desire, was flawless, her auburn hair, thick, wavy, and unbound, fell across their bodies like a soft blanket. She tilted her head and looked up at his lips, ran her tongue across her own, then met his eyes.

"Now will you bed me?" she asked.

Her face was soft and glowing; her breathing unsteady. She lifted her arm and her hand touched his cheek. Jasper knew in that moment he would deny her nothing that was within his power to give her, including his heart.

"I shall bed you with great pleasure, my lady."

Jasper had never been with a woman he wanted more, had never experienced this strange combination of excessive lust mingled with intense protection.

The bed seemed a long distance away, but he owed her the comfort of a soft mattress, the civility of clean, crisp sheets. He stood, then reached down and lifted her from the floor.

As he walked across the chamber, Claire twined her arms around his neck and began nibbling on his earlobe. It sent a driving beat of blood pulsing through his veins.

Depositing her in the center of the large bed, Jasper pulled away and divested himself of his boots, coat, waistcoat, and cravat. As he reached for the buttons on his shirt, he caught Claire's sultry smile.

"What is so amusing?"

"You." She shifted until she was on her knees, facing him. "You are taking off your garments so calmly and precisely, like a very proper English lord. I half expect to see your valet appear at any moment to remove the items and return them within the hour, freshly laundered and perfectly pressed."

Jasper frowned, then glanced over at the neatly folded

pile of clothes he had stacked on the chair. Stepping back, he swiftly yanked off his trousers, ripped off his shirt, and then tossed both garments on the floor.

"Is that better?"

"Infinitely."

Laughing, Jasper fell on the bed, reaching eagerly for his wife. She arched toward him, thrusting out her glorious breasts. Desire, hot and immediate, sizzled through him. He let his hands roam freely, his palm covering one full breast. "You are mine."

"I am. And you belong to me."

As if to prove her words, she closed her fingers around his length and pulled on his cock. Her fingers were warm, her palms soft. Jasper thrust eagerly into her hand, his penis thickening and growing larger with each stroke.

He reached for her, but Claire shifted away. With a mysterious smile on her face, she bent her head. Jasper hissed in a breath of shock when he felt her breath caress his aching hardness. She still held him tightly in one hand and stroked him lovingly, gliding up and down with her closed fist.

Then, suddenly, her tongue followed her hand, gliding, licking, and laving him from the base to the head. Once she completed this act several times, Claire slipped her lips around the head of his erect penis, took him full into her mouth, and sucked.

"Claire!" Astonishment laced his voice, but the onslaught of intense pleasure rendered any additional speech impossible.

His fingers curled through her hair and spasmed on her head. Sweat broke out on his forehead. He clenched his teeth in pleasure. She used her lips to alternate the pressure and her tongue to circle his most sensitive areas again and again.

At the moment when he felt he would come apart under the exquisite, agonizing pleasure of her ministrations, Jasper grabbed her shoulders and lifted her away.

Her hooded, sexy eyes met his gaze. "Why did you make me stop? I was starting to truly enjoy it."

Jasper shuddered with the effort of holding back his climax. She was killing him with her beguiling sexuality, her lustful experimentation, and open, honest passion.

"If you continue, then I won't be able to do this," he replied hoarsely.

He flipped her onto her back, spread her thighs wide, and entered her in one smooth thrust. She groaned. Jasper stilled instantly, fearing he had been too rough, but then she grasped his hips and tugged. Smiling, he propped himself on his elbows. He framed his hands around her face, holding it close so he could kiss her.

As their lips and tongues met, Jasper felt her long, luscious legs wrap around his hips, and he knew that she was more than ready for him to ride them both to ecstasy. He rocked his hips forward, concentrating on applying pressure to her most sensitive area.

Small moans sounded deep in her throat as she moved with him. The tight heat of her womanhood stole his breath as he gave into the sweet ache that shot through his entire body.

Jasper pressed a hand beneath Claire's hip and tilted her up to meet his next thrust. Harder and faster, he withdrew and thrust again, reaching with each surge for the pinnacle of ultimate bliss.

He quickly lost all sense of time and place and control. The communication between them was complete, yet it required no words or phrases. It was pure sensation, pure emotion, pure love.

Their bodies tensed at the same moment. They clung to each other in the inferno of passion, gasping and breathless, their senses merged, and their hearts thundering in perfect rhythm.

Jasper closed his eyes and drifted; then he lowered his head, pressing his face against Claire's throat. The stiffness that had surrounded his heart for years slid away, leaving him with a sense of peace and contentment.

A few minutes later, he left the bed to extinguish the candles and lock the bedchamber door. He wanted total privacy for the rest of the night and the morning.

Claire was nearly asleep when he spooned himself around her back, drawing her closer to his warm body. Closing his eyes, he contemplated the power that was growing between them—the appreciation of each other's unique qualities, the admiration for each other's strengths, and the understanding and acceptance of each other's weaknesses.

So this, he thought, *is love. How very extraordinary.*

Chapter Fifteen

It was not yet dawn when Claire awoke, missing Jasper's solid warmth. She turned suddenly in the large bed, rolling to her side. Her nose collided with something hard. She let out a startled yelp, then burst into laughter as she stared at her equally shocked husband. He was gingerly rubbing his own nose, and she quickly realized that was what she had knocked into.

"Sorry."

"My apologies."

They spoke at the same time, then smiled awkwardly at the happenstance, soon growing silent. Unsure of what to say, the pair simply stared at each other for several long moments.

A flash of uncertainty burned through Claire. She dipped her chin, feeling a sudden shyness at this new intimacy. She had never before slept with a man, or awakened with one by her side. It was a novel and altogether unique experience.

"I thought you had left," she said.

Jasper's eyes grew thoughtful. "I am through with running away."

His fingers reached out and cupped her jaw. His touch was sensual; his features tight with emotions. There was something in his eyes that made her feel glorious, as though she was the most extraordinary, amazing, wondrous creature on earth. Was that what he truly thought of her?

"I am very happy you stayed," she whispered.

"I actually had little choice. You exhausted me until I could barely move." His expression turned mischievous. "And, yet, as tired as I was, I found it nearly impossible to sleep. You, my dear little wife, snore like an old sea captain after a three-day drinking binge."

Claire pushed her pillow aside, gripped the edge tightly, then swung it overhead and brought it down clumsily on Jasper's head. He let out a bellow and reached for her weapon. They tousled for a moment for control of the feathered lump, but Jasper won easily.

Claire watched the pillow intently as it dangled from his left hand, waiting to spring out of the way the moment it came toward her, but Jasper tossed it out of the bed. She felt a momentary pang of disappointment.

"Aren't you going to retaliate?" she asked.

His brows knitted together in a frown. "You are a woman. I would never physically attack a female, even in jest."

"Oh." Claire was unsure how to react. On one hand, she wanted him to be less reserved and more playful, yet she could hardly fault his reasoning. "It pleases me to know you will treat me with such care and respect."

The muted light from the window illuminated Jasper's handsome features. Feeling a delightful sense of possession, Claire eased away a strand of golden hair from his forehead.

He smiled at her. "Of course, I have no compunction when it comes to tickling a woman."

Claire had no time to defend herself. Jasper lunged forward, his hands encircling her waist, his fingertips dancing along the edge of her skin. Within seconds, Claire was shrieking with laughter and scurrying to get away.

"Stop, oh, stop. I cannot breathe," Claire gasped out between bouts of giggles.

"Do you surrender?"

Claire twisted and turned, sinking deeper into the softness of the bed. She giggled something incomprehensible and tried to retaliate, but Jasper had wisely moved his torso out of her reach.

"Yes . . . I . . . surrender." Each word was puffed out in a short staccato rhythm as she fought for breath.

Fairly gloating in victory, Jasper collapsed beside her. He pressed a kiss on her neck. Claire threaded her fingers with his, to keep his hands occupied, then turned so that she faced him.

Jasper leaned forward and placed a soft kiss on the corner of her mouth. "I love hearing you laugh."

His eyes, sparkling with amusement, turned softer. Claire found her gaze drawn to the tempting line of his mouth. "And I love kissing you."

To prove her point, Claire lifted her arms, placed her hands on either side of his head, and kissed him with passionate urgency. Jasper responded immediately.

The kiss deepened and Claire leaned into its heat. Jasper's hands slid up to her shoulders, and he pulled her close until their naked flesh met, chest to chest. She drew in a quick breath as his fingers moved near her breast.

"Touch me," Claire whispered, brushing her breath over his ear. "Run your hands all over me."

She heard him say her name ever so softly as he eagerly obeyed her command; his hands roamed over her back, down to her hips, up her sides. His fingers felt hot as they skimmed her legs and thighs, and then slid down her stomach.

She loved it. Savoring each stroke, relishing each caress, Claire boldly opened her thighs, unafraid to show her sexual needs and desires.

The air was warm and sweet, and the bed was soft and slick. Jasper entered her body in one firm stroke, and Claire welcomed his strength with a cry of passion, a cry of love.

There was something masterful about the way their bodies merged together in a powerful wave of sensual desire. They moved in unison for an immeasurable amount of time, riding the storm of passion, conscious of each other's needs, each giving and receiving pleasure without reservation as they strove to become one.

Nearly overcome with emotion, Claire felt tears gather in her eyes as her climax crested. It came over her like a great tidal wave—an intense mixture of physical pleasure and emotional depth. Her pleasure somehow triggered his and she clung tightly to Jasper when she felt his body begin to shudder, savoring his moment of release nearly as much as her own.

Afterward, they lay wrapped in each other's arms. Claire's head pressed against Jasper's chest, and she listened to the slow, steady beat of his heart. Her heart, now.

With a contented smile, she closed her eyes and drifted back to sleep.

"You will not partner any man in a dance unless he is first approved by me," Jasper instructed. "If you have an interest in seeing any of the walks or exploring the gardens, you will tell me, and I shall accompany you. Though we are attending a private event, the promenades are often littered with lurking rakehells waiting for the opportunity to accost some unsuspecting female."

" 'Tis no wonder that most respectable ladies depart Vauxhall Gardens by two o'clock in the afternoon," Claire muttered.

"As well they should," Jasper replied.

Claire gritted her teeth at her husband's pompous tone. She had been looking forward to this evening for weeks, having heard and read much about the famous Vauxhall Gardens.

It was the perfect evening for an outdoor party, with pleasant temperatures and clear skies. Fireworks were planned, and Claire was hoping the tightrope walker, Mme. Saqui, who was paid an exorbitant fee of 100 guineas per week, would perform.

Yet Jasper's overbearing manner was becoming a true annoyance. Earlier he had told her he would not have allowed this outing if it had not involved a private party hosted by one of the most influential matrons of the *ton.*

Claire lifted her chin to meet her husband's gaze. He had not ceased issuing orders and commands since leaving the house. Though his concern was appreciated, Claire acknowledged that she was also feeling a small degree of annoyance. She did not like being considered a lackwit, and she did not enjoy being treated like a wayward child.

Given the bizarre events at the theater last night, she knew there was a need for extra caution and extra vigilance whenever she was out in public. After all, she was not a complete idiot.

She opened her mouth to express that very sentiment to her husband, but the words caught in her throat. They were traveling to the gardens by boat. Dusk was drawing on quickly, but the rays from the lantern hanging on the prow of the boat reflected off the water, illuminating his features.

The usual arrogance was obvious in the broad planes of Jasper's face, but it was tempered with great concern. And shining from his eyes was unmistakable love.

Claire's heart slammed against her chest, thumping painfully against her ribs. She wiped a nervous hand across her forehead, worried she would find it damp.

"Are you ill?" Jasper asked. "Should we return home?"

"I am fine."

The feelings revealed in his face shook her to her toes. In her heart, she believed he would someday come to love her. And now, though he had not spoken the words aloud, doubts that had lingered over the nature of his true feelings had vanished.

As they neared the step leading from the water, Claire could hear the distant sound of music. The air was filled with the heady scent of flowers. It caused a momentary distraction, but Claire's attention quickly returned to the man who carefully assisted her out of the boat.

She continued to hold Jasper's hand tightly once she reached solid ground and did not relinquish her grip until the rest of their group strolled together through the entrance.

"We should do a bit of exploring before we make an appearance at the party," Jasper's father suggested.

"Oh, yes," the countess quickly agreed. "I want to visit the arcades."

Arm in arm they set off down one of the many paths that were lit by gas lamps strung through the trees. Lady

Meredith and her husband fell in step behind them, and Jason joined his sister and brother-in-law.

Claire hesitated a moment before accepting her husband's offered arm. They had fallen behind the others, and she used this brief moment of privacy to lift her chin and whisper softly in his ear, "I love you, too, Jasper."

The party was in full swing when they finally arrived. They were met by their hostess, Lady Ansley, one of the *ton's* social leaders. She swept forward to greet them, making a great fuss over Jason, who she called the wayward son, as she scolded him for missing the beginning of the Season's society events.

"You must allow me to find you some suitable dancing partners," Lady Ansley said.

"I thank you for the kind offer, my lady," Jason replied with a steady smile. "I fear all the most discerning mothers will hide their daughters and race toward the exits the moment I show any interest."

Lady Ansley's lashes fluttered from behind her fan and she looked at him with a properly coy glance. "Not if I make the introductions."

"Precisely." Jason tugged the older woman's hand from her side and lifted it to his lips. She giggled like a young miss as he bent his head and placed a courtly kiss on her gloved knuckles.

Jasper worked hard to conceal his snort of disgust. His brother had a real talent for being fussed over by women of all ages. It was a reaction that had the power to quickly get under Jasper's skin, and tonight was no exception.

Yet Jasper was determined to keep his temper in

check. He had reached an uneasy truce with his brother, as they were now united in the cause of keeping Claire safe. In his gut, Jasper knew the day of reckoning between them was bound to come soon, but it would not happen tonight.

Jasper felt the gentle pressure of his wife's fingers on his sleeve and all thoughts of his brother fled.

"Your father has secured a table and wants us to join him in the supper alcove. He told me it was to the left of the Pavilion."

"Come, I'll lead the way."

Jasper was pleased to note there were many more lanterns, and thus more light in this area. Because there was not enough seating for all the guests in the section of alcoves allocated for the party, small tables had been arranged along the edge of the dance floor, each laid with a starched white cloth and set formally with the finest china, crystal, and silver. A colored lantern glowed at the center of each table.

When they arrived, their table was already laden with a lavish assortment of delicacies. Serving platters nearly overflowed with oysters, pork cutlets, salmon, prawns, hare with morels, and roast sweetbreads. Several bottles of chilled champagne and a rich red wine to wash it all down also cluttered the small space.

" 'Tis a far cry from the usual fare of salty ham, tough chicken, and stale biscuits that are offered here," Jasper commented as he filled his plate. "Lady Ansley's chef is a genius."

Lady Meredith laughed. "Jasper is right. One does not come to Vauxhall to enjoy the food."

"Ah, but tonight is the exception," the earl interjected. He refilled everyone's champagne goblet, emptying the bottle. "I am very pleased that Claire's first visit to the gardens is turning into such a delightful experience."

They all toasted and drank, then continued to feast, making noticeable headway in consuming the food. As they were finishing the meal, a handsome, older gentleman, dressed all in black, appeared at the entrance to the box.

"I would like to request the honor of a dance, Countess."

Jasper's mother smiled brightly, drained her champagne glass, and put out her hand. Seeing Claire glance with interest toward the dance floor, Jasper hastily wiped his mouth with his linen napkin, then led his wife out for the next dance.

I love you, too, Jasper. The words she had spoken to him moments before echoed in his mind as they paced through the steps. She had said them to him last night also, but earlier this evening she had added one very significant word. *Too.*

She knew. Jasper was unsure if he felt relief or annoyance that she understood his feelings better than he did. It really was rather disarming to admit that one's wife was perceptive enough to so easily know something that intimate and personal.

"Why are you scowling?" Claire whispered as they came together. "Is something amiss?"

You are right. I do love you. Jasper's heart pounded like cannon fire as the words swirled in his head. Yet he did not say them. This was hardly an appropriate time or place to declare his feelings for the first time.

Fortunately, the vigorous intricacies of the country dance made it difficult to converse. Jasper flashed a pleasant grin when he next came close to Claire, hoping to convince her all was well. She looked suspiciously into his eyes, but asked no further questions.

He was spared. For the moment.

A few minutes later, Lord Fairhurst stood at the edge of the dense crowd, unhappily gazing at the dance floor. Claire was currently being partnered by his father, would next dance with his brother, and then the marquess, so her safety was momentarily assured. Yet still he worried. Though this was supposed to be a private party, Vauxhall Gardens was a very public place, and it was all too easy for the uninvited to slip in with the guests.

A whirl of fashionable couples danced merrily by, and Jasper admitted that it was probably those individuals who had been invited that he needed to be most concerned about. With keen eyes, he scanned the crowd, suspecting he would find Squire Dorchester somewhere.

But, instead, his eyes discovered a very familiar female face. Before he could turn, his eyes met her gaze. Her lips compressed into a disapproving line, and Jasper waited, with a faint tinge of amusement, for her to turn her back and give him a direct cut.

She surprised him utterly by giving him a short, jerky nod of acknowledgment. Admiring the courage it took, he returned the gesture. Not a muscle moved on her plain face in reaction. Yet she continued to boldly return his gaze.

The music ended and the next set of couples began to take the floor. The few women clustered around Miss Anne Manning gradually disappeared, as they were claimed by male partners for the upcoming dance.

Anne stood alone. Following an impulse he did not

take the time to understand, Lord Fairhurst approached her.

"The next dance is about to begin, Miss Manning. If you are not otherwise engaged, I would be honored if you would partner me."

Anne blushed. There was an awkward silence that was finally broken when her mouth curved into a smile. In a soft voice barely above a whisper, she accepted his invitation. Jasper bowed and led her to the dance floor.

During the months that he had paid court to Rebecca, Jasper had taken little notice of her older sister. Though she often accompanied Rebecca as a chaperone, Anne's presence barely registered in his mind.

Anne rarely spoke, never offered any opinions, and seemed to scurry away anytime he was near. More often than not, she was like a ghost in the shadows, hovering on the edges, a dim presence that was faintly seen and barely acknowledged.

Once they had inadvertently left Anne behind after strolling the gravel paths in Hyde Park and did not realize her absence until their carriage had driven away. Embarrassed, Jasper had told his driver to immediately turn around. Anne had expressed no anger at the mishap, though she had appeared shaken and distressed. It was Rebecca who had displayed the emotions, scolding her sister for causing such an inconvenience.

Jasper wondered if this skittish behavior was an ingrained part of her nature, yet as the waltz began, Anne went readily into his arms. Perhaps he had misjudged her shyness. Or maybe she had finally managed to overcome it.

He caught her eyes as they whirled out of a turn, and she hastily lowered her gaze. They continued to dance for a few moments without speaking. He tried to remember if he had ever seen her with a beau, but could not recall any men showing her more than polite interest.

Jasper dipped his head closer to hers. "Are you enjoying yourself this evening?"

"Yes, very much," she responded, slightly breathless. "And you?"

"I find that the evening has much improved since you agreed to this waltz," Jasper responded, realizing it was true.

He had always liked to dance, and Anne was a surprisingly good partner. Jasper wound them around the slower moving couples, and she followed his lead gamely, never missing a step or losing her balance. As one couple drew precariously close, Jasper made a wide, sweeping turn to avoid a collision. That move earned him a sparkling little smile from Anne.

Her sudden animation caught his attention, and Jasper set himself to be his most charming. Anne responded immediately, laughing at his witticisms and even venturing to make a comment or two of her own.

The music drew to a close and they stopped dancing, though Jasper kept his arm loosely around Anne's shoulder to prevent her from being jostled by the crowd. He escorted her off the floor and returned her to her original spot, where a bevy of ladies were once again congregated.

Very aware of his audience, who were feigning disinterest behind their fans, yet listening to every word, Jasper executed a courtly bow. "Thank you for the dance, Miss Manning. I hope you enjoy the rest of your evening."

"And you also, my lord."

She turned away, hesitated, and then looked back over

her shoulder at him. Jasper noticed a happy glow in her eyes. The sight of her joy improved his mood. He suspected she received little happiness in her life and was pleased to play a small part in making this a pleasant evening for her.

Rebecca Manning waited impatiently until the third set of dancing began before slipping away from the party. Her father had given strict instructions to both his daughters, demanding that they stay clear of the secluded paths, but Rebecca had no intention of obeying that order.

Her emotions churned in a flutter of fear and excitement as she hurried away, knowing her father would be furious if she were discovered. Yet her father's pleasure was of little concern to her these days. Another man controlled her behavior, dominated her waking thoughts and actions, oftentimes so completely that Rebecca hardly recognized herself.

A part of her knew that Richard was pure wickedness, yet she ignored any internal signals to be cautious. The squire made her body burn to be near his, and she took foolish, unwise risks to please him, for he was the prize she yearned to have no matter how great the cost.

It took several moments for Rebecca's eyes to adjust to the deeper darkness of the Lover's Walk. Behind her, the distant lights of the party faded, along with the lively minuet the orchestra was playing. Following the instructions she had been given earlier, she gingerly walked along the path until she arrived at a recessed alcove with a small bench.

It was deserted. Rebecca let out a sigh of disappointment. She had expected her lover to be waiting for her.

She paced impatiently in the confined space, the smell of trailing tendrils of fragrant honeysuckle making her feel slightly ill. Her thoughts were scattered and distracted. She never heard the sound of footsteps approaching and had to stifle a scream when a masculine arm grasped her from behind and closed tightly around her waist.

"Are you alone?"

"Yes."

"Good." The squire pressed himself tightly against the full length of her back. Rebecca's breath caught. She felt her nipples peak and her body soften and quiver with expectation. Her almost immediate desire for him was always difficult to disguise.

She tried to turn and face him, hoping for a proper kiss, but the squire held her imprisoned. He drew a reckless hand through her upswept hair, and she heard several pins drop to the ground.

"We must be careful," she said breathlessly. "Anyone could come by and see us."

"I thought you liked that, Rebecca. Having someone watch."

She closed her eyes in shame, recalling a tryst they had shared earlier in the week when his servant, a lusty young stable lad, had watched from the shadows as Richard stripped her naked and mounted her like a stallion takes a mare.

The inhibitions of a lifetime had crumbled easily in the face of her newly awakened desire, for when she was with Richard, her needs, her desires, her cravings, ruled her every action.

" 'Twas only that one time," she whispered feebly. "I did it because you asked. I did it to please you."

"So you claim. But we both know the truth of the matter, do we not? You enjoyed it even more than I."

He bent his head and nipped the inside of her neck with his lips and teeth. Rebecca trembled with passion, but she tried again to hide it, willing herself to remain perfectly still. If Richard knew how much she desired him, he would cease his caresses immediately, just to punish her.

His hand reached down and bunched her skirts, wrinkling the fine silk of her gown. Rebecca did not care. Deliberately teasing her, his sly touch glided between her legs. His hand cupped possessively over her mound, and Rebecca whimpered with excitement.

He pulled back. She groaned, panting in frustration. Richard laughed. It was a harsh, ugly sound.

"You are hot for me tonight," he taunted. "But you shall not get what you need until you do as I say."

Rebecca's chin jutted mulishly. "Why must I wait? You should be doing your utmost to please me, in hopes that I will grant you a boon and do as you ask."

The squire snorted. "Do not try my patience by saying provoking things. I am in no mood for it."

Rebecca turned her head toward him and sulked. But she was too unsure of Richard to push her point further. "What do you want?"

His eyes lit with triumph. Rebecca lifted her face closer to his. Richard lowered his head and kissed her on the mouth. It was a brief meeting of the lips, so fleeting that, for an instant, she thought she might have imagined it.

Flustered, Rebecca pushed her shoulder boldly forward, trying to turn her body toward his as she searched for more. The squire jerked his head away.

"I want you to lure Lady Fairhurst down this secluded path, and then abandon her here."

Rebecca ceased her movements as a protest rose to her lips. "How am I going to accomplish such a ridiculous task? Given our rather awkward past history, Lady Fairhurst and I avoid each other by unspoken agreement. In fact, we have never even been formally introduced."

"There are over a hundred guests in attendance tonight. If you are so concerned about the proprieties, find someone to make a proper introduction."

Rebecca felt her blood begin to simmer. "Why? Why is it necessary for Lady Fairhurst to come here?"

Richard's hand began tangling the wisps of hair at the back of her neck. It hurt as he pulled at the strands, bruising the tender flesh on her neck. But she said nothing, fearing he would remove his hands entirely.

"Think, you little idiot! Has it not been your goal to humiliate Fairhurst? What better way to exact revenge than by compromising his bride? Will it not be scandalous for her to be discovered alone on a secluded path in the arms of a gentleman who is not her husband?"

Rebecca's temper flared as a sharp ache rose inside her. "You are planning on seducing her!" She let out a screech of anger and lunged at the squire, but Richard had not relinquished his hold, making it difficult for her to strike back. "I will not allow it!"

"Your extremes of emotions are so damn tedious," Richard retorted, his ever tightening grip now bordering on painful. "Remove that bloodthirsty look of jealousy from your eyes at once."

Rebecca trembled. More than anything she wanted to lash out, to make him feel the same anger and hurt that coursed through her veins, yet she worked hard to rein in her temper, fearing the consequences.

Even in her anger, she felt the hot, glowing embers of attraction for this man smolder. Richard was an enigma to her, but she was caught too tightly in his web to shake her fascination for him.

"You will do exactly as I tell you and all will go according to my plan," the squire continued. With surprising gentleness, he brushed back a stray lock of her hair, the light caress of his fingertips as intimate as the kisses she craved. "Arguing will only try my patience and waste time. Do you understand?"

Though she longed to disagree, Rebecca wisely jerked her head in agreement.

"Good." He reached out and traced her cheek with his fingers, the tender gesture at odds with the malice gleaming from his eyes. "I am pleased to discover that after these many weeks together you are finally learning that I always get what I want."

Chapter Sixteen

The first person Rebecca encountered upon returning to the party was her father. As she drew near, she could tell by the set of his jaw that he had been drinking and his mood was not pleasant.

Her initial instinct was to turn and run, but she quickly realized it was too late. He had already seen her.

"Where the blazes have you been?" Charles Manning barked. "I sent your sister to look for you over an hour ago."

"Father, please, lower your voice."

Rebecca tensed as an interested matron glanced their way and stood for a moment, watching them. Rebecca smiled brightly, hoping to convey that all was well.

Eventually, the woman was distracted by something else. Rebecca sighed inwardly, pleased to have avoided a scene. Until her father once again opened his mouth.

"Where have you been?" he repeated.

"Dancing," Rebecca lied. "First with Lord Hartley and later with Mr. Drummond."

"I saw Hartley not more than ten minutes ago. He never mentioned it."

Rebecca's heart leaped, and unexpected nerves tightened in her stomach, but she did not show a trace of her emotions. " 'Twas only a dance, Father. One of many that both of us have engaged in this evening. I'm sure Lord Hartley thought it was not significant enough to say anything to you."

Charles Manning's dark eyes narrowed in suspicion. "Why do I get the feeling that you are lying to me, Rebecca?" he asked, in a dark voice.

Her father's fingers closed around her wrist. He applied a strong amount of pressure, but this did not elicit the usual whimpering response from his daughter. For an instant, Rebecca felt frightened, but then her newly acquired hauteur surged back and she nearly broke into a smile. Her father's puny attempts at force were nothing compared with the squire's discipline.

She pulled her hand away. "I have told you where I was, Father. 'Tis your problem if you have difficulty accepting it as truth."

"You will not speak to me in such a disrespectful manner, young woman!"

He advanced menacingly, but Rebecca held her ground. Though he blistered and shouted and, every so often, struck his daughters, this was too public a place for such uncontrollable behavior. Like Rebecca, Charles Manning understood all too well the necessity of keeping up appearances.

"There you are," Anne interrupted. "I walked clear to the other side of the dance floor, yet had a suspicion that you would already be back here with Father."

Her voice was steady, but her twittering hands let Rebecca know that Anne had taken note of their father's fire-and-brimstone look.

Rebecca breathed a sigh of relief. For once she was actually glad to see her older sister. She needed a buffer and a distraction if she were to accomplish the squire's directive. Anne would provide that easily.

"Have you also questioned Anne as to her whereabouts this evening?" Rebecca asked when her sister joined them.

"Why would I bother?" Charles replied. He took a sloppy gulp of his whiskey, dribbling a small amount of liquid out of the side of his mouth. "I know Anne has been sitting in the shadows along with the other undesirable ladies for most of the night. I doubt she has been partnered for even one dance."

Rebecca smiled smugly, and then glanced at her sister. She was surprised to note a blush prickle Anne's cheeks. Had her sister for once been doing something she ought not?

Rebecca removed the handkerchief from her father's breast coat pocket and solicitously wiped his wet mouth. Then she linked her arm with his and bent her head to whisper to him in the confidential manner he preferred.

Fortunately for Rebecca, he was just enough in his cups not to recognize her blatant ploy to worm her way back into his favor.

"I never meant to cause you any problems," Rebecca insisted in a sweet tone. "You know I am always an obedient daughter, trusting in your judgment and following your orders. I really think you need to spend more time worrying about Anne, Father. Whatever are we going to do with her? 'Tis she who desperately needs your assistance in finding a husband."

"I do not require Father's help," Anne interjected.

Rebecca raised an astonished eyebrow at her sister. "Oh, really? Shall we all be miraculously surprised by a forthcoming declaration from a proper gentleman? Can we expect an official announcement soon?"

For some odd reason, this comment raised Anne's hackles. "That is my personal business."

"Stop baiting your sister," Charles instructed as he let out a weary sigh. " 'Tis hardly a fair contest."

For an instant, Rebecca was tempted to press on, but her objective was to mellow her father's mood. "Fetch Father some food," Rebecca demanded of Anne. "I am sure he would welcome the chance to sample some of Lady Ansley's fine cuisine. I have heard several of the other guests rave about this evening's offerings."

"Don't bother. We are leaving," Charles announced. "Gather your things together at once."

"But, Father, 'tis early," Rebecca said with an edge of panic, knowing if she left now she would be unable to follow Richard's orders. "Can we not at least stay until the fireworks? They are set to go off soon, at midnight."

"You can see them from the carriage window as we ride home."

"I want to watch them from the Pavilion."

"No." Charles glowered at Rebecca, the tic in his jaw emphasizing the strength of his resolve. But Rebecca was equally committed to having her own way. She favored her father with a smile that was little more than the baring of her teeth.

"I have promised the next set of dances to Squire Dorchester. I cannot leave until I fulfill my obligation."

"Send a note of apology to him in the morning," Charles instructed.

"That would be horribly rude," Rebecca answered in a stricken voice. "The squire has been a most attentive escort. You should be pleased that he has shown me such marked regard."

"Humph." Charles snorted and gave her a doubtful look. "I have not heard any proposals of marriage from the man's lips. Not that I would welcome his suit. With your looks, you can do far better than a mere country squire."

"He is a wealthy man from a respected lineage," Rebecca retorted hotly, defending her lover. "It would be an excellent match for me."

Charles Manning's eyes flared with anger. "I do not care how well his pockets are lined. He is not Fairhurst. His income cannot compare to the viscount's, and his title is merely a courtesy."

"Fairhurst is a prig," Rebecca said shortly. "His lineage may be more noble, but his family is infamous in certain circles. I believed he was different, and sadly have learned he is just as bad as many of his wretched ancestors. I count us lucky to have avoided forging a union with such a family. We are head and shoulders above them all."

"Fairhurst's connections in society and business would have been invaluable to me," Charles lamented. "Now that he is lost, we must make certain you contract an equal or better match."

"I cannot snare the requisite husband if I do not attend the proper events," Rebecca complained.

"We have attended tonight's party," Charles retorted. "And now we are leaving."

"But the evening's festivities have hardly begun."

"We have been here for hours, more than enough time for you to see and be seen. Besides, there will be a higher demand for your company if you are not so easily accessible."

Charles turned, but not before Rebecca saw the spiteful satisfaction glittering in his eyes. He was only insisting they leave because he knew how much she wanted to stay. Hateful man! Feeling an edge of desperation, Rebecca lost control of her tongue. "Stop being such a stubborn fool!"

She regretted the words the moment they left her lips. Her father was arrogant and vicious when thwarted. She was not generally so careless, but her mind was centered on finding Lady Fairhurst and leading her where the squire commanded.

Charles stiffened. When he turned to face her, the gleam in his eyes showed true fury. "No one tells me what to do. Especially my half-witted daughters. Do you understand me?" When she did not respond quickly enough, he shouted, "Do you?"

"Yes!"

Rebecca's chest was tight and her footsteps clumsy as she marched away. She briefly considered trying to lose herself in the crowd, but her father stayed so close on her heels, she realized he could grab her before she had a chance to disappear.

Richard would be furious at her failure to do his bidding, but there was no help for it. Lady Fairhurst's disgrace would have to wait until another day.

As Lord Fairhurst traversed the darkened path of the Lover's Walk, it reminded him of being a youngster playing a spirited game of hide and seek. All was quiet except for the crunch of his boots on the gravel path, the faint rustling of leaves in the tall trees overhead, and the occasional jittery female giggle echoing through the darkness.

It was that last, rather distinct sound, that made him very aware of the many couples half hidden in the shadows. He tried carefully to avoid them, assuming none would be especially interested in being "found."

Yet, as he rounded the turn in the path of one of the

lesser used byways, where the gas lamps strung in the trees were few and far between, he happened upon an intimate encounter that was progressing quickly beyond the usual stolen kiss or two.

A silver gleam of moonlight illuminated the ardent couple. The clever fellow had lured his partner into a most secluded spot, backing her into a corner surrounded by tall trees and thick shrubs. There were no avenues of escape, though judging by the looks of their passionate embrace, escape was the furthest thought from the woman's mind.

The man's coat had been removed and was presumably flung somewhere in the shadows. His shirt was undone and pulled free of his breeches, the stark white tails hanging along the sides of his hips.

His partner was cradled in his arms, melting bonelessly against him. Jasper assumed her clothing was in a similar state of undress, though he was too much of a gentleman to look closely.

Jasper started to back away, preparing to disappear before he was noticed, when he realized there was something very familiar about the man. Eyebrows raised, he squinted into the darkness, looking again at the couple, from one to the other.

Hell and damnation! Jasper loudly cleared his throat. Twice.

The woman remained unaware of his presence, apparently too engrossed in her passion to notice anything but the man who held her so tightly in his arms. But the man seemed to register that they were no longer alone, and that his pleasure was being interrupted. His back stiffened, and he slowly lifted his head.

Neither twin showed any emotions as their eyes met.

For a long moment silence prevailed. "Was there

something in particular you wanted?" Jason finally asked.

The sound of his voice startled his partner. She began to struggle, leaving his brother no choice but to dislodge himself from the embrace. Jasper caught sight of the woman's frantic face as she turned her back and attempted to smooth her garments into place.

Lady Sandra Norton was best known in society for two things—her unhappy marriage and her ample bosom. Apparently, his brother was taking full advantage of both.

After achieving some semblance of order to her person, Lady Norton was now faced with the impossible task of making a discreet exit. Because she was cornered in the alcove, the only route of escape led directly past Jasper.

Jason threw back his shoulders, his posture almost challenging. "There is no need to be worried about your reputation, sweetheart. Lord Fairhurst is the very soul of discretion. He would never lower himself to engage in common gossip," Jason declared loudly as he brushed a few leaves from the back of her cloak.

Lady Norton did not seem convinced. "Any unsavory rumors could quickly plunge me into disgrace," she replied nervously. "Lord Norton would be most upset."

Then you should have considered your actions more carefully before accompanying my brother to this secluded location, thought Jasper. But he did not speak his mind, saying instead, "I can assure you that no one will learn of this little interlude from me."

Lady Norton let out a shuddering gasp of relief. She spoke in low tones to Jason for a few moments, then buried her head under the hood of her cloak. Her eyes were luminous as she ran by Jasper.

Jason captured her elbow and made a move to accompany her, but she fended off his assistance. "No, please, I can find my way back on my own."

Her footsteps were barely audible as she hurried away. Jasper assumed she was running so quickly her feet hardly touched the ground.

Now alone, Jasper took a moment to study his brother. Jason stared right back.

"What drives you to be so reckless?" Jasper asked, breaking the lengthy silence. "Will you not be content until you carry the scars from the sword of a cuckolded husband on your body?"

"Better a sword than a pistol at my back while I say my wedding vows," Jason responded. "If I cannot dally with the matrons, that leaves the chits searching for a proper husband and their overbearing mamas. Them I avoid at all costs." Jason shoved his shirttails back into his breeches. "Do not be fooled by Lady Norton's flustered air of innocence. She came with me of her own free will, knowing exactly what to expect."

"And that makes it acceptable?" Jasper paced the small alcove. "Can you not confine your efforts to the younger widows instead of the married noblewomen? What if someone other than myself had discovered you? Lord Norton's fierce temper is well-known, rivaled only by his skill with both sword and pistol."

Jason shrugged, and Jasper felt his own shoulders tense. The last thing he wanted was to quarrel with his brother, but it was difficult to keep quiet when confronted with such self-destructive behavior.

Choosing Lady Norton for a potential affair was sheer insanity. Lord Norton was a possessive and jealous man. It was said that his quick temper accounted for his skills with both pistol and sword, because his lack of a reasonable response in countless situations provided him more experience on the dueling field than any member of the nobility.

Still, in the spirit of trying to keep some degree of peace between them, Jasper held back the scathing lecture playing through his mind.

This restraint clearly confused his brother. “Is that all you are going to say, my lord? No tirade about how I have nearly ruined the family with my thoughtless behavior, how I have proven myself once again to be a great disappointment?” Jason raked a hand through his mussed hair. “Bloody hell, brother, if you are not demanding that I act as contrite as a choirboy, you must finally be mellowing in your old age.”

Jasper breathed deeply, searching for calm. “There is no need for me to say a word, Jason. Clearly, you fully understand the dangers of your behavior. It only remains to see what you intend to do next.”

“Do?” Jason burst into laughter. “Why I shall do what I have always done. What we both have always done; that is, until you grew a sense of propriety and responsibility that is so large it could sink a frigate.” The laughter ceased. “I shall continue my life as a shameless sinner, rarely taken with noble thoughts or intentions.”

“That is not who you are, that is who you choose to be,” Jasper said quietly.

“No, that is the role I have been given,” Jason retorted. “You are Fairhurst, and one day will become the Earl of Stafford. And I, well, I am the reckless twin, the man who courts scandal at every turn, the one whose antics often become the topic of conversation in the most fashionable London drawing rooms, the man who proves that in the end Barrington blood will run true because it is tainted with generations of wastrels, rakes, and scoundrels."

Jason retrieved his coat from the shadows and shrugged into it before continuing. "We are two halves that make up one whole, Jasper. So remember this, if I were not so bad, then you would not have the opportunity to be so good."

Jasper folded his arms across his chest. "That is just an excuse for being irresponsible."

"Perhaps. But it works well for me."

Jasper gave his twin a wry smile. "For all your faults, I never took you for a coward."

Jason's face turned pale in the moonlight, his hands balled into fists at his side. His stare was like ice. "What did you call me?"

"A coward," Jasper repeated. "You have decided to waste your life rather than live it, to hide behind a facade of youthful indulgence rather than accept the responsibilities of a mature man."

Jasper dropped his arms to his side and waited with intense alertness for the explosion to come. But his brother surprised him by turning away.

"If I did not know better, I would think you were trying to provoke me into a duel," Jason scoffed.

"But that would cause a scandal, which I abhor," Jasper quipped, strangely let down by Jason's mild response. He was hoping to hit a nerve, to jolt his brother into facing the truth, but Jason refused to rise to the bait.

Suddenly, there was a screeching noise, followed by a loud burst. Both men glanced up and watched the shards of colored sparks illuminate the night sky. Standing side by side, they were silent for a long moment, each lost in their own thoughts.

"Where is Claire?" Jason asked.

"She is with Mother and Meredith. All three women were going to see the jugglers, and then wait in our supper alcove to watch the fireworks." As if on cue, another brilliantly colored shell burst in the sky. "I had better get back. We were planning on departing as soon as the fireworks ended. Will you be joining us?"

Jason paused, seeming to consider the suggestion. "No, 'tis early. I believe I shall stay at the party a while longer and see what other pleasures the evening holds."

Jasper was unable to help the slight stiffening of his back as he heard his brother's remarks, but he did not scold. He was disappointed, though not surprised, by Jason's answer. "Walk to the Pavilion with me. Mother will expect you to bid her good night."

Jason eyed him with cool wariness, but when his twin gestured toward the gravel path, he went. Both men were silent as they walked.

"There is something I have wanted to ask since you returned to London," Jasper said, turning his head. His gaze bore into Jason. "Why did you use my name on the marriage certificate when you married Claire?"

The question halted his twin dead in his tracks. His mouth thinned, then he cleared his throat. "For some unfathomable reason, I thought it was a good idea at the time. But I'll be damned if I can recall what prompted that decision now."

Jasper gave him a pained look. His ever flippant twin did not even have the good grace to look guilty. "I am serious."

"I was drunk?"

"I don't doubt that, but there has to be more to the story."

"Perhaps I enjoy manipulating people and don't give

a damn about the consequences," Jason responded, but his jaded grin did not reach his eyes.

Jasper's jaw knotted. "That might hold true when it comes to me, but I have seen you with Claire. You have a true regard for her. I cannot believe you would deliberately subject her to any unpleasantness."

He could tell by Jason's frown that this was not easy for him, but he refused to drop the matter. This was one stunt for which his brother needed to be held accountable.

"I met Claire purely by accident on my travels and found her to be an exceptionally fine woman. In the course of our friendship, I discovered that she could only gain financial independence through marriage. Dorchester was pressuring her to make a match, and she feared offending him and upsetting her parents."

"So you came to the rescue?" Jasper said in an ironic tone.

"In a manner of speaking." Jason rolled his shoulders in discomfort. "Claire and I agreed we never wanted a traditional marriage, and thus thought it best to live separate lives. I knew I was not going to be around, so I decided her best source of protection lay in a noble title. And since I did not have one of my own, I decided to borrow yours."

"And to hell with the legalities?" Jasper said in disgust, shaking his head at his brother's audacity. "Did it never cross your mind that the union might not be legal? Or even worse, that you had inadvertently tied *me* to a woman whom I had never met and knew nothing about?"

"Oh, for God's sake, give me some credit." Jason's cheeks puffed out; then he blew out a loud breath. "I consulted a solicitor in a neighboring village before the wedding. Even as I said my vows, I knew the ceremony was not binding for either you or me."

Jasper's brow shot up in shock. "You did this deliberately? And what about Claire? Was she ever going to be told the truth?"

Jason shifted uneasily from one foot to the other. "I planned on telling her eventually. But in the meantime, she would have obtained her freedom, her financial independence, and protection from Dorchester. With all those benefits, I saw no harm in the situation."

"No harm?" Jasper straightened his shoulders. "You deliberately deceived her. She believed it was a real marriage."

"She had to, or else the plan would have failed." Jason gazed steadily at his brother. "Claire had to be a wife in order to collect her inheritance, and I assumed her married state would discourage Dorchester. She is a terrible liar. I considered it, but then realized even if I could persuade her to enact the charade, she never would have been able to pretend to be my wife."

Jasper shook his head in amazement, hardly believing what he was hearing. His brother had knowingly entered into this deceptive union under the misguided notion that he was *helping* Claire? The logic of the argument was so perverse, it nearly made sense.

"What exactly were you planning to do, if after you told Claire of your duplicity, she disagreed with your tactics?"

Jason squirmed uncomfortably. "I figured when she finally learned the truth, she would be relieved to discover she was not saddled with me as her husband for the rest of her life."

"My God, Jason, you have done some ludicrous

things in your life, but this is the most idiotic, ill-conceived—"

"I do not understand what you are complaining about," Jason interrupted hotly. "My stunt has captured you a wife, an extraordinary woman that never would have entered your stuffy, narrow, proper little world if not for me. Clearly, you see her worth, or else you would not have *legally* married her at the earliest opportunity."

For an instant, Jasper could only gape at him. "Forgive me if I do not applaud your lunacy," he finally retorted, unable to keep the sarcasm from his voice.

Though a part of him knew he should be grateful to his brother for inadvertently bringing Claire into his life, Jasper could not so easily forgive or forget such reckless behavior. "Regardless of the outcome, this was an inexcusable breech of trust, as well as a mockery of the sacred institution of marriage. I cannot believe you would sink so low."

"And yet I should have guessed that somehow it would all turn out right for you, brother." Jason stifled a sigh, then thrust his chin out defiantly. "More than right, actually. Claire is a far better wife than you deserve."

The words gave Jasper pause. "I am well aware of that fact. 'Tis the only reason I am able to hold my fists by my side each time I see you."

"Not every time, brother." Jason tilted his head and reflectively rubbed his hand along his jaw, where the slight shadow of a bruise was still evident. "You sucker punched me the moment you had the opportunity."

"I was angry."

"Well, I hope you have gotten over it."

"I'm trying, but God knows you make it damn hard sometimes," Jasper replied gruffly. He leveled a stern glare at Jason, seeking to come to grips with the myriad of emotions that played inside him. "Yet no matter how impossible you are, no matter how incorrigible you act, it always boils down to one inescapable reality."

Jason eyed him askance. "And what, dare I ask, is that?"

"You are my brother, Jason, and despite how hard you push me, how desperately you try my patience, how intensely you seek to drive me to the very brink of sanity, I will never forsake you. The bond of blood and brotherhood we share, though it may at times be pulled and strained and stretched to its very limits, will never break." His face hardened. "Never."

There was a heartbeat of silence. For a second, Jasper regretted his words, worried that his honesty might have driven an even wider wedge between them. But then he recapitulated. He had spoken the truth. Perhaps that would make a difference.

Jason heaved a sigh. "I'm sorry, Jasper. I suppose I have been acting like a prize idiot."

Slowly, Jasper extended his hand. With a smile of relief, his brother clasped it firmly.

"You've changed," Jason remarked with surprise. "And thankfully for the better."

"Stop sounding so amazed." Jasper grinned; then he chuckled loudly. He reached out with his free hand and pulled his brother into a tight hug. "Yes, thanks to Claire, I have managed to change. Now, 'tis your turn."

Chapter Seventeen

"I do not understand why you insisted we meet here," Rebecca hissed, as she gave an uneasy glance around the dining room to ensure that no one in the vicinity was eavesdropping. " 'Tis far too risky. What if someone comes in and recognizes me? My father believes I am spending the afternoon at the dressmaker's. He will have apoplexy if he discovers I am out with you, unchaperoned."

Richard took another bite of his beef, then put down his knife and fork. "This establishment is too far away from the fashionable shopping district to be frequented by anyone of your acquaintance."

"I can believe that," Rebecca snapped, pushing away her uneaten plate of food. "The floor is filthy, the table linen stained. I shudder to think what sorts of vermin reside in the kitchen. How can you so eagerly ingest this slop?"

"It's delicious," Richard said. He cut another large chunk of rare roast beef and stuffed it in his mouth with an exaggerated motion, attacking his food with all the gusto of a starving man.

Rebecca squeezed her eyes shut and shuddered. Her revulsion brought a small smile to the squire's lips, the only bit of sunshine in this otherwise gray, rainy day when the weather matched his mood exactly. He was becoming tired of London, bored with Rebecca, and impatient to enact his long-awaited revenge against Claire and her noble husband.

"We should have arranged to meet somewhere more secluded, more private," Rebecca whined. Her hand slid across the table, and her nimble fingers began stroking the flesh of his exposed wrist. "I do not have to return home for two hours. 'Tis not too late for us to take a slow carriage ride around the park, with the shades drawn."

The look on her face told him if their chairs were closer together, she would most likely be reaching under the table to grab hold of his cock. Richard shuddered. Rebecca's invitation left him strangely disinterested. She had become far too predictable. It was almost as if he knew what she would say before she even opened her mouth. He took another bite of his meal and, not for the first time, wished she were not so necessary to his plans.

"Your eagerness delights me, but we must be careful." As he uttered the lie, Richard struggled to sound as reasonable and gentlemanly as possible.

He knew the value of being charming. Though she was pathetically obvious in her eagerness to please him, Rebecca possessed a vicious temper. Now was not the time to risk igniting it. Not when he was finally so close to achieving his revenge.

Rebecca made a sound that was not quite a sob. "There was a time, not too long ago, when you would have been the one insisting we take that carriage drive," she accused.

Though he managed to keep the bulk of his annoyance hidden, the squire's eyes made an insulting appraisal of his companion. "Stop pouting, dearest. It contorts your face into a most unattractive expression."

All pretense of upset vanished instantly. Rebecca's eyes blazed. "I want to leave. Immediately."

"Then do so. I shall not prevent it."

"Fine! The moment you make the arrangements for a hackney, I will depart," Rebecca said, interjecting ice into her voice.

Tension crackled in the air and all the pent-up frustration inside Richard rushed forward. *Oh, how he wanted to follow through with her demand and send her fleeing into the streets!* He was heartily sick of Rebecca Manning. She was spoiled, selfish, and vain. To his mind, she was in sore need of a sound thrashing, and he was just the man to do it.

They fell silent when the waiter approached with a second bottle of wine the squire had ordered earlier. "Just leave it on the table," he instructed.

Richard topped off their goblets. Rebecca shook her head, turning up her nose as though the liquid were putrid. "I don't want any wine. Tell the waiter to take it away."

The squire studied her for a moment, his head to one side, feigning interest in her obvious distress. His regard caused her anger to gradually soften, and Richard decided he needed to tell her what he required of her before it reemerged.

"Would you like me to order something else for you to drink? Or eat?" It took considerable effort to put an edge of concern in his voice.

"No." She continued to sulk, and he continued to act as though he gave a damn about it, even though his patience was wearing thin. Soon, the effort succeeded. Rebecca blinked hard. One hand fluttered up to her throat.

"Your moods are a constant puzzlement to me, Richard. I do not understand why you insist on treating me so deplorably."

Bloody hell, now she wanted to talk about his moods! The squire tapped his fingertips rhythmically on the tabletop, the only outward sign betraying his inner agitation. Rebecca was too absorbed in her own emotions to notice.

He pushed his plate away, suddenly losing his appetite; then lifted his goblet and took a big swallow of his wine. "Forgive me if I have distressed you in any way." The words nearly stuck in his throat, but he forced them out. "Though I have struggled to ignore it, I am still a bit annoyed over your failure last night to deliver Lady Fairhurst to me as you promised."

Rebecca shot him a furious look. "I have already explained that it was not my fault!"

Richard's body tensed. He was tired of excuses and tired of failure. He wanted, needed, to have Claire in his power. He had imagined over and over in his mind how he would taunt her, frighten her, play his all-time favorite game of cat-and-mouse with her, until her breathing was hoarse and thick and she begged him for mercy.

He wanted her shaken to her very foundations. He wanted her filled with regret that she had not seized the chance to become his wife when she had the opportunity. He wanted her to pay for cutting his pride to shreds, for slighting his attentions, for refusing to acknowledge that he was the one man who deserved to be her lord and master.

"You told me that your father prevented you from leading Lady Fairhurst to our little meeting spot at Vauxhall," the squire stated, bringing his thoughts back to the matter at hand. "Is that true?"

"Yes," Rebecca insisted. "He has taken note of your interest in me and that, in turn, has made him more overbearing and possessive."

Richard's mouth twisted into an odd smile. Rebecca's father must be dealt with, and he suspected it would appeal to her nature to have her father brought down a peg or two. "Then we must devise a plan to overcome this annoying obstacle."

"It won't be easy. He watches over me like a hawk."

"Ahh, a challenge." He sat back in his chair, eyeing her. "Something which we both exceed in overcoming."

"At times." She regarded him steadily. "Though I have been thinking that all of this seems to be far more trouble than it is worth. It might be best to drop it for now."

"No!"

Rebecca drew in a deep breath. "I do not understand why you are so obsessed with Lady Fairhurst."

Richard frowned. Her shortsighted jealousy was becoming tedious. "I was doing this for you, dearest. Although if you prefer to leave the happy couple alone, to let them bask in the attention and adoration of the *ton,* we shall drop the matter entirely. I suppose by now there are a few people who have forgotten that Fairhurst was to be your husband."

Rebecca absorbed his words in silence, and then spoke. "It would be fitting to see them both brought low."

"Yes, it would." Richard reached into his pocket and produced a cheroot. He leaned forward and lit it from the candle on the table, then feeling Rebecca's disapproving stare belatedly asked, "Do you mind, dearest?"

"I suppose not."

He inhaled, blew out a stream of smoke, then smiled most charmingly. "We need to review the next few days of society events and decide which will be the best occasion to carry out our little surprise for the viscount and his bride."

Rebecca frowned. "There are so many different parties. How can we possibly determine which of them Lord and Lady Fairhurst will attend?"

"Perhaps there is a servant in their household who could be enticed to aid us? For a fee, naturally," Richard suggested.

"I'm afraid we shall find no help from that quarter. Nearly all of Fairhurst's servants have been with the family for generations. They are a disgustingly loyal group."

The squire stared at her, thunderstruck. The only way Rebecca could possibly know that was if she had already tried—and failed—to bribe one of the servants to spy on Fairhurst.

Fascinating. Perhaps there was more to Rebecca than he originally thought.

"Then it might be best to decide which events we shall attend," Richard said. "The viscount and his wife are bound to appear at one or more of them."

They spent the next twenty minutes discussing the *ton's* social calender. It was assumed that either one or both of them would be included on the guest list for each of these parties, though Richard was not as certain of this as Rebecca.

Talking about afternoon picnics, musical evenings, and masquerade balls was hardly a stimulating topic, yet the squire felt a rush of excitement when he contemplated how he would crush this noble couple. Rebecca's attention, however, began to wander.

Regretfully, Richard realized further enticement would be necessary, especially when Rebecca ignored his question about Lady Brookstone's ball for the third time and flashed another of her insufferable sultry smiles his way.

Insatiable slut. It seemed that these days her mind was perpetually in the gutter. Richard was not interested in bedding her, but it might be necessary in order to gain her cooperation. To make his task more palatable, he would use Rebecca's body shamelessly while Claire occupied his mind and fired his blood with lust.

"The sooner we are finished with this business, the sooner we can take a carriage ride in the park." Richard spoke in a husky whisper designed to tease her desire. "With the window shades drawn."

She peered at him through her lashes, the tip of her tongue wetting her lips. "Will there be enough time?"

He traced her jaw with his finger and skimmed it down her neck. "Do you doubt I can make you come before the coach completes a full circuit of the park?"

Rebecca smiled weakly up at him. "I believe you can do anything you set your mind, and your delicious body, to doing," she replied in a deep, passion-roughened voice.

He took hold of her hand and smoothed his thumb over her palm. "I can. And I will. Because there is no other woman except you who can bring me such incredible pleasure."

The words were hollow, but Rebecca was too flushed with sexual excitement and triumph to notice.

But later, when he imagined it was Claire who straddled him so wantonly as he gripped her naked buttocks and pounded himself furiously inside her gloved warmth, so damn deep and tight, it was the squire who felt flush with triumph.

* * *

"Are you quite comfortable, Aunt Agnes?" Claire asked her elderly relative. "I told one of the footmen to pack a lap blanket in the carriage in case you felt a bit of a chill."

"I am managing," Great-Aunt Agnes replied in a sour humor, as she tugged the ribbon under her chin, checking the security of her bonnet. "Though I don't understand why you chose to take the barouche. I don't like open carriages. There's no privacy, no protection from the elements, and the constantly blowing breeze can ruin a perfectly fine hat."

Claire sighed. Sometimes it just wasn't worth the effort to try and please her great-aunt. "I thought you would enjoy the warm, fresh air and sunshine," Claire answered, wishing she had taken her husband's advice and used the family coach instead.

Great-Aunt Agnes's brows knit together in confusion. "You said you were taking me to a picnic."

"We are."

"Then why did you bring this carriage? Honestly, child, just how much fresh air and sunshine can a body tolerate?"

Claire forced a smile. It was either that or scream in frustration.

"If you prefer, I shall send John Coachman back to the house the moment he delivers us to Lord Castleman's manor," Jasper offered. "Then, Aunt Agnes, you will be assured of riding home from the picnic in comfort."

Great-Aunt Agnes smiled broadly. "That is very considerate of you, Fairhurst." She gave a little sigh and lifted her shoulders in a tiny shrug. "I would be more comfortable in a closed carriage, though I would certainly not want you to go to any trouble on my account."

" 'Tis no bother," Jasper replied.

It was difficult for Claire to keep a straight face. Her great-aunt enjoyed nothing more than having everyone dance to her tune, and it seemed as though her husband had fallen neatly into that trap.

She was about to lean over and tell him he had just been manipulated by an expert, when she noticed the faintest of smiles touch Jasper's lips. Their eyes met, and he gave her a look of amused understanding. Apparently, Jasper knew more about elderly women than she realized.

"When we arrive at the picnic, you must allow my brother to be your escort, Aunt Agnes," Jasper said. "He can introduce you to the most interesting guests."

Jason, who was seated beside the older woman in the carriage, quickly agreed. "It would be my pleasure."

"Oh, now don't be foolish," Great-Aunt Agnes protested, but Claire could see her aunt was tickled pink at the very notion of having a handsome young man at her beck and call for a few hours. "Mr. Barrington doesn't want to be saddled with an old woman like me. He will want to spend his time with the younger set, specifically the young women."

"Oh, my dear lady, bite your tongue." Jason placed the back of his hand against his forehead with an exaggerated, dramatic motion and sighed heavily.

Everyone laughed. Jason waited until they grew silent before continuing. "I confess, my motives for wanting your company are purely selfish. I am counting on you to protect me, Aunt Agnes. Though I have done everything in my power to prevent it, whenever I attend a society gathering, young, unmarried women tend to flirt shamelessly with me."

"Or fawn over you," Jasper interjected.

"Of course they do," Great-Aunt Agnes said primly.

"You are a very handsome young gentleman." Her keen gaze flicked between the brothers. "Actually, both of you are exceptionally handsome. It is nothing short of extraordinary to see the amazing resemblance you share. Claire, why did no one mention to me that your husband had an identical twin brother?"

"I suppose it just slipped everyone's mind," Claire replied vaguely.

Great-Aunt Agnes made a scornful sound. "I don't see how it could." She continued her study of the two brothers. "It must be odd to share your face with another individual, even if that person is your own flesh and blood. Tell me, has anyone ever mistaken one of you for the other?"

Claire noticed the brothers exchange a brief glance. The usual undercurrent of tension that always seemed to surround them was barely perceptible this afternoon, and Claire hoped that meant they had come to some sort of truce.

"Personally, I think the resemblance has faded over the years," Jason remarked.

"Oh, not at all," Great-Aunt Agnes insisted. "Why, you could easily exchange identities and fool any number of individuals. Even those who claim to know you best."

A small gasp escaped Claire's lips. Great-Aunt Agnes's seemingly innocent inquires were coming perilously close to uncovering the truth. "I think Jasper and Jason have long outgrown such childish pranks," Claire said with a forced smile.

"Nonsense. Men never tire of acting like imbeciles. 'Tis part of their nature." Great-Aunt Agnes spoke with her usual authority, reminding them all that the deep lines of age etched over her plump features in no way impaired her sharp tongue.

Fortunately, they were saved from further comments and questions about Jasper and Jason when Great-Aunt Agnes suddenly lapsed into a fit of coughing. Once recovered, she spoke passionately about how her feeble lungs could not possibly tolerate so much fresh air.

It was sunny and warm when they arrived at Lord Castleman's estate, which was situated just beyond the boundaries of London. With a little encouragement, Great-Aunt Agnes was persuaded to stay for the afternoon's festivities. Though touted as a picnic, there was nothing about the elegant affair that even marginally resembled the rustic outings most people experienced when eating out-of-doors.

On the vast expanse of manicured lawns behind the manor house, long, damask-covered tables were laid out in the shade of the tower oak trees. There were endless platters of artfully arranged food, both savory and sweet, and guests were encouraged to help themselves. Smaller tables were set out at intervals around the edges of the grounds, some in the shade, others in partial sun.

Musicians were clustered on the terrace, servants in full dress livery hustled to and from the main house carrying trays of food and drink. Great-Aunt Agnes immediately commandeered a sunny table for herself, and, as promised, Jason became her willing errand boy. He made a mad dash for the food, returning with a filled plate and two prominent matrons who were anxious to meet her.

Deciding she had endured more than enough of her great-aunt's company, Claire struck off on her own, after insisting that Jasper join a group of his male companions. Promising to meet later to eat lunch, the couple separated.

At first Claire was content to wander along the terraced gardens, following a flagstone path that curved around a row of close-clipped hedges. She exchanged polite nods with the other guests as she walked by, but Claire was glad no one stopped to engage her in conversation.

She had been introduced to so many people since coming out in society, it was nearly impossible to remember everyone's name. Their real names. In a fit of wicked humor, Claire had assigned many of society's fashionable elite some sort of nickname, and she strongly doubted they would find the humor in her addressing them as Lord Sour Breath or Lady Busybody.

Claire soon came upon a section of formal gardens. The area had been set with various straight paths leading to a marble fountain, complete with a statue of the Goddess Venus, at the center. Flower beds bursting with color and blooms lined the many paths, their sweet scents permeating the air.

Charmed with her discovery, Claire followed one of the paths up to the fountain, removed her glove, and thrust her hand into the cool, trickling water. It felt wonderfully wet and refreshing. After assuring herself that no one was close enough to see, Claire removed the other glove and cooled both hands.

For one wild moment, she was tempted to splash her face, but dignity prevailed. Reluctantly, she dried her hands with her handkerchief, pulled on her gloves, and then circled around the fountain to the path on the other side. She turned the corner of the high, neat box hedges and instantly tensed as a curious sensation sank into her.

It was not precisely fear, but more the instinctive internal warning of danger.

She was being watched.

Though the afternoon was bright with sunshine, Claire felt an icy shadow curl around her. Something, or rather someone, was causing an uncustomary anxiety to gnaw at her. It was all mixed up with an odd feeling of unease, the persistent and nagging feeling that she was being keenly observed—by someone hiding in the shadows.

Claire shaded her eyes and carefully surveyed the crush of guests. Everyone seemed to be having a delightful time. The music played softly in the background as people strolled along the paths and lawns, conversed in small groups, clustered around the elegant linen-covered tables, and sampled the array of food. Footmen circulated with wine and spirits for the gentlemen and fresh lemonade for the ladies.

Yet this feeling of discomfort held Claire immobile, chilling her flesh. Her heart was beating very fast.

"You seem upset. Is anything wrong, Claire?"

Startled, she glanced up at her husband's clouded expression. " 'Tis nothing." She experienced a sudden flash of guilt. Claire had no wish to ruin his enjoyment of the afternoon, especially when there was nothing of substance to report, for she was experiencing only a *feeling* of unease.

Lord Fairhurst came forward and took her hand in his. "Claire, tell me."

He uttered the words in a voice of fierce possessiveness. She smiled slightly, amazed at how it made her feel protected and safe, knowing he cared about her welfare so much.

"I know this will sound foolish, but if you insist." A

movement caught her eye and Claire turned her head, but the couple to her far left was engaged in an earnest conversation, seemingly oblivious to everything around them. Claire sighed, almost sorry she had broached the subject.

"I have the persistent feeling that someone is watching me, rather intently. Yet when I look about to identify them, no one appears to be taking any notice of me."

Jasper's brows rose fractionally. "Of course people are watching you. Staring, in fact. You are the most stunningly beautiful woman at the party."

Claire smiled, despite the queasy feelings that still invaded her stomach. "I am hardly the most attractive female in attendance, though I thank you for the compliment."

"It was sincerely given." Jasper gazed at her reflectively for a long interval. "Is Dorchester here? Has he approached you?"

"I have not seen him, but he could easily be one of the many guests."

Jasper frowned. "If you are feeling uncomfortable, we shall leave at once."

"And listen to Aunt Agnes prattle on about how she had to ride in the barouche for over an hour, only to be forced to abandon the picnic before she had eaten a proper luncheon and was introduced to everyone of importance?" Claire rolled her eyes meaningfully. "I think not."

"Good point. The last thing your aunt needs is more ammunition for her complaints."

"Precisely." Claire gave herself a mental shake. "Forgive me, Jasper. I'm just being silly. 'Tis a lovely affair and a glorious afternoon. You should return to your friends and enjoy yourself."

Jasper's nostrils flared. "You are the most levelheaded female I have ever known. If you are feeling uncomfortable, there must bc a reason."

"Perhaps I am still rattled over the incident at the theater."

"Perhaps." Though Jasper had agreed with her, he hardly looked convinced. "I think the best course is for me to remain by your side until we return home."

"Won't the other guests think that odd for a husband and wife to be so long in each other's company?"

"Hang it. Your safety and peace of mind are far more important than anything this misguided lot thinks."

Claire allowed herself a small smile. Though Jasper had yet to verbally declare his love for her, she was well satisfied with how their relationship was progressing. More and more, his selfless acts of caring demonstrated that she was an important and valuable part of his life and that he was committed to doing whatever was necessary to make her content.

And although he might not be able to fully understand or accept it, Claire knew, as she strolled through Lord Castleman's fragrant gardens clutching her husband's arm, that she and Jasper were linked together in an unbreakable bond.

Knowing that gave her the strength to smile and converse with the other guests as though everything was perfectly fine, even though she still felt the unease of unknown hostile eyes watching her every move.

Chapter Eighteen

Late afternoon was Claire's favorite time to be alone in the garden. There was still enough sunlight to keep the temperature pleasant and enough natural light to see the print of her book with ease.

The gardens were in keeping with the luxury of the mansion and were far more substantial than many others in London. There were pebble paths bordered by large trees, numerous neatly tended flower beds, secluded areas furnished with comfortable garden benches, and even several fountains.

This expanse of the open air and greenery reminded Claire of home. Though the sights and sounds of London had more than met her expectations, there were times when she felt homesick. She missed her parents, her sisters, even the family dog—a scamp of indeterminable breeding who was loyal, playful, and loving.

It was time for her to return. When she had broached the subject with Jasper last night, not a muscle had moved in his face. He did not deny her request outright, but did woodenly express concern at the idea of her traveling.

She had been surprised, even a bit hurt, at his response, believing they had progressed beyond such stiff formality.

"I miss my family, Jasper," she had insisted.

"Then send one of my coaches for them," he countered, his voice sounding gruff. "The house is large enough for everyone. I am certain we can make them welcome in London."

It was a generous offer, but impractical, especially considering her naturally disorganized family.

"It would take them weeks to be ready to make a journey to Town," Claire replied. "It will be far easier for the two of us to travel to see them. I prefer a long visit, but promise we shall leave as soon as you grow restless."

"You want me to accompany you? And then stay?"

A flurry of tenderness had engulfed Claire's heart at his flustered expression. He thought she meant to journey to Wiltshire without him? And stay there for an extended time on her own? Silly man. Did he not yet realize the extent of her commitment to him? Did he not know she could never bear to be parted from him for any length of time?

"I would never consider making the trip without you," she had answered.

She had looked at his face, into his eyes and saw relief in their depths. So, to further prove her point, Claire had swiftly removed her nightgown and walked naked into her husband's arms.

It had been an exhausting night. Again and again they had joined their bodies, nearly drowning themselves in the most exquisite pleasure imaginable. Passion had fueled their ardor, but there was something else, too, something more that connected their very souls.

Claire smiled now at the memory. They would leave for the country within a fortnight. She was looking forward to the trip. She was anxious for Jasper to meet her mother and father, yet nervous over having to explain the very bizarre condition of her marriage and to clarify the identity of her husband.

A breeze gusted by, rustling the treetops and murmuring the leaves. The hour was growing late. Claire retied the loosening strings on her bonnet; then turned to collect the book she had set beside her on the garden bench.

When she picked up the novel, the ribbon she had been using to mark her place slipped from the pages. Muttering to herself in annoyance, Claire bent to retrieve it, hoping it would not be too difficult to locate the last page she had read.

As she reached into the grass, something shiny caught her eye. A coin? A piece of jewelry? Curious, she brushed aside the long blades of grass and bent closer to the ground to examine the object.

A voice in the distance called out her name—a female voice, vaguely familiar, yet not easily placed. Still bent over, Claire turned her head toward the sound, but saw nothing on the horizon. Distracted by the object in the lawn, she returned her attention to the ground.

There was a whisper of movement behind her, but by the time Claire lifted her head to investigate, it was too late. Something hard struck her behind her ear. The pain exploded in her brain with a flash of color, and then darkness consumed her utterly.

Jasper gave the waiting footman an uncharacteristic smile as he handed over his hat and gloves. It seemed he was doing a fair amount of that lately—smiling. Oftentimes for no good reason. He supposed that was something else he could blame on his wife. She was making him ridiculously happy.

"Is Lady Fairhurst at home?" he inquired.

"She is in the garden, my lord."

Nodding his head in thanks, Jasper headed toward the back of the house. Tonight was the Henson's ball, an affair he would normally be looking forward to attending. Instead, the idea of a quiet, cozy dinner for two and a rousing evening of bedsport with his alluring wife held far greater appeal.

Hopefully, it would be an easy task to persuade Claire that this alternative plan was an excellent idea.

It was a novel experience for Jasper to have such tender feelings stirring almost constantly within him, to have a need nearly burning his blood to hold her and kiss her and feel her warmth and softness against his skin.

Allowing himself to feel that need instead of burying it beneath a stiff formality still gave him a sense of danger, but the fear was lessening each day. Being with Claire gave Jasper a feeling of bliss that went beyond the physical, and he had come to realize it was a risk worth taking, for it gave him the freedom to be with the one woman who filled his soul.

He suspected there were some in his family who believed he had completely changed, but Jasper did not see it that way. He believed he had finally grown up and realized that donning the manner of distance and stiff formality had been a fatally flawed plan, for it hid the best part of his nature: his passion.

With Claire's help, he had at long last come to believe he could trust that side of his nature; he could experience it without having it dominate his every movement; he could rejoice in the pleasure it brought him.

As he strode farther into the garden, Jasper reached into his jacket pocket and closed his hand over the jeweler's box snuggled inside. The ring he had commissioned for his wife was finally completed, and he was anxious to present it to her—the moment after he declared his unwavering love for her and his steadfast devotion to her happiness.

The first prickling of uneasiness struck when Jasper discovered Claire's favorite garden bench empty and her book left behind. She shared his passion for reading and cared for each novel she read as though it were a treasure. It was therefore odd to find a book of hers left out in the elements, unprotected.

Still, it might have been an oversight. Grasping the leather bound missive in his fist, Jasper bounded out of the garden and reentered the house. None of the servants were certain where Lady Fairhurst had gone, so he sent four footmen scouring through the rooms on the first and second floors in search of her, while he continued on to the chambers on the third floor.

He opened Claire's door and walked through the empty bedchamber to glance in the dressing room. It was also empty.

Pacing the floor with impatience, Jasper tugged on the bellpull. A young maid answered the call.

"Where is Lady Fairhurst's maid?"

"I have not seen her since lunchtime, my lord. 'Tis her half day off."

Frowning, Jasper dismissed the maid and instructed her to tell the butler, Mr. Brinks, he was needed immediately. Within minutes the butler arrived, flush faced and out of breath. Following close on his heels were the four footmen. Their grim expressions told Jasper what he did not want to hear—Lady Fairhurst was not in the house.

"When was the last time any of you saw her?" Jasper asked.

A stout, dark-haired footman stepped forward. "Following Mr. Brinks's instructions, I asked her Ladyship if she would like tea served in the garden fifteen minutes ago. She was sitting in the rose arbor, reading a book. She told me she would prefer to take her refreshments in her chamber and instructed them to be sent up at half past the hour."

All eyes turned toward the clock on the mantel. Jasper felt a chill rush through him. In just a few moments it would strike the appointed time. Where was Claire?

A knock came at the chamber door. Jasper half expected to see a servant carrying a ladened tea tray, but instead Jason casually strolled into the room. Jasper met his brother's gaze.

Instantly, Jason became alert. "What is wrong?"

"It's Claire. She's gone missing."

"Are you certain?"

"We have just combed the house and the grounds looking for her. She is not here."

"Perhaps she went out on an errand," Jason suggested. "Are any of the carriages gone?"

Jasper turned to his butler.

"Only the one that drove the countess to Bond Street late this morning," Mr. Brinks answered.

"Claire knows that I have been very worried for her safety," Jasper said. "She would not have left the house without telling someone. At least not of her own free will."

He gripped the book he still held in his hand so tight it began to bend, all the while trying to force his mind to remain calm while he tried to formulate a plan. But concentration was nearly impossible. God, where was she? What had happened to her?

"Assemble the household in the front foyer," Jason ordered. "Lord Fairhurst and I need to speak with the entire staff."

Jasper cast an eye of gratitude at his brother. The edges of fear were curling around his heart, making it difficult to keep a clear head.

The brothers entered the front foyer together, standing side by side before a curious and subdued household staff. Jason wasted no time informing the servants of Lady Fairhurst's disappearance and requesting information.

But the staff remained eerily quiet. All seemed visibly distressed; many had their mouths open in shock.

Jasper rubbed his face with his hands. "Anything you can remember, no matter how small, might be of help."

The seconds ticked by with agonizing slowness. Then a worried looking footman stepped forward.

"It might not seem like much, but since you've asked, there was a black coach parked at the top of the street earlier this afternoon. I took note of it because it was in an awkward spot, nearly blocking the corner. It seemed odd, too, since none of our neighbors or their visitors would choose such an inconvenient location to leave their coach."

"Did you see anyone disembark or enter this carriage?" Jasper asked.

"No."

Jason turned to the footman. "Was there a coat of arms on the door, or anything else distinct about the vehicle?"

The servant shook his head slowly, then lowered it in despair.

"Did anyone else see this carriage?" Jason asked.

There was a moment of silence, and then one of the underfootman said, "I think I did."

"How could you have seen the carriage?" Mr. Brinks

asked in an indignant tone. "You were supposed to be in the pantry polishing the silver all afternoon."

The servant dragged in a breath, held it for a second, then spoke. "I went out for some fresh air. 'Twas only for a moment, but I do remember that coach."

"Was Lady Fairhurst inside?" Jasper asked.

"Not that I could see. The driver was on top of the box, and there was at least one person inside because they stuck their head out of the window for a few seconds."

"Can you describe that person?"

"I only caught a fleeting glimpse, but it was a female. A lady, by the look of her bonnet."

"Did you know this woman?"

"I . . . uhm . . ." the man stammered, blushing slightly. There were a few beads of sweat forming at his hairline. "I believe it was Miss Manning, though I cannot be one hundred percent certain."

"Miss Manning?" Jason exclaimed.

Jasper let loose the curse that rose to his lips. This was not good news. If Claire was with Rebecca, then Dorchester would not be far behind. But where could they have taken her? And why?

"There is no need to jump to dire conclusions," Jason whispered. "A coach carrying Rebecca Manning is hardly a suspicious occurrence. Even if Claire were with her, it could all be very innocent."

"With Claire missing, everything is suspicious," Jasper countered.

He was practically numb with fear, distracted from everything by the worry of finding his wife. He had underestimated the danger, and that was inexcusable. Though Jasper longed to believe this was all an innocent mistake, he knew he must act as if the worst had occurred.

Giving no further explanation, he stormed from the

house, leaving behind his greatcoat, hat, and gloves. Jason followed quickly on his heels.

"Jasper, wait! You can hardly go chasing after every black coach in London. You might as well be searching for a needle in a haystack. Besides, if your servants are correct, this carriage left at least a half hour ago. We have no idea of its direction, or if Claire was even inside."

Jasper grimaced. "I am not going to try and find this carriage. I am going to Dardington's. Our brother-in-law arranged for the runners to keep a watch on Squire Dorchester. If Rebecca is involved, then the squire will also be a part of it. I pray to God that one of the runners can tell us where he is and that will, in turn, lead me to Claire."

"I'm coming with you," Jason declared. "We can take my phaeton. 'Tis the fastest carriage in London when I'm at the ribbons."

Minutes later, the brothers were careening through the crowded streets. Jason was indeed an expert whip, and Jasper was grateful for his brother's help, though he could not help but think that with every passing minute, the mysterious coach was slipping farther and farther away. Hanging on grimly to his seat, Jasper's mind was filled with thoughts of Claire. Where was she? Was she frightened? Hurt?

"Try not to worry," Jason murmured as he hauled on the reins and skillfully negotiated a sharp curve. "We'll get her back."

Jasper nodded. The confident words reminded him he was not alone. That thought helped renew his hope and focus his mind on rescue. They would discover Claire's whereabouts, assemble a plan, and bring her safely home.

The alternative was simply unimaginable.

* * *

The noisy rattle of carriage wheels crunching on a gravel path pulled Claire back to consciousness. Groggily, she lifted her head, and then winced as a searing pain shot through her skull. Gingerly, she reached to touch the most tender area, her fingers encountering raw skin and a growing lump.

She began to sit up, and for a moment, everything spun around sickeningly. Claire waited until it stopped, and then she gradually lifted herself upright.

"Ah, so you are finally awake. Good. I had to pay the driver an extra shilling to carry you from the garden to the coach. You must outweigh me by at least a stone. But now that added expense can be saved once we reach our destination."

Claire blinked furiously, and the woman sitting on the opposite side of the carriage slowly came into focus.

"Miss Manning?"

"You do know my name! Richard claimed you would not, but I knew better." Her voice was smug, superior, as was her grin.

"Richard?" Claire mumbled in confusion.

The smug smile vanished. "Squire Dorchester to you."

Dear Lord! Claire's heart began pounding with dread. Her head hurt terribly, and her body felt so weary she could barely move. Yet Claire knew she must struggle to keep her wits about her.

"Is that where we are going? To meet the squire?"

"Wouldn't you like to know?" Rebecca Manning's laugh was short and brittle.

Claire's nerves jangled in her stomach at the sound. What was happening? She doubted very much that she had been kidnapped to be held for ransom. Miss Manning certainly had reason to dislike her, but this seemed an extreme action for a woman.

Claire did not know Rebecca Manning at all, yet she could not credit this was entirely her plan. This seemed more like an act Richard Dorchester would devise, and it was his involvement and intentions that Claire truly feared.

They soon stopped in a wooded area, in what might have been a park. Since she had lost consciousness, Claire was unsure of how many miles they had traveled. Judging by the position of the sun, it had been at least an hour, maybe longer. She wondered how far from the city they had come.

"Get out."

Claire lifted her chin defiantly and stared at her captor. "No."

Rebecca Manning sputtered unbecomingly; then she reached beneath the folds of her cloak and extracted a lethal-looking knife. The long blade flashed menacingly in the fading light of the carriage interior.

"Get out," Miss Manning repeated.

Claire swallowed involuntarily, her eyes never leaving the knife blade. Though it seemed impossible to believe a lady would ever use such a diabolical weapon, Claire knew she could not risk further injury. With great reluctance, she obeyed the command.

After they exited the carriage, Claire glanced up at the coachman. Though she expected no less, her spirits sank further when he deliberately avoided her eyes. There was no help to be found from him.

"Return for me at the appointed time, in the appointed location," Miss Manning commanded, tossing up a small leather pouch of coins. "You shall be paid the rest then."

The pouch disappeared beneath the driver's cloak. Then he flicked the reins, sparing them no further glance. Miss Manning stood close by Claire's side as the carriage slowly disappeared. Claire shivered, rubbing her arms. Her head continued to throb, and she felt woozy. Even if she had the strength to flee, she had no idea where to run.

"Walk."

With the tip of a knife blade placed firmly in her back, Claire started walking, and they immediately entered a thick forest of large oak trees. For a moment, she felt as though she were back home in the country. There were no city sounds of carts or carriages or pedestrian traffic to be heard. It was eerily quiet all around them, an almost silent woods.

They rounded a bend and the trees thinned, forming a clearing. They crossed a wide lawn, then headed down a long slope toward a lake. There were a few large trees scattered along the banks, their slouching limbs dipping into the water.

Raising her head, Claire anxiously scanned the darkening horizon. Miss Manning had planned well. Even if someone was in the vicinity, with twilight fast approaching, little could be seen of them.

There was no one in sight when they reached the water's edge. For a fleeting moment, Claire dared to hope that she would simply be abandoned in this secluded area and forced to find her way out alone. But a rustling behind one of the large oak trees soon dashed that hope.

"You're late."

Both women whirled in the direction of the voice.

"Why are you here?" Rebecca screeched in annoyance.

"I could ask you the same question, dear sister," the

female voice replied. "You told me that you were going to Gunther's for an ice."

Hope surged through Claire. She had expected to find the odious Squire Dorchester, but instead Miss Manning's sister Anne stood before them, apparently much to Rebecca's surprise. Was it too much to hope that the plan had been foiled and rescue was in sight?

Rebecca scowled. "Where I go is none of your business. Stop meddling in my affairs and leave at once."

"Not without Lady Fairhurst."

Rebecca lost her temper. "You stupid cow! Be gone or you will ruin everything!"

"How can I ruin what I have planned?"

The words brought Rebecca up short. She paused, gazing at her sister as if she'd never seen her before. "What nonsense are you babbling?"

Anne's feverish eyes gleamed viciously. "For once I am in control, little sister. How I have relished outwitting you. And now you will listen to me. You will do as I say!"

Anne advanced steadily with each word. When she stood close enough, she slapped Rebecca across the face, sending her reeling to the ground, the force of the blow knocking her bonnet askew.

Her hand pressed to her reddened cheek, Rebecca stared up at Anne, shock etched on her face. "You hit me!"

Rebecca's cry was loud enough to send the birds scouring from the trees.

"Be glad that is all I have done, dear sister." Anne pulled a small object from the pocket of her gown. It was a pistol, small and deadly, made for a woman's hand. "If you anger me further, I shall not hesitate to use this."

Claire swallowed the gasp that rose in her throat as Anne brandished the weapon in front of Rebecca's nose.

Rebecca, however, had not yet grasped the magnitude of the danger. Her palm still resting against her bruised cheek, she glared at her sister with undisguised disgust.

"I will tell you one final time. Leave here immediately. This matter does not concern you."

"I am staying."

Rebecca's gaze skittered around. "The squire will be furious when he arrives and finds you here," she threatened. "I shall not protect you from his wrath. In fact, I shall enjoy watching him punish you when he discovers that you have struck me."

Anne made a clucking noise with her tongue. "I have seen the bruises you try so hard to conceal. Why should the squire care if someone else hits you? Or does he reserve that privilege only for himself?"

Claire noticed Rebecca's hand move to her shoulder and caught the shadowy glimpse of a fading bruise. It sickened her to realize that Anne spoke the truth. Claire felt no sense of triumph at the verification of Dorchester's true character, for even she would never have believed he was capable of such brutality.

Rebecca slowly straightened, and then rose to her feet. "Your ignorance has sealed your fate, Anne. I shall do nothing to spare you. Nothing." She bared her teeth in a cruel smile. "He will laugh when he sees your little gun. And then he will beat you until you are bloody and begging for mercy."

Anne did not appear frightened at her sister's threats. "You are starting to bore me," she announced as she circled around Rebecca's left side. Then, suddenly, Anne lifted her arm high in the air and brought the butt end of the pistol sharply down on the back of Rebecca's head.

Claire heard a dull thud as the blow sent Rebecca crashing to her knees. She struggled for a moment, swaying drunkenly, shaking her head, and trying to rise. But, instead, she fell forward. Once she hit the ground, she remained still.

Her head will ache even more than mine, Claire thought with a flash of sympathy.

Anne nudged Rebecca's inert form with the toe of her walking boot. There was no sound or movement from the prone form. Anne turned toward Claire and let out a nervous giggle. Claire tensed.

"You seem upset by my actions," Anne said in a puzzled voice. "I do not understand why. My sister and her lover would have made you suffer great physical pain. I would never do anything so cruel."

"I never thought that you would." Claire felt herself flinch as the lie crossed her lips. "But Rebecca spoke the truth about the squire. I fear his anger, as should you. We must leave immediately, before he arrives and discovers us."

Anne giggled again. "There is nothing to fear from Dorchester. I have already taken care of him."

With a cryptic smile, Anne beckoned Claire closer. Fearfully, Claire approached. Needles of panic drove into her when she saw Anne's handiwork. Anne had indeed taken care of the squire. He sat hidden from view at the base of a huge tree, his back pressed against the trunk. His hands and feet were bound with a thick rope, his mouth gagged and his head slumped forward at an unnatural angle.

"Is he dead?" Claire whispered.

"Not yet." Anne let out a small sigh. "You know, I have never murdered anyone. You shall be the first. Then Dorchester. Then Rebecca."

The blood drained from Claire's head and a buzzing filled her ears. She fought to keep her expression impassive and her gaze level, but she could not control the icy chills that ran up and down her spine.

Anne sounded perfectly reasonable, but her words were lunacy. Panic beat in Claire's chest, making it difficult to think. Still, she knew her only chance of survival was to stall for time.

"You told your sister that all of this was your plan."

"Yes. I arranged everything very cleverly." Anne bowed her head demurely. "How unseemly of me to be so boastful. But all has gone even better than I expected."

"It has?"

Anne nodded, clearly eager to tell her story. "You see, I needed to get you alone, and I could not manage that without help. So I tricked Rebecca into coming to my aid."

"You tricked her?" Claire prompted.

"I did!" A bubble of laughter escaped from Anne's thin lips. "I sent Rebecca a note, instructing her to bring you here, and signed it in Dorchester's hand. Though it was a difficult task to remove you from your home without being seen, I knew she would find a way to get it done. She has fallen completely under the squire's spell and will do anything he asks of her."

"And what of Dorchester? How did you get him here?"

"I brought him here on the pretext of a tryst and sent him a letter forged with Rebecca's signature." Anne snorted disgustedly. "They have met before in this very spot. I followed her one afternoon and watched them fornicating on the banks of the lake like a pair of wild animals. 'Twas nearly inhuman."

Claire shuddered at the disturbing image, knowing she could not possibly comment. Yet she had to keep Anne talking. "Is that why you want to . . . to kill them? Because you disapprove of their relationship?"

Anne tilted her head back and laughed. The sound chilled Claire to her bones.

"My sister and the squire are a well-matched pair. Spawns of the devil, both of them. They do not deserve to live." Anne lifted her chin and struck a righteous pose. "Dorchester tried to provoke a fight with Lord Fairhurst at the duke's ball. And my sister was unforgivably cruel to Lord Fairhurst when he tried to explain how he had inadvertently found himself married to you."

Claire stared at Anne in confusion. "I can assure you these incidents did not unduly disturb my husband."

Anne's face crumpled. "You don't understand. I would have been content to be his sister-in-law—to stand in the shadows, to receive only brotherly affection and regard. It would have been enough. He would have been a part of my family, a part of my future, but my sister could not even manage that, the damn fool."

Claire watched in fascination as tears of anguish brimmed in Anne's eyes.

"I do not wish to harm you," Anne continued. "But there is no other way. I must do what is necessary to be near him. Once you are dead, he shall turn to me in his grief." Anne gulped in a large breath and a dreamy, faraway look entered her eyes. "Then, after a proper phase of mourning has elapsed, I shall become Lord Fairhurst's wife."

Chapter Nineteen

Time had never crawled so slowly. Jason drove to the marquess's home at neck-breaking speed. Pedestrians shouted curses and nearly dove to get out of the way; heavy carriages and carts pulled up short and maneuvered to one side as quickly as possible. It was a miracle they didn't end up in a ditch.

Yet for Jasper it was still too slow. *Damn, can't my brother drive any faster?* Every minute that passed brought Claire closer to danger and left his heart paralyzed with terror.

At last, the marquess's mansion came into view. Jasper leaped from the phaeton as the horses slowed, taking the front stone steps two at a time. Grim-faced and determined, he stormed the front door, demanding to see Lord Dardington. Fortunately for the young footman, wide-eyed and alarmed at such agitated, unexpected behavior, the marquess was at home.

Not waiting to be escorted, Jasper, with his brother hot on his heels, raced to the marquess's study. The sound of running feet echoed though the vast hallway as a footman valiantly tried to outdistance them, fearing he would be sacked if he did not properly announce the guests.

The door to the marquess's study opened with a crash.

Startled, Dardington glanced up from the paperwork he was reviewing.

"What the hell—"

"Claire is missing," Jasper declared. "I think she was somehow tricked or coerced into getting into a carriage with Rebecca Manning." Chest heaving, Jasper took a deep breath. "I cannot believe that Miss Manning would act alone. Dorchester must also be involved."

A flash of surprise and concern crossed Lord Dardington's handsome features. "What can I do to help?"

"We need information," Jasper replied, his face hardening. "I need to contact the runners who are watching Dorchester. Immediately."

"The men are instructed to alert me at once if they observe anything unusual or out of the ordinary. Barring that, they issue a weekly report." The marquess unlocked the center drawer of his inlaid mahogany desk and pulled out a stack of papers.

Jasper took the papers and scanned them swiftly. "These are nearly a week old. When do you expect your next report?"

The marquess glanced at the mantel clock. "It should be here any minute. Bow Street prides itself on punctuality."

The study remained tense with silence as the three men waited. Finally, the study door opened and a large, rather odd-looking man entered. Tall and broad shouldered, he was dressed in a cheaply tailored brown jacket and trousers. His face was half-covered by a bushy gray beard and mustache, and he moved with a slowness of manner that made Jasper grind his teeth.

"We are interested in anything you can tell us about the squire," Lord Dardington demanded, forgoing any introductions.

The runner frowned thoughtfully. "I have my latest report right here. As always, I've put in everything that I thought was significant."

Jasper snatched the papers and quickly scanned the newest report. "This is useless," he exclaimed, throwing the pages to the floor. "We need to know where the squire is at this moment."

The runner scratched his head. "I suspect he is still in Hyde Park, though he might have returned to his lodging when I was on my way here."

Patience totally exhausted, Jasper sprang forward, grabbing the runner by the front of his jacket. "Why was this activity not reported immediately?"

The man sputtered and coughed, pushing ineffectively at the hands that held him so tightly. " 'Tis not uncommon for the squire to meet his lady-love in the park. He seems to enjoy taking his pleasure in a more, um . . . unconventional manner. I've seen them there together numerous times. I didn't think it was necessary to make special mention of it, since I included it in my weekly accounting."

"His lady-love? Do you mean Miss Manning?" Jasper asked.

"Yes, that's her. Miss Rebecca Manning."

"Was she there today?" Dardington asked.

The runner glanced from Jasper to the marquess in confusion. "At the park?"

"Yes, man, at the park!" Jasper shouted, twisting his hands tighter on the lapels of the runner's jacket and jerking him forward.

"Not that I saw."

"Jasper, stop it," Jason interrupted, pulling at his brother's shoulder.

Struggling to get his fear and agitation under control, Jasper released the man and he staggered back a little.

"I can show you the spot, if you like," the runner offered, his expression faintly wary.

"Let's go," Jasper exclaimed.

"Wait!" the marquess shouted. "We need weapons."

Lord Dardington unlocked a wooden cabinet and withdrew several pistols. He passed them over to the twins, who shoved them into the waistband of their trousers. Once armed with the pistols, each man secured a knife in his boot. The marquess turned from the cabinet, paused, swung back around, reached in, and added a second gun to his arsenal.

Then, looking more like a gang of pirates than a trio of English noblemen, they hurried out the door.

It was a horrible way to die.

The water of the lake was an uninviting, ominous presence—black, silent, and still. With nothing beneath her feet, it would quickly close over her head. She would fight valiantly to stay afloat, to gasp and sputter for breath, for life, but it would not matter. Eventually, her strength would fail, and she would sink slowly to a watery grave.

"A gunshot will be noisy and a knife blade messy," Anne said. "This will be a far more dignified end."

Claire felt the hard steel barrel of the pistol press into her back. Reluctantly, she took a small step forward. The edge of the water lapped against her slippers, soaking the silk and chilling her feet.

"Think of how Lord Fairhurst will suffer when my body is discovered," Claire said, turning slightly to face her captor. "If you truly love him, you would spare him such pain."

"I do not want him to suffer." Anne's plain face was remorseful. "He will feel distressed over the mysterious death of his wife because he honors his husbandly duties. But his heart will not be saddened. He does not love you. He did not choose you to be his wife. His twin brother did."

Agitated, Anne shoved the barrel of the gun harder into Claire's back. Claire advanced another small step. The water covered her ankles.

Her fingers dug into her palms as she tried to think of a topic of conversation that would keep Anne talking. "Lord Fairhurst is a determined man, with a persistent nature. He will not rest until he discovers who was responsible for my death. And he will see that they are punished."

"I am counting on it." Anne broke into a slight smile, and then pressed her hand over her heart. "He is a heroic man, who cannot abide leaving something this important unsolved. That is why I brought the squire out here. I needed a third body to complete the circle of violence and explain these deaths.

"I will shoot him and leave the pistol clutched in Rebecca's hand. I will stab her and leave the knife in the squire's fist. Once the bodies are discovered, there will be endless speculation as to the chain of events, but it must eventually be concluded that they somehow killed each other."

Claire swallowed hard. "What about me?"

An ironic grin touched Anne's lips. "Your body will be found in the lake, unbruised. No gunshot wounds, no knife wounds. There will be no clues as to how you got there, though, eventually, the coachman who drove you and my sister here today will come forward to tell what he knows."

Claire gave a slow, confused shake of her head. "The coachman?"

"He is the cousin of my maid. I recommended that Rebecca use him several weeks ago when she needed a driver who would take her to her trysts with Dorchester, while remaining discreet. None of our servants would be so bold. Since then, the coachman has been ferrying her all about Town for her secret rendezvous."

Even though she was clouded by fear, Claire had to concede it was a diabolically clever plan. The driver had only seen Rebecca and herself. He could truthfully say that he last saw both of them alive, walking into the forest off the gravel path where he left them.

"You will never be suspected of having any involvement," Claire whispered in amazement.

"Exactly." Anne's chilling smile returned. "Our shared grief over the shocking and sudden deaths of our beloved family members will bring Lord Fairhurst closer to me. I will comfort him, and when he is ready to hear it, I shall confide my theories of these horrific events to him.

"Perhaps you were trying to escape, but lost your footing and fell in the water. Perhaps you were pushed or forced into the lake by Rebecca or the squire, or the both of them. Perhaps the squire dishonored you so completely that you took your own life rather than face the shame of what had occurred."

"What if I refuse to go in the water?" Claire dared to ask, dismayed that her voice came out in a rusty croak.

Anne stared at her dumbly. "It will greatly distress Lord Fairhurst if you are found with a bullet through your chest." She cocked the hammer of the pistol with a resounding click. "But I will do whatever is necessary to achieve my heart's desire."

Claire wet her lips. Her feet, completely submerged in the water, were numb. Anne was clearly mad, but unfortunately sane enough to carry out her plans.

Claire tried to imagine how Jasper would react to news of her death. Crushed was too minor an emotion. He would feel as she would if the situation were reversed—utterly devastated.

Claire remembered the kiss she had shared with him after breakfast that morning. She expected a warm, quick kiss, but his lips had clung to hers, and for the briefest of moments, she thought he was going to declare his love for her.

When he did not, Claire had almost broached the subject herself, but she stopped, telling herself that it was unnecessary to hear the words because she knew the truth. He did love her. He showed her his love many times each day, with his looks of affection, his acts of kindness and consideration, and his passionate physical desire that had become an almost compulsive need.

But now, with death facing her so starkly, so coldly, Claire deeply regretted not hearing the words fall from his lips. And she wished she had told him more often of her own feelings.

Dying young and with regrets. Was there anything more tragic?

In the distance, Claire heard an animal cry. It was such a sharp, distinctive sound that she wondered if it might be a signal. Was it possible that Jasper had found her?

"Take another step forward."

"Miss Manning, please—"

"I will hear no pleas for mercy!" Anne screeched. She

seemed lost in her anger for a moment; then she pulled the tattered edges of her dignity about her and became once again a proper English lady.

Intent on murder.

"Move forward."

Claire's stomach lurched, and she clenched her fist against her abdomen. She was not about to quietly go to her death, like a lamb to the slaughter. She had far too much to live for. But her options for escape seemed nonexistent. She could try to run, but she was certain Anne would shoot her at the first sign of escape.

She could try to overpower her captor, but again, at this close range, the risk of being shot was great. Her best chance of survival was to quietly, and without a fuss, slip into the lake. As darkness continued to fall, it might be possible to maneuver to shallow water and await rescue.

If only she knew how to swim!

The first few steps were not too hard. The ground beneath Claire's feet was soft and slippery, but it held her weight. The water was icy cold, shocking Claire's awareness, yet it helped to keep her senses on heightened alert.

She heard the animal sound again, this time closer. The water had reached her waist. When she moved, it lapped against her breasts. Her soggy skirts felt very heavy. Though she struggled to stand upright, they pulled her down, deeper into the water. *Hurry, Jasper. Hurry.*

Then suddenly, the ground beneath her disappeared. Claire gasped in fright, flaying her arms wildly as her feet struggled to find the bottom. But it was gone. The black waters of the lake closed over her head, and she sank down into the wet cold.

Terror invaded her very soul. She could not see; she could not breathe. Kicking her legs, she struggled to bring herself to the surface. The top of her head, then her eyes cleared the water, and Claire tilted her neck far back, exposing her nose and mouth to the blessed air.

Dragging in a breath, she looked up and saw the stars twinkling in the heavens. Night had truly fallen.

Her heart pounding with fear, Claire tried to remain calm. She floated for a few seconds; then she felt herself being dragged under the water. Holding her breath, she let herself sink down. She began thrashing her legs and arms to lift her body to the surface.

It worked. Again, her head broke above the water just long enough to catch a few lungfuls of precious air. As she sunk down for the third time, Claire felt a sharp pain in her side. Were there fish or toads or other water creatures lurking in these depths that could bite her?

The next time it took longer to reach the surface. Her legs felt as if there were heavy irons shackled to them; her arms and shoulders ached; her lungs were burning. She gulped, taking in a mouthful of water and very little air.

Coughing, choking, Claire felt herself go under again. The pain in her side sharpened. The air in her lungs was gone. She was fighting a losing battle. Her wet skirts hampered her movement; their heavy weight anchored her, making it impossible to paddle to a shallow depth.

Claire never doubted that Jasper was on his way to rescue her, but he would arrive too late. Anne had been too clever. This spot was too isolated to be easily found, and Anne would be long gone when the bodies were finally discovered.

Claire hoped Jason would be with her beloved. Though

he did not realize it, Jasper would need his brother's strength to survive this ordeal.

Claire focused her mind on her last memory of him leaving the breakfast room that morning with a smile of affection on his handsome face and her lips still tingling from the warmth of his kiss.

Forgive me, my love, for leaving you.

Her head began to throb, and she felt a thundering in her ears. Claire sunk deeper and deeper, but thoughts of Jasper spurred her to a last burst of energy. Using all her strength, she kicked her legs and pulled through the water with her arms, again and again and again. But when she lifted her face for a breath of air, there was only water.

It was a horrible way to die.

The Bow Street Runner, George Harris, led the three men to a little-known gravel path on the outer edges of Hyde Park.

"The squire usually instructs the carriage to leave him here," he told the men, "and then he walks the rest of the way. Miss Manning does the same."

" 'Tis nearly dark and the forest is very dense," the marquess commented. "Are you certain this is the right spot?"

The runner nodded. "I've been here enough times, though never this late at night."

"Can you lead us to the area where they rendezvous, Harris?" Jasper asked, his face hopeful.

The runner nodded again.

Intent on keeping a fast pace without making too much noise, Jasper barely noticed his surroundings as they tromped, in single file, through the thick woods. When they broke clear of the trees, Harris hesitated.

Impatient with the delay, Jasper strode toward the runner. Jason grasped his brother's arm, halting him, and pointed toward the clearing. "Is that Claire?"

Jasper squinted in the darkness, barely making out the silhouette of a lone woman standing on the perimeter of a large lake.

"I don't think so. Claire is taller. Maybe it's Rebecca."

"Do you see anyone else in the vicinity?" the marquess asked as he withdrew one of the pistols from his waistband and came to stand beside the brothers.

"No."

"This is the place," Harris declared as he joined them. "They usually carry on their activities in the open area of the meadow, but I don't see them."

"We've spotted a woman near the lake," the marquess said. "She can't be here alone. I'll circle around one side and Harris will circle around the other, while you and Jason question this mysterious female."

"No weapons," Jasper commanded as his twin extracted a pistol. "Whoever this is, we don't want to scare her. Besides, in this darkness, a stray bullet could easily strike the wrong person."

Jason agreed. Side by side, the brothers strode across the clearing, a sliver of moonlight illuminating the way.

As they drew near, Jasper's muscles tensed, ready for . . . anything.

The woman did not hear their approach. She stood with her back toward them, shrouded in a gloomy shadow as clouds passed over the moon. Yet, when they drew close enough, Jasper realized he knew her. He halted, stunned.

"Good God, 'tis Anne Manning," he whispered to his brother. "What the bloody hell is she doing here?"

"Could she also be involved with the squire?"

Jasper's face contorted in a grimace. "I find that nearly impossible to believe. Yet, thus far, nothing has made sense."

The sound of their voices must have alerted her to their presence, for she turned in their direction. The clouds drifted and the moonlight shone clear. Anne Manning's face was a portrait of shock.

Yet she recovered swiftly. "Gentlemen, my goodness, you startled me." Though she spoke to both men, her gaze remained locked on Lord Fairhurst.

"Are you alone?" Jasper demanded.

"Yes." A tear slipped from beneath Miss Manning's lashes and fell down her cheek. She did not wipe it away. "How clever of you to have found me. I have been so frightened. I was out riding late this afternoon when my mare was spooked by a rabbit. When she reared in surprise, I was thrown. Fortunately, I was not badly injured, though my mount cantered away and left me stranded. I assumed help would be sent once the horse was captured. Is there a large party searching for me?"

Neither man answered. Though she seemed genuine, there were too many peculiar circumstances to accept it as truth.

"You were riding alone in this rather desolate area when you were unseated?" Jasper asked. "Where was your groom?"

"I sent him home." Miss Manning looked down. "I know 'tis not entirely proper, but I find this section of the park so peaceful, so serene. I often ride here alone because it reminds me of the country."

"You come here often, yet how strange that you are not dressed for riding," Jason commented wryly.

Miss Manning gave a prim sniff, but she offered no explanation. Unease settled in Jasper's chest as Harris and the marquess emerged from the cover of darkness.

"I think you'll be interested in seeing what I've discovered, my lord," the runner proclaimed. "Miss Rebecca Manning is lying in the thick grass on the opposite side of the lake. She's breathing, but despite my best efforts, I could not rouse her."

"And I have I found the squire," the marquess announced. "He's out cold and all trussed up like a Christmas goose."

"Claire?" Jasper asked.

Both men shook their heads. Jasper took a menacing step forward. "It seems that you have quite a bit of explaining to do, Miss Manning." All pretense of civility vanished. "Where is Claire? What have you done with her?"

"I have no idea what you are talking about, my lord. I have not seen Lady Fairhurst since Lord Jordan's ball, three nights ago."

"You're lying." Jasper grabbed Anne by the shoulders and squeezed tightly. "Where is she?"

"I told you. I do not know. Please, you must—"

"There!" Jason shouted. "In the middle of the lake! Something is moving!"

Flinging Miss Manning aside, Jasper eyed the water. Jason was right. Something of substantial size was floating just beneath the surface in the middle of the lake. A body?

"Claire," Jasper whispered in horror.

"It could just be a tree branch," the marquess warned.

But Jasper was not listening. He had already ripped

off his jacket and was struggling to remove his boots. The moment they were gone, he sprinted to the water and dove beneath the surface.

Total darkness engulfed him. With long, smooth strokes he swam forward, but his searching hands found nothing but lily pads. Jasper's stomach hardened into a knot. He broke the surface and turned frantically in a circle, straining for a glimpse of what he believed was his wife.

"Wait, Jasper!" his brother yelled from the bank. "You are creating too many waves and ripples. Stay as still as you can for a minute."

Obediently, Jasper treaded water, his breath coming in harsh gasps.

"I see it!" Jason shouted. "Directly to your left, about fifty yards."

Following his brother's commands, Jasper swam to the spot and dove. Arms spread wide, he blindly reached out until his hand struck something large and solid. In an instant, he knew it was a body. Claire.

Summoning all his strength, he yanked her to the surface. Her stillness frightened him, but he wasted no time swimming to shore with his precious burden. As he neared the bank, Jason jumped in, boots and all, and helped carry Claire to dry land.

"She's not breathing and her heartbeat is very faint," Jason declared in a worried voice. "I think she's swallowed a great amount of water."

Jasper stumbled out of the lake and rushed to his wife's side. Turning her carefully onto her stomach, he applied pressure to her lower back. Nothing happened.

Frantically, he moved his hands higher and tried again. With steadfast determination, he repeated the process over and over. "Breathe, damn it. Breathe."

Finally, Claire moaned, her body convulsed, and she expelled a significant amount of water. It was the most joyous sound Jasper had ever heard.

He lifted her into a sitting position and cradled her tenderly in his arms. She began coughing and shivering each time she drew a shuddering breath. Jason removed his dry jacket and handed it to his brother. Jasper quickly wrapped it around Claire. Then his fingers skimmed over her face, shoulders, and arms.

"Are you hurt?" he asked urgently.

Teeth chattering, body shivering, Claire pressed her face against Jasper's wet chest. She moved her head until she could hear the beat of his heart, closing her eyes in relief. *She was safe.*

"I prayed you would come," she croaked.

Jasper eased her damp hair back from her face and pressed his lips to her forehead. "I was nearly out of my mind fearing I would not arrive in time. Thank God one of the servants saw Rebecca's coach, or else we would have had no clues at all."

Claire shuddered. "This has been a hellish nightmare. Miss Manning is frightfully unbalanced. We always thought it was the squire who might be a threat, but it has been Anne who has been watching me, stalking me, waiting for the chance to get rid of me."

"I blame myself," Jasper muttered. "I handled the—"

A woman screamed. They turned and saw one of the Manning sisters launch herself in attack at the other. The momentum sent both women tumbling to the ground. There was a sickening thud when they landed, one on top of the other.

"My God!" Jasper exclaimed.

Claire tried to stand, but the aftermath of shock had

left her weak at the knees. She clung to her husband's arm, and he helped her to her feet.

"Rebecca's been stabbed," Jason declared, as he knelt beside the women. "When she regained her senses, Harris brought her here, but at the sight of her sister she became enraged and attacked."

Clutching her side, Rebecca, sitting atop her sister, made a feeble attempt to rise, then slumped forward. Her body remained completely still.

"Will she recover?" Jasper asked.

"She is bleeding rather profusely." Jason pulled Rebecca off Anne and laid her carefully in the grass. "Do you have a handkerchief?"

Jasper removed a soggy piece of linen from his pocket and silently handed it to his brother. Claire did the same. Jason tied them together, and then added his own monogrammed handkerchief, forming a small tourniquet, which he affixed around the wound. "She needs immediate care. Dardington has gone for help. He should arrive shortly."

"What about Anne?" Claire asked.

Harris bent to examine the body. Anne was on her back, staring up at the moon with unseeing eyes. She looked mildly surprised.

"There's no need to rush for help for this one," the runner replied. "Her neck is broken."

Claire let out a jagged gasp. Pressing her hand to her mouth, she turned away from the corpse. "May God have mercy on her soul."

"The magistrate is going to have a hell of a time trying to sort all of this out," Harris commented. "And he will have plenty of questions for you and Lady Fairhurst."

"Tell him we shall speak with him tomorrow." Jasper

tightened his protective hold, and Claire leaned gratefully into his strength. "I am taking my wife home."

Claire let out a small sigh as she luxuriated in the moist heat that enveloped her tired, aching body. After her harrowing ordeal in the lake, she thought she would fear all but the smallest amounts of water, but soaking in this oversized tub had been nothing but pleasure. Especially since she was sharing her bath with her husband.

"Are you getting sleepy?"

The sound of Jasper's deep voice drifted through the room. Claire tilted her head back until it rested upon his shoulder. "I am almost too tired to be sleepy."

Jasper picked up a small square of linen, dipped it in the water, and ran it languidly over Claire's shoulders and breasts. "We'll stay until the water cools."

Claire nodded. She was simply too relaxed to move. Sitting between his legs in the hard cradle of his body, she could clearly feel his arousal firmly pressing against the small of her back. It gave her an oddly sensual feeling of comfort.

"So Anne Manning actually believed I would turn to her if you were gone?" Jasper asked as he leaned forward and pressed a kiss on Claire's temple.

"She did. My death was the only way for her to achieve her goal, which was to be with you."

Claire felt Jasper shudder. He reached out and stroked her cheek with the back of his fingers. "I thought Rebecca was involved because I handled our breakup so poorly and I believed her to be under the squire's influence. I never suspected Anne."

"Neither did anyone else." Claire ran her fingers lazily over Jasper's arm, which was resting on the side of the tub. She liked feeling the crisp texture of his hair and the solid muscle beneath. "What happened to the squire?"

"Though she was badly wounded, Rebecca became hysterical when she saw him. She started shouting and accusing him of all manner of degradation. The squire pretended to ignore her, but all who witnessed the display could see he was badly shaken.

"I suspect he shall leave London as soon as he can make the arrangements, though I believe news of his downfall will eventually reach Wiltshire. Once it does, he will no longer be considered a man of influence. I doubt any of the good folk in your village will have anything to do with him. In all likelihood, he will be forced out of the community in disgrace."

"We shall make sure of it," Claire insisted. "Then this nightmare will truly be over."

"I deeply regret not arriving sooner." Jasper's arms squeezed her harder, gathering her even closer, as though he would never let her go. "I have never before suffered such agonized worry for another person in my life. Each time I think of you struggling in that lake, it makes me shudder."

"I was terrified," Claire admitted. "Not so much of death, but of knowing that I would never again see you or hold you or have a chance to tell you how much I love you."

Claire shifted sideways and glanced up at Jasper's face. "I also deeply regretted never hearing from your lips the truth about your feelings for me."

He looked at her uncertainly, giving no indication of what he was feeling. Claire gnawed at the inside of her cheek, trying to contain her rising sense of discomfort.

Had she been wrong? Was he still determined to contain all of his passion? Did he intend to continue to enforce a rigid control of all his emotions? Was tonight's rescue only a reflection of his sense of husbandly duty and obligation?

"I bought you a ring," he blurted out.

"A ring? But I already have a wedding ring."

"I know. It's just—" Jasper shook his head and muttered beneath his breath. "I am making a muddle of this."

Claire inhaled and exhaled slowly. "Just speak the truth."

Jasper took her face between his hands. Claire's heart sped up. She saw a tremor pass across his shoulders as if he had taken a chill.

"I love you, Claire," Jasper said. "My heart is yours. My soul is yours. Hell, my very life is yours. And I pray that for the rest of our lives you will never cease looking at me with something special glowing in your eyes."

Claire responded with a watery smile. A tear trickled from the outside of her eye and fell over her cheek. Jasper's thumb brushed across the wet path.

"Oh, my love," Claire whispered. "I shall always feel this way about you."

She leaned into his arms and gloried in the comforting familiarity. This was not only a man she loved, this was a man she needed. Claire lifted her head expectantly and their lips met in a gentle, loving kiss that spoke of a lifetime of possibilities.

Epilogue

On the morning of her wedding day, Claire stood at her bedchamber window looking down on her parent's garden and admired the fullness of the summer blooms. Thanks to a perfect mix of sunshine and rain this season, the garden had blossomed into pure delight, a heady combination of color and fragrance.

Shouting from the rose arbor drew Claire's gaze, and she smiled as she watched the two household servants being mercilessly bullied by the family cook. The three were in the process of preparing for the wedding breakfast, which was to be served in the garden in a few short hours. Though Cook was not in any way responsible for setting out and arranging the tables and chairs, she nevertheless was in the thick of the action, shouting orders and demanding changes.

"You look radiant," Claire's mother declared as she entered the chamber. "Are you feeling all fluttery and nervous?"

Claire laughed merrily. "Well, Mother, since this is my *third* wedding ceremony, I hardly have a right to be nervous."

"Oh my, I suppose it is." The older woman smoothed the train of Claire's pale green gown. "You don't mind, do you?"

Claire shook her head. All things considered, her parents were taking her very bizarre marital status with amazing good humor. Initially, Claire had been uncertain how to explain the mix-up with her husband, but in the end, explanations had been fairly simple.

Jasper, with Claire at his side, patiently told her parents the entire truth, beginning with his twin's deception and concluding with his own vow to be a loving, protective, and faithful husband to their daughter. Her parents were immediately won over by Lord Fairhurst's honest charm and sincere desire to give Claire all that was within his power.

Yet Claire fully believed that it was the loving glow of happiness radiating from her eyes each time they fell upon her husband that made her parents fully accept their new son-in-law.

It was agreed from the beginning that the details of these strange happenings were to be kept among themselves. Even Claire's sisters were not informed. It was, of course, revealed to all that Lord Fairhurst had a twin brother, but no one in the family or the village suspected the men had switched places when the original wedding had occurred earlier in the year.

Claire's parents had suffered a few moments of distress when they realized they had not in truth witnessed their eldest daughter's marriage, and upon seeing that distress, Jasper immediately suggested they repeat the ceremony. To avoid any awkward questions, Jasper's family was invited to the village and they arrived declaring their joy at the opportunity to see their son wed, because they had missed the ceremony in the winter.

To keep family harmony intact, it was also decided to include Great-Aunt Agnes in the event. The elderly relative seemed pleased to be invited, though she had a comment, criticism, and suggestion for nearly every aspect of the day, including a loud protest about the wedding breakfast being held out-of-doors. Her opinions were born stoically by Claire's parents.

A commotion at the door interrupted the bride's preparations as a handsomely attired man entered the room.

"Oh, dear, it invites bad luck if the groom sees his bride before the ceremony." Claire's mother moved herself in front of her daughter, attempting to shield her from view, and then paused. "Though I am unsure if that superstition holds true since you are already married. What do you think, Claire?"

"I think it is an unnecessary point, Mother, since it is Jason who has come to see me, not my bridegroom."

The older woman let out a nervous laugh. "Is it? Gracious, I still cannot tell these two fine, handsome gentlemen apart."

Claire crossed the room, set her arms on her brother-in-law's shoulders, and gave him a kiss on the cheek. "This is a lovely surprise."

"You look stunning, Claire. Even more beautiful than on *our* wedding day."

She smiled, yet suspected her eyes were suspiciously bright. These days, even the smallest bout of emotions seemed to set off her tears. "A winter, spring, and now summer wedding ceremony. Do you think this sort of fashion trend will catch on with the London crowd?"

"Hardly. That group balks at the very thought of marriage."

"I always knew they were fools."

They laughed together. "I have brought you a small token from your bridegroom." With a dramatic flourish, Jason presented her with a bouquet of tiny white roses tied together with trailing ribbons of emerald green that matched the exact shade of the ribbons trimming her gown.

"The details of my dress were supposed to be kept a secret," Claire remarked suspiciously.

"And so they were, except for the colors you were wearing." Jason lowered his voice to a serious tone. "Jasper wanted the flowers to complement your attire, so he bribed Madame Renude for the information. You know my brother cannot be denied anything he truly desires."

"I find that to be one of his more endearing qualities." Claire blushed and buried her nose in the fragrant blossoms.

There was a momentary silence. Jason opened his mouth twice, but said nothing. Claire wondered if he felt uncomfortable speaking in her mother's hearing.

"Would you please check if the carriage is ready, Mother? I do not want to be late arriving at the church."

The tension in the room seemed to build the moment they were alone, but Claire waited patiently.

"I will be leaving shortly after the festivities today and assumed this would be the only chance we would have to speak privately." Jason shot her a grim look as the silence lengthened. "I need to know that you forgive me," he finally blurted out. "For everything."

"Dear Jason, I confess when I agreed to your marriage proposal those many months ago, I never thought my life would have turned out the way that it has." Claire hastily wiped away the single tear that trickled down her cheek. "I was not a person who held a strong belief in fate, but I know it was my destiny to be with Jasper. That never would have happened without you.

"There is nothing to forgive, but if it pleases you to

hear it, then I will say that I hold no ill will toward you and am very proud to be your sister by marriage."

She lifted her face, and he kissed her cheek. "My brother is a damn lucky man," he whispered.

Claire's hands were shaking, so she crossed her arms over her waist. "My greatest wish is that one day you will also find a love as strong and true. 'Tis no more than you deserve."

For a split-second Jason looked horrified; then his charming, frivolous mask slipped into place.

"The carriage is waiting at the front drive, and your father says we need to leave right now," her mother said, as she bustled back into the room. "Come along, dear, we don't want to be late."

A few minutes later, Claire was sitting in the open carriage with her parents, watching the hedgerows pass by. In keeping with tradition, Lord Fairhurst had arranged for a pair of matched grays to pull the coach. Their shining coats gleamed in the sunshine as they pranced merrily down the winding lane, their bridle and reins festively dressed in ribbons and flower garlands.

Claire took a deep breath and drank in her surroundings. The temperature was neither too hot nor too cold; the sky was a perfect, cloudless blue; and the wind carried a subtle, refreshing breeze. It truly was the ideal day for a wedding, and she realized, with some surprise, that though this was indeed her third ceremony, it was the first time she actually *felt* like a bride.

There was a sizable crowd of well-wishers gathered around the churchyard gate. Though everyone understood this was to be a small, private ceremony, many wanted to wish the couple well and were eager to catch a glimpse of Claire's very aristocratic, very handsome in-laws.

There were a few cheers and shouts of congratulations as Claire stepped out of the carriage. Claire waved enthusiastically to one and all. When she reached the church steps, the peal of the pipe organ greeted her. Before she was allowed to enter the church vestibule, her mother fussed with the hem of her train and adjusted the veil on her bonnet a final time. Then with one last emotional smile for the blushing bride, she hastened to her seat.

Claire gripped her delicate bouquet in one hand, and then absently ran the other hand down the front of her gown. For a few seconds, her palm lingered lovingly over her lower abdomen. Though she knew she was hardly the first woman to walk toward her bridegroom carrying his unborn child safely in her womb, she believed she was the happiest. It had not been easy keeping the secret, but she knew it would add even more meaning to this special day when she shared the news with Jasper later that night in the privacy of their bedchamber.

The music swelled, and Claire held tightly to her father's arm as they embarked upon the walk up the aisle to the altar. Any trace of residual nerves vanished the moment she spotted Jasper, so handsome and severe in dark blue with white linen, his eyes bright with warmth and love.

They clasped hands and turned together to face the rector.

"Dearly beloved," he began.

A few female sniffles were heard, and then everyone let out appreciative sighs of joy when at the end of the ceremony, the couple first gazed into each other's eyes before pressing their lips together in a passionate kiss. They emerged from the church to shouts and cheers and a shower of flower petals hurled by family, friends, and well-wishers.

Once alone in the carriage, they exchanged several heated kisses, and then stared into each other's eyes like two moonstruck youths in the first throes of discovering their love.

The wedding breakfast was a loud, boisterous party, with numerous toasts, laughter, jokes, and Meredith's girls racing around the garden. Claire sat contentedly at the place of honor and enjoyed every moment of the cheerful scene of celebration, at times wondering how it was possible for happiness to be so strong and full that it nearly took her breath away.

Jasper reached under the table and grabbed her hand, intertwining their fingers. "Happy?"

Not trusting her voice, Claire nodded and smiled. This truly had been a magical day.

"I just said good-bye to my brother, and he asked me to give you his regards," Jasper continued. "Though he regretted leaving the party, he needed to depart while there was still a fair amount of daylight."

"Is he on his way back to London?"

"No, he is off to the wilds of York, to deal with a problem on one of my estates."

"Your man of affairs was ineffective in solving the situation?" Claire questioned.

Jasper swirled the wine in his goblet before lifting it to his lips and taking a long swallow. "There are complications that require authority I do not afford my servants, and since I loathed the idea of leaving my bride, I have sent my brother in my place."

"It pleases me greatly to hear that you trust him so completely."

Jasper smiled, and Claire recognized a trace of his old

cynicism. "The situation is so dire, I doubt even Jason can make matters any worse."

"Well, I still think it was kind of Jason to agree to come to your aid."

"He owes me."

"Does he now?" Claire playfully pulled the goblet out of her husband's hand and took a small sip of wine. "I believe it is you who owes Jason. After all, if not for him, you and I would not be married. For the third time."

He tipped his head closer so that their foreheads were nearly touching. "Legally, this is our second wedding ceremony, but I am not about to quibble. I approve of anything that serves to bind you tighter to me."

"You do?"

"Oh, yes. I am impulsively romantic," he declared, looking thoroughly amused at the very notion.

"You are nothing of the sort," Claire replied with a giggle. "And that is perfectly fine, because I love you just as you are."

The corners of his eyes crinkled as his smile widened. "And I love you, Claire. More than you will ever know."

Then Lord Fairhurst, a man known far and wide for his proper attitude and stuffy manners, lifted his wife out of her chair, placed her onto his lap, enfolded her intimately within his arms, and gave her a fierce, searing kiss that all who witnessed agreed was just barely within the bounds of decorum.

ABOUT THE AUTHOR

Adrienne Basso lives with her family in New Jersey. She is the author of six Zebra historical romances set in the Regency period and is currently working on her next historical romance to be published in 2006. She is also working on a vampire novella, which will appear in *Highland Vampire,* coming in trade paperback in September 2005. Adrienne loves to hear from readers, and you may write to her c/o Zebra Books. Please include a self-addressed stamped envelope if you wish a response.